March Violets

PHILIP KERR

PENGUIN BOOKS

PENGUIN BOOKS

UK | USA | Canada | Ireland | Australia
India | New Zealand | South Africa

Penguin Books is part of the Penguin Random House group of companies
whose addresses can be found at global.penguinrandomhouse.com.

First published by Viking 1989
Published in Penguin Books 1990
Reissued in this edition 2015

004

Copyright © Philip Kerr, 1989

The moral right of the copyright holders has been asserted

Printed and bound in Great Britain by Clays Ltd, Elcograf S.p.A.

A CIP catalogue record for this book is available from the British Library

ISBN: 978-0-241-97601-2

PENGUIN BOOKS

MARCH VIOLETS

Philip Kerr wrote more than thirty novels over his lifetime, including the hugely popular Children of the Lamp series for children, but he is best remembered as the creator of the iconic Berlin-based detective Bernie Gunther, who first appeared in his Berlin Noir series.

Born in Edinburgh, Kerr read Law as an undergraduate before completing a Master's degree in Law and Philosophy, most of this German, and it was then that he first became interested in German twentieth-century history. He went on to work as a copywriter at various advertising agencies, including Saatchi & Saatchi, but spent most of his time researching an idea he'd had for a novel about a Berlin-based policeman. And following several trips to Germany – and a great deal of walking around the streets of Berlin – his first novel, *March Violets*, was published in 1989 and introduced the world to the tough-talking private eye Bernie Gunther. Ian Rankin said of him: 'His Bernie Gunther novels are extraordinary, a mix of great storytelling and brilliant research, with a believable (a)moral hero.'

Kerr wrote a further thirteen books featuring the much-loved German detective, set during the 1930s, the Second World War and the Cold War. His writing has been universally lauded and Kerr was the recipient of many awards, including the RBA International Prize for Crime Writing and the CWA Ellis Peters Historic Crime Award. He was also listed amongst Granta's 'Best Young British Novelists'. He was married to fellow novelist Jane Thynne, with whom he had three children. He lived in London with his family until his death in 2018.

For my mother

BERLIN, 1936

FIRST MAN: Have you noticed how the March Violets have managed to completely overtake Party veterans like you and me?

SECOND MAN: You're right. Perhaps if Hitler had also waited a little before climbing on to the Nazi bandwagon he'd have become Führer quicker too.

Schwarze Korps, November 1935

Stranger things happen in the dark dreams of the Great Persuader . . .

This morning, at the corner of Friedrichstrasse and Jägerstrasse, I saw two men, SA men, unscrewing a red *Der Stürmer* showcase from the wall of a building. *Der Stürmer* is the anti-Semitic journal that's run by the Reich's leading Jew-baiter, Julius Streicher. The visual impact of these display cases, with their semi-pornographic line-drawings of Aryan maids in the voluptuous embraces of long-nosed monsters, tends to attract the weaker-minded reader, providing him with cursory titillation. Respectable people have nothing to do with it. Anyway, the two SA men placed the Stürmerkästen in the back of their lorry next to several others. They did their work none too carefully, because there were at least a couple which had broken glass covers.

An hour later I saw the same two men removing another one of these Stürmerkästen from outside a tram-stop in front of the Town Hall. This time I went up to them and asked what they were doing.

'It's for the Olympiad,' said one. 'We're ordered to take them all down so as not to shock the foreign visitors who will be coming to Berlin to see the Games.'

In my experience, such sensitivity on the part of the authorities is unheard of.

I drove home in my car – it's an old black Hanomag – and changed into my last good suit: made of light-grey flannel cloth, it cost me 120 marks when I bought it three years ago, and it is of a quality that is becoming increasingly rare in this country; like butter, coffee and soap, new wool material is ersatz, more often than not. The new material is serviceable enough, all right, just not very hard-wearing, and rather ineffective when it comes to keeping out the cold in winter. Or, for that matter, in summer.

I checked my appearance in the bedroom mirror and then picked up my best hat. It's a wide-brimmed hat of dark-grey felt, and is encircled by a black baratvea band. Common enough. But like the Gestapo, I wear my hat differently from other men, with the brim lower in front than at the back. This has the effect of hiding my eyes of course, which makes it more difficult for people to recognize me. It's a style that originated with the Berlin Criminal Police, the Kripo, which is where I acquired it.

I slipped a packet of Murattis into my jacket pocket, and, tucking a gift-wrapped piece of Rosenthal porcelain carefully under my arm, I went out.

The wedding took place at the Luther Kirche on Dennewitz Platz, just south of Potsdamer Railway Station, and a stone's throw from the home of the bride's parents. The father, Herr Lehmann, was an engine driver out of Lehrter Station, and drove the 'D-Zug', the express train, to Hamburg and back four times a week. The bride, Dagmar, was my secretary, and I had no idea what I was going to do without her. Not that I cared to know, either: I'd often thought of marrying Dagmar myself. She was pretty and good at organizing me, and in my own odd way I suppose that I loved her; but then at thirty-eight I was probably too old for her, and maybe just a shade too dull. I'm not much given to having a wild time, and Dagmar was the sort of girl who deserved some fun.

So here she was, marrying this flyer. And on the face of it he was everything that a girl could have wished for: he was young, handsome and, in the grey-blue uniform of the National Socialist Flying Corps, he looked to be the epitome of the dashing young Aryan male. But I was disappointed when I met him at the wedding reception. Like most Party members, Johannes Buerckel had the look and the air of a man who took himself very seriously indeed.

2

It was Dagmar who made the introduction. Johannes, true to type, brought his heels together with a loud click and bowed his head curtly before shaking my hand.

'Congratulations,' I said to him. 'You're a very fortunate fellow. I'd have asked her to marry me, only I don't think I look as good as you in uniform.'

I took a closer look at his uniform: on the left breast-pocket he wore the silver SA Sports Badge and the Pilots Badge; above these two decorations was the ubiquitous 'Scary' Badge – the Party Badge; and on his left arm he wore the swastika armband. 'Dagmar told me you were a pilot with Lufthansa on temporary attachment to the Ministry of Aviation, but I had no idea . . . What did you say he was, Dagmar?'

'A Sports Flyer.'

'Yes, that's it. A Sports Flyer. Well, I had no idea you fellows were in uniform.'

Of course it didn't take a detective to work out that 'Sports Flyer' was one of those fancy Reich euphemisms, and that this particular one related to the secret training of fighter pilots.

'He does look splendid, doesn't he?' said Dagmar.

'And you look beautiful, my dear,' cooed the groom dutifully.

'Forgive me for asking, Johannes, but is Germany's air force now to be officially recognized?' I said.

'Flying Corps,' said Buerckel. 'It's a Flying Corps.' But that was the whole of his answer. 'And you, Herr Günther – a private detective, eh? That must be interesting.'

'Private investigator,' I said, correcting him. 'It has its moments.'

'What sort of things do you investigate?'

'Almost anything, except divorce. People act funny when they're being cheated by their wives or their husbands, or when they're the ones doing the cheating. I was once engaged by a woman to tell her husband that she was planning to leave him. She was afraid he'd pop her. So I told him, and, what do you know, the son of a bitch tried to pop me. I spent three weeks in St Gertrauden Hospital with my neck in a brace. That finished me with matrimonial work permanently. These days I do anything from insurance investigations to guarding wedding presents to finding missing persons – that's the ones the police don't already know about, as well as the ones they do. Yes, that's one area of my business that's seen a real improvement since the National Socialists took power.' I smiled as affably as I could, and wiggled my eyebrows suggestively. 'I guess we've all done well out of National Socialism, haven't we? Proper little March Violets.'

'You mustn't take any notice of Bernhard,' said Dagmar. 'He has an odd sense of humour.' I would have said more, but the band started to play and Dagmar wisely led Buerckel on to the dance-floor, where they were applauded warmly.

Bored with the sekt that was on offer, I went into the bar in search of a real drink. I ordered a Bock and a Klares chaser, which is a shot of the clear, colourless potato-based alcohol I have a taste for, and I drank these fairly quickly and ordered the same again.

'Thirsty work, weddings,' said the little man next to me: it was Dagmar's father. He turned his back to the bar and watched his daughter proudly. 'Looks a proper picture, doesn't she, Herr Günther?'

'I don't know what I'm going to do without her,' I said. 'Perhaps you can persuade her to change her mind and stay on with me. I'm sure they must need the money. Young couples always need money when they first marry.'

Herr Lehmann shook his head. 'I'm afraid that there is only one kind of labour for which Johannes and his National Socialist government think a woman is qualified, and that's the kind she has at the end of a nine-month term.' He lit his pipe and puffed philosophically. 'Anyway,' he said. 'I suppose they'll be applying for one of those Reich Marriage Loans, and that would stop her from working, wouldn't it?'

'Yes, I suppose you're right,' I said, and downed the chaser. I saw his face say that he never had me marked as a drunk and so I said, 'Don't let this stuff fool you, Herr Lehmann. I just use it as a mouthwash, only I'm too damned lazy to spit the stuff out.' He chuckled at that, and slapped me on the back and ordered us two large ones. We drank those and I asked him where the happy couple were going on their sparkle.

'To the Rhine,' he said. 'Wiesbaden. Frau Lehmann and myself went to Königstein for ours. It's a lovely part of the world. He's not long back, though, and then he's off on some Strength Through Joy trip, courtesy of the Reich Labour Service.'

'Oh? Where to?'

'Mediterranean.'

'You believe that?'

The old man frowned. 'No,' he said grimly. 'I haven't mentioned it to Dagmar, but I reckon he's off to Spain . . .'

'. . . and war.'

'And war, yes. Mussolini has helped Franco, so Hitler's not going to miss out on the fun, is he? He won't be happy until he's got us into another bloody war.'

After that we drank some more, and later on I found myself dancing with a nice little stocking-buyer from Grunfeld's Department Store. Her name was Carola and I persuaded her to leave with me and we went over to Dagmar and Buerckel to wish them luck. It was rather odd, I thought, that Buerckel should choose that moment to make a reference to my war record.

'Dagmar tells me that you were on the Turkish front.' Was he, I wondered, a little bit worried about going to Spain? 'And that you won an Iron Cross.'

I shrugged. 'Only a second class.' So that was it, I thought; the flyer was hungry for glory.

'Nevertheless,' he said, 'an Iron Cross. The Führer's Iron Cross was a second class.'

'Well, I can't speak for him, but my own recollection is that provided a soldier was honest – comparatively honest – and served at the front, it was really rather easy towards the end of the war to collect a second class. You know, most of the first-class medals were awarded to men in cemeteries. I got my Iron Cross for staying out of trouble.' I was warming to my subject. 'Who knows,'

I said. 'If things work out, you might collect one yourself. It would look nice on a handsome tunic like that.'

The muscles in Buerckel's lean young face tightened. He bent forwards and caught the smell of my breath.

'You're drunk,' he said.

'*Si*,' I said. Unsteady on my feet, I turned away. '*Adios, hombre.*'

It was late, gone one o'clock, when finally I drove back to my apartment in Trautenaustrasse, which is in Wilmersdorf, a modest neighbourhood, but still a lot better than Wedding, the district of Berlin in which I grew up. The street itself runs north-east from Güntzelstrasse past Nikolsburger Platz, where there is a scenic sort of fountain in the middle of the square. I lived, not uncomfortably, at the Prager Platz end.

Ashamed of myself for having teased Buerckel in front of Dagmar, and for the liberties I had taken with Carola the stocking-buyer in the Tiergarten near the goldfish pond, I sat in my car and smoked a cigarette thoughtfully. I had to admit to myself that I had been more affected by Dagmar's wedding than previously I would have thought possible. I could see there was nothing to be gained by brooding about it. I didn't think that I could forget her, but it was a safe bet that I could find lots of ways to take my mind off her.

It was only when I got out of the car that I noticed the large dark-blue Mercedes convertible parked about twenty metres down the street, and the two men who were leaning on it, waiting for someone. I braced myself as one of the men threw away his cigarette and walked quickly towards me. As he drew nearer I could see that he was too well-groomed to be Gestapo and that the other one was wearing a chauffeur's uniform, although he would have looked a lot more comfortable in a leopard-skin leotard, with his music-hall weightlifter's build. His less than discreet presence lent the well-dressed and younger man an obvious confidence.

'Herr Günther? Are you Herr Bernhard Günther?' He stopped in front of me and I shot him my toughest look, the sort that would make a bear blink: I don't care for people who solicit me outside my house at one in the morning.

'I'm his brother. He's out of town right now.' The man smiled broadly. He didn't buy that.

'Herr Günther, the private investigator? My employer would like a word with you.' He pointed at the big Mercedes. 'He's waiting in the car. I spoke to the concierge and she told me that you were expected back this evening. That was three hours ago, so you can see we've been waiting quite some time. It really is very urgent.'

I lifted my wrist and flicked my eyes at my watch.

'Friend, it's 1.40 in the morning, so whatever it is you're selling, I'm not interested. I'm tired and I'm drunk and I want to go to bed. I've got an office on Alexanderplatz, so do me a favour and leave it till tomorrow.'

The young man, a pleasant, fresh-faced fellow with a button-hole, blocked my path. 'It can't wait until tomorrow,' he said, and then smiled winningly. 'Please speak to him, just for a minute, I beg you.'

'Speak to whom?' I growled, looking over at the car.

'Here's his card.' He handed it over and I stared stupidly at it like it was a winning raffle-ticket. He leaned over and read it for me, upside-down. '"Dr Fritz Schemm, German Lawyer, of Schemm & Schellenberg, Unter den Linden, Number 67." That's a good address.'

'Sure it is,' I said. 'But a lawyer out at this time of night and from a smart firm like that? You must think I believe in fairies.' But I followed him to the car anyway. The chauffeur opened the door. Keeping one foot on the running board, I peered inside. A man smelling of cologne leaned forward, his features hidden in the shadows, and when he spoke, his voice was cold and inhospitable, like someone straining on a toilet-bowl.

'You're Günther, the detective?'

'That's right,' I said, 'and you must be –' I pretended to read his business card, '– Dr Fritz Schemm, German Lawyer.' I uttered the word 'German' with a deliberately sarcastic emphasis. I've always hated it on business cards and signs because of the implication of racial respectability; and even more so now that – at least as far as

8

lawyers are concerned – it is quite redundant, since Jews are forbidden to practise law anyway. I would no more describe myself as a 'German Private Investigator' than I would call myself a 'Lutheran Private Investigator' or an 'Antisocial Private Investigator' or a 'Widowed Private Investigator', even though I am, or was at one time, all of these things (these days I'm not often seen in church). It's true that a lot of my clients are Jews. Their business is very profitable (they pay on the nail), and it's always the same – Missing Persons. The results are pretty much the same too: a body dumped in the Landwehr Canal courtesy of the Gestapo or the SA; a lonely suicide in a rowboat on the Wannsee; or a name on a police list of convicts sent to a KZ, a Concentration Camp. So right away I didn't like this lawyer, this German Lawyer.

I said: 'Listen, Herr Doktor, like I was just telling your boy here, I'm tired and I've drunk enough to forget that I've got a bank manager who worries about my welfare.' Schemm reached into his jacket pocket and I didn't even shift, which shows you how blue I must have been. As it was he only took out his wallet.

'I have made inquiries about you and I am informed that you offer a reliable service. I need you now for a couple of hours, for which I will pay you 200 Reichsmarks: in effect a week's money.' He laid his wallet on his knee and thumbed two blues onto his trouser-leg. This couldn't have been easy, since he had only one arm. 'And afterwards Ulrich will drive you home.'

I took the notes. 'Hell,' I said, 'I was only going to go to bed and sleep. I can do that anytime.' I ducked my head and stepped into the car. 'Let's go, Ulrich.'

The door slammed and Ulrich climbed into the driver's seat, with Freshface alongside of him. We headed west.

'Where are we going?' I said.

'All in good time, Herr Günther,' he said. 'Help yourself to a drink, or a cigarette.' He flipped open a cocktail cabinet which looked as though it had been salvaged from the *Titanic* and produced a cigarette box. 'These are American.'

I said yes to the smoke but no to the drink: when people are as ready to part with 200 marks as Dr Schemm had been, it pays to keep your wits about you.

'Would you be so kind as to light me, please?' said Schemm, fitting a cigarette between his lips. 'Matches are the one thing I cannot manage. I lost my arm with Ludendorff at the capture of the fortress of Liège. Did you see any active service?' The voice was fastidious, suave even: soft and slow, with just a hint of cruelty. The sort of voice, I thought, that could lead you into incriminating yourself quite nicely, thank you. The sort of voice that would have done well for its owner had he worked for the Gestapo. I lit our cigarettes and settled back into the Mercedes's big seat.

'Yes, I was in Turkey.' Christ, there were so many people taking an interest in my war record all of a sudden, that I wondered if I hadn't better apply for an Old Comrades Badge. I looked out of the window and saw that we were driving towards the Grunewald, an area of forest that lies on the west side of the city, near the River Havel.

'Commissioned?'

'Sergeant.' I heard him smile.

'I was a major,' he said, and that was me put firmly in my place. 'And you became a policeman after the war?'

'No, not right away. I was a civil servant for a while, but I couldn't stand the routine. I didn't join the force until 1922.'

'And when did you leave?'

'Listen, Herr Doktor, I don't remember you putting me on oath when I got into the car.'

'I'm sorry,' he said. 'I was merely curious to discover whether you left of your own accord, or . . .'

'Or was pushed? You've got a lot of forehead asking me that, Schemm.'

'Have I?' he said innocently.

'But I'll answer your question. I left. I dare say if I'd waited long enough they'd have weeded me out like all the others. I'm not a National Socialist, but I'm not a fucking Kozi either; I dislike Bolshevism just like the Party does, or at least I think it does. But that's not quite good enough for the modern Kripo or Sipo or whatever it's called now. In their book if you're not for it you must be against it.'

'And so you, a Kriminalinspektor, left Kripo,' he paused, and then added in tones of affected surprise, 'to become the house detective at the Adlon Hotel.'

'You're pretty cute,' I sneered, 'asking me all these questions when you already know the answers.'

'My client likes to know about the people who work for him,' he said smugly.

'I haven't taken the case yet. Maybe I'll turn it down just to see your face.'

'Maybe. But you'd be a fool. Berlin has a dozen like you – private investigators.' He named my profession with more than a little distaste.

'So why pick me?'

'You have worked for my client before, indirectly. A couple of years ago you conducted an insurance investigation for the Germania Life Assurance Company, of which my client is a major shareholder. While the Kripo were still whistling in the dark you were successful in recovering some stolen bonds.'

'I remember it.' And I had good reason to. It had been one of my first cases after leaving the Adlon and setting up as a private investigator. I said: 'I was lucky.'

'Never underestimate luck,' said Schemm pompously. Sure, I thought: just look at the Führer.

By now we were on the edge of the Grunewald Forest in Dahlem, home to some of the richest and most influential people in the country, like the Ribbentrops. We pulled up at a huge wrought-iron gate which hung between massive walls, and Freshface had to hop out to wrestle it open. Ulrich drove on through.

'Drive on,' ordered Schemm. 'Don't wait. We're late enough as it is.' We drove along an avenue of trees for about five minutes before arriving at a wide gravel courtyard around which were set on three sides a long centre building and the two wings that comprised the house. Ulrich stopped beside a small fountain and jumped out to open the doors. We got out.

Circling the courtyard was an ambulatory, with a roof supported by thick beams and wooden columns, and this was patrolled by a man with a pair of evil-looking Dobermanns. There wasn't much light apart from the coachlamp by the front door, but as far as I could see the house was white with pebbledash walls and a deep mansard roof – as big as a decent-sized hotel of the sort that I couldn't afford. Somewhere in the trees behind the house a peacock was screaming for help.

Closer to the door I got my first good look at the doctor. I suppose he was quite a handsome man. Since he was at least fifty, I suppose you would say that he was distinguished-looking. Taller than he had seemed when sitting in the back of the car, and dressed fastidiously, but with a total disregard for fashion. He wore a stiff collar you could have sliced a loaf with, a pin-striped suit of a light-grey shade, a creamy-coloured waistcoat and spats; his only hand was gloved in grey kid, and on his neatly cropped square grey head he wore a large grey hat with a brim that surrounded the high, well-pleated crown like a castle moat. He looked like an old suit of armour.

He ushered me towards the big mahogany door, which swung open to reveal an ashen-faced butler who stood aside as we crossed the threshold and stepped into the wide entrance hall. It was the kind of hall that made you feel lucky just to have got through the door. Twin flights of stairs with gleaming white banisters led up to the upper floors, and on the ceiling hung a chandelier that was bigger than a church-bell and gaudier than a stripper's earrings. I made a mental note to raise my fees.

The butler, who was an Arab, bowed gravely and asked me for my hat.

'I'll hang on to it, if you don't mind,' I said, feeding its brim through my fingers. 'It'll help to keep my hands off the silver.'

'As you wish, sir.'

Schemm handed the butler his own hat as if to the manor born. Maybe he was, but with lawyers I always assume that they came by their wealth and position through avarice and by means nefarious: I never yet met one that I could trust. His glove he neatly removed with an almost double-jointed contortion of his fingers, and dropped it into his hat. Then he straightened his necktie and asked the butler to announce us.

We waited in the library. It wasn't big by the standards of a Bismarck or a Hindenburg, and you couldn't have packed more than six cars between the Reichstag-sized desk and the door. It was decorated in early Lohengrin, with its great beams, granite chimney-piece in which a log crackled quietly, and wall-mounted weaponry. There were plenty of books, of the sort you buy by the metre: lots of German poets and philosophers and jurists with whom I can claim a degree of familiarity, but only as the names of streets and cafés and bars.

I took a hike around the room. 'If I'm not back in five minutes, send out a search party.'

Schemm sighed and sat down on one of the two leather sofas that were positioned at right angles to the fire. He picked a magazine off the rack and pretended to read. 'Don't these little cottages give you claustrophobia?' Schemm sighed petulantly, like an old maiden aunt catching the smell of gin on the pastor's breath.

'Do sit down, Herr Günther,' he said.

I ignored him. Fingering the two hundreds in my trouser pocket to help me stay awake, I meandered over to the desk and glanced over its green-leather surface. There was a copy of the *Berliner Tageblatt*, well read, and a pair of half-moon spectacles; a pen; a heavy brass ashtray containing the butt of a well-chewed cigar and, next to it, the box of Black Wisdom Havanas from which it had been taken; a pile of correspondence and several silver-framed photographs. I glanced over at Schemm, who was making heavy weather of his magazine and his eyelids, and then picked up one of the framed photographs. She was dark and pretty, with a full

13

figure, which is just how I like them, although I could tell that she might find my after-dinner conversation quite resistible: her graduation robes told me that.

'She's beautiful, don't you think?' said a voice that came from the direction of the library door and caused Schemm to get up off the sofa. It was a singsong sort of voice with a light Berlin accent. I turned to face its owner and found myself looking at a man of negligible stature. His face was florid and puffy and had something so despondent in it that I almost failed to recognize it. While Schemm was busy bowing I mumbled something complimentary about the girl in the photograph.

'Herr Six,' said Schemm with more obsequy than a sultan's concubine, 'may I introduce Herr Bernhard Günther.' He turned to me, his voice changing to suit my depressed bank balance. 'This is Herr Doktor Hermann Six.' It was funny, I thought, how it was that in more elevated circles everyone was a damned doctor. I shook his hand and found it held for an uncomfortably long time as my new client's eyes looked into my face. You get a lot of clients who do that: they reckon themselves as judges of a man's character, and after all they're not going to reveal their embarrassing little problems to a man who looks shifty and dishonest: so it's fortunate that I've got the look of someone who is steady and dependable. Anyway, about the new client's eyes: they were blue, large and prominent, and with an odd sort of watery brightness in them, as if he had just stepped out of a cloud of mustard gas. It was with some shock that it dawned on me that the man had been crying.

Six released my hand and picked up the photograph I'd just been looking at. He stared at it for several seconds and then sighed profoundly.

'She was my daughter,' he said, with his heart in his throat. I nodded patiently. He replaced the photograph face down on the desk, and pushed his monkishly-styled grey hair across his brow. 'Was, because she is dead.'

'I'm sorry,' I said gravely.

'You shouldn't be,' he said. 'Because if she were alive you wouldn't be here with the chance to make a lot of money.' I listened: he was talking my language. 'You see, she was murdered.' He paused for dramatic effect: clients do a lot of that, but this one was good.

'Murdered,' I repeated dumbly.

'Murdered.' He tugged at one of his loose, elephantine ears before thrusting his gnarled hands into the pockets of his shapeless navy-blue suit. I couldn't help noticing that the cuffs of his shirt were frayed and dirty. I'd never met a steel millionaire before (I'd heard of Hermann Six; he was one of the major Ruhr industrialists), but this struck me as odd. He rocked on the balls of his feet, and I glanced down at his shoes. You can tell a lot by a client's shoes. That's the only thing I've picked up from Sherlock Holmes. Six's were ready for the Winter Relief – that's the National Socialist People's Welfare Organization where you send all your old clothes. But then German shoes aren't much good anyway. The ersatz leather is like cardboard; just like the meat, and the coffee, and the butter, and the cloth. But coming back to Herr Six, I didn't have him marked as so stricken by grief that he was sleeping in his clothes. No; I decided he was one of these eccentric millionaires that you sometimes read about in the newspapers: they spend nothing on anything, which is how they come to be rich in the first place.

'She was shot dead, in cold blood,' he said bitterly. I could see we were in for a long night. I got out my cigarettes.

'Mind if I smoke?' I asked. He seemed to recover himself at that.

'Do excuse me, Herr Günther,' he sighed. 'I'm forgetting my manners. Would you like a drink or something?' The 'or something' sounded just fine, like a nice four-poster, perhaps, but I asked for a mocha instead. 'Fritz?'

Schemm stirred on the big sofa. 'Thank you, just a glass of water,' he said humbly. Six pulled the bell-rope, and then selected a fat black cigar from the box on the desk. He ushered me to a seat, and I dumped myself on the other sofa, opposite Schemm. Six took a taper and pushed it at a flame. Then he lit his cigar and sat down beside the man in grey. Behind him the library door opened and a young man of about thirty-five came into the room. A pair of rimless glasses worn studiously at the end of a broad, almost negroid nose belied his athletic frame. He snatched them off, stared awkwardly at me and then at his employer.

'Do you want me in this meeting, Herr Six?' he said. His accent was vaguely Frankfurt.

'No, it's all right, Hjalmar,' said Six. 'You get off to bed, there's a good fellow. Perhaps you'd ask Farraj to bring us a mocha and a glass of water, and my usual.'

'Um, right away, Herr Six.' Again he looked at me, and I couldn't work out whether my being there was a source of vexation to him or not, so I made a mental note to speak to him when I got the chance.

'There is one more thing,' said Six, turning round on the sofa. 'Please remind me to go through the funeral arrangements with you first thing tomorrow. I want you to look after things while I'm away.'

'Very well, Herr Six,' and with that he wished us goodnight and left.

'Now then, Herr Günther,' said Six after the door had closed. He spoke with the Black Wisdom stuck in the corner of his mouth, so that he looked like a fairground barker and sounded like a child with a piece of candy. 'I must apologize for bringing you here at this unearthly hour; however, I'm a busy man. Most important of all, you must understand that I am also a very private one.'

'All the same, Herr Six,' I said, 'I must have heard of you.'

'That is very probable. In my position I have to be the patron of many causes and the sponsor of many charities – you know the sort of thing I'm talking about. Wealth does have its obligations.'

So does an outside toilet, I thought. Anticipating what was coming, I yawned inside myself. But I said: 'I can certainly believe it,' with such an affectation of understanding that it caused him to hesitate for a short moment before continuing with the well-worn phrases I had heard so many times before. 'Need for discretion'; and 'no wish to involve the authorities in my affairs'; and 'complete respect for confidentiality', etc., etc. That's the thing about my job. People are always telling you how to conduct their case, almost as if they didn't quite trust you, almost as if you were going to have to improve your standards in order to work for them.

'If I could make a better living as a not-so-private investigator, I'd have tried it a long time ago,' I told him. 'But in my line of business a big mouth is bad for business. Word would get around, and one or two well-established insurance companies and legal practices who I can call regular clients would go elsewhere. Look, I know you've had me checked out, so let's get down to business, shall we?' The interesting thing about the rich is that they like being told where to get off. They confuse it with honesty. Six nodded appreciatively.

At this point, the butler cruised smoothly into the room like a rubber wheel on a waxed floor and, smelling faintly of sweat and something spicy, he served the coffee, the water and his master's brandy with the blank look of a man who changes his earplugs six times a day. I sipped my coffee and reflected that I could have told Six that my nonagenarian grandmother had eloped with the Führer and the butler would have continued to serve the drinks without so much as flexing a hair follicle. When he left the room I swear I hardly noticed.

'The photograph you were looking at was taken only a few years ago, at my daughter's graduation. Subsequently she became a schoolteacher at the Arndt Grammar School in Berlin-Dahlem.' I found a pen and prepared to take notes on the back of Dagmar's wedding invitation. 'No,' he said, 'please don't take notes, just listen. Herr Schemm will provide you with a complete dossier of information at the conclusion of this meeting.

'Actually, she was rather a good schoolteacher, although I ought to be honest and tell you that I could have wished for her to have done something else with her life. Grete – yes, I forgot to tell you her name – Grete had the most beautiful singing voice, and I wanted her to take up singing professionally. But in 1930 she married a young lawyer attached to the Berlin Provincial Court. His name was Paul Pfarr.'

'Was?' I said. My interruption drew the profound sigh from him once again.

'Yes. I should have mentioned it. I'm afraid he's dead too.'

'Two murders, then,' I said.

'Yes,' he said awkwardly. 'Two murders.' He took out his wallet and a snapshot. 'This was taken at their wedding.'

There wasn't much to tell from it except that, like most society wedding-receptions, it had been held at the Adlon Hotel. I recognized the Whispering Fountain's distinctive pagoda, with its carved elephants from the Adlon's Goethe Garden. I stifled a real yawn. It wasn't a particularly good photograph, and I'd had more than enough of weddings for one day and a half. I handed it back.

'A fine couple,' I said, lighting another Muratti. Six's black cigar lay smokeless and flat on the round brass ashtray.

'Grete was teaching until 1934 when, like many other women, she lost her job – a casualty of the government's general discrimination against working women in the employment drive. Meanwhile Paul landed a job at the Ministry of the Interior. Not long afterwards my first wife Lisa died, and Grete became very depressed. She started drinking and staying out late. But just a few weeks ago she seemed her old self again.' Six regarded his brandy morosely and then threw it back in one gulp. 'Three nights ago, however, Paul and Grete died in a fire at their home in Lichterfelde-Ost. But before the house caught fire they were each shot, several times, and the safe ransacked.'

'Any idea what was in the safe?'

'I told the fellows from Kripo that I had no idea what it contained.'

I read between the lines and said: 'Which wasn't quite true, right?'

'I have no idea as to most of the safe's contents. There was one item, however, which I did know about and failed to inform them of.'

'Why did you do that, Herr Six?'

'Because I would prefer that they didn't know.'

'And me?'

'The item in question affords you with an excellent chance of tracking down the murderer ahead of the police.'

'And what then?' I hoped he wasn't planning some private little execution, because I didn't feel up to wrestling with my conscience, especially when there was a lot of money involved.

'Before delivering the murderer into the hands of the authorities you will recover my property. On no account must they get their hands on it.'

'What exactly are we talking about?'

Six folded his hands thoughtfully, then unfolded them again, and then swathed himself with his arms like a party-girl's wrap. He looked quizzically at me.

'Confidentially, of course,' I growled.

'Jewels,' he said. 'You see, Herr Günther, my daughter died intestate, and without a will all her property goes to her husband's estate. Paul did make a will, leaving everything to the Reich.' He shook his head. 'Can you believe such stupidity, Herr Günther? He left everything. Everything. One can hardly credit it.'

'He was a patriot then.'

Six failed to perceive the irony in my remark. He snorted with derision. 'My dear Herr Günther, he was a National Socialist. Those people think that they are the first people ever to love the Fatherland.' He smiled grimly. 'I love my country. And there is nobody who gives more than I do. But I simply cannot stand the thought that the Reich is to be enriched even further at my expense. Do you understand me?'

'I think so.'

'Not only that, but the jewels were her mother's, so quite apart from their intrinsic value, which I can tell you is considerable, they are also of some sentimental account.'

'How much are they worth?'

Schemm stirred himself to offer up some facts and figures.

'I think I can be of some assistance here, Herr Six,' he said, delving into a briefcase that lay by his feet, and producing a buff-coloured file which he laid on the rug between the two sofas. 'I have here the last insurance valuations, as well as some photographs.' He lifted a sheet of paper and read off the bottom-line figure with no more expression than if it had been the amount of his monthly newspaper account. 'Seven hundred and fifty thousand Reichsmarks.' I let out an involuntary whistle. Schemm winced at that, and handed me some photographs. I had seen bigger stones, but only in photographs of the pyramids. Six took over with a description of their history.

'In 1925 the world jewel market was flooded with gems sold by Russian exiles or put on sale by the Bolsheviks, who had discovered a treasure trove walled up in the palace of Prince Youssoupov, husband to the niece of the Tsar. I acquired several pieces in Switzerland that same year: a brooch, a bracelet and, most precious of all, a diamond collet necklace consisting of twenty brilliants. It was made by Cartier and weighs over one hundred carats. It goes without saying, Herr Günther, that it will not be easy to dispose of such a piece.'

'No, indeed.' It might seem cynical of me, but the sentimental value of the jewels was now looking quite insignificant beside their monetary value. 'Tell me about the safe.'

'I paid for it,' said Six. 'Just as I paid for the house. Paul didn't have a great deal of money. When Grete's mother died I gave her the jewels, and at the same time I had a safe installed so that she could keep them there when they weren't in the vault at the bank.'

'So she had been wearing them quite recently?'

'Yes. She accompanied my wife and myself to a ball just a few nights before she was killed.'

'What kind of safe was it?'

'A Stockinger. Wall-mounted, combination lock.'

'And who knew the combination?'

'My daughter, and Paul, of course. They had no secrets from

each other, and I believe he kept certain papers to do with his work there.'

'Nobody else?'

'No. Not even me.'

'Do you know how the safe was opened, if there were any explosives used?'

'I believe there were no explosives used.'

'A nutcracker then.'

'How's that?'

'A professional safe-cracker. Mind you, it would have to be someone very good to puzzle it.' Six leaned forward on the sofa.

'Perhaps,' he said, 'the thief forced Grete or Paul to open it, then ordered them back to bed, where he shot them both. And afterwards he set fire to the house in order to cover his tracks – throw the police off the scent.'

'Yes, that's possible,' I admitted. I rubbed a perfectly circular area of smooth skin on my otherwise stubbly face: it's where a mosquito bit me when I was in Turkey, and ever since then I've never had to shave it. But quite often I find myself rubbing it when I feel uneasy about something. And if there's one thing guaranteed to make me feel uneasy, it's a client playing detective. I didn't rule out what he was suggesting might have happened, but it was my turn to play the expert: 'Possible, but messy,' I said. 'I can't think of a better way of raising the alarm than making your own private Reichstag. Playing Van der Lubbe and torching the place doesn't sound like the sort of thing a professional thief would do, but then neither does murder.' There were a lot of holes in that of course: I had no idea that it was a professional; not only that, but in my experience it's rare that a professional job also involves murder. I just wanted to hear my own voice for a change.

'Who would have known she had jewels in the safe?' I asked.

'Me,' said Six. 'Grete wouldn't have told anyone. I don't know if Paul had.'

'And did either of them have any enemies?'

'I can't answer for Paul,' he said, 'but I'm sure that Grete didn't have an enemy in the world.' While I could accept the possibility that Daddy's little girl always brushed her teeth and said her prayers at night, I found it hard to ignore how vague Six was about his son-in-law. That made the second time he was uncertain about what Paul would have done.

'What about you?' I said. 'A rich and powerful man like yourself must have his fair share of enemies.' He nodded. 'Is there anyone who might hate you bad enough to want to get back at you through your daughter?'

He re-kindled his Black Wisdom, puffed at it and then held it away from him between the tips of his fingers. 'Enemies are the inevitable corollary of great wealth, Herr Günther,' he told me. 'But these are business rivals I'm talking about, not gangsters. I don't think any of them would be capable of something as cold-blooded as this.' He stood up and went to attend to the fire. With a large brass poker he dealt vigorously with the log that was threatening to topple out of the grate. While Six was off-guard I jabbed him with one about the son-in-law.

'Did you and your daughter's husband get on?'

He twisted round to look at me, poker still in hand, and face slightly flushed. It was all the answer that I needed, but still he tried to throw some sand in my eyes. 'Why ever do you ask such a question?' he demanded.

'Really, Herr Günther,' said Schemm, affecting shock at my asking such an insensitive question.

'We had our differences of opinion,' said Six. 'But what man can be expected sometimes not to agree with his son-in-law?' He put down the poker. I kept quiet for a minute. Eventually he said: 'Now then, with regard to the conduct of your investigations, I would prefer it if you would confine your activities specifically to searching for the jewels. I don't care for the idea of you snooping around in the affairs of my family. I'll pay your fees, whatever they are –'

'Seventy marks a day, plus expenses,' I lied, hoping that Schemm hadn't checked it out.

'What is more, the Germania Life Assurance and Germania Insurance Companies will pay you a recovery fee of five per cent. Is that agreeable to you, Herr Günther?' Mentally I calculated the figure to be 37,500. With that sort of money I was set. I found myself nodding, although I didn't care for the ground rules he was laying down: but then for nearly 40,000 it was his game.

'But I warn you, I'm not a patient man,' he said. 'I want results, and I want them quickly. I have written out a cheque for your immediate requirements.' He nodded to his stooge, who handed me a cheque. It was for 1,000 marks and made out to cash at the Privat Kommerz Bank. Schemm dug into his briefcase again and handed me a letter on the Germania Life Assurance Company's notepaper.

'This states that you have been retained by our company to investigate the fire, pending a claim by the estate. The house was insured by us. If you have any problems you should contact me. On no account are you to bother Herr Six, or to mention his name. Here is a file containing any background information you may need.'

'You seem to have thought of everything,' I said pointedly.

Six stood up, followed by Schemm, and then, stiffly, by me. 'When will you start your investigations?' he said.

'First thing in the morning.'

'Excellent.' He clapped me on the shoulder. 'Ulrich will drive you home.' Then he walked over to his desk, sat down in his chair and settled down to go through some papers. He didn't pay me any more attention.

When I stood in the modest hall again, waiting for the butler to turn up with Ulrich, I heard another car draw up outside. This one was too loud to be a limousine, and I guessed that it was some kind of sports job. A door slammed, there were footsteps on the gravel and a key scraped in the lock of the front door. Through it came a woman I recognized immediately as the UFA Film Studio star, Ilse Rudel. She was wearing a dark sable coat and an evening dress of blue satin-organza. She looked at me, puzzled, while I just gawped back at her. She was worth it. She had the kind of body I'd only ever dreamed about, in the sort of dream I'd often dreamed of having again. There wasn't much I couldn't imagine it doing, except the ordinary things like work and getting in a man's way.

'Good morning,' I said, but the butler was there with his cat-burglar's steps to take her mind off me and help her out of the sable.

'Farraj, where is my husband?'

'Herr Six is in the library, madam.' My blue eyes popped a good deal at that, and I felt my jaw slacken. That this goddess should be married to the gnome sitting in the study was the sort of thing that bolsters your faith in Money. I watched her walk towards the library door behind me. Frau Six – I couldn't get over it – was tall and blonde and as healthy-looking as her husband's Swiss bank account. There was a sulkiness about her mouth, and my acquaintance with the science of physiognomy told me that she was used to having her own way: in cash. Brilliant clips flashed on her perfect ears, and as she got nearer the air was filled with the scent of 4711 cologne. Just as I thought she was going to ignore me, she glanced in my direction and said coolly: 'Goodnight, whoever you are.' Then the library swallowed her whole before I had a chance to do the same. I rolled my tongue up and tucked it back into my mouth. I looked at my watch. It was 3.30. Ulrich reappeared.

'No wonder he stays up late,' I said, and followed him through the door.

3

The following morning was grey and wet. I woke with a whore's drawers in my mouth, drank a cup of coffee and went through the morning's *Berliner Borsenzeitung*, which was even more difficult to understand than usual, with sentences as long and as hard-to-incomprehensible as a speech from Hess.

Shaved and dressed and carrying my laundry bag, I was at Alexanderplatz, the chief traffic centre of east Berlin, less than an hour later. Approached from Neue Königstrasse, the square is flanked by two great office blocks: Berolina Haus to the right, and Alexander Haus to the left, where I had my office on the fourth floor. I dropped off my laundry at Adler's Wet-Wash Service on the ground floor before going up.

Waiting for the lift, it was hard to ignore the small noticeboard that was situated immediately next to it, to which were pinned an appeal for contributions to the Mother and Child Fund, a Party exhortation to go and see an anti-Semitic film and an inspiring picture of the Führer. This noticeboard was the responsibility of the building's caretaker, Herr Gruber, a shifty little undertaker of a man. Not only is he the block air-defence monitor with police powers (courtesy of Orpo, the regular uniformed police), he is also a Gestapo informer. Long ago I decided that it would be bad for business to fall out with Gruber and so, like all the other residents of Alexander Haus, I gave him three marks a week, which is supposed to cover my contributions to whichever new money-making scheme the DAF, the German Labour Front, has dreamed up.

I cursed the lift's lack of speed as I saw Gruber's door open just enough to permit his peppered-mackerel of a face to peer down the corridor.

'Ah, Herr Günther, it's you,' he said, coming out of his office. He edged towards me like a crab with a bad case of corns.

'Good morning, Herr Gruber,' I said, avoiding his face. There was something about it that always reminded me of Max Schreck's screen portrayal of Nosferatu, an effect that was enhanced by the rodent-like washing movements of his skeletal hands.

'There was a young lady who came for you,' he said. 'I sent her up. I do hope that was convenient, Herr Günther.'

'Yes –'

'If she's still there, that is,' he said. 'That was at least half an hour ago. Only I knew Fräulein Lehmann is no longer working for you, so I had to say that there was no telling when you would turn up, you keeping such irregular hours.' To my relief the lift arrived and I drew open the door and stepped in.

'Thank you, Herr Gruber,' I said, and shut the door.

'Heil Hitler,' he said. The lift started to rise up the shaft. I called: 'Heil Hitler.' You don't miss the Hitler Salute with someone like Gruber. It's not worth the trouble. But one day I'm going to have to beat the crap out of that weasel, just for the sheer pleasure of it.

I share the fourth floor with a 'German' dentist, a 'German' insurance broker, and a 'German' employment agency, the latter having provided me with the temporary secretary who I now presumed was the woman seated in my waiting room. Coming out of the lift I hoped that she wasn't battle-scarred ugly. I didn't suppose for a minute that I was going to get a juicy one, but then I wasn't about to settle for any cobra either. I opened the door.

'Herr Günther?' She stood up, and I gave her the once-over: well, she wasn't as young as Gruber had led me to believe (I guessed her to be about forty-five) but not bad, I thought. A bit warm and cosy maybe (she had a substantial backside), but I happen to prefer them like that. Her hair was red with a touch of grey at the sides and on the crown, and tied back in a knot. She wore a suit of plain grey cloth, a white high-necked blouse and a black hat with a Breton brim turned up all around the head.

'Good morning,' I said, as affably as I could manage on top of the mewling tomcat that was my hangover. 'You must be my temporary secretary.' Lucky to get a woman at all, and this one looked half-reasonable.

'Frau Protze,' she declared, and shook my hand. 'I'm a widow.'

'Sorry,' I said, unlocking the door to my office. 'What part of Bavaria are you from?' The accent was unmistakable.

'Regensburg.'

'That's a nice town.'

'You must have found buried treasure there.' Witty too, I thought; that was good: she'd need a sense of humour to work for me.

I told her all about my business. She said it all sounded very exciting. I showed her into the adjoining cubicle where she was to sit on that backside.

'Actually, it's not so bad if you leave the door to the waiting room open,' I explained. Then I showed her the washroom along the corridor and apologized for the shards of soap and the dirty towels. 'I pay seventy-five marks a month and I get a tip like this,' I said. 'Damn it, I'm going to complain to that son-of-a-bitch of a landlord.' But even as I said it I knew I never would.

Back in my office I flipped open my diary and saw that the day's only appointment was Frau Heine, at eleven o'clock.

'I've an appointment in twenty minutes,' I said. 'Woman wants to know if I've managed to trace her missing son. He's a Jewish U-Boat.'

'A what?'

'A Jew in hiding.'

'What did he do that he has to hide?' she said.

'You mean apart from being a Jew?' I said. Already I could see that she had led quite a sheltered life, even for a Regensburger, and it seemed a shame to expose the poor woman to the potentially distressing sight of her country's evil-smelling arse. Still, she was all grown-up now, and I didn't have the time to worry about it.

'He just helped an old man who was being beaten up by some thugs. He killed one of them.'

'But surely if he was helping the old man –'

27

'Ah, but the old man was Jewish,' I explained. 'And the two thugs belonged to the SA. Strange how that changes everything, isn't it? His mother asked me to find out if he was still alive and still at liberty. You see, when a man is arrested and beheaded or sent to a KZ, the authorities don't always bother to inform his family. There are a lot of MPs – missing persons – from Jewish families these days. Trying to find them is a large part of my business.' Frau Protze looked worried.

'You help Jews?' she said.

'Don't worry,' I said. 'It's perfectly legal. And their money is as good as anyone's.'

'I suppose so.'

'Listen, Frau Protze,' I said. 'Jews, gypsies, Red Indians, it's all the same to me. I've got no reason to like them, but I don't have any reason to hate them either. When he walks through that door, a Jew gets the same deal as anyone else. Same as if he were the Kaiser's cousin. But it doesn't mean I'm dedicated to their welfare. Business is business.'

'Certainly,' said Frau Protze, colouring a little. 'I hope you don't think I have anything against the Jews.'

'Of course not,' I said. But of course that is what everybody says. Even Hitler.

'Good God,' I said, when the U-Boat's mother had left my office. 'That's what a satisfied customer looks like.' The thought depressed me so much that I decided to get out for a while.

At Loeser & Wolff I bought a packet of Murattis, after which I cashed Six's cheque. I paid half of it into my own account; and I treated myself to an expensive silk dressing-gown at Wertheim's just for being lucky enough to land as sweet an earner as Six.

Then I walked south-west, past the railway station from which a train now rumbled forth heading towards the Jannowitz Bridge, to the corner of Königstrasse where I had left my car.

Lichterfelde-Ost is a prosperous residential district in south-west Berlin much favoured by senior civil servants and members of the armed forces. Ordinarily it would have been way out of a young couple's price league, but then most young couples don't have a multi-millionaire like Hermann Six for a father.

Ferdinandstrasse ran south from the railway line. There was a policeman, a young Anwärter in the Orpo, standing guard outside Number 16, which was missing most of the roof and all of its windows. The bungalow's blackened timbers and brickwork told the story eloquently enough. I parked the Hanomag and walked up to the garden gate, where I flipped out my identification for the young bull, a spotty-looking youth of about twenty. He looked at it carefully, naively, and said redundantly: 'A private investigator, eh?'

'S'right. I've been retained by the insurance company to investigate the fire.' I lit a cigarette and watched the match suggestively as it burned towards my fingertips. He nodded, but his face appeared troubled. It cleared all of a sudden as he recognized me.

'Hey, didn't you use to be in Kripo up at the Alex?' I nodded, my nostrils trailing smoke like a factory chimney. 'Yes, I thought I recognized the name – Bernhard Günther. You caught Gormann, the Strangler, didn't you? I remember reading about it in the newspapers. You were famous.' I shrugged modestly. But he was right. When I caught Gormann I was famous for a while. I was a good bull in those days.

The young Anwärter took off his shako and scratched the top of his squarish head. 'Well, well,' he said; and then: 'I'm going to join Kripo. That is, if they'll have me.'

'You seem a bright enough fellow. You should do all right.'

'Thanks,' he said. 'Hey, how about a tip?'

'Try Scharhorn in the three o'clock at the Hoppegarten.' I shrugged. 'Hell, I don't know. What's your name, young fellow?'

'Eckhart,' he said. 'Wilhelm Eckhart.'

'So, Wilhelm, tell me about the fire. First of all, who's the pathologist on the case?'

'Some fellow from the Alex. I think he was called Upmann or Illmann.'

'An old man with a small chin-beard and rimless glasses?' He nodded. 'That's Illmann. When was he here?'

'Day before yesterday. Him and Kriminalkommissar Jost.'

'Jost? It's not like him to get his flippers dirty. I'd have thought it would take more than just the murder of a millionaire's daughter to get him off his fat arse.' I threw my cigarette away, in the opposite direction from the gutted house: there didn't seem any point in tempting fate.

'I heard it was arson,' I said. 'Is that true, Wilhelm?'

'Just smell the air,' he said.

I inhaled deeply, and shook my head.

'Don't you smell the petrol?'

'No. Berlin always smells like this.'

'Maybe I've just been standing here a long time. Well, they found a petrol can in the garden, so I guess that seals it.'

'Look, Wilhelm, would you mind if I just took a quick look around? It would save me having to fill out some forms. They'll have to let me have a look sooner or later.'

'Go right ahead, Herr Günther,' he said, opening the front gate. 'Not that there's much to see. They took bags of stuff away with them. I doubt there's anything that would be of interest to you. I don't even know why I'm still here.'

'I expect it's to watch out in case the murderer returns to the scene of the crime,' I said tantalizingly.

'Lord, do you think he might?' breathed the boy.

I pursed my lips. 'Who knows?' I said, although personally I had never heard of such a thing. 'I'll take a look anyway, and thanks, I appreciate it.'

'Don't mention it.'

He was right. There wasn't much to see. The man with the matches had done a proper job. I looked in at the front door, but there was so much debris I couldn't see anywhere for me to step. Round to the side I found a window that gave onto another room where the going wasn't so difficult underfoot. Hoping that I might at least find the safe, I climbed inside. Not that I needed to be there at all. I just wanted to form a picture inside my head. I work better that way: I've got a mind like a comic book. So I wasn't too disappointed when I found that the police had already taken the safe away, and that all that was left was a gaping hole in the wall. There was always Illmann, I told myself.

Back at the gate I found Wilhelm trying to comfort an older woman of about sixty, whose face was stained with tears.

'The cleaning woman,' he explained. 'She turned up just now. Apparently she's been away on holiday and hadn't heard about the fire. Poor old soul's had a bit of a shock.' He asked her where she lived.

'Neuenburger Strasse,' she sniffed. 'I'm all right now, thank you, young man.' From her coat pocket she produced a small lace handkerchief which seemed as improbable in her large, peasant hands as an antimacassar in those of Max Schmeling, the boxer, and quite inadequate for the task which lay before it: she blew her pickled-walnut of a nose with the sort of ferocity and volume that made me want to hold my hat on my head. Then she wiped her big, broad face with the soggy remnant. Smelling some information about the Pfarr household, I offered the old pork chop a lift home in my car.

'It's on the way,' I said.

'I wouldn't want to put you to any trouble.'

'It's no trouble at all,' I insisted.

'Well, if you are sure, that would be very kind of you. I have had a bit of a shock.' She picked up the box that lay at her feet, each one of which bulged over the top of its well-polished black walking shoe like a butcher's thumb in a thimble. Her name was Frau Schmidt.

'You're a good sort, Herr Günther,' said Wilhelm.

'Nonsense,' I said, and so it was. There was no telling what information I might glean from the old woman about her late employers. I took the box from her hands. 'Let me help you with that,' I said. It was a suit-box, from Stechbarth's, the official tailor to the services, and I had the idea that she might have been bringing it for the Pfarrs. I nodded silently at Wilhelm, and led the way to the car.

'Neuenburger Strasse,' I repeated as we drove off. 'That's off Lindenstrasse, isn't it?' She confirmed that it was, gave me some directions and was silent for a moment. Then she started weeping again.

'What a terrible tragedy,' she sobbed.

'Yes, yes, it's most unfortunate.'

I wondered how much Wilhelm had told her. The less the better, I thought, reasoning that the less shocked she was, at least at this stage, the more I would get out of her.

'Are you a policeman?' she asked.

'I'm investigating the fire,' I said evasively.

'I'm sure you must be too busy to drive an old woman like me across Berlin. Why don't you drop me on the other side of the bridge and I'll walk the rest. I'm all right now, really I am.'

'It's no trouble. Anyway, I'd quite like to talk to you about the Pfarrs – that is, if it wouldn't upset you.' We crossed the Landwehr Canal and came onto Belle-Alliance Platz, in the centre of which rises the great Column of Peace. 'You see, there will have to be an inquest, and it would help me if I knew as much about them as possible.'

'Yes, well I don't mind, if you think I can be of assistance,' she said.

When we got to Neuenburger Strasse, I parked the car and followed the old woman up to the second floor of an apartment building that was several storeys high.

Frau Schmidt's apartment was typical of the older generation of people in this city. The furniture was solid and elaborate – Berliners spend a lot of money on their tables and chairs – and there was a big porcelain-tiled stove in the living room. A copy of an engraving by Dürer, which was as common in the Berliner's home as an aquarium in a doctor's waiting room, hung dully above a dark red Biedermeier sideboard on which were placed various photographs (including one of our beloved Führer) and a little silk swastika mounted in a large bronze frame. There was also a drinks tray, from which I took a bottle of schnaps and poured a small glassful.

'You'll feel better after you've drunk this,' I said, handing her the glass, and wondering whether or not I dared take the liberty of pouring myself one too. Enviously, I watched her knock it back in one. Smacking her fat lips she sat down on a brocaded chair by the window.

'Feel up to answering a few questions?'

She nodded. 'What do you want to know?'

'Well for a start, how long had you known Herr and Frau Pfarr?'

'Hmm, let's see now.' A silent movie of uncertainty flickered on the woman's face. The voice emptied slowly out of the Boris Karloff mouth, with its slightly protruding teeth, like grit from a bucket. 'It must be a year, I suppose.' She stood up again and removed her coat, revealing a dingy, floral-patterned smock. Then she coughed for several seconds, tapping herself on the chest as she did so.

All this time I stood squarely in the middle of the room, my hat on the back of my head and my hands in my pockets. I asked her what sort of couple the Pfarrs had been.

'I mean, were they happy? Argumentative?' She nodded to both of these suggestions.

'When I first went to work there, they were very much in love,' she said. 'But it wasn't long after that that she lost her job as a schoolteacher. Quite cut up about it, she was. And before long they were arguing. Not that he was there very often when I was. But when he was, then more often than not they'd have words, and I don't mean squabbles, like most couples. No, they had loud, angry arguments, almost as if they hated each other, and a couple of times I found her crying in her room afterwards. Well, I really don't know what it was they had to be unhappy about. They had a lovely home – it was a pleasure to clean it, so it was. Mind you, they weren't flashy. I never once saw her spending lots of money on things. She had lots of nice clothes, but nothing showy.'

'Any jewellery?'

'I believe she had some jewellery, but I can't say as I remember her wearing it, but then I was only there in the daytime. On the other hand, there was an occasion when I moved his jacket and some earrings fell onto the floor, and they weren't the sort of earrings that she would have worn.'

'How do you mean?'

'These were for pierced ears, and Frau Pfarr only ever wore clips. So I drew my own conclusions, but said nothing. It was none of my business what he got up to. But I reckon she had her suspicions. She wasn't a stupid woman. Far from it. I believe that's what drove her to drink as much as she did.'

'Did she drink?'

'Like a sponge.'

'What about him? He worked at the Ministry of the Interior, didn't he?'

She shrugged. 'It was some government place, but I couldn't tell you what it was called. He was something to do with the law – he had a certificate on the wall of his study. All the same, he was very quiet about his work. And very careful not to leave papers lying around so that I might see them. Not that I would have read them, mind. But he didn't take the chance.'

'Did he work at home much?'

'Sometimes. And I know he used to spend time at that big office building on Bülowplatz – you know, the one that used to be the headquarters for them Bolsheviks.'

'You mean the DAF building, the headquarters of the German Labour Front. That's what it is now that the Kozis have been thrown out of it.'

'That's right. Now and again Herr Pfarr would give me a lift there, you see. My sister lives in Brunnenstrasse and normally I'd catch a Number 99 to Rosenthaler Platz after work. Now and then Herr Pfarr was kind enough to run me as far as Bülowplatz, where I'd see him go in the DAF building.'

'You saw them last – when?'

'It's two weeks yesterday. I've been on holiday, see. A Strength Through Joy trip to Rugen Island. I saw her, but not him.'

'How was she?'

'She seemed quite happy for a change. Not only that, but she didn't have a drink in her hand when she spoke to me. She told me that she was planning a little holiday to the spas. She often went there. I think she got dried out.'

'I see. And so this morning you went to Ferdinandstrasse via the tailors, is that correct, Frau Schmidt?'

'Yes, that's right. I often did little errands for Herr Pfarr. He was usually too busy to get to the shops, and so he'd pay me to get things for him. Before I went on holiday there was a note asking me to drop his suit off at his tailors and that they knew all about it.'

'His suit, you say.'

'Well, yes, I think so.' I picked up the box.

'Mind if I take a look?'

'I don't see why not. He's dead after all, isn't he?'

Even before I had removed the lid I had a pretty good idea of what was in the box. I wasn't wrong. There was no mistaking the midnight black that echoed the old élitist cavalry regiments of the Kaiser's army, the Wagnerian double-lightning flash on the right collar-patch and the Roman-style eagle and swastika on the left sleeve. The three pips on the left collar-patch denoted the wearer of the uniform as a captain, or whatever the fancy rank that captains were called in the SS was. There was a piece of paper pinned to the right sleeve. It was an invoice from Stechbarth's, addressed to Hauptsturmführer Pfarr, for twenty-five marks. I whistled.

'So Paul Pfarr was a black angel.'

'I'd never have believed it,' said Frau Schmidt.

'You mean you never saw him wearing this?'

She shook her head. 'I never even saw it hanging in his wardrobe.'

'Is that so.' I wasn't sure whether I believed her or not, but I could think of no reason why she should lie about it. It was not uncommon for lawyers – German lawyers, working for the Reich – to be in the SS: I imagined Pfarr wearing his uniform on ceremonial occasions only.

It was Frau Schmidt's turn to look puzzled. 'I meant to ask you how the fire started.'

I thought for a minute and decided to let her have it without any of the protective padding, in the hope that the shock would stop her asking some awkward questions that I couldn't answer.

'It was arson,' I said quietly. 'They were both murdered.' Her jaw dropped like a cat-flap, and her eyes moistened again, as if she had stepped into a draught.

'Good God,' she gasped. 'How terrible. Whoever could do such a thing?'

'That's a good question,' I said. 'Do you know if either of them had any enemies?' She sighed deeply and then shook her head. 'Did you ever overhear either of them arguing with someone other than each other? On the telephone, perhaps? Somebody at the door? Anything.' She continued to shake her head.

'Wait a minute, though,' she said slowly. 'Yes, there was one occasion, several months ago. I heard Herr Pfarr arguing with another man in his study. It was pretty heated and, I can tell you, some of the language they used was not fit to be heard by decent folk. They were arguing about politics. At least I think it was politics. Herr Six was saying some terrible things about the Führer which –'

'Did you say Herr Six?'

'Yes,' she said. 'He was the other man. After a while he came storming out of the study and through the front door with a face like pig's liver. Nearly knocked me over he did.'

'Can you remember what else was said?'

'Only that each accused the other of trying to ruin him.'

'Where was Frau Pfarr when all this happened?'

'She was away, on one of her trips, I think.'

'Thank you,' I said. 'You've been most helpful. And now I must be getting back to Alexanderplatz.' I turned towards the door.

'Excuse me,' said Frau Schmidt. She pointed to the tailor's box. 'What shall I do with Herr Pfarr's uniform?'

'Mail it,' I said, putting a couple of marks on the table. 'To Reichsführer Himmler, Prinz Albrecht Strasse, Number 9.'

4

Simeonstrasse is only a couple of streets away from Neuenburger Strasse, but where the windows of the buildings in the latter are lacking paint, in Simeonstrasse they are lacking glass. Calling it a poor area is a bit like saying that Joey Goebbels has a problem finding his size in shoes.

Tenement buildings five- and six-storeys high closed in on a narrow crocodile's back of deep cobblestones like two granite cliffs, linked only by the rope-bridges of washing. Sullen youths, each one of them with a roll-up hanging in ashes from his thin lips like a trail of shit from a bowl-bored goldfish, buttressed the ragged corners of gloomy alleyways, staring blankly at the colony of snot-nosed children who hopped and skipped along the pavements. The children played noisily, oblivious to the presence of these older ones and taking no notice of the crudely daubed swastikas, hammers and sickles and general obscenities that marked the street walls and which were their elders' dividing dogmas. Below the level of the rubbish-strewn streets and under the shadow of the sun-eclipsing edifices which enclosed them were the cellars that contained the small shops and offices that served the area.

Not that it needs much in the way of service. There is no money in an area like this, and for most of these concerns business is about as brisk as a set of oak floorboards in a Lutheran church hall.

It was into one of these small shops, a pawnbroker, that I went, ignoring the large Star of David daubed on the wooden shutters that protected the shop window from breakage. A bell rang as I opened and shut the door. Doubly deprived of daylight, the shop's only source of illumination was an oil lamp hanging from the low ceiling, and the general effect was that of the inside of an old sailing ship. I browsed around, waiting for Weizmann, the proprietor, to appear from the back of the shop.

There was an old Pickelhaube helmet, a stuffed marmot, in a glass case, that looked as if it had perished of anthrax, and an old Siemens vacuum-cleaner; there were several cases full of military medals – mostly second-class Iron Crosses like mine own, twenty odd volumes of Kohler's *Naval Calendar*, full of ships long since sunk or sent to the breaker's yard, a Blaupunkt radio, a chipped bust of Bismarck and an old Leica. I was inspecting the case of medals when a smell of tobacco, and Weizmann's familiar cough, announced his present appearance.

'You should look after yourself, Weizmann.'

'And what would I do with a long life?' The threat of Weizmann's wheezing cough was ever present in his speech. It lay in wait to trip him like a sleeping halberdier. Sometimes he managed to catch himself; but this time he fell into a spasm of coughing that sounded hardly human at all, more like someone trying to start a car with an almost flat battery, and as usual it seemed to afford him no relief whatsoever. Nor did it require him to remove the pipe from his tobacco-pouch of a mouth.

'You should try inhaling a little bit of air now and then,' I told him. 'Or at least something you haven't first set on fire.'

'Air,' he said. 'It goes straight to my head. Anyway, I'm training myself to do without it: there's no telling when they'll ban Jews from breathing oxygen.' He lifted the counter. 'Come into the back room, my friend, and tell me what service I can do for you.' I followed him round the counter, past an empty bookcase.

'Is business picking up then?' I said. He turned to look at me. 'What happened to all the books?' Weizmann shook his head sadly.

'Unfortunately, I had to remove them. The Nuremberg Laws –' he said with a scornful laugh, '– they forbid a Jew to sell books. Even secondhand ones.' He turned and passed on through to the back room. 'These days I believe in the law like I believe in Horst Wessel's heroism.'

'Horst Wessel?' I said. 'Never heard of him.'

Weizmann smiled and pointed at an old Jacquard sofa with the stem of his reeking pipe. 'Sit down, Bernie, and let me fix us a drink.'

'Well, what do you know? They still let Jews drink booze. I was almost feeling sorry for you back there when you told me about those books. Things are never as bad as they seem, just as long as there's a drink about.'

'That's the truth, my friend.' He opened a corner cabinet, found the bottle of schnaps and poured it carefully but generously. Handing me my glass he said, 'I'll tell you something. If it wasn't for all the people who drink, this country really would be in a hell of a state.' He raised his glass. 'Let us wish for more drunks and the frustration of an efficiently run National Socialist Germany.'

'To more drunks,' I said, watching him drink it, almost too gratefully. He had a shrewd face, with a mouth that wore a wry smile, even with the chimneystack. A large, fleshy nose separated eyes that were rather too closely set together, and supported a pair of thick, rimless glasses. The still-dark hair was brushed neatly to the right of a high forehead. Wearing his well-pressed blue pin-striped suit, Weizmann looked not unlike Ernst Lubitsch, the comic actor turned film director. He sat down at an old rolltop and turned sideways to face me.

'So what can I do for you?'

I showed him the photograph of Six's necklace. He wheezed a little as he looked at it, and then coughed his way into a remark.

'If it's real –' He smiled and nodded his head from side to side. 'Is it real? Of course it's real, or why else would you be showing me such a nice photograph. Well then, it looks like a very fine piece indeed.'

'It's been stolen,' I said.

'Bernie, with you sitting there I didn't think it was stuck up a tree waiting for the fire service.' He shrugged. 'But, such a fine-looking necklace – what can I tell you about it that you don't already know?'

'Come on, Weizmann. Until you got caught thieving you were one of Friedlaender's best jewellers.'

'Ah, you put it so delicately.'

'After twenty years in the business you know bells like you know your own waistcoat pocket.'

'Twenty-two years,' he said quietly, and poured us both another glass. 'Very well. Ask your questions, Bernie, and we shall see what we shall see.'

'How would someone go about getting rid of it?'

'You mean some other way than just dropping it in the Land-wehr Canal? For money? It would depend.'

'On what?' I said patiently.

'On whether the person in possession was Jewish or Gentile.'

'Come on, Weizmann,' I said. 'You don't have to keep wringing the yarmulke for my benefit.'

'No, seriously, Bernie. Right now the market for gems is at rock bottom. There are lots of Jews leaving Germany who, to fund their emigration, must sell the family jewels. At least, those who are lucky enough to have any to sell. And, as you might expect, they get the lowest prices. A Gentile could afford to wait for the market to become more buoyant. A Jew could not.' Coughing in small explosive bursts, he took another, longer look at Six's photo-graph and gave a chesty little shrug.

'Way out of my league, I can tell you that much. Sure, I buy some small stuff. But nothing big enough to interest the boys from the Alex. Like you, they know about me, Bernie. There's my time in the cement for a start. If I was to step badly out of line they'd have me in a KZ quicker than the drawers off a Kit-Kat showgirl.' Wheezing like a leaky old harmonium, Weizmann grinned and handed the photograph back to me.

'Amsterdam would be the best place to sell it,' he said. 'If you could get it out of Germany, that is. German customs officers are a smuggler's nightmare. Not that there aren't plenty of people in Berlin who would buy it.'

'Like who, for instance?'

'The two-tray boys – one tray on top and one under the counter – they might be interested. Like Peter Neumaier. He's got a nice little shop on Schlüterstrasse, specializing in antique jewellery.

This might be his sort of thing. I've heard he's got plenty of flea and can pay it in whatever currency you like. Yes, I'd have thought he'd certainly be worth checking out.' He wrote the name down on a piece of paper. 'Then we have Werner Seldte. He may appear to be a bit Potsdam, but he's not above buying some hot bells.' Potsdam was a word of faint opprobrium for people who, like the antiquated pro-Royalists of that town, were smug, hypocritical and hopelessly dated in both intellectual and social ideas. 'Frankly, he's got fewer scruples than a backstreet angelmaker. His shop is on Budapester Strasse or Ebertstrasse or Hermann Goering Strasse or whatever the hell the Party calls it now.

'Then there are the dealers, the diamond merchants who buy and sell from classy offices where a browser for an engagement ring is about as popular as a pork chop in a rabbi's coat pocket. These are the sort of people who do most of their business on the gabbler.' He wrote down some more names. 'This one, Laser Oppenheimer, he's a Jew. That's just to show that I'm fair and that I've got nothing against Gentiles. Oppenheimer has an office on Joachimsthaler Strasse. Anyway, the last I heard of him he was still in business.

'There's Gert Jeschonnek. New to Berlin. Used to be based in Munich. From what I've heard, he's the worst kind of March Violet – you know, climbing on board the Party wagon and riding it to make a quick profit. He's got a very smart set of offices in that steel monstrosity on Potsdamer Platz. What's it called –?'

'Columbus Haus,' I said.

'That's it. Columbus Haus. They say that Hitler doesn't much care for modern architecture, Bernie. Do you know what that means?' Weizmann gave a little chuckle. 'It means that he and I have something in common.'

'Is there anyone else?'

'Maybe. I don't know. It's possible.'

'Who?'

'Our illustrious Prime Minister.'

'Goering? Buying hot bells? Are you serious?'

'Oh yes,' he said firmly. 'That man has a passion for owning expensive things. And he's not always as fussy as he could be regarding how he gets hold of them. Jewels are one thing I know he has a weakness for. When I was at Friedlaender's he used to come into the shop quite often. He was poor in those days – at least, too poor to buy much. But you could see he would have bought a great deal if he had been able to.'

'Jesus Christ, Weizmann,' I said. 'Can you imagine it? Me dropping in at Karinhall and saying, "Excuse me, Herr Prime Minister, but you wouldn't happen to know anything about a valuable diamond necklace that some coat has clawed from a Ferdinandstrasse residence in the past few days? I trust you would have no objections to me taking a look down your wife Emmy's dress and seeing if she's got them hidden somewhere between the exhibits?"'

'You'd have the devil's own job to find anything down there,' wheezed Weizmann excitedly. 'That fat sow is almost as big as he is. I'll bet she could breastfeed the entire Hitler Youth and still have milk enough left for Hermann's breakfast.' He began a fit of coughing which would have carried off another man. I waited until it had found a lower gear, and then produced a fifty. He waved it away.

'What did I tell you?'

'Let me buy something, then.'

'What's the matter? Are you running out of crap all of a sudden?'

'No, but –'

'Wait, though,' he said. 'There is something you might like to buy. A finger lifted it at a big parade on Unter den Linden.' He got up and went into the small kitchen behind the office. When he came back he was carrying a packet of Persil.

'Thanks,' I said, 'but I send my stuff to the laundry.'

'No, no, no,' he said, pushing his hand into the powder. 'I hid it in here just in case I had any unwelcome visitors. Ah, here we are.' He withdrew a small, flat, silvery object from the packet, and polished it on his lapel before laying it flat on my palm. It was an oval-shaped disc about the size of a matchbox. On one side was the

42

ubiquitous German eagle clutching the laurel crown that encircled the swastika; and on the other were the words Secret State Police, and a serial number. At the top was a small hole by which the bearer of the badge could attach it to the inside of his jacket. It was a Gestapo warrant-disc.

'That ought to open a few doors for you, Bernie.'

'You're not joking,' I said. 'Christ, if they caught you with this –'

'Yes, I know. It would save you a great deal of slip money, don't you think? So if you want it, I'll ask fifty for it.'

'Fair enough,' I said, although I wasn't sure about carrying it myself. What he said was true: it would save on bribes; but if I was caught using it I'd be on the first train to Sachsenhausen. I paid him the fifty. 'A bull without his beer-token. God, I'd like to have seen the bastard's face. That's like a horn-player without a mouthpiece.' I stood up to go.

'Thanks for the information,' I said. 'And in case you didn't know, it's summertime up on the surface.'

'Yes, I noticed that the rain was a little warmer than usual. At least a rotten summer is one thing they can't blame on the Jews.'

'Don't you believe it,' I said.

5

There was chaos back at Alexanderplatz, where a tram had derailed. The clock in the tall, red-brick tower of St George's was striking three o'clock, reminding me that I hadn't eaten anything since a bowl of Quaker Quick Flakes ('For the Youth of the Nation') for breakfast. I went to the Café Stock; it was close by Wertheim's Department Store, and in the shadow of the S-Bahn railway viaduct.

The Café Stock was a modest little restaurant with an even more modest bar in the far corner. Such was the size of the eponymous proprietor's bibulous belly that there was only just room for him to squeeze behind the bar; and as I came through the door it was there that I found him standing, pouring beers and polishing glasses, while his pretty little wife waited on the tables. These tables were often taken by Kripo officers from the Alex, and this had the effect of obliging Stock to play up his commitment to National Socialism. There was a large picture of the Führer on the wall, as well as a printed sign that said, 'Always give the Hitler Salute.'

Stock wasn't always that way, and before March 1933 he had been a bit of a Red. He knew that I knew it, and it always worried him that there were others who would remember it too. So I didn't blame him for the picture and the sign. Everyone in Germany was somebody different before March 1933. And as I'm always saying, 'Who isn't a National Socialist when there's a gun pointed at his head?'

I sat down at an empty table and surveyed the rest of the clientele. A couple of tables away were two bulls from the Queer Squad, the Department for the Suppression of Homosexuality: a bunch of what are little better than blackmailers. At a table next to them, and sitting on his own, was a young Kriminalassistent from the station at Werdersche Market, whose badly pock-marked face

I remembered chiefly for his having once arrested my informer, Neumann, on suspicion of theft.

Frau Stock took my order of pig's knuckle with sauerkraut briskly and without much in the way of pleasantry. A shrewish woman, she knew and disapproved of my paying Stock for small snippets of interesting gossip about what was going on at the Alex. With so many officers coming in and out of the place, he often heard quite a lot. She moved off to the dumb-waiter and shouted my order down the shaft to the kitchen. Stock squeezed out from behind his bar and ambled over. He had a copy of the Party newspaper, the *Völkischer Beobachter*, in his fat hand.

'Hallo, Bernie,' he said. 'Lousy weather we're having, eh?'

'Wet as a poodle, Max,' I said. 'I'll have a beer when you're ready.'

'Coming right up. You want to look at the paper?'

'Anything in it?'

'Mr and Mrs Charles Lindbergh are in Berlin. He's the fellow that flew across the Atlantic.'

'It sounds fascinating, really it does. I suppose the great aviator will be opening a few bomber factories while he's here. Maybe even take a test-flight in a shiny new fighter. Perhaps they want him to pilot one all the way to Spain.'

Stock looked nervously over his shoulder and gestured for me to lower my voice. 'Not so loud, Bernie,' he said, twitching like a rabbit. 'You'll get me shot.' Muttering unhappily, he went off to get my beer.

I glanced at the newspaper he had left on my table. There was a small paragraph about the 'investigation of a fire on Ferdinand-strasse, in which two people are known to have lost their lives', which made no mention of their names, or their relation to my client, or that the police were treating it as a murder investigation. I tossed it contemptuously onto another table. There's more real news on the back of a matchbox than there is in the *Völkischer Beo-bachter*. Meanwhile, the detectives from the Queer Squad were leaving; and Stock came back with my beer. He held the glass up for my attention before placing it on the table.

'A nice sergeant-major on it, like always,' he said.

'Thanks.' I took a long drink and then wiped some of the sergeant-major off my upper lip with the back of my hand. Frau Stock collected my lunch from the dumb-waiter and brought it over. She gave her husband a look that should have burned a hole in his shirt, but he pretended not to have seen it. Then she went to clear the table that was being vacated by the pockmarked Kriminalassistant. Stock sat down and watched me eat.

After a while I said, 'So what have you heard? Anything?'

'A man's body fished out of the Landwehr.'

'That's about as unusual as a fat railwayman,' I told him. 'The canal is the Gestapo's toilet, you know that. It's got so that if someone disappears in this goddamn city, it's quicker to look for him at the lighterman's office than police headquarters or the city morgue.'

'Yes, but this one had a billiard cue – up his nose. It penetrated the bottom of his brain they reckoned.'

I put down my knife and fork. 'Would you mind laying off the gory details until I've finished my food?' I said.

'Sorry,' said Stock. 'Well, that's all there is really. But they don't normally do that sort of thing, do they, the Gestapo?'

'There's no telling what is considered normal on Prinz Albrecht Strasse. Perhaps he'd been sticking his nose in where it wasn't wanted. They might have wanted to do something poetic.' I wiped my mouth and laid some change on the table which Stock collected up without bothering to count it.

'Funny to think that it used to be the Art School – Gestapo headquarters, I mean.'

'Hilarious. I bet the poor bastards they work over up there go to sleep as happy as little snowmen at the notion.' I stood up and went to the door. 'Nice about the Lindberghs though.'

I walked back to the office. Frau Protze was polishing the glass on the yellowing print of Tilly that hung on the wall of my waiting room, contemplating with some amusement the predicament of the hapless Burgomeister of Rothenburg. As I came through the door the phone started to ring. Frau Protze smiled at me and then stepped smartly into her little cubicle to answer it, leaving me to look afresh at the clean picture. It was a long time since I'd really looked at it. The Burgomeister, having pleaded with Tilly, the sixteenth-century commander of the Imperial German Army, for his town to be spared destruction, was required by his conqueror to drink six litres of beer without drawing breath. As I remembered the story, the Burgomeister had pulled off this prodigious feat of bibbing and the town had been saved. It was, as I had always thought, so characteristically German. And just the sort of sadistic trick some SA thug would play. Nothing really changes that much.

'It's a lady,' Frau Protze called to me. 'She won't give her name, but she insists on speaking to you.'

'Then put her through,' I said, stepping into my office. I picked up the candlestick and the earpiece.

'We met last night,' said the voice. I cursed, thinking it was Carola, the girl from Dagmar's wedding reception. I wanted to forget all about that little episode. But it wasn't Carola. 'Or perhaps I should say this morning. It was pretty late. You were on your way out and I was just coming back after a party. Do you remember?'

'Frau –' I hesitated, still not quite able to believe it.

'Please,' she said, 'less of the Frau. Ilse Rudel, if you don't mind, Herr Günther.'

'I don't mind at all,' I said. 'How could I not remember?'

'You might,' she said. 'You looked very tired.' Her voice was as sweet as a plate of Kaiser's pancakes. 'Hermann and I, we often forget that other people don't keep such late hours.'

'If you'll permit me to say so, you looked pretty good on it.'

'Well, thank you,' she cooed, sounding genuinely flattered. In my experience you can never flatter any woman too much, just as you can never give a dog too many biscuits.

'And how can I be of service?'

'I'd like to speak to you on a matter of some urgency,' she said. 'All the same, I'd rather not talk about it on the telephone.'

'Come and see me here, in my office?'

'I'm afraid I can't. I'm at the studios in Babelsberg right now. Perhaps you would care to come to my apartment this evening?'

'Your apartment?' I said. 'Well, yes, I'd be delighted. Where is it?'

'Badenschestrasse, Number 7. Shall we say nine o'clock?'

'That would be fine.' She hung up. I lit a cigarette and smoked it absently. She was probably working on a film, I thought, and imagined her telephoning me from her dressing room wearing only a robe, having just finished a scene in which she'd been required to swim naked in a mountain lake. That took me quite a few minutes. I've got a good imagination. Then I got to wondering if Six knew about the apartment. I decided he did. You don't get to be as rich as Six was without knowing your wife had her own place. She probably kept it on in order to retain a degree of independence. I guessed that there wasn't much she couldn't have had if she really put her mind to it. Putting her body to it as well probably got her the moon and a couple of galaxies on top. All the same, I didn't think it was likely that Six knew or would have approved of her seeing me. Not after what he had said about me not poking into his family affairs. Whatever it was she wanted to talk to me urgently about was certainly not for the gnome's ears.

I called Müller, the crime reporter on the *Berliner Morgenpost*, which was the only half-decent rag left on the news-stand. Müller was a good reporter gone to seed. There wasn't much call for the old style of crime-reporting; the Ministry of Propaganda had seen to that.

'Look,' I said after the preliminaries, 'I need some biographical information from your library files, as much as you can get and as soon as possible, on Hermann Six.'

'The steel millionaire? Working on his daughter's death, eh, Bernie?'

'I've been retained by the insurance company to investigate the fire.'

'What have you got so far?'

'You could write what I know on a tram ticket.'

'Well,' said Müller, 'that's about the size of the piece we've got on it for tomorrow's edition. The Ministry has told us to lay off it. Just to record the facts, and keep it small.'

'How's that?'

'Six has got some powerful friends, Bernie. His sort of money buys an awful lot of silence.'

'Were you onto anything?'

'I heard it was arson, that's about all. When do you need this stuff?'

'Fifty says tomorrow. And anything you can dig up on the rest of the family.'

'I can always use a little extra money. Be talking to you.'

I hung up and shoved some papers inside some old newspapers and then dumped them in one of the desk drawers that still had a bit of space. After that I doodled on the blotter and then picked up one of the several paperweights that were lying on the desk. I was rolling its cold bulk around my hands when there was a knock at the door. Frau Protze edged into the room.

'I wondered if there was any filing that needed to be done.' I pointed at the untidy stacks of files that lay on the floor behind my desk.

'That's my filing system there,' I said. 'Believe it or not, they are in some sort of order.' She smiled, humouring me no doubt, and nodded attentively as if I was explaining something that would change her life.

'And are they all work in progress?'

I laughed. 'This isn't a lawyer's office,' I said. 'With quite a few of them, I don't know whether they are in progress or not. Investigation isn't a fast business with quick results. You have to have a lot of patience.'

'Yes, I can see that,' she said. There was only one photograph on my desk. She turned it round to get a better look at it. 'She's very beautiful. Your wife?'

'She was. Died on the day of the Kapp Putsch.' I must have made

49

that remark a hundred times. Allying her death to another event like that, well, it plays down how much I still miss her, even after sixteen years. Never successfully however. 'It was Spanish influenza,' I explained. 'We were together for only ten months.' Frau Protze nodded sympathetically.

We were both silent for a moment. Then I looked at my watch. 'You can go home if you like,' I told her.

When she had gone I stood at my high window a long time and watched the wet streets below, glistening like patent leather in the late afternoon sunlight. The rain had stopped and it looked as though it would be a fine evening. Already the office workers were making their ways home, streaming out of Berolina Haus opposite, and down into the labyrinth of underground tunnels and walkways that led to the Alexanderplatz U-Bahn station.

Berlin. I used to love this old city. But that was before it had caught sight of its own reflection and taken to wearing corsets laced so tight that it could hardly breathe. I loved the easy, carefree philosophies, the cheap jazz, the vulgar cabarets and all of the other cultural excesses that characterized the Weimar years and made Berlin seem like one of the most exciting cities in the world.

Behind my office, to the south-east, was Police Headquarters, and I imagined all the good hard work that was being done there to crack down on Berlin's crime. Villainies like speaking disrespectfully of the Führer, displaying a 'Sold Out' sign in your butcher's shop window, not giving the Hitler Salute, and homosexuality. That was Berlin under the National Socialist Government: a big, haunted house with dark corners, gloomy staircases, sinister cellars, locked rooms and a whole attic full of poltergeists on the loose, throwing books, banging doors, breaking glass, shouting in the night and generally scaring the owners so badly that there were times when they were ready to sell up and get out. But most of the time they just stopped up their ears, covered their blackened eyes and tried to pretend that there was nothing wrong. Cowed with fear, they spoke very little, ignoring the carpet moving underneath their feet, and their laughter was the thin, nervous kind that always accompanies the boss's little joke.

Policing, like autobahn construction and informing, is one of the new Germany's growth industries; and so the Alex is always busy. Even though it was past closing time for most of the departments that had dealings with the public, there were still a great many people milling about the various entrances to the building when I got there. Entrance Four, for the Passport Office, was especially busy. Berliners, many of them Jewish, who had queued all day for an exit visa, were even now emerging from this part of the Alex, their faces happy or sad according to the success of their enterprise.

I walked on down Alexanderstrasse and passed Entrance Three, in front of which a couple of traffic police, nicknamed 'white mice' because of their distinctive short white coats, were climbing off their powder-blue BMW motorcycles. A Green Minna, a police-van, came racing down the street, Martin-horn blaring, in the direction of Jannowitz Bridge. Oblivious to the noise, the two white mice swaggered in through Entrance Three to make their reports.

I went in by Entrance Two, knowing the place well enough to have chosen the entrance where I was least likely to be challenged by someone. If I was stopped, I was on my way to Room 32a, the Lost Property Office. But Entrance Two also serves the police morgue.

I walked nonchalantly along a corridor and down into the basement, past a small canteen to a fire exit. I pushed the bar on the door down and found myself in a large cobbled courtyard where several police cars were parked. One of these was being washed by a man wearing gumboots who paid me no attention as I crossed the yard and ducked into another doorway. This led to the boiler room, and I stopped there for a moment while I made a mental check of my bearings. I hadn't worked at the Alex for ten years not to know my way around. My only concern was that I might meet someone who knew me. I opened the only other door that led out of the boiler room and ascended a short staircase into a corridor, at the end of which was the morgue.

When I entered the morgue's outer office I encountered a sour smell that was reminiscent of warm, wet poultry flesh. It mixed with the formaldehyde to make a sickly cocktail that I felt in my stomach at the same time as I drew it into my nostrils. The office, barely furnished with a couple of chairs and a table, contained nothing to warn the unwary of what lay beyond the two glass doors, except the smell and a sign which simply read 'Morgue: Entrance Forbidden'. I opened the doors a crack and looked inside.

In the centre of a grim, damp room was an operating-table that was also part trough. On opposite sides of a stained ceramic gulley were two marble slabs, set slightly at an angle so that fluids from a corpse could drain into the centre and be washed down a drain by water from one of the two tall murmuring taps that were situated at each end. The table was big enough for two corpses laid head-to-toe, one on each side of the drain; but there was only one cadaver, that of a male, which lay under the knife and the surgical saw. These were wielded by a bent, slight man with thin dark hair, a high forehead, glasses, a long hooked nose, a neat moustache and a small chin-beard. He was wearing gumboots, a heavy apron, rubber gloves and a stiff collar and a tie.

I stepped quietly through the doors, and contemplated the corpse with professional curiosity. Moving closer I tried to see what had caused the man's death. It was clear that the body had been lying in water, since the skin was sodden and peeling away on the hands and feet, like gloves and socks. Otherwise it was in largely reasonable condition, with the exception of the head. This was black in colour and completely featureless, like a muddy football, and the top part of the cranium had been sawn away and the brain removed. Like a wet Gordian knot, it now lay in a kidney-shaped dish awaiting dissection.

Confronted with violent death in all its ghastly hues, contorted attitudes and porcine fleshiness, I had no more reaction than if I had been looking in the window of my local 'German' butcher's shop, except that this one had more meat on display. Sometimes I was surprised at the totality of my own indifference to the sight of the stabbed, the drowned, the crushed, the shot, the burned and the bludgeoned, although I knew well how that insensitivity had come about. Seeing so much death on the Turkish front and in my service with Kripo, I had almost ceased to regard a corpse as being in any way human. This acquaintance with death had persisted since my becoming a private investigator, when the trail of a missing person so often led to the morgue at St Gertrauden, Berlin's largest hospital, or to a salvage-man's hut near a levee on the Landwehr Canal.

I stood there for several minutes, staring at the gruesome scene in front of me, and puzzled as to what had produced the condition of the head and the differing one of the body, before eventually Dr Illmann glanced round and saw me.

'Good God,' he growled. 'Bernhard Günther. Are you still alive?' I approached the table, and blew a breath of disgust.

'Christ,' I said. 'The last time I came across body odour this bad, a horse was sitting on my face.'

'He's quite a picture, isn't he?'

'You're telling me. What was he doing, frenching a polar bear? Or maybe Hitler kissed him.'

'Unusual, isn't it? Almost as if the head were burned.'

'Acid?'

'Yes.' Illmann sounded pleased, like I was a clever pupil. 'Very good. It's difficult to say what kind, but most probably hydrochloric or sulphuric.'

'Like someone didn't want you to know who he was.'

'Precisely so. Mind you, it doesn't disguise the cause of death. He had a broken billiard cue forced up one of his nostrils. It pierced the brain, killing him instantly. Not a very common way of killing a man; indeed, in my experience it is unique. However, one learns not to be surprised at the various ways in which murderers choose to kill their victims. But I'm sure you're not surprised. You always did have a good imagination for a bull, Bernie. To say nothing of your nerve. You know, you've got a hell of a nerve just walking in here like this. It's only my sentimental nature that stops me from having you thrown out on your ear.'

'I need to talk to you about the Pfarr case. You did the PM, didn't you?'

'You're well informed,' he said. 'As a matter of fact the family reclaimed the bodies this morning.'

'And your report?'

'Look, I can't talk here. I'll be through with our friend on the slab in a while. Give me an hour.'

'Where?'

'How about the Künstler Eck, on Alt Kölln. It's quiet there and we won't be disturbed.'

'The Künstler Eck,' I repeated. 'I'll find it.' I turned back towards the glass doors.

'Oh, and Bernie. Make sure you bring a little something for my expenses?'

The independent township of Alt Kölln, long since absorbed by the capital, is a small island on the River Spree. Largely given up to museums, it has thus earned itself the sobriquet 'Museum Island'. But I have to confess that I have never seen the inside of one of them. I'm not much interested in The Past and, if you ask me, it is this country's obsession with its history that has partly put us where we are now: in the shit. You can't go into a bar without some arsehole going on about our pre-1918 borders, or harking back to Bismarck and when we kicked the stuffing out of the French. These are old sores, and to my mind it doesn't do any good to keep picking at them.

From the outside, there was nothing about the place that would have attracted the passer-by to drop in for a casual drink: not the door's scruffy paintwork, nor the dried-up flowers in the window-box; and certainly not the poorly handwritten sign in the dirty window which read: 'Tonight's speech can be heard here.' I cursed, for this meant that Joey the Cripp was addressing a Party rally that evening, and as a result there would be the usual traffic chaos. I went down the steps and opened the door.

There was even less about the inside of the Künstler Eck that would have persuaded the casual drinker to stay awhile. The walls were covered with gloomy wood carvings – tiny models of cannons, death's heads, coffins and skeletons. Against the far wall was a large pump-organ painted to look like a graveyard, with crypts and graves yielding up their dead, at which a hunchback was playing a piece by Haydn. This was as much for his own benefit as anyone else's, since a group of storm-troopers were singing 'My Prussia Stands So Proud and Great' with sufficient gusto as to almost completely drown the hunchback's playing. I've seen some odd things in Berlin in my time, but this was like something from a Conrad Veidt film, and not a very good one at that. I expected the one-armed police-captain to come in at any moment.

Instead I found Illmann sitting alone in a corner, nursing a bottle of Engelhardt. I ordered two more of the same and sat down as the storm-troopers finished their song and the hunchback commenced a massacre of one of my favourite Schubert sonatas.

'This is a hell of a place to choose,' I said grimly.

'I'm afraid that I find it curiously quaint.'

'Just the place to meet your friendly neighbourhood body-snatcher. Don't you see enough of death during the day that you have to come to drink in a charnel-house like this?'

He shrugged unabashedly. 'It is only with death around me that I am constantly reminded that I am alive.'

'There's a lot to be said for necrophilia.' Illmann smiled, as if agreeing with me.

'So you want to know about the poor Hauptsturmführer and his little wife, eh?' I nodded. 'This is an interesting case, and, I don't mind telling you, the interesting ones are becoming increasingly rare. With all the people who wind up dead in this city you would think I was busy. But of course, there is usually little or no mystery about how most of them got that way. Half the time I find myself presenting the forensic evidence of a homicide to the very people who committed it. It's an upside down world that we live in.' He opened his briefcase and took out a blue ring-file. 'I brought the photographs. I thought you would want to see the happy couple. I'm afraid they're a pair of real stokers. I was only able to make the identification from their wedding rings, his and hers.'

I flicked through the file. The camera angles changed but the subject remained the same: two gun-metal grey corpses, bald like Egyptian pharaohs, lay on the exposed and blackened springs of what had once been a bed, like sausages left too long under the grill.

'Nice album. What were they doing, having a punch-up?' I said, noticing the way in which each corpse had its fists raised like a bare-knuckle fighter.

'A common enough observation in a death like this.'

'What about those cuts in the skin? They look like knife wounds.'

'Again, what one would expect,' said Illmann. 'The heat in a conflagration causes the skin to split open like a ripe banana. That is, if you can remember what a banana looks like.'

'Where did you find the petrol cans?'

He raised his eyebrows quizzically. 'Oh, you know about those, do you? Yes, we found two empty cans in the garden. I don't think they'd been there very long. They weren't rusted and there was still a small amount of petrol which remained unevaporated in the bottom of one of them. And according to the fire officer there was a strong smell of petrol about the place.'

'Arson, then.'

'Undoubtedly.'

'So what made you look for bullets?'

'Experience. With a post-mortem following a fire, one always keeps in mind the possibility that there has been an attempt to destroy evidence. It's standard procedure. I found three bullets in the female, two in the male and three in the headboard of the bed. The female was dead before the fire started. She was hit in the head and the throat. Not so the male. There were smoke particles in the air passages and carbon monoxide in the blood. The tissues were still pink. He was hit in the chest and in the face.'

'Has the gun been found yet?' I asked.

'No, but I can tell you that it was most probably a 7.65 mm automatic, and something quite hard on its ammunition, like an old Mauser.'

'And they were shot from what sort of distance?'

'I should say the murderer was about 150 cm from the victims when firing the weapon. The entry and exit wounds were consist-ent with the murderer having stood at the bottom of the bed; and, of course, there are the bullets in the headboard.'

'Just the one weapon, you think?' Illmann nodded. 'Eight bul-lets,' I said. 'That's a whole magazine for a pocket pistol, isn't it? Somebody was making very sure. Or else they were very angry. Christ, didn't the neighbours hear anything?'

'Apparently not. If they did, they probably thought it was just the Gestapo having a little party. The fire wasn't reported until 3.10 a.m., by which time there was no chance of bringing it under control.'

The hunchback abandoned his organ recital as the storm-troopers launched into a rendition of 'Germany, Thou Art Our Pride'. One of them, a big burly fellow with a scar on his face the length and consistency of a piece of bacon-rind walked round the bar, waving his beer and demanding that the rest of the Künstler Eck's customers join in the singing. Illmann did not seem to mind and sang in a loud baritone. My own singing showed a consider-able want of key and alacrity. Loud songs do not a patriot make. The trouble with these fucking National Socialists, especially the young ones, is that they think they have got a monopoly on patri-otism. And even if they don't have one now, the way things are going, they soon will.

When the song was over, I asked Illmann some more questions. 'They were both naked,' he told me, 'and had drunk a good deal. She had consumed several Ohio Cocktails, and he'd had a large amount of beer and schnaps. More than likely they were quite drunk when they were shot. Also, I took a high vaginal swab in the female and found recent semen, which was of the same blood type as the male. I think they'd had quite an evening. Oh yes, she was eight weeks pregnant. Ah, life's little candle burns but briefly.'

'Pregnant.' I repeated the word thoughtfully. Illmann stretched and yawned.

'Yes,' he said. 'Want to know what they had for dinner?'

'No,' I said firmly. 'Tell me about the safe instead. Was it open or shut?'

'Open.' He paused. 'You know, it's interesting, you didn't ask me how it was opened. Which leads me to suppose that you already knew that beyond a bit of scorching, the safe was undamaged; that if the safe was opened illegally, then it was done by someone who knew what he was doing. A Stockinger safe is no pushover.'

'Any piano players on it?' Illmann shook his head.

'It was too badly scorched to take any prints,' he said.

'Let us assume,' I said, 'that immediately prior to the deaths of the Pfarrs, the safe contained – what it contained, and that it was, as it should have been, locked up for the night.'

'Very well.'

'Then there are two possibilities: one is that a professional nut-cracker did the job and then killed them; and the other is that someone forced them to open it and then ordered them back to bed where he shot them. Still, it's not like a pro to have left the safe door open.'

'Unless he was trying hard to look like an amateur,' said Illmann. 'My own opinion is that they were both asleep when they were shot. Certainly from the angle of bullet entry I would say that both of them were lying down. Now if you were conscious, and someone had a gun on you, it's more than likely you would be sitting up in bed. And so I would conclude that your intimidation theory is unlikely.' He looked at his watch and finished his beer.

Patting my leg, he added warmly, 'It's been good, Bernie. Just like the old days. How pleasant to talk to someone whose idea of detective work does not involve a spotlight and a set of brass knuckles. Still. I won't have to put up with the Alex for much longer. Our illustrious Reichskriminaldirektor, Arthur Nebe, is retiring me, just as he's retired the other old conservatives before me.'

'I didn't know you were interested in politics,' I said.

'I'm not,' he said. 'But isn't that how Hitler got elected in the first place: too many people who didn't give a shit who was running the country? The funny thing is that I care even less now than I did before. Catch me joining those March Violets on the bandwagon. But I won't be sorry to leave. I'm tired of all the squabbling that goes on between Sipo and Orpo as to who controls Kripo. It gets very confusing when it comes to filing a report, not knowing whether or not one should be involving our uniformed friends in Orpo.'

'I thought Sipo and the Gestapo were in the Kripo driving seat.'

'At the higher levels of command that is the case,' Illmann confirmed. 'But at the middle and lower levels the old administrative chains of command still operate. At the municipal level, local police presidents, who are part of Orpo, are also responsible for Kripo. But the word is that Orpo's head is giving undercover encouragement to any police president who is prepared to frustrate the thumbscrew boys in Sipo. In Berlin, that suits our own police president. He and the Reichskriminaldirektor, Arthur Nebe, hate each other's guts. Ludicrous, isn't it? And now, if you don't mind, I really must be going.'

'What a way to run a fucking bullring,' I said.

'Believe me, Bernie, you're well out of it.' He grinned happily. 'And it can get a lot worse yet.'

Illmann's information cost me a hundred marks. I've never found that information comes cheap, but lately the cost of private investigation does seem to be going up. It's not difficult to see why. Everyone is making some sort of a twist these days. Corruption in one form or another is the most distinctive feature of life under National Socialism. The government has made several revelations about the corruption of the various Weimar political parties, but these were as nothing compared to the corruption that exists now. It flourishes at the top, and everyone knows it. So most people figure that they are due a share themselves. I don't know of anyone who is as fastidious about such things as they used to be. And that includes me. The plain truth of it is that people's sensitivity to corruption, whether it's black-market food or obtaining favours from a government official, is about as blunt as a joiner's pencil stub.

6

That evening it seemed as though almost all of Berlin was on its way to Neukölln to witness Goebbels conduct the orchestra of soft, persuasive violins and brittle, sarcastic trumpets that was his voice. But for those unlucky enough not to have sight of the Popular Enlightener, there were a number of facilities provided throughout Berlin to ensure that they could at least have the sound. As well as the radios required by law in restaurants and cafés, on most streets there were loudspeakers mounted on advertising pillars and lamp-posts; and a force of radio wardens was empowered to knock on doors and enforce the mandatory civic duty to listen to a Party broadcast.

Driving west on Leipzigerstrasse, I met the torchlight parade of Brownshirt legions as it marched south down Wilhelmstrasse, and I was obliged to get out of my car and salute the passing standard. Not to have done so would have been to risk a beating. I guess there were others like me in that crowd, our right arms extended like so many traffic policemen, doing it just to avoid trouble and feeling a bit ridiculous. Who knows? But come to think of it, political parties were always big on salutes in Germany: the Social Democrats had their clenched fist raised high above the head; the Bolshies in the KPD had their clenched fist raised at shoulder level; the Centrists had their two-fingered, pistol-shaped hand signal, with the thumb cocked; and the Nazis had fingernail inspection. I can remember when we used to think it was all rather ridiculous and melodramatic, and maybe that's why none of us took it seriously. And here we all were now, saluting with the best of them. Crazy.

Badenschestrasse, running off Berliner Strasse, is just a block short of Trautenau Strasse, where I have my own apartment. Proximity is their only common factor. Badenschestrasse, Number 7 is one of the most modern apartment blocks in the city, and about as exclusive as a reunion dinner for the Ptolemies.

I parked my small and dirty car between a huge Deusenberg and a gleaming Bugatti and went into a lobby that looked like it had left a couple of cathedrals short of marble. A fat doorman and a storm-trooper saw me, and, deserting their desk and their radio which was playing Wagner prior to the Party broadcast, they formed a human barrier to my progress, anxious that I might want to insult some of the residents with my crumpled suit and self-inflicted manicure.

'Like it says on the sign outside,' growled Fatso, 'this is a private building.' I wasn't impressed with their combined effort to get tough with me. I'm used to being made to feel unwelcome, and I don't bounce easily.

'I didn't see any sign,' I said truthfully.

'We don't want any trouble, Mister,' said the storm-trooper. He had a delicate-looking jaw that would have snapped like a dead twig with only the briefest of introductions to my fist.

'I'm not selling any,' I told him. Fatso took over.

'Well, whatever it is you're selling, they don't want any here.'

I smiled thinly at him. 'Listen, Fatso, the only thing that's stopping me from pushing you out of my way is your bad breath. It'll be tricky for you, I know, but see if you can work the telephone, and ring up Fräulein Rudel. You'll find she's expecting me.' Fatso pulled the huge brown-and-black moustache that clung to his curling lip like a bat on a crypt wall. His breath was a lot worse than I could have imagined.

'For your sake, swanktail, you'd better be right,' he said. 'It'd be a pleasure to throw you out.' Swearing under his breath he wobbled back to his desk and dialled furiously.

'Is Fräulein Rudel expecting someone?' he said, moderating his tone. 'Only, she never told me.' His face fell as my story checked out. He put the phone down and swung his head at the lift door.

'Third floor,' he hissed.

There were only two doors, at opposite ends of the third. There was a velodrome of parquet-floor between them and, as if I was expected, one of the doors was ajar. The maid ushered me into the drawing room.

'You'd better take a seat,' she said grumpily. 'She's still dressing and there's no telling how long she'll be. Fix yourself a drink if you want.' Then she disappeared and I examined my surroundings.

The apartment was no larger than a private airfield and looked about as cheap a set as something out of Cecil B. de Mille, of whom there was a photograph jostling for pride of place with all the others on the grand piano. Compared with the person who had decorated and furnished the place, the Archduke Ferdinand had been blessed with the taste of a troupe of Turkish circus dwarves. I looked at some of the other photographs. Mostly they were stills of Ilse Rudel taken from her various films. In a lot of them she wasn't wearing very much – swimming nude or peering coyly from behind a tree which hid the more interesting parts. Rudel was famous for her scantily clad roles. In another photograph she was sitting at a table in a smart restaurant with the good Dr Goebbels; and in another, she was sparring with Max Schmeling. Then there was one in which she was being carried in a workman's arms, only the 'workman' just happened to be Emil Jannings, the famous actor. I recognized it as a still from *The Builder's Hut*. I like the book a lot better than I had liked the film.

At the hint of 4711 I turned around, and found myself shaking the beautiful film star by the hand.

'I see you've been looking at my little gallery,' she said, re-arranging the photographs I had picked up and examined. 'You must think it terribly vain of me to have so many pictures of myself on display, but I simply can't abide albums.'

'Not at all,' I said. 'It's very interesting.' She flashed me the smile that made thousands of German men, myself included, go weak at the chin.

'I'm so glad you approve.' She was wearing a pair of green-velvet lounging pyjamas with a long, gold, fringed sash, and high-heeled green morocco slippers. Her blonde hair was done up

63

in a braided knot at the back of her head, as was fashionable; but unlike most German women, she was also wearing makeup and smoking a cigarette. That sort of thing is frowned on by the BdM, the Women's League, as being inconsistent with the Nazi ideal of German Womanhood; however, I'm a city boy: plain, scrubbed, rosy faces may be just fine down on the farm, but like nearly all German men I prefer my women powdered and painted. Of course, Ilse Rudel lived in a different world to other women. She probably thought the Nazi Women's League was a hockey association.

'I'm sorry about those two fellows on the door,' she said, 'but you see, Josef and Magda Goebbels have an apartment upstairs, so security has to be extra tight, as you can imagine. Which reminds me, I promised Josef that I'd try and listen to his speech, or at least a bit of it. Do you mind?'

It was not the sort of question that you ever asked; unless you happened to be on first-name terms with the Minister of Propaganda and Popular Enlightenment, and his lady wife. I shrugged.

'That's fine by me.'

'We'll only listen for a few minutes,' she said, switching on the Philco that stood on top of a walnut drinks cabinet. 'Now then. What can I get you to drink?' I asked for a whisky and she poured me one that was big enough for a set of false teeth. She poured herself a glass of Bowle, Berlin's favourite summer drink, from a tall, blue-glass pitcher, and joined me on a sofa that was the colour and contours of an underripe pineapple. We clinked glasses and, as the tubes of the radio set warmed up, the smooth tones of the man from upstairs slipped slowly into the room.

First of all, Goebbels singled out foreign journalists for criticism, and rebuked their 'biased' reporting of life in the new Germany. Some of his remarks were clever enough to draw laughter and then applause from his sycophantic audience. Rudel smiled uncertainly, but remained silent, and I wondered if she understood what her club-footed neighbour from upstairs was talking about. Then he raised his voice and proceeded to declaim against the traitors – whoever they were, I didn't know – who were trying to sabotage the national revolution. Here she stifled a yawn. Finally, when Joey got going on his favourite subject, the glorification of the Führer, she jumped up and switched the radio off.

'Goodness me, I think we've heard enough from him for one evening.' She went over to the gramophone and picked up a disc.

'Do you like jazz?' she said, changing the subject. 'Oh, it's all right, it's not negro jazz. I love it, don't you?' Only non-negro jazz is permitted in Germany now, but I often wonder how they can tell the difference.

'I like any kind of jazz,' I said. She wound up the gramophone and put the needle into the groove. It was a nice relaxed sort of piece with a strong clarinet and a saxophonist who could have led a company of Italians across no man's land in a barrage.

I said: 'Do you mind me asking why you keep this place?'

She danced back to the sofa and sat down. 'Well, Herr Private Investigator, Hermann finds my friends a little trying. He does a lot of work from our house in Dahlem, and at all hours: I do most of my entertaining here, so as not to disturb him.'

'Sounds sensible enough,' I said. She blew a column of smoke at me from each exquisite nostril, and I took a deep breath of it; not because I enjoyed the smell of American cigarettes, which I do, but because it had come from inside her chest, and anything to do with that chest was all right by me. From the movement underneath her jacket I had already concluded that her breasts were large and unsupported.

'So,' I said, 'what was it that you wanted to see me about?' To my surprise, she touched me lightly on the knee.

'Relax,' she smiled. 'You're not in a hurry, are you?' I shook my head and watched her stub out her cigarette. There were already several butts in the ashtray, all heavily marked with lipstick, but none of them had been smoked for more than a few puffs, and it occurred to me that she was the one who needed to relax, and that maybe she was nervous about something. Me perhaps. As if confirming my theory she jumped up off the sofa, poured herself another glass of Bowle and changed the record.

'Are you all right with your drink?'

'Yes,' I said, and sipped some. It was good whisky, smooth and peaty, with no backburner in it. Then I asked her how well she had known Paul and Grete Pfarr. I don't think the question surprised her. Instead, she sat close to me, so that we were actually touching, and smiled in a strange way.

'Oh, yes,' she said whimsically. 'I forgot. You're the man who's investigating the fire for Hermann, aren't you?' She did some more grinning, and added: 'I suppose the case has the police baffled.' There was a note of sarcasm in her voice. 'And then you come along, the Great Detective, and find the clue that solves the whole mystery.'

'There's no mystery, Fräulein Rudel,' I said provocatively. It threw her only slightly.

'Why, surely the mystery is, who did it?' she said.

'A mystery is something that is beyond human knowledge and comprehension, which means that I should be wasting my time in even trying to investigate it. No, this case is nothing more than a puzzle, and I happen to like puzzles.'

'Oh, so do I,' she said, almost mocking me, I thought. 'And please, you must call me Ilse while you're here. And I shall call you by your Christian name. What is it?'

'Bernhard.'

'Bernhard,' she said, trying it for size, and then shortening it, 'Bernie.' She gulped a large mouthful of the champagne and sauterne mixture she was drinking, picked out a strawberry from the top of her glass and ate it. 'Well, Bernie, you must be a very good private investigator to be working for Hermann on something as important as this. I thought you were all seedy little men who followed husbands and looked through keyholes at what they got up to, and then told their wives.'

'Divorce cases are just about the one kind of business that I don't handle.'

'Is that a fact?' she said, smiling quietly to herself. It irritated me quite a bit, that smile; in part because I felt she was patronizing me, but also because I wanted desperately to stop it with a kiss. Failing that, the back of my hand. 'Tell me something. Do you make much money doing what you do?' Tapping me on the thigh to indicate that she hadn't finished her question, she added: 'I don't mean to sound rude. But what I want to know is, are you comfortable?'

I took note of my opulent surroundings before answering. 'Me, comfortable? Like a Bauhaus chair, I am.' She laughed at that. 'You didn't answer my question about the Pfarrs,' I said.

'Didn't I?'

'You know damn well you didn't.'

She shrugged. 'I knew them.'

'Well enough to know what Paul had against your husband?'

'Is that really what you're interested in?' she said.

'It'll do for a start.'

She gave an impatient little sigh. 'Very well. We'll play your game, but only until I get bored of it.' She raised her eyebrows questioningly at me, and although I had no idea what she was talking about, I shrugged and said:

'That's fine by me.'

'It's true, they didn't get on, but I haven't the haziest why. When Paul and Grete first met, Hermann was against their getting married. He thought Paul wanted a nice platinum tooth – you know, a rich wife. He tried to persuade Grete to drop him. But Grete wouldn't hear of it. After that, by all accounts they got on fine. At least until Hermann's first wife died. By then I'd been seeing him for some time. It was when we got married that things really started to cool off between the two of them. Grete started drinking. And their marriage seemed little more than a fig-leaf, for decency's sake – Paul being at the Ministry and all that.'

'What did he do there, do you know?'

'No idea.'

'Did he nudge around?'

'With other women?' She laughed. 'Paul was good-looking, but a bit lame. He was dedicated to his work, not another woman. If he did, he kept it very quiet.'

'What about her?'

Rudel shook her golden head, and took a large gulp of her drink. 'Not her style.' But she paused for a moment and looked more thoughtful. 'Although . . .' She shrugged. 'It probably isn't anything.'

'Come on,' I said. 'Unpack it.'

'Well, there was one time in Dahlem, when I was left with just the tiniest suspicion that Grete might have had something going with Haupthändler.' I raised an eyebrow. 'Hermann's private secretary. This would have been about the time when the Italians had entered Addis Ababa. I remember that only because I went to a party at the Italian Embassy.'

'That would have been early in May.'

'Yes. Anyway, Hermann was away on business, so I went by myself. I was filming at UFA the next morning and had to be up early. I decided to spend the night at Dahlem, so I would have a bit more time in the morning. It's a lot easier getting to Babelsberg from there. Anyway, when I got home I poked my head around the drawing-room door in search of a book I had left there, and who should I find sitting in the dark but Hjalmar Haupthändler and Grete.'

'What were they doing?'

'Nothing. Nothing at all. That's what made it so damned suspicious. It was two o'clock in the morning and there they were, sitting at opposite ends of the same sofa like a couple of school children on their first date. I could tell they were embarrassed to see me. They gave me some cabbage about just chatting and was that really the time. But I didn't buy it.'

'Did you mention it to your husband?'

'No,' she said. 'Actually, I forgot about it. And even if I hadn't, I wouldn't have told him. Hermann is not the sort of person who could have just left it alone to sort itself out. Most rich men are like that, I think. Distrustful, and suspicious.'

'I'd say he must trust you a great deal to let you keep your own apartment.'

She laughed scornfully. 'God, what a joke. If you knew what

I have to put up with. But then you probably know all about us, you being a private investigator.' She didn't let me answer. 'I've had to sack several of my maids because they were being bribed by him to spy on me. He's really a very jealous man.'

'Under similar circumstances I'd probably act the same way,' I told her. 'Most men would be jealous of a woman like you.' She looked me in the eye, and then at the rest of me. It was the sort of provocative look that only whores and phenomenally rich and beautiful film stars can get away with. It was meant to get me to climb aboard her bones like a creeper on to a trellis. A look that made me want to gore a hole in the rug. 'Frankly, you probably like to make a man jealous. You strike me as the kind of woman who holds out her hand to signal a left and then makes a right, just to keep him guessing. Are you ready to tell me why you asked me here tonight?'

'I've sent the maid home,' she said, 'so stop thrashing words and kiss me, you big idiot.' Normally I'm not too good at taking orders, but on this occasion I didn't quarrel. It's not every day that a film star tells you to kiss her. She gave me the soft, luscious inside of her lips, and I let myself equal their competence, just to be polite. After a minute I felt her body stir, and when she pulled her mouth away from my lamprey-like kiss her voice was hot and breathless.

'My, that was a real slow-burner.'

'I practise on my forearm.' She smiled and raised her mouth up to mine, kissing me like she intended to lose control of herself and so that I would stop holding something back from her. She was breathing through her nose, as if she needed more oxygen, gradually getting serious about it, and me keeping pace with her, until she said:

'I want you to fuck me, Bernie.' I heard each word in my fly. We stood up in silence, and taking me by the hand she led me to the bedroom.

'I've got to go to the bathroom first,' I said. She was pulling the pyjama-jacket over her head, her breasts wobbling: these were real film star's chicks and for a moment I couldn't take my eyes off them. Each brown nipple was like a British Tommy's helmet.

'Don't be too long, Bernie,' she said, dropping first her sash, and then the trousers, so that she stood there in just her knickers.

But in the bathroom I took a long, honest look in the mirror, which was one whole wall, and asked myself why a living goddess like the one turning down the white satin sheets needed me of all people to help justify an expensive laundry account. It wasn't my choirboy's face, or my sunny disposition. With my broken nose and my car-bumper of a jaw, I was handsome only by the standards of a fairground boxing-booth. I didn't imagine for a minute that my blond hair and blue eyes made me fashionable. She wanted something else besides a brush, and I had a shrewd idea what it was. The trouble was I had an erection that, temporarily at least, was very firmly in command.

Back in the bedroom, she was still standing there, waiting for me to come and help myself. Impatient of her, I snatched her knickers down, pulling her onto the bed, where I prised her sleek, tanned thighs apart like an excited scholar opening a priceless book. For quite a while I pored over the text, turning the pages with my fingers and feasting my eyes on what I had never dreamed of possessing.

We kept the light on, so that finally I had a perfect view of myself as I plugged into the crisp fluff between her legs. And afterwards she lay on top of me, breathing like a sleepy but contented dog, stroking my chest almost as if she was in awe of me.

'My, but you're a well-built man.'

'Mother was a blacksmith,' I said. 'She used to hammer a nail into a horse's shoe with the flat of her hand. I get my build from her.' She giggled.

'You don't say much, but when you do you like to joke, don't you?'

'There are an awful lot of dead people in Germany looking very serious.'

'And so very cynical. Why is that?'

'I used to be a priest.'

She fingered the small scar on my forehead where a piece of shrapnel had creased me. 'How did you get this?'

'After church on Sundays I'd box with the choirboys in the sacristy. You like boxing?' I remembered the photograph of Schmeling on the piano.

'I adore boxing,' she said. 'I love violent, physical men. I love going to the Busch Circus and watching them train before a big fight, just to see if they defend or attack, how they jab, if they've got guts.'

'Just like one of those noblewomen in ancient Rome,' I said, 'checking up on her gladiators to see if they're going to win before she puts a bet on.'

'But of course. I like winners. Now you . . .'

'Yes?'

'I'd say you could take a good punch. Maybe take quite a few. You strike me as the durable, patient sort. Methodical. Prepared to soak up more than a little punishment. That makes you dangerous.'

'And you?' She bounced excitedly on my chest, her breasts wobbling engagingly, although, for the moment at least, I had no more appetite for her body.

'Oh, yes, yes,' she cried excitedly. 'What sort of fighter am I?'

I looked at her from the corner of one eye. 'I think you would dance around a man and let him expend quite a bit of energy before coming back at him with one good punch to win on a knock-out. A win on points would be no sort of contest for you. You always like to put them down on the canvas. There's just one thing that puzzles me about this bout.'

'What's that?'

'What makes you think I'd take a dive?'

She sat up in bed. 'I don't understand.'

'Sure you do.' Now that I'd had her it was easy enough to say. 'You think your husband hired me to spy on you, isn't that right? You don't believe I'm investigating the fire at all. That's why you've been planning this little tryst all evening, and now I imagine

I'm supposed to play the poodle, so that when you ask me to lay off I'll do just what you say, otherwise I might not get any more treats. Well, you've been wasting your time. Like I said, I don't do divorce work.'

She sighed and covered her breasts with her arms. 'You certainly can pick your moments, Herr Sniffer Dog,' she said.

'It's true, isn't it?'

She sprang out of bed and I knew that I was watching the whole of her body, as naked as a pin without a hat, for the last time; from here on in I would have to go to the cinema to catch those tantalizing glimpses of it, like all the other fellows. She went over to the cupboard and snatched a gown from a hanger. From the pocket she produced a packet of cigarettes. She lit one and smoked it angrily, with one arm folded across her chest.

'I could have offered you money,' she said. 'But instead I gave you myself.' She took another nervous puff, hardly inhaling it at all. 'How much do you want?'

Exasperated, I slapped my naked thigh, and said: 'Shit, you're not listening, spoon-ears. I told you. I wasn't hired to go peeking through your keyhole and find out the name of your lover.'

She shrugged with disbelief. 'How did you know I had a lover?' she said.

I got out of bed, and started to dress. 'I didn't need a magnifying glass and a pair of tweezers to pick that one up. It stands to reason that if you didn't already have a lover, then you wouldn't be so damned nervous of me.' She gave me a smile that was as thin and dubious as the rubber on a secondhand condom.

'No? I bet you're the sort who could find lice on a bald head. Anyway, who said I was nervous of you? I just don't happen to care for the interruption of my privacy. Look, I think you had better push off.' She turned her back to me as she spoke.

'I'm on my way.' I buttoned up my braces and slipped my jacket on. At the bedroom door, I made one last try to get through to her.

'For the last time, I wasn't hired to check up on you.'

'You've made a fool of me.'

I shook my head. 'There's not enough sense in anything you've said to fill a hollow tooth. With all your milkmaid's calculations, you didn't need my help to make a fool of yourself. Thanks for a memorable evening.' As I left her room she started to curse me with the sort of eloquence you expect only from a man who has just hammered his thumb.

I drove home feeling like a ventriloquist's mouth ulcer. I was sore at the way things had turned out. It's not every day that one of Germany's great film stars takes you to bed and then throws you out on your ear. I'd like to have had more time to grow familiar with her famous body. I was a man who had won the big prize at the fair, only to be told there had been a mistake. All the same, I said to myself, I ought to have expected something like that. Nothing resembles a street snapper so much as a rich woman.

Once inside my apartment I poured myself a drink and then boiled some water for a bath. After that, I put on the dressing-gown I'd bought in Wertheim's and started to feel good again. The place was stuffy, so I opened a few windows. Then I tried reading for a while. I must have fallen asleep, because a couple of hours had passed by the time I heard the knock at the door.

'Who is it?' I said, going into the hall.

'Open up. Police,' said a voice.

'What do you want?'

'To ask you some questions about Ilse Rudel,' he said. 'She was found dead at her apartment an hour ago. Murdered.' I snatched the door open and found the barrel of a Parabellum poking me in the stomach.

'Back inside,' said the man with the pistol. I retreated, raising my hands instinctively.

He wore a Bavarian-cut sports coat of light-blue linen, and a canary-yellow tie. There was a scar on his pale young face, but it was neat and clean-looking, and probably self-inflicted with a

73

razor in the hope that it might be mistaken for a student's duelling scar. Accompanied by a strong smell of beer, he advanced into my hallway, closing the door behind him.

'Anything you say, sonny,' I said, relieved to see that he looked less than comfortable with the Parabellum. 'You had me fooled there with that story about Fräulein Rudel. I shouldn't have fallen for it.'

'You bastard,' he snarled.

'Mind if I put my hands down? Only my circulation isn't what it used to be.' I dropped my hands to my sides. 'What's this all about?'

'Don't deny it.'

'Deny what?'

'That you raped her.' He adjusted his grip on the gun, and swallowed nervously, his Adam's apple tossing around like a honeymoon couple under a thin pink sheet. 'She told me what you did to her. So you needn't try and deny it.'

I shrugged. 'What would be the point? In your shoes I know who I would believe. But listen, are you sure you know what you're doing? Your breath was waving a red flag when you tiptoed in here. The Nazis may seem a bit liberal in some things, but they haven't done away with capital punishment, you know. Even if you're hardly old enough to be expected to hold your drink.'

'I'm going to kill you,' he said, licking his dry lips.

'Well, that's all right, but do you mind not shooting me in the belly?' I pointed at his pistol. 'It's by no means certain that you'd kill me, and I'd hate to spend the rest of my life drinking milk. No, if I were you I'd go for a head shot. Between the eyes if you can manage it. A difficult shot, but it would kill me for sure. Frankly, the way I feel right now, you'd be doing me a favour. It must be something I've eaten, but my insides feel like the wave machine at Luna Park.' I farted a great, meaty trombone of a fart in confirmation.

'Oh, Jesus,' I said, waving my hand in front of my face. 'See what I mean?'

'Shut up, you animal,' said the young man. But I saw him raise the barrel and level it at my head. I remembered the Parabellum from my army days, when it had been the standard service pistol. The Pistol .08 relies on the recoil to fire the striker, but with the first shot the firing mechanism is always comparatively stiff. My head made a smaller target than my stomach, and I hoped that I'd have enough time to duck.

I threw myself at his waist, and as I did so I saw the flash and felt the air of the 9 mm bullet as it zipped over my head and smashed something behind me. My weight carried us both crashing into the front door. But if I had expected him to be less than capable of putting up a stiff resistance, I was mistaken. I took hold of the wrist with the gun and found the arm twisting towards me with a lot more strength than I had credited it with. I felt him grab the collar of my dressing-gown and twist it. Then I heard it rip.

'Shit,' I said. 'That does it.' I pushed the gun towards him, and succeeded in pressing the barrel against his sternum. Putting my whole weight onto it I hoped to break a rib, but instead there was a muffled, fleshy report as it fired again, and I found myself covered in his steaming blood. I held his limp body for several seconds before I let it roll away from me.

I stood up and took a look at him. There was no doubt that he was dead, although blood continued to bubble up from the hole in his chest. Then I went through his pockets. You always want to know who's been trying to kill you. There was a wallet containing an ID card in the name of Walther Kolb, and 200 marks. It didn't make sense to leave the money for the boys from Kripo, so I took 150 to cover the cost of my dressing-gown. Also, there were two photographs; one of these was an obscene postcard in which a man was doing things to a girl's bottom with a length of rubber tube; and the other was a publicity still of Ilse Rudel, signed, 'with much love'. I burned the photograph of my former bedmate, poured myself a stiff one and, marvelling at the picture of the erotic enema, I called the police.

A couple of bulls came down from the Alex. The senior officer, Oberinspektor Tesmer, was a Gestapo man; the other, Inspektor

Stahlecker, was a friend, one of my few remaining friends in Kripo, but with Tesmer around there wasn't a chance of an easy ride.

'That's my story,' I said, having told it for the third time. We were all seated round my dining table on which lay the Parabellum and the contents of the dead man's pockets. Tesmer shook his head slowly, as if I had offered to sell him something he wouldn't have a chance of shifting himself.

'You could always part exchange it for something else. Come on, try again. Maybe this time you'll make me laugh.' With its thin, almost non-existent lips, Tesmer's mouth was like a slash in a length of cheap curtain. And all you saw through the hole were the points of his rodent's teeth, and the occasional glimpse of the ragged, grey-white oyster that was his tongue.

'Look, Tesmer,' I said. 'I know it looks a bit beat up, but take my word for it, it's really very reliable. Not everything that shines is any good.'

'Try shifting some of the fucking dust off it then. What do you know about the canned meat?'

I shrugged. 'Only what was in his pockets. And that he and I weren't going to get along.'

'That wins him quite a few extra points on my card,' said Tesmer.

Stahlecker sat uncomfortably beside his boss, and tugged nervously at his eyepatch. He had lost an eye when he was with the Prussian infantry, and at the same time had won the coveted 'pour le mérite' for his bravery. Me, I'd have hung onto the eye, although the patch did look rather dashing. Combined with his dark colouring and bushy black moustache, it served to give him a piratical air, although his manner was altogether more stolid: slow even. But he was a good bull, and a loyal friend. All the same, he wasn't about to risk burning his fingers while Tesmer was doing his best to see if I'd catch fire. His honesty had previously led him to express one or two ill-advised opinions about the NSDAP during the '33 elections. Since then he'd had the sense to keep his mouth shut, but he and I both knew that the Kripo Executive was just looking for an excuse to hang him out to dry. It was only his outstanding war record that had kept him in the force this long.

'And I suppose he tried to kill you because he didn't like your cologne,' said Tesmer.

'You noticed it too, huh?' I saw Stahlecker smile a bit at that, but so did Tesmer, and he didn't like it.

'Günther, you've got more lip than a nigger with a trumpet. Your friend here may think you're funny, but I just think you're a cunt, so don't fuck me around. I'm not the sort with a sense of humour.'

'I've told you the truth, Tesmer. I opened the door and there was Herr Kolb with the lighter pointing at my dinner.'

'A Parabellum on you, and yet you still managed to take him. I don't see any fucking holes in you, Günther.'

'I'm taking a correspondence course in hypnotism. Like I said, I was lucky, he missed. You saw the broken light.'

'Listen, I don't mesmerize easy. This fellow was a professional. Not the sort to let you have his lighter for a bag of sherbet.'

'A professional what – haberdasher? Don't talk out of your navel, Tesmer. He was just a kid.'

'Well, that makes it worse for you, because he isn't going to do any more growing up.'

'Young he may have been,' I said, 'but he was no weakling. I didn't bite my lip because I find you so damned attractive. This is real blood, you know. And my dressing-gown. It's torn, or hadn't you noticed?'

Tesmer laughed scornfully. 'I thought you were just a sloppy dresser.'

'Hey, this is a fifty-mark gown. You don't think I'd tear it just for your benefit, do you?'

'You could afford to buy it, then you could also afford to lose it. I always thought your kind made too much money.' I leaned back in my chair. I remembered Tesmer as one of Police Major Walther Wecke's hatchet-men, charged with rooting out conservatives and

77

Bolsheviks from the force. A mean bastard if ever there was one. I wondered how Stahlecker managed to survive.

'What is it you earn, Günther? Three? Four hundred marks a week? Probably make as much as me and Stahlecker put together, eh, Stahlecker?' My friend shrugged non-committally.

'I dunno.'

'See?' said Tesmer. 'Even Stahlecker doesn't have any idea how many thousands a year you make.'

'You're in the wrong job, Tesmer. The way you exaggerate, you should work for the Ministry of Propaganda.' He said nothing. 'All right, all right, I get it. How much is it going to cost me?' Tesmer shrugged, trying to control the grin that threatened to break out on his face.

'From a man with a fifty-mark gown? Let's say a round hundred.'

'A hundred? For that cheap little garter-handler? Go and take another look at him, Tesmer. He doesn't have a Charlie Chaplin moustache and a stiff right arm.'

Tesmer stood up. 'You talk too much, Günther. Let's hope your mouth begins to fray at the edges before it gets you into serious trouble.' He looked at Stahlecker and then back at me. 'I'm going for a piss. Your old pitman here has got until I come back into the room to persuade you, otherwise . . .' He pursed his lips and shook his head. As he walked out, I called after him:

'Make sure you lift the seat.' I grinned at Stahlecker.

'How are you doing, Bruno?'

'What is it, Bernie? Have you been drinking? You blue or something? Come on, you know how difficult Tesmer could make things for you. First you plum the man with all that smart talk, and now you want to play the black horse. Pay the bastard.'

'Look, if I don't black horse him a little and drag my heels about paying him that kind of mouse, then he'll figure I'm worth a lot more. Bruno, as soon as I saw that son of a bitch I knew that the evening was going to cost me something. Before I left Kripo he and Wecke had me marked. I haven't forgotten and neither has he. I still owe him some agony.'

'Well, you certainly made it expensive for yourself when you mentioned the price of that gown.'

'Not really,' I said. 'It cost nearer a hundred.'

'Christ,' breathed Stahlecker. 'Tesmer is right. You *are* making too much money.' He thrust his hands deep into his pockets and looked squarely at me. 'Want to tell me what really happened here?'

'Another time, Bruno. It was mostly true.'

'Excepting one or two small details.'

'Right. Listen, I need a favour. Can we meet tomorrow? The matinée at the Kammerlichtspiele in the Haus Vaterland. Back row, at four o'clock.'

Bruno sighed, and then nodded. 'I'll try.'

'Before then see if you can't find out something about the Paul Pfarr case.' He frowned and was about to speak when Tesmer returned from the lavatory.

'I hope you wiped the floor.'

Tesmer pointed a face at me in which belligerence was moulded like cornice-work on a Gothic folly. The set of his jaw and the spread of his nose gave him about as much profile as a piece of lead piping. The general effect was early-Paleolithic.

'I hope you decided to get wise,' he growled. There would have been more chance of reasoning with a water buffalo.

'Seems like I don't have much choice,' I said. 'I don't suppose there's any chance of a receipt?'

7

Just off Kronprinzenallee, on the edge of Dahlem, was the huge wrought-iron gate to Six's estate. I sat in the car for a while and watched the road. Several times I closed my eyes and found my head nodding. It had been a late night. After a short nap I got out and opened the gate. Then I ambled back to the car and turned onto the private road, down a long, gentle slope and into the cool shade cast by the dark pine trees lining its gravelled length.

In daylight Six's house was even more impressive, although I could see now that it was not one but two houses, standing close together: beautiful, solidly built Wilhelmine farmhouses.

I pulled up at the front door, where Ilse Rudel had parked her BMW the night I had first seen her, and got out, leaving the door open just in case the two Dobermanns put in an appearance. Dogs are not at all keen on private investigators, and it's an antipathy that is entirely mutual.

I knocked on the door. I heard it echo in the hall and, seeing the closed shutters, I wondered if I'd had a wasted journey. I lit a cigarette and stood there, just leaning on the door, smoking and listening. The place was about as quiet as the sap in a gift-wrapped rubber tree. Then I heard some footsteps, and I straightened up as the door opened to reveal the Levantine head and round shoulders of the butler, Farraj.

'Good morning,' I said brightly. 'I was hoping that I'd find Herr Haupthändler in.' Farraj looked at me with the clinical distaste of a chiropodist regarding a septic toenail.

'Do you have an appointment?' he asked.

'Not really,' I said, handing him my card. 'I was hoping he might give me five minutes, though. I was here the other night, to see Herr Six.' Farraj nodded silently, and returned my card.

'My apologies for not recognizing you, sir.' Still holding the door, he retreated into the hall, inviting me to enter. Having closed it behind him, he looked at my hat with something short of amusement.

'No doubt you will wish to keep your hat again, sir.'

'I think I had better, don't you?' Standing closer to him, I could detect the very definite smell of alcohol, and not the sort they serve in exclusive gentlemen's clubs.

'Very good, sir. If you'll just wait here for a moment, I'll find Herr Haupthändler and ask him if he can see you.'

'Thanks,' I said. 'Do you have an ashtray?' I held my cigarette ash aloft like a hypodermic syringe.

'Yes, sir.' He produced one made of dark onyx that was the size of a church Bible, and which he held in both hands while I did the stubbing out. When my cigarette was extinguished he turned away and, still carrying the ashtray, he disappeared down the corridor, leaving me to wonder what I was going to say to Haupthändler if he would see me. There was nothing in particular I had in mind, and not for one minute did I imagine that he would be prepared to discuss Ilse Rudel's story about him and Grete Pfarr. I was just poking around. You ask ten people ten dumb questions, and sometimes you hit a raw nerve somewhere. Sometimes, if you weren't too bored to notice, you managed to recognize that you were on to something. It was a bit like panning for gold. Every day you went down to the river and went through pan after pan of mud. And just occasionally, provided you kept your eyes peeled, you found a dirty little stone that was actually a nugget.

I went to the bottom of the stairs and looked up the stairwell. A large circular skylight illuminated the paintings on the scarlet-coloured walls. I was looking at a still life of a lobster and a pewter pot when I heard footsteps on the marble floor behind me.

'It's by Karl Schuch you know,' said Haupthändler. 'Worth a great deal of money.' He paused, and added: 'But very, very dull. Please, come this way.' He led the way into Six's library.

'I'm afraid I can't give you very long. You see, I still have a great many things to do for the funeral tomorrow. I'm sure you understand.' I sat down on one of the sofas and lit a cigarette. Haupthändler folded his arms, the leather of his nutmeg-brown sports jacket creaking across his sizeable shoulders, and leaned against his master's desk.

'Now what was it that you wished to see me about?'

'Actually, it's about the funeral,' I said, improvising on what he had given me. 'I wondered where it was to be held.'

'I must apologize, Herr Günther,' he said. 'I'm afraid it hadn't occurred to me that Herr Six would wish you to attend. He's left all the arrangements to me while he's in the Ruhr, but he didn't think to leave any instructions regarding a list of mourners.'

I tried to look awkward. 'Oh, well,' I said, standing up. 'Naturally, with a client such as Herr Six I should like to have been able to pay my respects to his daughter. It is customary. But I'm sure he will understand.'

'Herr Günther,' said Haupthändler, after a short silence. 'Would you think it terrible of me if I were to give you an invitation now, by hand?'

'Not at all,' I said. 'If you are sure it won't inconvenience your arrangements.'

'It's no trouble,' he said. 'I have some cards here.' He walked around the desk and pulled open a drawer.

'Have you worked for Herr Six long?'

'About two years,' he said absently. 'Prior to that I was a diplomat with the German Consular Service.' He took out a pair of glasses from his breast pocket and placed them on the end of his nose before writing out the invitation.

'And did you know Grete Pfarr well?'

He glanced up at me briefly. 'I really didn't know her at all,' he said. 'Other than to say hallo to.'

'Do you know if she had any enemies, jealous lovers, that sort of thing?' He finished writing the card, and pressed it on the blotter.

'I'm quite sure she didn't,' he said crisply, removing his glasses and returning them to his pocket.

'Is that so? What about him? Paul.'

'I can tell you even less about him, I'm afraid,' he said, slipping the invitation into an envelope.

'Did he and Herr Six get on all right?'

'They weren't enemies, if that's what you're implying. Their differences were purely political.'

'Well, that amounts to something quite fundamental these days, wouldn't you say?'

'Not in this case, no. Now if you'll excuse me, Herr Günther, I really must be getting on.'

'Yes, of course.' He handed me the invitation. 'Well, thanks for this,' I said, following him out into the hall. 'Do you live here too, Herr Haupthändler?'

'No, I have an apartment in town.'

'Really? Where?' He hesitated for a moment.

'Kurfürstenstrasse,' he said eventually. 'Why do you ask?'

I shrugged. 'I ask too many questions, Herr Haupthändler,' I said. 'Forgive me. It's habit, I'm afraid. A suspicious nature goes with the job. Please don't be offended. Well, I must be going.' He smiled thinly, and as he showed me to the door he seemed relaxed; but I hoped I had said enough to put a few ripples on his pond.

The Hanomag seems to take an age to reach any sort of speed, so it was with a certain amount of misplaced optimism that I took the Avus 'Speedway' back to the centre of town. It costs a mark to get on this highway, but the Avus is worth it: ten kilometres without a curve, all the way from Potsdam to Kurfürstendamm. It's the one road in the city on which the driver who fancies himself as Carraciola, the great racing driver, can put his foot down and hit speeds of up to 150 kilometres an hour. At least, they could in the days before BV Aral, the low-octane substitute petrol that's not much better than meths. Now it was all I could do to get ninety out of the Hanomag's 1.3 litre engine.

I parked at the intersection of Kurfürstendamm and Joachimsthaler Strasse, known as 'Grunfeld Corner' because of the department store of the same name which occupies it. When Grunfeld, a Jew, still owned his store, they used to serve free lemonade at the Fountain in the basement. But since the State dispossessed him, as it has with all the Jews who owned big stores, like Wertheim, Hermann Tietz and Israel, the days of free lemonade have gone. If that weren't bad enough, the lemonade you now have to pay for and once got free doesn't taste half as good, and you don't have to have the sharpest taste-buds in the world to realize that they're cutting down on the sugar. Just like they're cheating on everything else.

I sat drinking my lemonade and watching the lift go up and down the tubular glass shaft that allowed you to see out into the store as you rode from floor to floor, in two minds whether or not to go up to the stocking counter and see Carola, the girl from Dagmar's wedding. It was the sour taste of the lemonade that put me in mind of my own debauched behaviour, and that decided me against it. Instead I left Grunfeld's and walked the short distance down Kurfürstendamm and onto Schlüterstrasse.

A jewellers is one of the few places in Berlin where you can expect to find people queueing to sell rather than to buy. Peter Neumaier's Antique Jewellers was no exception. When I got there the line wasn't quite outside the door, but it was certainly rubbing the glass; and it was older and sadder looking than most of the queues that I was used to standing in. The people waiting there were from a mixture of backgrounds, but mostly they had two things in common: their Judaism and, as an inevitable corollary, their lack of work, which was how they came to be selling their valuables in the first place. At the top of the queue, behind a long glass counter, were two stone-faced shop assistants in good suits. They had a neat line in appraisal, which was to tell the prospective seller how poor the piece actually was and how little it was likely to fetch on the open market.

'We see stuff like this all the time,' said one of them, wrinkling his lips and shaking his head at the spread of pearls and brooches on the counter beneath him. 'You see, we can't put a price on sentimental value. I'm sure you understand that.' He was a young fellow, half the age of the deflating old mattress of a woman before him, and good-looking too, although in need of a shave, perhaps. His colleague was less forthcoming with his indifference: he sniffed so that his nose took on a sneer, he shrugged a half shrug of his coathanger-sized shoulders, and he grunted unenthusiastically. Silently, he counted out five one-hundred-mark notes from a roll in his skinny miser's hand that must have been worth thirty times as much. The old man he was buying from was undecided about whether or not he should accept what must have been a derisory offer, and with a trembling hand he pointed at the bracelet lying on the piece of cloth he had wrapped it up in.

'But look here,' said the old man, 'you've got one just like it in the window for three times what you're offering.'

The Coathanger pursed his lips. 'Fritz,' he said, 'how long has that sapphire bracelet been in the window?' It was an efficient double-act, you had to say that much.

'Must be six months,' responded the other. 'Don't buy another one, this isn't a charity you know.' He probably said that several times a day. Coathanger blinked with slow boredom.

'See what I mean? Look, go somewhere else if you think you can get more for it.' But the sight of the cash was too much for the old man, and he capitulated. I walked to the head of the line and said that I was looking for Herr Neumaier.

'If you've got something to sell, then you'll have to wait in line with all the rest of them,' muttered Coathanger.

'I have nothing to sell,' I said vaguely, adding, 'I'm looking for a diamond necklace.' At that Coathanger smiled at me like I was his long-lost rich uncle.

'If you'll just wait one moment,' he said unctuously, 'I'll just see if Herr Neumaier is free.' He disappeared behind a curtain for a minute, and when he returned I was ushered through to a small office at the end of the corridor.

Peter Neumaier sat at his desk, smoking a cigar that belonged properly in a plumber's tool-bag. He was dark, with bright blue eyes, just like our beloved Führer, and was possessed of a stomach that stuck out like a cash register. The cheeks of his face had a red, skinned look, as if he had eczema, or had simply stood too close to his razor that morning. He shook me by the hand as I introduced myself. It was like holding a cucumber.

'I'm pleased to meet you, Herr Günther,' he said warmly. 'I hear you're looking for some diamonds.'

'That's correct. But I should tell you that I'm acting on behalf of someone else.'

'I understand,' Neumaier grinned. 'Did you have a particular setting in mind?'

'Oh, yes indeed. A diamond necklace.'

'Well, you have come to the right place. There are several diamond necklaces I can show you.'

'My client knows precisely what he requires,' I said. 'It must be a diamond collet necklace, made by Cartier.' Neumaier laid his cigar in the ashtray, and breathed out a mixture of smoke, nerves and amusement.

'Well,' he said. 'That certainly narrows the field.'

'That's the thing about the rich, Herr Neumaier,' I said. 'They always seem to know exactly what they want, don't you think?'

'Oh, indeed they do, Herr Günther.' He leaned forwards in his chair and, collecting his cigar, he said: 'A necklace such as you describe is not the sort of piece that comes along every day. And of course it would cost a great deal of money.' It was time to stick the nettle down his trousers.

'Naturally, my client is prepared to pay a great deal of money. Twenty-five per cent of the insured value, no questions asked.'

He frowned. 'I'm not sure I understand what you're talking about,' he said.

'Come off it, Neumaier. We both know that there's a lot more to your operation than the heart-warming little scene you're putting on out front there.'

He blew some smoke and looked at the end of his cigar. 'Are you suggesting that I buy stolen merchandise, Herr Günther, because if you are –'

'Keep your ears stiff, Neumaier, I haven't finished yet. My client's flea is solid. Cash money.' I tossed the photograph of Six's diamonds at him. 'If some mouse walks in here trying to sell it, you give me a call. The number's on the back.'

Neumaier regarded it and me distastefully and then stood up. 'You are a joke, Herr Günther. With a few cups short in your cupboard. Now get out of here before I call the police.'

'You know, that's not a bad idea,' I said. 'I'm sure they'll be very impressed with your public spirit when you offer to open up your safe and invite them to inspect the contents. That's the confidence of honesty, I suppose.'

'Get out of here.'

I stood up and walked out of his office. I hadn't intended to handle it that way, but I hadn't liked what I'd seen of Neumaier's operation. In the shop Coathanger was half-way through offering an old woman a price for her jewel-box that was less than she might have got for it at the Salvation Army hostel. Several of the Jews waiting behind her looked at me with an expression that was a mixture of hope and hopelessness. It made me feel about as comfortable as a trout on a marble slab, and for no reason that I could think of, I felt something like shame.

Gert Jeschonnek was a different proposition. His premises were on the eighth floor of Columbus Haus, a nine-storeyed building on Potsdamer Platz which has a strong emphasis on the horizontal line. It looked like something a long-term prisoner might have made, given an endless supply of matches, and at the same time it put me in mind of the nearly eponymous building near Tempelhof Airport that is Columbia Haus – the Gestapo prison in Berlin. This country shows its admiration for the discoverer of America in the strangest ways.

The eighth floor was home to a whole country-club of doctors, lawyers and publishers, who were only just getting by on 30,000 a year.

The double entrance doors to Jeschonnek's office were made of polished mahogany, on which appeared in gold lettering, 'GERT JESCHONNEK. PRECIOUS STONE MERCHANT'. Beyond these was an L-shaped office with walls that were a pleasant shade of pink, on which were hung several framed photographs of diamonds, rubies and various gaudy little baubles that might have stimulated the greed of a Solomon or two. I took a chair and waited for an anaemic young man sitting behind a typewriter to finish on the telephone. After a minute he said:

'I'll call you back, Rudi.' He replaced the receiver and looked at me with an expression that was just a few centimetres short of surly.

'Yes?' he said. Call me old-fashioned, but I have never liked male secretaries. A man's vanity gets in the way of serving the needs of another male, and this particular specimen wasn't about to win me over.

'When you've finished filing your nails, perhaps you'd tell your boss that I'd like to see him. The name's Günther.'

'Do you have an appointment?' he said archly.

'Since when does a man who's looking for some diamonds need to make an appointment? Tell me that, would you?' I could see that he found me less amusing than a boxful of smoke.

'Save your breath to cool your soup,' he said, and came round the desk to go through the only other door. 'I'll find out if he can see you.' While he was out of the room I picked up a recent issue of *Der Stürmer* from the magazine rack. The front page had a drawing of a man in angel's robes holding an angel's mask in front of his face. Behind him was his devil's tail, sticking out from underneath his surplice, and his 'angel's' shadow, except that this now revealed the profile behind the mask to be unmistakably Jewish. Those *Der Stürmer* cartoonists love to draw a big nose, and this one was a real pelican's beak. A strange thing to find in a respectable businessman's office, I thought. The anaemic young man emerging from the other office provided the simple explanation.

'He won't keep you very long,' he said, adding, 'He buys that to impress the kikes.'

'I'm afraid I don't follow.'

'We get a lot of Jewish custom in here,' he explained. 'Of course, they only want to sell, never to buy. Herr Jeschonnek thinks that if they see that he subscribes to *Der Stürmer*, it will help him to drive a harder bargain.'

'Very shrewd of him,' I said. 'Does it work?'

'I guess so. You'd better ask him.'

'Maybe I will at that.'

There wasn't much to see in the boss's office. Across a couple of acres of carpet was a grey steel safe that had once been a small battleship, and a Panzer-sized desk with a dark leather top. The desk had very little on it except a square of felt, on which lay a ruby that was big enough to decorate a Maharajah's favourite elephant, and Jeschonnek's feet, wearing immaculate white spats, and these swung under the table as I came through the door.

Gert Jeschonnek was a burly hog of a man, with small piggy eyes and a brown beard cropped close to his sunburned face. He wore a light-grey double-breasted suit that was ten years too young for him, and in the lapel was a Scary Badge. He had March Violet plastered all over him like insect repellent.

'Herr Günther,' he said brightly, and for a moment he was almost standing at attention. Then he crossed the floor to greet me. A purplish butcher's hand pumped mine own, which showed patches of white when I let it go. He must have had blood like treacle. He smiled a sweet smile and then looked across my shoulder to his anaemic secretary who was about to close the door on us. Jeschonnek said:

'Helmut. A pot of your best strong coffee please. Two cups, and no delays.' He spoke quickly and precisely, beating time with his hand like a teacher of elocution. He led me over to the desk, and the ruby, which I figured was there to impress me, in the same way as the copies of *Der Stürmer* were there to impress his Jewish custom. I pretended to ignore it, but Jeschonnek was not to be denied his little performance. He held the ruby up to the light in his fat fingers, and grinned obscenely.

'An extremely fine cabochon ruby,' he said. 'Like it?'

'Red isn't my colour,' I said. 'It doesn't go with my hair.' He laughed and replaced the ruby on the velvet, which he folded up and returned to his safe. I sat down on a big armchair in front of his desk.

'I'm looking for a diamond necklace,' I said. He sat down opposite me.

'Well, Herr Günther, I'm the acknowledged expert on diamonds.' His head gave a proud little flourish, like a racehorse, and I caught a powerful whiff of cologne.

'Is that so?' I said.

'I doubt if there's a man in Berlin who knows as much about diamonds as I do.' He thrust his stubbly chin at me, as if challenging me to contradict him. I almost threw up.

'I'm glad to hear it,' I said. The coffee arrived and Jeschonnek glanced uncomfortably after his secretary as he minced out of the room.

'I cannot get used to having a male secretary,' he said. 'Of course, I can see that the proper place for a woman is in the home, bringing up a family, but I have a great fondness for women, Herr Günther.'

'I'd take a partner before I'd take on a male secretary,' I said. He smiled politely.

'Now then, I believe you're in the market for a diamond.'

'Diamonds,' I said, correcting him.

'I see. On their own, or in a setting?'

'Actually I'm trying to trace a particular piece which has been stolen from my client,' I explained, and handed him my card. He stared at it impassively. 'A necklace, to be precise. I have a photograph of it here.' I produced another photograph and handed it to him.

'Magnificent,' he said.

'Each one of the baguettes is one carat,' I told him.

'Quite,' he said. 'But I don't see how I can help you, Herr Günther.'

'If the thief should try and offer it to you, I'd be grateful if you would contact me. Naturally, there is a substantial reward. I have been authorized by my client to offer twenty-five per cent of the insured value for recovery, no questions asked.'

'May one know the name of your client, Herr Günther?'

I hesitated. 'Well,' I said. 'Ordinarily, a client's identity is confidential. But I can see that you are the kind of man who is used to respecting confidentiality.'

'You're much too kind,' he said.

'The necklace is Indian, and belongs to a princess who is in Berlin for the Olympiad, as the guest of the Government.' Jeschonnek began to frown as he listened to my lies. 'I have not met the princess myself, but I am told that she is the most beautiful creature that Berlin has ever seen. She is staying at the Adlon Hotel, from where the necklace was stolen several nights ago.'

'Stolen from an Indian princess, eh?' he said, adding a smile to his features. 'Well, I mean, why was there nothing in the newspapers about this? And why are the police not involved?' I drank some of my coffee to prolong a dramatic pause.

'The management of the Adlon is anxious to avoid a scandal,' I said. 'It's not so very long ago that the Adlon suffered a series of unfortunate robberies committed there by the celebrated jewel-thief Faulhaber.'

'Yes, I remember reading about that.'

'It goes without question that the necklace is insured, but where the reputation of the Adlon is concerned, that is hardly the point, as I am sure you will understand.'

'Well, sir, I shall certainly contact you immediately if I come across any information that may help you,' said Jeschonnek, producing a gold watch from his pocket. He glanced at it deliberately. 'And now, if you'll excuse me, I really must be getting on.' He stood up and held out his pudgy hand.

'Thanks for your time,' I said. 'I'll see myself out.'

'Perhaps you'd be kind enough to ask that boy to step in here when you go out,' he said.

'Sure.'

He gave me the Hitler Salute. 'Heil Hitler,' I repeated dumbly.

In the outside office the anaemic boy was reading a magazine. My eyes caught sight of the keys before I'd finished telling him that his boss required his presence: they were lying on the desk next to the telephone. He grunted and wrenched himself out of his seat. I hesitated at the door.

'Oh, do you have a piece of paper?'

He pointed to the pad on which the keys were lying. 'Help yourself,' he said, and went into Jeschonnek's office.

'Thanks, I will.' The key-ring was labelled 'Office'. I took a cigarette case out of my pocket and opened it. In the smooth surface of the modelling clay I made three impressions – two sides and a vertical – of both keys. I suppose that you could say I did it on impulse. I'd hardly had time to digest everything that Jeschonnek had said; or rather, what he hadn't said. But then I always carry that piece of clay, and it seems a shame not to use it when the opportunity presents itself. You would be surprised how often a key that I've had made with that mould comes in useful.

Outside, I found a public telephone and called the Adlon. I still remembered lots of good times at the Adlon, and lots of friends, too.

'Hello, Hermine,' I said, 'it's Bernie.' Hermine was one of the girls on the Adlon's switchboard.

'You stranger,' she said. 'We haven't seen you in ages.'

'I've been a bit busy,' I said.

'So's the Führer, but he still manages to get around and wave to us.'

'Maybe I should buy myself an open-top Mercedes and a couple of outriders.' I lit a cigarette. 'I need a small favour, Hermine.'

'Ask.'

'If a man telephones and asks you or Benita if there is an Indian princess staying at the hotel, would you please say that there is? If he wants to speak to her, say she's not taking any calls.'

'That's all?'

'Yes.'

'Does this princess have a name?'

'You know the names of any Indian girls?'

'Well,' she said, 'I saw a film the other week which had this Indian girl in it. Her name was Mushmi.'

'Let it be Princess Mushmi then. And thanks, Hermine. I'll be speaking to you soon.'

I went into the Pschorr Haus restaurant and ate a plate of bacon and broad beans, and drank a couple of beers. Either Jeschonnek knew nothing about diamonds, or he had something to hide. I'd told him that the necklace was Indian, when he ought to have recognized it as being by Cartier. Not only that, but he had failed to contradict me when I described the stones incorrectly as baguettes. Baguettes are square or oblong, with a straight edge; but Six's necklace consisted of brilliants, which are round. And then there was the caratage; I'd said that each stone was a carat in weight, when they were obviously several times larger.

It wasn't much to go on; and mistakes are made: it's impossible always to pick up a stick by the right end; but all the same, I had this feeling in my socks that I was going to have to visit Jeschonnek again.

8

After leaving Pschorr Haus, I went into the Haus Vaterland, which as well as housing the cinema where I was to meet Bruno Stahlecker, is also home to an almost infinite number of bars and cafés. The place is popular with the tourists, but it's too old-fashioned to suit my taste: the great ugly halls, the silver paint, the bars with their miniature rainstorms and moving trains; it all belongs to a quaint old European world of mechanical toys and music-hall, leotarded strong-men and trained canaries. The other thing that makes it unusual is that it's the only bar in Germany that charges for admission. Stahlecker was less than happy about it.

'I had to pay twice,' he grumbled. 'Once at the front door, and again to come in here.'

'You should have flashed your Sipo pass,' I said. 'You'd have got in for nothing. That's the whole point of having it, isn't it?' Stahlecker looked blankly at the screen.

'Very funny,' he said. 'What is this shit, anyway?'

'Still the newsreel,' I told him. 'So what did you find out?'

'There's the small matter of last night to be dealt with yet.'

'My word of honour, Bruno, I never saw the kid before.' Stahlecker sighed wearily. 'Apparently this Kolb was a small-time actor. One or two bit-parts in films, in the chorus-line in a couple of shows. Not exactly Richard Tauber. Now why would a fellow like that want to kill you? Unless maybe you've turned critic and gave him a few bad notices.'

'I've got no more understanding of theatre than a dog has of laying a fire.'

'But you do know why he tried to kill you, right?'

'There's this lady,' I said. 'Her husband hired me to do a job for him. She thought that I'd been hired to look through her keyhole.

So last night she has me round to her place, asks me to lay off and accuses me of lying when I tell her that I'm not concerned who she's sleeping with. Then she throws me out. Next thing I know there's this pear-head standing in my doorway with a lighter poked in my gut, accusing me of raping the lady. We dance around the room a while, and in the process the gun goes off. My guess is that the kid was in a swarm about her, and that she knew it.'

'And so she put him up to it, right?'

'That's the way I see it. But try and make it stick and see how far you'd get.'

'I don't suppose you're going to tell me the name of this lady, or her husband, are you?' I shook my head. 'No, I thought not.'

The film was starting: called *The Higher Order*, it was one of those patriotic little entertainments that the boys in the Ministry of Propaganda had dreamed up on a bad day. Stahlecker groaned.

'Come on,' he said. 'Let's go and get a drink. I don't think I can stand watching this shit.'

We went to the Wild West Bar on the first floor, where a band of cowboys were playing *Home on the Range*. Painted prairies covered the walls, complete with buffalo and Indians. Leaning up against the bar, we ordered a couple of beers.

'I don't suppose any of this would have something to do with the Pfarr case, would it, Bernie?'

'I've been retained to investigate the fire,' I explained. 'By the insurance company.'

'All right,' he said. 'I'll tell you this just the once, and then you can tell me to go to hell. Drop it. It's a hot one, if you'll pardon the expression.'

'Bruno,' I said, 'go to hell. I'm on a percentage.'

'Just don't say I didn't warn you when they throw you into a KZ.'

'I promise. Now unpack it.'

'Bernie, you've got more promises than a debtor has for the bailiff.' He sighed and shook his head. 'Well, here's what there is.

'This Paul Pfarr fellow was a high-flyer. Passed his juridicial in 1930, saw preparatory service in the Stuttgart and Berlin Provincial

Courts. In 1933, this particular March Violet joins the SA, and by 1934 he is an assessor judge in the Berlin Police Court, trying cases of police corruption, of all things. The same year he is recruited into the SS and in 1935 he also joins the Gestapo, supervising associations, economic unions and of course the DAF, the Reich Labour Service. Later that year he is transferred yet again, this time to the Ministry of the Interior, reporting directly to Himmler, with his own department investigating corruption amongst servants of the Reich.'

'I'm surprised that they notice.'

'Apparently Himmler takes a very dim view of it. Anyway, Paul Pfarr was charged with paying particular attention to the DAF, where corruption is endemic.'

'So he was Himmler's boy, eh?'

'That's right. And his ex-boss takes an even dimmer view of people working for him getting canned than he does of corruption. So a couple of days ago the Reichskriminaldirektor appoints a special squad to investigate. It's an impressive team: Gohrmann, Schild, Jost, Dietz. You get mixed up in this, Bernie, and you won't last longer than a synagogue window.'

'They got any leads?'

'The only thing I heard was that they were looking for a girl. It seems as though Pfarr might have had a mistress. No name, I'm afraid. Not only that, but she's disappeared.'

'You want to know something?' I said. 'Disappearing is all the rage. Everyone's doing it.'

'So I heard. I hope you aren't the fashionable sort, then.'

'Me? I must be one of the only people in this city not to own a uniform. I'd say that makes me very unfashionable.'

Back at Alexanderplatz I visited a locksmith and gave him the mould to make a copy of Jeschonnek's office keys. I'd used him many times before, and he never asked any questions. Then I collected my laundry and went up to the office.

I wasn't half-way through the door before a Sipo pass had flashed in front of my face. In the same instant I caught sight of the Walther inside the man's unbuttoned grey-flannel jacket.

'You must be the sniffer,' he said. 'We've been waiting to speak to you.' He had mustard-coloured hair, coiffed by a competition sheepshearer, and a nose like a champagne cork. His moustache was wider than the brim on a Mexican's hat. The other one was the racial archetype with the sort of exaggerated chin and cheekbones he'd copied off a Prussian election poster. They both had cool, patient eyes, like mussels in brine, and sneers like someone had farted, or told a particularly tasteless joke.

'If I'd known, I'd have gone to see a couple of movies.' The one with the pass and the haircut stared blankly at me.

'This here is Kriminalinspektor Dietz,' he said.

The one called Dietz, who I guessed to be the senior officer, was sitting on the edge of my desk, swinging his leg and looking generally unpleasant.

'You'll excuse me if I don't get out my autograph-book,' I said, and walked over to the corner by the window where Frau Protze was standing. She sniffed and pulled out a handkerchief from the sleeve of her blouse, and blew her nose. Through the material she said:

'I'm sorry, Herr Günther, they just barged in here and started ransacking the place. I told them I didn't know where you were, or when you would be back, and they got quite nasty. I never knew that policemen could behave so disgracefully.'

'They're not policemen,' I said. 'More like knuckles with suits. You'd better run along home now. I'll see you tomorrow.'

She sniffed some more. 'Thank you, Herr Günther,' she said. 'But I don't think I'll be coming back. I don't think my nerves are up to this sort of thing. I'm sorry.'

'That's all right. I'll mail what I owe you.' She nodded, and having stepped round me she almost ran out of the office. The haircut snorted with laughter and kicked the door shut behind her. I opened the window.

'There's a bit of a smell in here,' I said. 'What do you fellows do when you're not scaring widows and searching for the petty-cash box?'

Dietz jerked himself off my desk and came over to the window. 'I heard about you, Günther,' he said, looking out at the traffic. 'You used to be a bull, so I know that you know the official paper on just how far I can go. And that's still a hell of a long way yet. I can stand on your fucking face for the rest of the afternoon, and I don't even have to tell you why. So why don't you cut the shit and tell me what you know about Paul Pfarr, and then we'll be on our way again.'

'I know he wasn't a careless smoker,' I said. 'Look, if you hadn't gone through this place like an earth-tremor, I might have been able to find a letter from the Germania Life Assurance Company engaging me to investigate the fire pending any claim.'

'Oh, we found that letter,' said Dietz. 'We found this, too.' He took my gun out of his jacket pocket and pointed it playfully at my head.

'I've got a licence for it.'

'Sure you have,' he said, smiling. Then he sniffed the muzzle, and spoke to his partner. 'You know, Martins, I'd say this pistol has been cleaned; and recently, too.'

'I'm a clean boy,' I said. 'Take a look at my fingernails if you don't believe me.'

'Walther PPK, 9 mm,' said Martins, lighting a cigarette. 'Just like the gun that killed poor Herr Pfarr and his wife.'

'That's not what I heard.' I went over to the drinks cabinet. I was surprised to see that they hadn't helped themselves to any of my whisky.

'Of course,' said Dietz, 'we were forgetting that you've still got friends over at the Alex, weren't we.' I poured myself a drink. A little too much to swallow in less than three gulps.

'I thought they got rid of all those reactionaries,' said Martins. I surveyed the last mouthful of whisky.

'I'd offer you boys a drink, only I wouldn't want to have to throw away the glasses afterwards.' I tossed the drink back.

Martins flicked away his cigarette and, clenching his fists, he stepped forward a couple of paces. 'This bum specializes in lip like a yid does in nose,' he snarled. Dietz stayed where he was, leaning on the window. But when he turned around there was tabasco in his eyes.

'I'm running out of patience with you, mulemouth.'

'I don't get it,' I said. 'You've seen the letter from the Assurance people. If you think it's a fake, then check it out.'

'We already did.'

'Then why the double act?' Dietz walked over and looked me up and down like I was shit on his shoe. Then he picked up my last bottle of good scotch, weighed it in his hand and threw it against the wall above the desk. It smashed with the sound of a canteen of cutlery dropping down a stairwell, and the air was suddenly redolent with alcohol. Dietz straightened his jacket after the exertion.

'We just wanted to impress you with the need to keep us informed of what you're doing, Günther. If you find out anything, and I mean anything, then you better speak to us. Because if I find out you've been giving us any fig-leaf, then I'll have you in a KZ so quick, your fucking ears will whistle.' He leaned towards me and I caught the smell of his sweat. 'Understand, mulemouth?'

'Don't stick your jaw too far out, Dietz,' I said, 'or I'll feel obliged to slap it.'

He smiled. 'I'd like that sometime. Really I would.' He turned to his partner. 'Come on,' he said. 'Let's get out of here before I kick him in the eggs.'

I'd just finished clearing up the mess when the phone rang. It was Müller from the *Berliner Morgenpost* to say that he was sorry, but beyond the sort of material that the obituaries people collected over the years, there really wasn't much in the files about Hermann Six to interest me.

'Are you giving me the up and down, Eddie? Christ, this fellow is a millionaire. He owns half the Ruhr. If he stuck his finger up his arse he'd find oil. Somebody must have got a look through his keyhole at some time.'

'There was a reporter a while back who did quite a bit of spade-work on all of those big boys on the Ruhr: Krupp, Voegler, Wolff, Thyssen. She lost her job when the Government solved the unemployment problem. I'll see if I can find out where she's living.'

'Thanks, Eddie. What about the Pfarrs? Anything?'

'She was really into spas. Nauheim, Wiesbaden, Bad Homburg, you name it, she'd splashed some there. She even wrote an article about it for *Die Frau*. And she was keen on quack medicine. There's nothing about him, I'm afraid.'

'Thanks for the gossip, Eddie. Next time I'll read the society page and save you the trouble.'

'Not worth a hundred, huh?'

'Not worth fifty. Find this lady reporter for me and then I'll see what I can do.'

After that I closed the office and returned to the key shop to collect my new set of keys and my tin of clay. I'll admit it sounds a bit theatrical; but honestly, I've carried that tin for several years, and short of stealing the actual key itself, I don't know of a better way of opening locked doors. A delicate mechanism of fine steel with which you can open any kind of lock, I don't have. The truth is that with the best modern locks, you can forget picking: there are no slick, fancy little wonder tools. That stuff is for the film-boys at UFA. More often than not a burglar simply saws off the bolt-head, or drills around it and removes a piece of the goddam door. And that reminded me: sooner or later I was going to have to check out just who there was in the fraternity of nutcrackers with the talent to have opened the Pfarrs' safe. If that was how it was done. Which meant that there was a certain scrofulous little tenor who was long overdue for a singing lesson.

I didn't expect to find Neumann at the dump where he lived in Admiralstrasse, in the Kottbusser Tor district, but I tried there anyway. Kottbusser Tor was the kind of area that had worn about as well as a music-hall poster, and Admiralstrasse, Number 43 was the kind of place where the rats wore ear-plugs and the cockroaches had nasty coughs. Neumann's room was in the basement at the back. It was damp. It was dirty. It was foul. And Neumann wasn't there.

The concierge was a snapper who was over the hill and down a disused mine-shaft. Her hair was every bit as natural as parade goose-stepping down the Wilhelmstrasse, and she'd evidently been wearing a boxing-glove when she'd applied the crimson lipstick to her paperclip of a mouth. Her breasts were like the rear ends of a pair of dray horses at the end of a long hard day. Maybe she still had a few clients, but I thought it was a better bet that I'd see a Jew at the front of a Nuremberg pork-butcher's queue. She stood in the doorway to her apartment, naked under the grubby towelling robe which she left open, and lit a half-smoked cigarette.

'I'm looking for Neumann,' I said, doing my level best to ignore the two coat-pegs and the Russian boyar's beard that were being displayed for my benefit. You felt the twang and itch of syphilis in your tail just looking at her. 'I'm a friend of his.' The snapper yawned cheesily and, deciding that I'd seen enough for free, she closed her robe and tied the cord.

'You a bull?' she sniffed.

'Like I said, I'm a friend.' She folded her arms and leaned on the doorway.

'Neumann doesn't have any friends,' she said, looking at her dirty fingernails and then back at my face. I had to give her that one. 'Except for me, maybe, and that's only because I feel sorry for the little twitcher. If you were a friend of his you'd tell him to see a doctor. He isn't right in the head, you know.' She took a long drag on her cigarette and then flicked the butt past my shoulder.

'He's not tapped,' I said. 'He just has a tendency to talk to himself. A bit strange, that's all.'

'If that's not tapped then I don't know what the hell is,' she said. There was something in that too.

'You know when he'll be back?'

The snapper shrugged. A hand that was all blue veins and knuckle-duster rings took hold of my tie; she tried to smile coyly, only it came out as a grimace. 'Maybe you'd care to wait for him,' she said. 'You know, twenty marks buys an awful lot of time.'

Retrieving my tie I took out my wallet and thumbed her a five. 'I'd like to. Really I would. But I must be getting on my way. Perhaps you'd tell Neumann that I was looking for him. The name is Günther. Bernhard Günther.'

'Thank you, Bernhard. You're a real gentleman.'

'Do you have any idea where he might be?'

'Bernhard, your guess is as good as mine. You could chase him from Pontius to Pilate and still not find him.' She shrugged and shook her head. 'If he's broke he'll be somewhere like the X Bar, or the Rucker. If he's got any mouse in his pocket he'll be trying to nudge a bit of plum at the Femina or the Café Casanova.' I started down the stairs. 'And if he's not at any of those places then he'll be at the racetrack.' She followed me out onto the landing and down some of the steps. I got into my car with a sigh of relief. It's always difficult getting away from a snapper. They never like to see trade walking out of the door.

I don't have much faith in experts; or, for that matter, in the statements of witnesses. Over the years I've come to belong to the school of detection that favours good, old-fashioned, circumstantial evidence of the kind that says a fellow did it because he was the type who'd do that sort of thing anyway. That, and information received.

Keeping a tenor like Neumann is something that requires trust and patience; and just as the first of these does not come naturally to Neumann, so the second does not come naturally to me: but only where he is concerned. Neumann is the best informer I've ever had, and his tips are usually accurate. There were no lengths to which I would not go to protect him. On the other hand, it does not follow that you can rely on him. Like all informers he would sell his own sister's plum. You get one to trust you, that's the hard bit; but you could no more trust one yourself than I could win the Sierstorpff Stakes at the Hoppegarten.

I started at the X Bar, an illegal jazz club where the band were sandwiching American hits between the opening and closing chords of whatever innocuous and culturally acceptable Aryan number took their fancy; and they did it well enough not to trouble any Nazi's conscience regarding so-called inferior music.

In spite of his occasionally strange behaviour, Neumann was one of the most nondescript, anonymous-looking people I had ever seen. It was what made him such an excellent informer. You had to look hard to see him, but that particular night, there was no sign of him at the X. Nor at the Allaverdi, nor the Rucker Bar in the rough end of the red-light district.

It wasn't yet dark, but already the dope dealers had surfaced. To be caught selling cocaine was to be sent to a KZ, and for my money they couldn't catch too many of them; but as I knew from experience, that wasn't easy: the dealers never carried coke on them; instead they would hide it in a stash nearby, in a secluded alley or doorway. Some of them posed as war cripples selling cigarettes; and some of them were war cripples selling cigarettes, wearing the yellow armlet with its three black spots that had persisted from Weimar days. This armlet conferred no official status, however; only the Salvation Army received official permission to peddle wares on street corners, but the laws against vagrancy were not strictly enforced anywhere except the more fashionable areas of the city, where the tourists were likely to go.

'Ssigars, and ssigarettes,' hissed a voice. Those familiar with this 'coke signal' would answer with a loud sniff; often they found that they had bought cooking salt and aspirin.

The Femina, on Nurnberger Strasse, was the sort of spot you went when you were looking for some female company if you didn't mind them big and florid and thirty marks for the privilege. Table telephones made the Femina especially suitable for the shy type, so it was just Neumann's sort of place, always presuming that he had some money. He could order a bottle of sekt and invite a girl to join him without so much as moving from his table. There were even pneumatic tubes through which small presents could be blown into the hand of a girl at the opposite end of the club. Apart from money, the only thing a man needed at the Femina was good eyesight.

I sat at a corner table and glanced idly at the menu. As well as the list of drinks, there was a list of presents that could be purchased from the waiter, for sending through the tubes: a powder compact for one mark fifty; a matchbox-container for a mark; and perfume for five. I couldn't help thinking that money was likely to be the most popular sort of present you could send rocketing over to whichever party girl caught your eye. There was no sign of Neumann, but I decided to stick it out for a while in case he showed up. I signalled the waiter and ordered a beer.

There was a cabaret, of sorts: a chanteuse with orange hair, and a twangy voice like a Jew's harp; and a skinny little comedian with joined-up eyebrows, who was about as risqué as a wafer on an ice-cream sundae. There was less chance of the crowd at the Femina enjoying the acts than there was of it rebuilding the Reichstag: it laughed during the songs; and it sang during the comedian's monologues; and it was no nearer the palm of anyone's hand than if it had been a rabid dog.

Looking round the room I found there were so many false eye-lashes flapping at me that I was beginning to feel a draught. Several tables away a fat woman rippled the fingers of a pudgy hand at me, and misinterpreting my sneer for a smile, she started to struggle out of her seat. I groaned.

'Yessir?' answered the waiter. I pulled a crumpled note out of my pocket and tossed it on to his tray. Without bothering to wait for my change I turned and fled.

There's only one thing that unnerves me more than the company of an ugly woman in the evening, and that's the company of the same ugly woman the following morning.

I got into the car and drove to Potsdamer Platz. It was a warm, dry evening, but the rumbling in the purple sky told me that the weather was about to change for the worse. I parked on Leipziger

Platz in front of the Palast Hotel. Then I went inside and telephoned the Adlon.

I got through to Benita, who said that Hermine had left her a message, and that about half an hour after I had spoken to her a man had called asking about an Indian princess. It was all I needed to know.

I collected my raincoat and a flashlight from the car. Holding the flash under the raincoat I walked the fifty metres back to Potsdamer Platz, past the Berlin Tramway Company and the Ministry of Agriculture, towards Columbus Haus. There were lights on the fifth and seventh floors, but none on the eighth. I looked in through the heavy plate-glass doors. There was a security guard sitting at the desk reading a newspaper, and, further along the corridor, a woman who was going over the floor with an electric polisher. It started to rain as I turned the corner onto Hermann Goering Strasse, and made a left onto the narrow service alley that led to the underground car-park at the back of Columbus Haus.

There were only two cars parked – a DKW and a Mercedes. It seemed unlikely that either of them belonged to the security guard or the cleaner; more probably, their owners were still at work in offices on the floors above. Behind the two cars, and under a bulkhead light, was a grey, steel door with the word 'Service' painted on it; it had no handle, and was locked. I decided that it was probably the sort of lock that had a spring bolt that could be withdrawn by a knob on the inside, or by means of a key on the outside, and I thought that there was a good chance that the cleaner might leave the building through this door.

I checked the doors of the two parked cars almost absent-mindedly, and found that the Mercedes was not locked. I sat in the driver's seat, and fumbled for the light switch. The two huge lamps cut through the shadows like the spots at a Party rally in Nuremberg. I waited. Several minutes passed. Bored, I opened the glove-box. There was a road map, a bag of mints and a Party membership book with stamps up to date. It identified the bearer as one

Henning Peter Manstein. Manstein had a comparatively low Party number, which belied the youthfulness of the man in the photograph on the book's ninth page. There was quite a racket in the sale of early Party numbers, and there was no doubting that was how Manstein had come by his. A low number was essential to quick political advancement. His handsome young face had the greedy look of a March Violet stamped all over it, as clearly as the Party insignia embossed across the corner of the photograph.

Fifteen minutes passed before I heard the sound of the service door opening. I sprang out of the seat. If it was Manstein, then I was going to have to make a run for it. A wide pool of light spilled onto the floor of the garage, and the cleaning woman came through the door.

'Hold the door,' I called. I switched off the headlights and slammed the car door. 'I've left something upstairs,' I said. 'I thought for a minute I was going to have to walk all the way round to the front.' She stood there dumbly, holding the door open as I approached. When I drew near her she stepped aside, saying:

'I have to walk all the way to Nollendorf Platz. I don't have no big car to take me home.'

I smiled sheepishly, like the idiot I imagined Manstein to be. 'Thanks very much,' I said, and muttered something about having left my key in my office. The cleaning woman hovered a little and then released the door to me. I stepped inside the building and let it go. It closed behind me, and I heard the loud click of the cylinder lock as the bolt hit the chamber.

Two double doors with porthole windows led into a long, brightly lit corridor that was lined with stacks of cardboard boxes. At the far end was a lift, but there was no way of using it without alerting the guard. So I sat down on the stairs and removed my shoes and socks, putting them on again in reverse order, with the socks over the shoes. It's an old trick, favoured by burglars, for muffling the sound of shoe-leather on a hard surface. I stood up and began the long climb.

By the time I got to the eighth floor my heart was pounding

with the effort of the climb and having to breathe quietly. I waited at the edge of the stairs, but there was no sound from any of the offices next to Jeschonnek's. I shone the flash at both ends of the corridor, and then walked down to his door. Kneeling down I looked for some wires that might give a clue to there being an alarm, but there were none; I tried first one key, and then the other. The second one was almost turning, so I pulled it out and smoothed the points with a small file. I tried again, this time successfully. I opened the door and went in, locking it behind me in case the security guard decided to do his rounds. I pointed the flash onto the desk, over the pictures and across to the door to Jeschonnek's private office. Without the least resistance to the levers, the key turned smoothly in my fingers. Covering the name of my locksmith with mental blessings, I walked over to the window. The neon sign on top of Pschorr Haus cast a red glow over Jeschonnek's opulent office, so there wasn't much need for the flash. I turned it off.

I sat down at the desk and started to look for I didn't know what. The drawers weren't locked, but they contained little that was of any interest to me. I got quite excited when I found a red leather-bound address book, but I read it all the way through, recognizing just the one name: that of Hermann Goering, only he was care of a Gerhard Von Greis at an address on Derfflingerstrasse. I remembered Weizmann the pawnbroker saying something about Fat Hermann having an agent who sometimes bought precious stones on his behalf, so I copied out Von Greis's address and put it in my pocket.

The filing cabinet wasn't locked either, but again I drew a blank; plenty of catalogues of gems and semi-precious stones, a Lufthansa flight table, a lot of papers to do with currency exchange, some invoices and some life assurance policies, one of which was with the Germania Life.

Meanwhile, the big safe sat in the corner, impregnable, and mocking my rather feeble attempts to uncover Jeschonnek's secrets, if he had any. It wasn't difficult to see why the place wasn't fitted with an alarm. You couldn't have opened that box if you'd had a truck-load of dynamite. There wasn't much left, apart from the waste-paper basket. I emptied the contents on the desk, and started to poke through the scraps of paper: a Wrigley's chewing-gum wrapper, the morning's *Völkischer Beobachter*, two ticket-halves from the Lessing Theater, a till receipt from the KDW department store and some rolled-up balls of paper. I smoothed them out. On one of these was the Adlon's telephone number, and underneath the name 'Princess Mushmi', which had been question-marked and then crossed out several times; next to it was written my own name. There was another telephone number written next to my name, and this had been doodled around so that it looked like an illumination from a page in a medieval Bible. The number was a mystery to me, although I recognized it was Berlin West. I picked up the receiver and waited for the operator.

'Number please?' she said.

'J 1–90–33.'

'Trying to connect you.' There was a brief silence on the line, and then it started ringing.

I have an excellent memory when it comes to recognizing a face, or a voice, but it might have taken me several minutes to place the cultured voice with its light Frankfurt accent that answered the telephone. As it was, the man identified himself immediately he had finished confirming the number.

'I'm so sorry,' I mumbled indistinctly. 'I have the wrong number.' But as I replaced the receiver I knew that it was anything but.

9

It was in a grave close to the north wall of the Nikolai Cemetery on Prenzlauer Allee, and only a short distance away from the memorial to National Socialism's most venerated martyr, Horst Wessel, that the bodies were buried, one on top of the other, following a short service at Nikolai Kirche on nearby Molken Market.

Wearing a stunning black hat that was like a grand piano with the lid up, Ilse Rudel was even more beautiful in mourning than she was in bed. A couple of times I caught her eye, but tight-lipped, like she had my neck between her teeth, she looked straight through me as if I was a piece of dirty glass. Six himself maintained an expression that was more angry than grief-stricken: with eyebrows knotted and head bowed, he stared down into the grave as though he were trying by a supernatural effort of will to make it yield up the living body of his daughter. And then there was Haupthändler, who looked merely thoughtful, like a man for whom there were other matters that were more pressing, such as the disposal of a diamond necklace. The appearance on the same sheet of paper in Jeschonnek's waste-paper basket of Haupthändler's home telephone number with that of the Adlon Hotel, my own name and that of the bogus princess, demonstrated a possible chain of causation: alarmed by my visit, and yet puzzled by my story, Jeschonnek had telephoned the Adlon to confirm the existence of the Indian princess, and then, having done so, he had telephoned Haupthändler to confront him with a set of facts regarding the ownership and theft of the jewels which was at variance with that which might originally have been explained to him.

Perhaps. At least, it was enough to be going on with.

At one point Haupthändler stared impassively at me for several seconds; but I could read nothing in his features: no guilt, no fear, no ignorance of the connection I had established between him and Jeschonnek, nor any suspicion of it either. I saw nothing that made me think he was incapable of having committed a double murder. But he was certainly no cracksman; so had he somehow persuaded Frau Pfarr to open it for him? Had he made love to her in order to get at her jewels? Given Ilse Rudel's suspicion that they might have been having an affair, it had to be counted as one possibility.

There were some other faces that I recognized. Old Kripo faces: Reichskriminaldirektor Arthur Nebe; Hans Lobbe, the head of Kripo Executive; and one face which, with its rimless glasses and small moustache, looked more as if it belonged to a punctilious little schoolmaster than to the head of the Gestapo and Reichsführer of the SS. Himmler's presence at the funeral confirmed Bruno Stahlecker's impression – that Pfarr had been the Reichsführer's star pupil, and that he wasn't about to let the murderer get away with it.

Of a woman on her own, who might have been the mistress that Bruno had mentioned as having been kept by Paul Pfarr, there was no sign. Not that I really expected to see her, but you never can tell.

After the burial Haupthändler was ready with a few words of advice from his, and my employer, 'Herr Six sees little need for you to have concerned yourself in what is essentially a family affair. I'm also to remind you that you are being remunerated on the basis of a daily fee.'

I watched the mourners get into their big black cars, and then Himmler and the top bulls in Kripo get into theirs. 'Look, Haupthändler,' I said. 'Forget the sledge ride. Tell your boss that if he thinks he's getting a cat in a sack, then he can cut me loose now. I'm not here because I like fresh air and eulogies.'

'Then why are you here, Herr Günther?' he said.

'Ever read *The Song of the Niebelungen*?'

'Naturally.'

'Then you'll remember that the Niebelung warriors wished to avenge the murder of Siegfried. But they couldn't tell who they should hold to account. So the trial of blood was begun. The Burgundian warriors passed one by one before the bier of the hero. And when it was the murderer Hagen's turn, Siegfried's wounds flowed with blood again, so revealing Hagen's guilt.'

Haupthändler smiled. 'That's hardly the stuff of modern criminal investigation, is it?'

'Detection should observe the little ceremonies, Herr Haupthändler, be they apparently anachronistic. You might have noticed that I was not the only person involved in finding a solution to this case who attended this funeral.'

'Are you seriously suggesting that someone here could have killed Paul and Grete Pfarr?'

'Don't be so bourgeois. Of course it is possible.'

'It's preposterous, that's what it is. All the same, do you have someone in mind for the role of Hagen yet?'

'It's under consideration.'

'Then I trust you will be able to report your having identified him to Herr Six before very long. Good day to you.'

I had to admit one thing. If Haupthändler had killed the Pfarrs then he was as cool as a treasure chest in fifty fathoms of water.

I drove down Prenzlauer Strasse on to Alexanderplatz. I collected my mail and went up to the office. The cleaning woman had opened the window, but the smell of booze was still there. She must have thought I washed in the stuff.

There were a couple of cheques, a bill and a hand-delivered note from Neumann telling me to meet him at the Café Kranzler at twelve o'clock. I looked at my watch. It was almost 11.30.

In front of the German War Memorial a company of Reichswehr were making trade for chiropodists to the accompaniment of a brass band. Sometimes I think that there must be more brass bands in Germany than there are motor-cars. This one struck up with *The Great Elector's Cavalry March* and set off at a lick towards the Brandenburger Tor. Everyone who was watching was getting in some arm exercise, so I hung back, pausing in a shop doorway to avoid having to join them.

I walked on, following the parade at a discreet distance and reflecting on the last alterations to the capital's most famous avenue: changes that the Government has deemed to be necessary to make Unter den Linden more suitable for military parades like the one I was watching. Not content with removing most of the lime trees which had given the avenue its name, they had erected white Doric columns on top of which sat German eagles; new lime trees had been planted, but these were not even as tall as the street lamps. The central lane had been widened, so that military columns might march twelve abreast, and was strewn with red sand so that their jackboots did not slip. And tall white flagpoles were being erected for the imminent Olympiad. Unter den Linden had always been flamboyant, without much harmony in its mixture of architectural designs and styles; but that flamboyance was now made brutal. The bohemian's fedora had become a Pickelhaube.

The Café Kranzler, on the corner of Friedrichstrasse, was popular with the tourists and prices were accordingly high; so it was not the sort of place that I would have expected Neumann to have chosen for a meet. I found him twitching over a cup of mocha and an abandoned piece of cake.

'What's the matter?' I said, sitting down. 'Lost your appetite?'

Neumann sneered at his plate. 'Just like this Government,' he said. 'It looks damn good, but tastes of absolutely nothing. Lousy ersatz cream.' I waved to the waiter and ordered two coffees. 'Look, Herr Günther, can we make this quick? I'm going over to Karlshorst this afternoon.'

'Oh? Got a tip, have you?'

'Well, as a matter of fact –'

I laughed. 'Neumann, I wouldn't bet on a horse that you were going to back if it could out-pace the Hamburg Express.'

'So fuck off, then,' he snapped.

If he was a member of the human race at all, Neumann was its least attractive specimen. His eyebrows, twitching and curling like two poisoned caterpillars, were joined together by an irregular scribble of poorly matched hair. Behind thick glasses that were almost opaque with greasy thumbprints, his grey eyes were shifty and nervous, searching the floor as if he expected that at any moment he would be lying flat on it. Cigarette smoke poured out from between teeth that were so badly stained with tobacco they looked like two wooden fences.

'You're not in trouble, are you?' Neumann's face adopted a phlegmatic expression.

'I owe some people some flea, that's all.'

'How much?'

'Couple of hundred.'

'So you're going to Karlshorst to try and win some of it, is that it?'

He shrugged. 'And what if I am?' He put out his cigarette and searched his pockets for another. 'You got a nail? I've run out.' I tossed a packet across the table.

'Keep it,' I said, lighting us both. 'A couple of hundred, eh? You know, I just might be able to help you out there. Maybe even leave you some on top. That is, if I get the right information.'

Neumann raised his eyebrows. 'What sort of information?'

I drew on my cigarette, and held it deep within my lungs. 'The name of a puzzler. A first class professional nutcracker who might have done a job about a week ago; stolen some bells.'

He pursed his lips and shook his head slowly. 'I haven't heard anything, Herr Günther.'

'Well, if you do, make sure you let me know.'

'On the other hand,' he said, lowering his voice, 'I could tell you something that would put you well in with the Gestapo.'

'What's that?'

'I know where a Jewish U-Boat is hiding out.' He smiled smugly.

'Neumann, you know I'm not interested in that crap.' But as I spoke, I thought of Frau Heine, my client, and her son. 'Hold on a moment,' I said. 'What's the Jew's name?' Neumann gave me a name, and grinned, a disgusting sight. His was an order of life not much higher than the calcareous sponge. I pointed my finger squarely at his nose. 'If I get to hear that U-Boat's been pulled in, I won't have to know who informed on him. I promise you, Neumann, I'll come round and tear your fucking eyelids off.'

'What's it to you?' he whined. 'Since when have you been the knight in Goldberg armour?'

'His mother is a client of mine. Before you forget you ever heard about him, I want the address where he is so I can tell her.'

'All right, all right. But that's got to be worth something, hasn't it?' I took out my wallet and gave him a twenty. Then I wrote down the address that Neumann gave me.

'You'd disgust a dung-beetle,' I said. 'Now, what about this nutcracker?'

He frowned exasperatedly at me. 'Look, I said I didn't have anything.'

'You're a liar.'

'Honest, Herr Günther, I don't know nothing. If I did, I'd tell you. I need the money, don't I?' He swallowed hard and wiped the sweat from his brow with a public health-hazard of a handkerchief. Avoiding my eyes, he stubbed out his cigarette, which was only half-smoked.

'You don't act like someone who knows nothing,' I said. 'I think you're scared of something.'

'No,' he said flatly.

'Ever hear of the Queer Squad?' He shook his head. 'You might say they used to be colleagues of mine. I was thinking that if I found out you'd been holding out on me, I'd have a word with them. Tell them you were a smelly little para 175.' He looked at me with a mixture of surprise and outrage.

'Do I look like I suck lemons? I'm not queer, you know I'm not.'

'Yes, but they don't. And who are they going to believe?'

'You wouldn't do that.' He grabbed my wrist.

'From what I hear of it, left-handers don't have too good a time of it in the KZs.' Neumann stared glumly into his coffee.

'You evil bastard,' he sighed. 'A couple of hundred you said, and a bit more.'

'A hundred now, and two more if it's on the level.' He started to twitch.

'You don't know what you're asking, Herr Günther. There's a ring involved. They'd kill me for sure if they found out I'd fingered them.' Rings were unions of ex-convicts, dedicated officially to the rehabilitation of criminals; they had respectable club names, and their rules and regulations spoke of sporting activities and social gatherings. Not infrequently, a ring would host a lavish dinner (they were all very rich) at which defence lawyers and police officials would appear as guests of honour. But behind their semi-respectable façades the rings were nothing more than the institutions of organized crime in Germany.

'Which one is it?' I asked.

'The "German Strength".'

'Well, they won't find out. Anyway, none of them are as powerful as they used to be. There's only one ring that's doing good business these days and that's the Party.'

'Vice and drugs may have taken a bit of a hammering,' he said, 'but the rings still run the gambling, the currency rackets, the black market, new passports, loan-sharking and dealing in stolen goods.' He lit another cigarette. 'Believe me, Herr Günther, they're still strong. You don't want to get in their way.' He lowered his voice and leaned towards me. 'I've even heard a strong whisper that they canned some old Junker who was working for the Prime Minister. How do you like that, eh? The bulls don't even know that he's dead yet.'

I racked my brain and came across the name that I had copied from Gert Jeschonnek's address book. 'This Junker's name; it wouldn't have been Von Greis, would it?'

'I didn't hear no name. All I know is that he's dead, and that the bulls are still looking for him.' He flicked his ash negligently at the ashtray.

'Now tell me about the nutcracker.'

'Well, it seems like I did hear something. About a month ago, a fellow by the name of Kurt Mutschmann finishes two years' cement at Tegel Prison. From what I've heard about him, Mut-schmann is a real craftsman. He could open the legs of a nun with rigor mortis. But the polyps don't know about him. You see, he got put inside because he clawed a car. Nothing to do with his regular line of work. Anyway, he's a German Strength man, and when he came out the ring was there to look after him. After a while they set him up with his first job. I don't know what it was. But here's the interesting part, Herr Günther. The boss of German Strength, Red Dieter, has now got a contract out on Mutschmann, who is nowhere to be found. The word is that Mutschmann double-crossed him.'

'Mutschmann was a professional, you say.'

'One of the best.'

'Would you say murder was part of his portfolio?'

'Well,' said Neumann, 'I don't know the man myself. But from what I've heard, he's an artist. It doesn't sound like his number.'

'What about this Red Dieter?'

'He's a right bastard. He'd kill a man like someone else would pick their nose.'

'Where do I find him?'

'You won't tell him it was me who told you, will you, Herr Günther? Not even if he were to put a gun to your head.'

'No,' I lied; loyalty goes only so far.

'Well, you could try the Rheingold Restaurant on Potsdamer Platz. Or the Germania Roof. And if you take my advice you'll carry a lighter.'

'I'm touched by your concern for my well-being, Neumann.'

'You're forgetting the money,' he said, correcting me. 'You said I'd get another 200 if it checked out.' He paused, and then added: 'And a hundred now.' I took out my wallet again and thumbed him a couple of fifties. He held the two notes up to the window to scrutinize the watermarks.

'You must be joking.'

Neumann looked at me blankly. 'What about?' He pocketed the money quickly.

'Forget it.' I stood up and dropped some loose change onto the table. 'One more thing. Can you remember when you heard about the contract on Mutschmann?' Neumann looked as thoughtful as he could manage.

'Well, now that I come to think of it, it was last week, about the time that I heard about this Junker getting killed.'

I walked west down Unter den Linden towards Pariser Platz and the Adlon.

I went through the hotel's handsome doorway and into the sumptuous lobby with its square pillars of dark, yellow-clouded marble. Everywhere there were tasteful *objets d'art*; and in every corner there was the gleam of yet more marble. I went into the bar, which was full of foreign journalists and embassy people, and asked the barman, an old friend of mine, for a beer and the use of his telephone. I called Bruno Stahlecker at the Alex.

'Hallo, it's me, Bernie.'

'What do you want, Bernie?'

'How about Gerhard Von Greis?' I said. There was a long pause. 'What about him?' Bruno's voice sounded vaguely challenging, as if he was daring me to know more than I was supposed to.

'He's just a name on a piece of paper to me at the moment.'

'That all?'

'Well, I heard he was missing.'

'Would you mind telling me how?'

'Come on, Bruno, why are you being so coy about it? Look, my little song-bird told me, all right? Maybe if I knew a bit more I might be able to help.'

'Bernie, there are two hot cases in this department right now, and you seem to be involved in both of them. That worries me.'

'If it will make you feel better, I'll have an early night. Give me a break, Bruno.'

'This makes two in one week.'

'I owe you.'

'You're damn right you do.'

'So what's the story?'

Stahlecker lowered his voice. 'Ever heard of Walther Funk?'

'Funk? No, I don't think I have. Wait a minute, isn't he some big noise in the business world?'

'He used to be Hitler's economic advisor. He's now Vice-President of the Reich Chamber of Culture. It would seem that he and Herr Von Greis were a bit warm on each other. Von Greis was Funk's boyfriend.'

'I thought the Führer couldn't stand queers?'

'He can't stand cripples either, so what will he do when he finds out about Joey Goebbels's club foot?' It was an old joke, but I laughed anyway.

'So the reason for tiptoes is because it could be embarrassing for Funk, and therefore embarrassing for the Government, right?'

'It's not just that. Von Greis and Goering are old friends. They saw service together in the war. Goering helped Von Greis get his first job with I. G. Farben Chemicals. And lately he'd been acting as Goering's agent. Buying art and that sort of thing. The Reichs-kriminaldirektor is keen that we find Von Greis as soon as possible. But it's over a week now, and there's been no sign of him. He and Funk had a secret love-nest on Privatstrasse that Funk's wife didn't know about. But he hasn't been there for days.' From my pocket I removed the piece of paper on which I had copied down an address from the book in Jeschonnek's desk drawer: it was a number in Derfflingerstrasse.

'Privatstrasse, eh? Was there any other address?'

'Not as far as we know.'

'Are you on the case, Bruno?'

'Not any more I'm not. Dietz has taken over.'

'But he's working on the Pfarr case, isn't he?'

'I guess so.'

'Well, doesn't that tell you something?'

'I don't know, Bernie. I'm too busy trying to put a name to some guy with half a billiard cue up his nose to be a real detective like you.'

'Is that the one they fished out of the river?'

Bruno sighed irritatedly. 'You know, one time I'm going to tell you something you don't already know about.'

'Illmann was talking to me about it. I bumped into him the other night.'

'Yeah? Where was that?'

'In the morgue. I met your client there. Good-looking fellow. Maybe he's Von Greis.'

'No, I thought of that. Von Greis had a tattoo on his right forearm: an imperial eagle. Look, Bernie, I've got to go. Like I said a hundred times, don't hold out on me. If you hear anything, let me know. The way the boss is riding me, I could use a break.'

'Like I said, Bruno, I owe you one.'

'Two. You owe me two, Bernie.'

I hung up and made another call, this time to the governor of Tegel Prison. I made an appointment to see him and then ordered another beer. While I was drinking it I did some doodling on a piece of paper, the algebraic kind that you hope will help you think more clearly. When I finished doing that, I was more confused than ever. Algebra was never my strong subject. I knew I was getting somewhere, but I thought I would worry about where that was only when I arrived.

10

Derfflingerstrasse was convenient for the brand-new Air Ministry situated at the south end of Wilhelmstrasse and the corner of Leipzigerstrasse, not to mention the Presidential Palace on nearby Leipzigerplatz: convenient for Von Greis to wait upon his master in his capacities as Chief of the Luftwaffe and as Prime Minister of Prussia.

Von Greis's apartment was on the third floor of a smart apartment-block. There was no sign of a concierge, so I went straight on up. I hit the door-knocker and waited. After a minute or so had elapsed I bent down to look through the letter-box. To my surprise I found the door swinging open as I pushed back the flap on its tight spring.

I didn't need my deerstalker-hat to realize that the place had been turned over, from top to bottom. The long hallway's parquet floor was covered with books, papers, envelopes and empty wallet files, as well as a considerable amount of broken glass which was referable to the empty doors of a large secretaire bookcase.

I walked past a couple of doors and stopped dead as I heard a chair scrape in the grate of one of the rooms ahead of me. Instinctively I reached for my gun. The pity was, it was still in my car. I was going for a heavy cavalry sabre mounted on the wall when behind me I heard a piece of glass crack underneath someone's foot, and a stinging blow to the back of my neck sent me plunging through a hole in the earth.

For what seemed like hours, although it must only have been a few minutes, I lay at the bottom of a deep well. Fumbling my way back to consciousness I became aware of something in my pockets, and then a voice from a long way off. Then I felt someone lift me under the shoulders, drag me for a couple of miles and shove my face under a waterfall.

I shook my head and squinted up to look at the man who had hit me. He was almost a giant, with a lot of mouth and cheeks, like he'd stuffed each of them with a couple of slices of bread. There was a shirt round his neck, but it was the kind that belonged properly in a barber's chair, and the kind of neck that ought to have been harnessed to a plough. The arms of his jacket had been stuffed with several kilos of potatoes, and they ended prematurely, revealing wrists and fists that were the size and colour of two boiled lobsters. Breathing deeply, I shook my head painfully. I sat up slowly, holding my neck with both hands.

'Christ, what did you hit me with? A length of railway track?'

'Sorry about that,' said my attacker, 'but when I saw you going for that sabre I decided to slow you down a bit.'

'I guess I'm lucky you didn't decide to knock me out, otherwise . . .' I nodded at my papers which the giant was holding in his great paws. 'Looks like you know who I am. Mind telling me who you are? It seems like I ought to know you.'

'Rienacker, Wolf Rienacker. Gestapo. You used to be a bull, didn't you? Up at the Alex.'

'That's right.'

'And now you're a sniffer. So what brought you up here?'

'Looking for Herr Von Greis.' I glanced about the room. There was a lot of mess, but it didn't seem that there was much missing. A silver epergne stood immaculate on a sideboard, the empty drawers of which were lying on the floor; and there were several dozen oil paintings leaning in neat ranks against the walls. Clearly whoever had ransacked the place hadn't been after the usual variety of loot, but something in particular.

'I see.' He nodded slowly. 'You know who owns this apartment?'

I shrugged. 'I had supposed it was Herr Von Greis.'

Rienacker shook his bucket-sized head. 'Only some of the time. No, the apartment is owned by Hermann Goering. Few people know about it, very few.' He lit a cigarette and threw me the packet. I lit one and smoked it gratefully. I noticed that my hand was shaking.

'So the first mystery,' continued Rienacker, 'is how you did.

The second is why you wanted to speak to Von Greis at all. Could be that you were after the same thing that the first mob were after? The third mystery is where Von Greis is now. Maybe he's hiding, maybe someone's got him, maybe he's dead. I don't know. This place was done over a week ago. I came back here this afternoon to have another poke around in case there was something I missed the first time, and to do some thinking, and what do you know, you come through the door.' He took a long drag on his cigarette. In his enormous ham of a fist it looked like a baby's tooth. 'It's my first real break on this case. So how's about you start talking?'

I sat up and straightened my tie and tried to fix my sodden collar. 'Let me just figure this out,' I said. 'I've got this friend up at the Alex who told me that the police don't know about this place, and yet here you are staking it out. Which leads me to suppose that you, or whoever it is you're working for, likes it that way. You'd prefer to find Von Greis, or at least get your hands on what makes him so popular, before they do. Now, it wasn't the silver, and it wasn't the paintings, because they're still here.'

'Go on.'

'This is Goering's apartment, so I guess that makes you Goering's bloodhound. There's no reason Goering should have any regard for Himmler. After all, Himmler won control of the police and the Gestapo from him. So it would make sense for Goering to want to avoid involving Himmler's men more than was necessary.'

'Aren't you forgetting something? I work for the Gestapo.'

'Rienacker, I may be easy to slug, but I'm not stupid. We both know that Goering has lots of friends in the Gestapo. Which is hardly surprising, since he set it up.'

'You know, you should have been a detective.'

'My client thinks much the same way as yours about involving the bulls in his business. Which means that I can level with you, Rienacker. My man is missing a picture, an oil painting, which he acquired outside any of the recognized channels, so you see, it would be best if the police didn't know anything about it.' The big bull said nothing, so I kept on going.

'Anyway, a couple of weeks ago, it was stolen from his home. Which is where I fit in. I've been hanging around some of the dealers, and the word I hear is that Hermann Goering is a keen art buyer – that somewhere in the depths of Karinhall he has a collection of old masters, not all of them acquired legitimately. I heard that he had an agent, Herr Von Greis, in all matters relating to the purchase of art. So I decided to come here and see if I could speak to him. Who knows, the picture I'm looking for might very well be one of the ones stacked up against that wall.'

'Maybe it is,' said Rienacker. 'Always supposing I believe you. Who's the painting by, and what's the subject?'

'Rubens,' I said, enjoying my own inventiveness. 'A couple of nude women standing by a river. It's called *The Bathers*, or something like that. I've a photograph back at the office.'

'And who is your client?'

'I'm afraid I can't tell you that.'

Rienacker wielded a fist slowly. 'I could try persuading you perhaps.'

I shrugged. 'I still wouldn't tell you. It's not that I'm the honourable type, protecting my client's reputation, and all that crap. It's just that I'm on a pretty substantial recovery fee. This case is my big chance to make some real flea, and if it costs me a few bruises and some broken ribs then that's the way it will have to be.'

'All right,' said Rienacker. 'Take a look at the pictures if you want. But if it is there I'll have to clear it first.' I got back onto my wobbly legs and went over to the paintings. I don't know a great deal about Art. All the same, I recognize quality when I see it, and most of the pictures in Goering's apartment were the genuine article. To my relief there was nothing that had a nude woman in it, so I wasn't required to make a guess as to whether Rubens had done it or not.

'It's not here,' I said finally. 'But thanks for letting me take a look.' Rienacker nodded.

In the hallway I picked up my hat and placed it back on my throbbing head. He said: 'I'm at the station on Charlottenstrasse. Corner of Französische Strasse.'

'Yes,' I said, 'I know it. Above Lutter and Wegner's Restaurant, isn't it?' Rienacker nodded. 'And yes, if I hear anything, I'll let you know.'

'See that you do,' he growled, and let me out.

When I got back to Alexanderplatz, I found that I had a visitor in my waiting room.

She was well-built and quite tall, in a suit of black cloth that lent her impressive curves the contours of a well-made Spanish guitar. The skirt was short and narrow and tight across her ample behind, and the jacket was cut to give a high-waisted line, with the fullness gathered in to fit under her substantial bust. On her shiny black head of hair she wore a black hat with a brim turned up all the way round, and in her hands she held a black cloth bag with a white handle and clasp, and a book which she put down as I came into the waiting room.

The blue eyes and perfectly lipsticked mouth smiled with disarming friendliness.

'Herr Günther, I imagine.' I nodded dumbly. 'I'm Inge Lorenz. A friend of Eduard Müller. Of the *Berliner Morgenpost*?' We shook hands. I unlocked the door to my office.

'Come in and make yourself comfortable,' I said. She took a look around the room and sniffed the air a couple of times. The place still smelt like a bartender's apron.

'Sorry about the smell. I'm afraid I had a bit of an accident.' I went to the window and pushed it open. When I turned round I found her standing beside me.

'An impressive view,' she observed.

'It's not bad.'

'Berlin Alexanderplatz. Have you read Döblin's novel?'

'I don't get much time for reading nowadays,' I said. 'Anyway, there's so little that's worth reading.'

'Of course it's a forbidden book,' she said, 'but you should read it, while it's in circulation again.'

'I don't understand,' I said.

'Oh, but haven't you noticed? Banned writers are back in the

124

bookshops. It's because of the Olympiad. So that tourists won't think things are quite as repressive here as has been made out. Of course, they'll disappear again as soon as it's all over but, if only because they are forbidden, you should read them.'

'Thanks. I'll bear it in mind.'

'Do you have a cigarette?'

I flipped open the silver box on the desk and held it up by the lid for her. She took one and let me light her.

'The other day, in a café on Kurfürstendamm, I absent-mindedly lit one, and some old busybody came up to me and reminded me of my duty as a German woman, wife or mother. Fat chance, I thought. I'm nearly thirty-nine, hardly the age to start producing new recruits for the Party. I'm what they call a eugenic dud.' She sat down in one of the armchairs and crossed her beautiful legs. I could see nothing that was dud about her, except maybe the cafés she frequented. 'It's got so that a woman can't go out wearing a bit of make-up for fear of being called a whore.'

'You don't strike me as being the type to worry much about what people call you,' I said. 'And as it happens, I like a woman to look like a lady, not a Hessian milkmaid.'

'Thank you, Herr Günther,' she said smiling. 'That's very sweet of you.'

'Müller says you used to be a reporter on the DAZ.'

'Yes, that's right. I lost my job during the Party's "Clear Women out of Industry" campaign. An ingenious way of solving Germany's unemployment problem, don't you think? You just say that a woman already has a job, and that's looking after the home and the family. If she doesn't have a husband then she'd better get one, if she knows what's good for her. The logic is frightening.'

'How do you support yourself now?'

'I did freelance a bit. But right now, well frankly, Herr Günther, I'm broke, which is why I'm here. Müller says you're digging for some information on Hermann Six. I'd like to try and sell what I know. Are you investigating him?'

'No. Actually, he's my client.'

'Oh.' She seemed slightly taken aback at this.

'There was something about the way he hired me that made me want to know a lot more about him,' I explained, 'and I don't just mean the school he went to. I suppose you could say that he irritated me. You see, I don't like being told what to do.'

'Not a very healthy attitude these days.'

'I guess not.' I grinned at her. 'Shall we say fifty marks then, for what you know?'

'Shall we say a hundred, and then you won't be disappointed?'

'How about seventy-five and dinner?'

'It's a deal.' She offered me her hand and we shook on it.

'Is there a file or something, Fräulein Lorenz?'

She tapped her head. 'Please call me Inge. And it's all up here, down to the last detail.'

And then she told me.

'Hermann Six was born, the son of one of the wealthiest men in Germany, in April 1881, eight years to the day before our beloved Führer entered this world. Since you mentioned school, he went to the König Wilhelm Gymnasium in Berlin. After that he went into the stock exchange, and then into his father's business, which, of course, was the Six Steel Works.

'Along with Fritz Thyssen, the heir to another great family fortune, young Six was an ardent nationalist, organizing the passive resistance to the French occupation of the Ruhr in 1923. For this both he and Thyssen were arrested and imprisoned. But there the similarity between the two ends, for unlike Thyssen, Six has never cared for Hitler. He was a Conservative Nationalist, never a National Socialist, and any support he may have given the Party has been purely pragmatic, not to say opportunistic.

'Meanwhile he married Lisa Voegler, a former State Actress in the Berlin State Theatre. They had one child, Grete, born in 1911. Lisa died of tuberculosis in 1934, and Six married Ilse Rudel, the actress.' Inge Lorenz stood up and started to walk about the room as she spoke. Watching her made it difficult to concentrate: when she turned away my eyes were on her behind; and when she turned to face me they were on her belly.

'I said that Six doesn't care for the Party. That's true. He is equally opposed, however, to the trade-union cause, and appreciated the way in which the Party set about neutralizing it when it first came to power. But it's the so-called Socialism of the Party that really sticks in his throat. And the Party's economic policy. Six was one of several leading businessmen present at a secret meeting in early 1933 held in the Presidential Palace, at which future National Socialist economic policy was explained by Hitler and Goering. Anyway, these businessmen responded by contributing several million marks to Party coffers on the strength of Hitler's promise to eliminate the Bolsheviks and restore the army. It was a courtship that did not last long. Like a lot of Germany's industrialists, Six favours expanding trade and increased commerce. Specifically, with regard to the steel industry he prefers to buy his raw materials abroad, because it's cheaper. Goering does not agree, however, and believes that Germany should be self-sufficient in iron ore, as in everything else. He believes in a controlled level of consumption and exports. It's easy to see why.' She paused, waiting for me to furnish her with the explanation that was so easy to see.

'Is it?' I said.

She tutted and sighed and shook her head all at once. 'Well, of course it is. The simple fact of the matter is that Germany is preparing for war, and so conventional economic policy is of little or no relevance.'

I nodded intelligently. 'Yes, I see what you mean.' She sat down on the arm of her chair, and folded her arms.

'I was speaking to someone who still works on the DAZ,' she said, 'and he says that there's a rumour that in a couple of months, Goering will assume control over the second four-year economic plan. Given his declared interest in the setting up of state-owned raw material plants to guarantee the supply of strategic resources, such as iron ore, one can imagine that Six is less than happy about that possibility. You see, the steel industry suffered from considerable over-capacity during the depression. Six is reluctant to sanction the investment that is required for Germany to become self-sufficient in iron ore because he knows that as soon as the rearmament boom finishes, he'll find himself massively over-capitalized, producing expensive iron and steel, itself the result of the high cost of producing and using domestic iron ore. He'll be unable to sell German steel abroad because of the high price. Of course, it goes without saying that Six wants business to keep the initiative in the German economy. And my guess is that he'll be doing his best to persuade the other leading businessmen to join him in opposing Goering. If they fail to back him, there's no telling what he's capable of. He's not above fighting dirty. It's my suspicion, and it's only a suspicion, mind, that he has contacts in the underworld.'

The stuff on German economic policy was of marginal consequence, I thought; but Six and the underworld, well that really got me interested.

'What makes you say that?'

'Well, first there was the strike-breaking that occurred during the steel strikes,' she said. 'Some of the men who beat up workers had gangland connections. Many of them were ex-convicts, members of a ring, you know, one of those criminal rehabilitation societies.'

'Can you remember the name of this ring?' She shook her head.

'It wasn't German Strength, was it?'

'I don't remember.' She thought some more. 'I could probably dig up the names of the people involved, if that would help.'

'If you can,' I said, 'and anything else you can produce on that strike-breaking episode, if you wouldn't mind.'

There was a lot more, but I already had my seventy-five-marks worth. Knowing more about my private, secretive client, I felt that I was properly in the driving seat. And now that I'd heard her out, it occurred to me that I could make use of her.

'How would you like to come and work for me? I need someone to be my assistant, someone to do the digging around in public records and to be here now and then. I think it would suit you. I could pay you, say, sixty marks a week. Cash, so we wouldn't have to inform the labour people. Maybe more if things work out. What do you say?'

'Well if you're sure . . .' She shrugged. 'I could certainly use the money.'

'That's settled then.' I thought for a minute. 'Presumably, you still have a few contacts on papers, in government departments?' She nodded. 'Do you happen to know anyone in the DAF, the German Labour Service?'

She thought for a minute, and fiddled with the buttons on her jacket. 'There was someone,' she said, ruminatively. 'An ex-boyfriend, an SA man. Why do you ask?'

'Give him a call, and ask him to take you out this evening.'

'But I haven't seen or spoken to him in months,' she said. 'And it was bad enough getting him to leave me alone the last time. He's a real leech.' Her blue eyes glanced anxiously at me.

'I want you to find out anything you can about what Six's son-in-law, Paul Pfarr, was so interested in that he was there several times a week. He had a mistress, too, so anything you can find out about her as well. And I mean anything.'

'I'd better wear an extra pair of knickers, then,' she said. 'The man has hands like he thinks he should have been a midwife.' For the briefest of moments I allowed myself a small pang of jealousy, as I imagined him making a pass at her. Perhaps in time I might do the same.

'I'll ask him to take me to see a show,' she said, summoning me from my erotic reverie. 'Maybe even get him a little drunk.'

'That's the idea,' I said. 'And if that fails, offer the bastard money.'

Tegal Prison lies to the north-west of Berlin and borders a small lake and the Borsig Locomotive Company housing-estate. As I drove onto Seidelstrasse, its red-brick walls heaved into sight like the muddy flanks of some horny-skinned dinosaur; and when the heavy wooden door banged shut behind me, and the blue sky vanished as though it had been switched off like an electric light, I began to feel a certain amount of sympathy for the inmates of what is one of Germany's toughest prisons.

A menagerie of warders lounged around the main entrance hall, and one of these, a pug-faced man smelling strongly of carbolic soap and carrying a bunch of keys that was about the size of the average car tyre, led me through a Cretan labyrinth of yellowing, toilet-bricked corridors and into a small cobbled courtyard in the centre of which stood the guillotine. It's a fearsome-looking object, and always sends a chill down my spine when I see it again. Since the Party had come to power, it had seen quite a bit of action, and even now it was being tested, no doubt in preparation for the several executions that were posted on the gate as scheduled for dawn the next morning.

The warder led me through an oak door and up a carpeted stairway, to a corridor. At the end of the corridor, the warder stood outside a polished mahogany door and knocked. He paused for a second or two and then ushered me inside. The prison governor, Dr Konrad Spiedel, rose from behind his desk to greet me. It was several years since I had first made his acquaintance, when he'd been governor of Brauweiler Prison, near Köln, but he had not forgotten the occasion:

'You were seeking information on the cellmate of a prisoner,' he recalled, nodding towards an armchair. 'Something to do with a bank robbery.'

'You've a good memory, Herr Doktor,' I said.

'I confess that my recall is not entirely fortuitous,' he said. 'The same man is now a prisoner within these walls, on another charge.' Spiedel was a tall, broad-shouldered man of about fifty. He wore a Schiller tie and an olive-green Bavarian jacket; and in his button-hole, the black-and-white silk bow and crossed swords that denoted a war veteran.

'Oddly enough, I'm here on the same sort of mission,' I explained. 'I believe that until recently you had a prisoner here by the name of Kurt Mutschmann. I was hoping that you could tell me something about him.'

'Mutschmann, yes, I remember him. What can I tell you except that he kept out of trouble while he was here, and seemed quite a reasonable fellow?' Spiedel stood up and went over to his filing cabinet, and rummaged through several sections. 'Yes, here we are. Mutschmann, Kurt Hermann, aged thirty-six. Convicted of car theft April 1934, sentenced to two years' imprisonment. Address given as Cicerostrasse, Number 29, Halensee.'

'Is that where he went on discharge?'

'I'm afraid your guess is as good as mine. Mutschmann had a wife, but during his imprisonment it would seem from his record that she visited him only the one time. It doesn't look like he had much to look forward to on the outside.'

'Did he have any other visitors?'

Spiedel consulted the file. 'Just the one, from the Union of Ex-Convicts, a welfare organization we are led to believe, although I have my doubts as to the authenticity of that organization. A man by the name of Kasper Tillessen. He visited Mutschmann on two occasions.'

'Did Mutschmann have a cellmate?'

'Yes, he shared with 7888319, Bock, H.J.' He retrieved another file from the drawer. 'Hans Jürgen Bock, aged thirty-eight. Convicted of assaulting and maiming a man in the old Steel Workers Union in March 1930, sentenced to six years' imprisonment.'

'Do you mean that he was a strike-breaker?'

'Yes, he was.'

'You wouldn't happen to have the particulars of that case, would you?'

Spiedel shook his head. 'I'm afraid not. The case file has been sent back to Criminal Records at the Alex.' He paused. 'Hmm. This might help you, though. On discharge Bock gave the address where he was intending to stay as "Care of Pension Tillessen, Chamisso-platz, Number 17, Kreuzberg". Not only that but this same Kasper Tillessen paid Bock a visit on behalf of the Union of Ex-Convicts.' He looked at me vaguely. 'That's about it, I'm afraid.'

'I think I've got enough,' I said brightly. 'It was kind of you to give me some of your time.'

Spiedel adopted an expression of great sincerity, and with some solemnity he said: 'Sir, it was my pleasure to help the man who brought Gormann to justice.'

I reckon that in ten years from now, I'll still be trading off that Gormann business.

When a man's wife visits him only once in two years' cement, then she doesn't bake him a sponge-cake to celebrate his freedom. But it was possible that Mutschmann had seen her after his release, if only to knock the shit out of her, so I decided to check her out anyway. You always eliminate the obvious. That's fundamental to detection.

Neither Mutschmann nor his wife lived at the address in Cice-rostrasse any more. The woman I spoke to there told me that Frau Mutschmann had re-married, and was living in Ohmstrasse on the Siemens housing-estate. I asked her if anyone else had been around looking for her, but she told me that there hadn't.

It was 7.30 by the time I got to the Siemens housing-estate. There are as many as a thousand houses on it, each of them built of the same whitewashed brick, and providing accommodation for the families of the employees of the Siemens Electrical Com-pany. I couldn't imagine anything less congenial than living in a house that had all the character of a sugar lump; but I knew that in the Third Reich there were many worse things being done in the name of progress than the homogenizing of workers' dwellings.

As I stood outside the front door, my nose caught the smell of cooking meat, pork I thought, and suddenly I realized how hungry I was; and how tired. I wanted to be at home, or seeing some easy, brainless show with Inge. I wanted to be anywhere other than confronting the flint-faced brunette who opened the door to me. She wiped her mottled pink hands on her grubby apron and eyed me suspiciously.

'Frau Buverts?' I said, using her new married name, and almost hoping she wasn't.

'Yes,' she said crisply. 'And who might you be? Not that I need to ask. You've got bull stapled to each dumb ear. So I'll tell you once, and then you can clear off. I haven't seen him in more than eighteen months. And if you should find him, then tell him not to come after me. He's as welcome here as a Jew's prick up Goering's arse. And that goes for you, too.'

It's the small manifestations of ordinary good humour and common courtesy that make the job so worthwhile.

Later that night, between 11 and 11.30, there was a loud knock at my front door. I hadn't had a drink, but the sleep I'd been having was deep enough to make me feel as if I had. I walked unsteadily into the hall, where the faint chalky outline of Walther Kolb's body on the floor brought me out of my sleepy stupor and prompted me to go back and get my spare gun. There was another knock, louder this time, followed by a man's voice.

'Hey, Günther, it's me, Rienacker. Come on, open up, I want to talk to you.'

'I'm still aching from our last little chat.'

'Aw, you're not still sore about that, are you?'

'I'm fine about it. But as far as my neck is concerned, you're strictly *persona non grata*. Especially at this time of night.'

'Hey, no hard feelings, Günther,' said Rienacker. 'Look, this is important. There's money in it.' There was a long pause, and when

Rienacker spoke again, there was an edge of irritation in his bass voice. 'Come on, Günther, open up, will you? What the fuck are you so scared of? If I was arresting you, I'd have busted the door down by now.' There was some truth in that, I thought, so I opened the door, revealing his massive figure. He glanced coolly at the gun in my hand, and nodded as if admitting that for the moment I still had an advantage.

'You weren't expecting me, then,' he said drily.

'Oh, I knew it was you all right, Rienacker. I heard your knuckles dragging on the stairs.'

He snorted a laugh that was mainly tobacco smoke. Then he said: 'Get dressed, we're going for a ride. And better leave the hammer.'

I hesitated. 'What's the matter?'

He grinned at my discomfiture. 'Don't you trust me?'

'Now why do you say that? The nice man from the Gestapo knocks on my door at midnight, and asks me if I'd like to take a spin in his big shiny-black motor-car. Naturally I just go weak at the knees because I know that you've booked us the best table at Horcher's.'

'Someone important wants to see you,' he yawned. 'Someone very important.'

'They've named me for the Olympic shit-throwing team, right?' Rienacker's face changed colour and his nostrils flared and contracted quickly, like two emptying hot-water bottles. He was starting to get impatient.

'All right, all right,' I said. 'I suppose I'm going whether I like it or not. I'll get dressed.' I went towards the bedroom. 'And no peeking.'

It was a big black Mercedes, and I climbed in without a word. There were two gargoyles in the front seat, and lying on the floor in the back, his hands cuffed behind him, was the semi-conscious body of a man. It was dark, but from his moans I could tell that he'd taken quite a beating. Rienacker got in behind me. With the movement of the car, the man on the floor stirred and made a half attempt to get up. It earned him the toe of Rienacker's boot against his ear.

'What did he do? Leave his fly button undone?'

'He's a fucking Kozi,' said Rienacker, outraged, as if he had arrested an habitual child molester. 'A midnight fucking postman. We caught him red-handed, pushing Bolshie leaflets for the KPD through letter-boxes in this area.'

I shook my head. 'I see the job is just as hazardous as it always was.'

He ignored me, and shouted to the driver: 'We'll drop this bastard off, and then go straight onto Leipzigerstrasse. Mustn't keep his majesty waiting.'

'Drop him off where? Schöneberger Bridge?'

Rienacker laughed. 'Maybe.' He produced a hip flask from his coat pocket and took a long pull from it. I'd had just such a leaflet put through my own letter-box the previous evening. It had been devoted largely to ridiculing no less a person than the Prussian Prime Minister. I knew that in the weeks leading up to the Olympiad, the Gestapo were making strenuous efforts to smash the communist underground in Berlin. Thousands of Kozis had been arrested and sent to KZ camps like Oranienburg, Columbia Haus, Dachau and Buchenwald. Putting two and two together, it suddenly came to me with a shock just who it was I was being taken to see.

At Grolmanstrasse Police Station, the car stopped, and one of the gargoyles dragged the prisoner out from under our feet. I didn't think much for his chances. If ever I saw a man destined for a late-night swimming lesson in the Landwehr, it was him. Then we drove east on Berlinerstrasse and Charlottenburger Chaussee, Berlin's east-west axis, which was decorated with a lot of black, white and red bunting in celebration of the forthcoming Olympiad. Rienacker eyed it grimly.

'Fucking Olympic Games,' he sneered. 'Waste of fucking money.'

'I'm forced to agree with you,' I said.

'What's it all for, that's what I'd like to know. We are what we are, so why pretend we're not? All this pretence really pisses me off. You know, they're even drafting in snappers from Munich and Hamburg because Berlin trade in female flesh has been so hard hit by the Emergency Powers. And nigger jazz is legal again. What do you make of that, Günther?'

'Say one thing, do another. That's this Government all over.'

He looked at me narrowly. 'I wouldn't go around saying that sort of thing, if I were you,' he said.

I shook my head. 'It doesn't matter what I say, Rienacker, you know that. Just as long as I can be of service to your boss. He wouldn't care if I were Karl Marx and Moses in one, if he thought I could be of use to him.'

'Then you'd better make the most of it. You'll never get another client as important as this one.'

'That's what they all say.'

Just short of the Brandenburger Tor, the car turned south onto Hermann Goering Strasse. At the British Embassy all the lights were burning and there were several dozen limousines drawn up out front. As the car slowed and turned into the driveway of the big building next door, the driver wound down the window to let the storm-trooper on guard identify us, and we heard the sound of a big party drifting across the lawn.

We waited, Rienacker and I, in a room the size of a tennis court. After a short while a tall thin man wearing the uniform of an officer in the Luftwaffe told us that Goering was changing, and that he would see us in ten minutes.

It was a gloomy palace: overbearing, grandiose and affecting a bucolic air that belied its urban location. Rienacker sat down in a medieval-looking chair, saying nothing as I took a look around, but watching me closely.

'Cosy,' I said, and stood in front of a Gobelin tapestry depicting several hunting scenes that could just as easily have accommodated a scene featuring a full-scale version of the Hindenburg. The room's only light came from a lamp on the huge Renaissance-style desk which was composed of two silver candelabra with parchment shades; it illuminated a small shrine of photographs: there was one of Hitler wearing the brown shirt and leather cross belt of an SA man, and looking more than a little like a boy scout; and there were photographs of two women, whom I guessed were Goering's dead wife Karin, and his living wife Emmy. Next to the photographs was a large leather-bound book, on the front of which was a coat of arms, which, I presumed, was Goering's own. This was a mailed fist grasping a bludgeon, and it struck me how much more appropriate than the swastika it would have been for the National Socialists.

I sat down beside Rienacker, who produced some cigarettes. We waited for an hour, perhaps longer, before we heard voices outside the door, and hearing it open, we both stood up. Two men in Luftwaffe uniform followed Goering into the room. To my astonishment, I saw that he was carrying a lion cub in his arms. He kissed it on the head, pulled its ears and then dropped it on to the silk rug.

'Off you go and play, Mucki, there's a good little fellow.' The cub growled happily, and gambolled over to the window, where he started to play with the tassel on one of the heavy curtains.

Goering was shorter than I had imagined, which made him seem that much bulkier. He wore a sleeveless green-leather hunting jacket, a white flannel shirt, white drill trousers and white tennis shoes.

'Hallo,' he said, shaking my hand and smiling broadly. There was something slightly animal about him, and his eyes were a hard, intelligent blue. The hand wore several rings, one of them a big ruby. 'Thank you for coming. I'm so sorry you've been kept waiting. Affairs of state, you understand.' I said that it was quite all right, although in truth I hardly knew what to say. Close up, I was struck by the smooth, almost babyish quality of his skin, and I wondered if it was powdered. We sat down. For several minutes he continued to appear delighted at my being there, almost childishly so, and after a while he felt obliged to explain himself.

'I've always wanted to meet a real private detective,' he said.

'Tell me, have you ever read any of Dashiell Hammett's detective stories? He's an American, but I think he's wonderful.'

'I can't say I have, sir.'

'Oh, but you should. I shall lend you a German edition of *Red Harvest*. You'll enjoy it. And do you carry a gun, Herr Günther?'

'Sometimes, sir, when I think I might need it.'

Goering beamed like an excited schoolboy. 'Are you carrying it now?'

I shook my head. 'Rienacker here thought it might scare the cat.'

'A pity,' said Goering. 'I should like to have seen the gun of a real shamus.' He leaned back in his chair, which looked as though it might once have belonged to a bumper-sized Medici pope, and waved his hand.

'Well then, to business,' he said. One of the aides brought forward a file and laid it before his master. Goering opened it and studied the contents for several seconds. I figured that it was about me. There were so many files on me around these days that I was beginning to feel like a medical case-history.

'It says here that you used to be a policeman,' he said. 'Quite an impressive record, too. You'd have been a kommissar by now. Why did you leave?' He removed a small lacquered pillbox from his jacket and shook a couple of pink pills onto his fat palm as he waited for me to reply. He took them with a glass of water.

'I didn't much care for the police canteen, sir.' He laughed loudly. 'But with respect, Herr Prime Minister, I'm sure you are well aware of why I left, since at that time you were yourself in command of the police. I don't recall making a secret of my opposition to the purging of so-called unreliable police officers. Many of those men were my friends. Many of them lost their pensions. A couple even lost their heads.'

Goering smiled slowly. With his broad forehead, cold eyes, low growling voice, predatory grin and lazy belly, he reminded me of nothing so much as a big, fat, man-eating tiger; and as if telepathically conscious of the impression he was making on me, he leaned forwards in his chair, scooped up the lion cub from off the rug and cradled it on his sofa-sized lap. The cub blinked sleepily, hardly stirring as its owner stroked its head and thumbed its ears. He looked like he was admiring his own child.

'You see,' he said. 'He is not in anyone's shadow. And he's not afraid to speak his mind. That is the great virtue of independence. There's no reason on earth why this man should do me a service. He's got the guts to remind me of that when another man would have stayed silent. I can trust a man like that.'

I nodded at the file on his desk. 'I'd lay a bet that it was Diels who put that little lot together.'

'And you'd be right. I inherited this file, your file, with a great many others, when he lost his position as Gestapo chief to that little shit of a chicken farmer. It was the last great service that he was to do for me.'

'Do you mind my asking what happened to him?'

'Not at all. He is still in my employment, although occupying a lesser position, as an inland-shipping administrator with the Hermann Goering Works in Cologne.' Goering repeated his own name without the least trace of hesitation or embarrassment; he must have thought it was the most natural thing in the world that a factory should bear his name.

'You see,' he said proudly, 'I look after the people who have done me a service. Isn't that so, Rienacker?'

The big man's answer came back with the speed of a pilota ball. 'Yes sir, Herr Prime Minister, you most certainly do.' Full marks, I thought as a servant bearing a large tray of coffee, Moselle and eggs Benedict for the Prime Minister came into the room. Goering tucked in as if he hadn't eaten all day.

'I may no longer be head of the Gestapo,' he said, 'but there are many in the security police, like Rienacker here, who are still loyal to me, rather than to Himmler.'

'A great many,' piped Rienacker loyally.

'Who keep me informed about what the Gestapo is doing.' He dabbed daintily at his wide mouth with a napkin. 'Now then,' he said. 'Rienacker tells me that you turned up at my apartment in

Derfflingerstrasse this afternoon. It is, as he may already have told you, an apartment that I have placed at the disposal of a man who in certain matters is my confidential agent. His name is, as I believe you know, Gerhard Von Greis, and he has been missing for over a week. Rienacker says that you thought that he might have been approached by someone trying to sell a stolen painting. A Rubens nude, to be precise. What made you think that my agent was worth contacting, and how you managed to track him down to that particular address I have no idea. But you impress me, Herr Günther.'

'Thank you very much, Herr Prime Minister.' Who knows? I thought; with a little practice I could sound just like Rienacker.

'Your record as a police officer speaks for itself, and I don't doubt that as a private investigator you are no less competent.' He finished eating, swallowed a glassful of Moselle and lit an enormous cigar. He showed no signs of weariness, unlike the two aides and Rienacker, and I was starting to wonder what the pink pills had been. He blew a doughnut-sized smoke-ring. 'Günther, I want to become your client. I want you to find Gerhard Von Greis, preferably before Sipo does. Not that he's committed any crime, you understand. It's just that he is the custodian of some confidential information which I have no wish to see fall into Himmler's hands.'

'What kind of confidential information, Herr Prime Minister?'

'I'm afraid I can't tell you that.'

'Look, sir,' I said. 'If I'm going to row the boat I like to know if there are any leaks in it. That's the difference between me and a regular bull. He doesn't get to ask why. It's the privilege of independence.'

Goering nodded. 'I admire directness,' he said. 'I don't just say that I'm going to do something, I do it and I do it properly. I don't suppose there's any point in hiring you unless I take you fully into my confidence. But you must understand, that imposes certain obligations on you, Herr Günther. The price of betraying my trust is a high one.'

I didn't doubt it for a minute. I got so little sleep these days,

I didn't think that losing some more on account of what I knew about Goering was going to make any difference. I couldn't back off. Besides, there was likely to be some good money in it, and I try not to walk away from money if I can possibly help it. He took another two of the little pink pills. He seemed to take them as often as I might have smoked a cigarette.

'Sir, Rienacker will tell you that when he and I met in your apartment this afternoon, he asked me to tell him the name of the man I was working for, the man who owns the Rubens nude. I wouldn't tell him. He threatened to beat it out of me. I still wouldn't tell him.'

Rienacker leaned forwards. 'That's correct, Herr Prime Minister,' he offered.

I continued with my pitch. 'Every one of my clients gets the same deal. Discretion and confidentiality. I wouldn't stay in business for very long if it was any other way.'

Goering nodded. 'That's frank enough,' he said. 'Then let me be equally frank. Many positions in the bureaucracy of the Reich fall to my patronage. Consequently, I'm often approached by a former colleague, a business contact, to grant a small favour. Well, I don't blame people for trying to get on. If I can, I help them. But of course I will ask a favour in return. That is the way the world works. At the same time, I have built up a large store of intelligence. It is a reservoir of knowledge that I draw on to get things done. Knowing what I know, it is easier to persuade people to share my point of view. I have to take the larger view, for the good of the Fatherland. Even now there are many men of influence and power who do not agree with what the Führer and myself have identified as the priorities for the proper growth of Germany, so that this wonderful country of ours may assume its rightful place in the world.' He paused. Perhaps he was expecting me to jump up and give the Hitler Salute and burst into a couple of verses of *Horst Wessel*; but I stayed put, nodding patiently, waiting for him to come to the point.

'Von Greis was the instrument of my will,' he said silkily, 'as well as of my foible. He was both my purchasing agent, and my fund raiser.'

'You mean he was an up-market squeeze-artist.'

Goering winced and smiled at the same time. 'Herr Günther, it does you much credit to be so honest, and so objective, but please try not to make it compulsive. I am a blunt man myself, but I don't make a virtue out of it. Understand this: everything is justified in the service of the State. Sometimes one must be hard. It was, I think, Goethe who said that one must either conquer and rule, or serve and lose, suffer or triumph, be the anvil or the hammer. Do you understand?'

'Yes, sir. Look, it might help if I knew who Von Greis had dealings with.'

Goering shook his head. 'I really can't tell you that. It's my turn to get on the soapbox and talk about Discretion and Confidentiality. To that extent, you'll have to work in the dark.'

'Very well, sir, I'll do my best. Do you have a photograph of the gentleman?'

He reached into a drawer and produced a small snapshot which he handed to me. 'This was taken five years ago,' he said. 'He hasn't changed a great deal.'

I looked at the man in the picture. Like many German men, he wore his fair hair cropped relentlessly close to the skull, except for an absurd kiss-curl decorating his broad forehead. The face, crumpled in many places like an old cigarette-packet, wore a waxed moustache, and the general effect was of the cliché German Junker to be found in the pages of a back number of *Jugend*.

'Also, he has a tattoo,' added Goering. 'On his right arm. An imperial eagle.'

'Very patriotic,' I said. I put the photograph in my pocket, and asked for a cigarette. One of Goering's aides offered me one from the great silver box, and lit it with his own lighter. 'I believe that the police are working on the idea that his disappearance might have something to do with his being a homosexual.' I said nothing about the information that Neumann had given me concerning the German Strength ring having murdered a nameless aristocrat. Until I could check his story, there was no point in throwing away what might turn out to be a good card.

'That is indeed a possibility.' Goering's admission sounded uncomfortable. 'It's true, his homosexuality led him to some dangerous places and, on one occasion, it even brought him to the attention of the police. However, I was able to see that the charge was dropped. Gerhard was not deterred by what should have been a salutary experience. There was even a relationship with a prominent bureaucrat to contend with. Foolishly, I allowed it to continue in the hope that it would force Gerhard to become more discreet.'

I took this information with several pinches of salt. I thought it much more likely that Goering had allowed the relationship to continue in order that he might compromise Funk – a lesser political rival – with the aim of putting him into his back pocket. That is, if he wasn't there already.

'Did Von Greis have any other boyfriends?'

Goering shrugged and looked at Rienacker, who stirred, and said: 'There was nobody in particular, as far as we know. But it's difficult to say for sure. Most of the warm boys have been driven underground by the Emergency Powers. And most of the old queer clubs like the Eldorado have been closed. All the same, Herr Von Greis still managed to pursue a number of casual liaisons.'

'There is one possibility,' I said. 'That on a nocturnal visit to some out of the way corner of the city for sex, the gentleman was picked up by the local Kripo, beaten up and tossed into a KZ. You might not hear about it for several weeks.' The irony of the situation was not lost on me: that I should be discussing the disappearance of the servant of the man who was himself the architect of so many other disappearances. I wondered if he could see it too. 'Frankly, sir, one to two weeks is not a long time to be missing in Berlin these days.'

'Inquiries in that direction are already being made,' said Goering. 'But you are right to mention it. Apart from that, it's up to you now. From what inquiries Rienacker has made about you, missing persons would seem to be your speciality. My aide here will provide you with money, and anything else you may require. Is there anything else?'

I thought for a moment. 'I'd like to put a tap on a telephone.'

I knew that the Forschungsamt, the Directorate of Scientific Research, which took care of wire-taps, was subordinate to Goering. Housed in the old Air Ministry building, it was said that even Himmler had to obtain Goering's permission to put a wire-tap on someone, and I strongly suspected that it was through this particular facility that Goering continued to add to the 'reservoir of intelligence' that Diels had left to his erstwhile master.

Goering smiled. 'You are well-informed. As you wish.' He turned and spoke to his aide. 'See to it. It is to be given priority. And make sure that Herr Günther is given a daily transcript.'

'Yes, sir,' said the man. I wrote out a couple of numbers on a piece of paper and handed it to him. Then Goering stood up.

'This is your most important case,' he said, putting his hand lightly on my shoulder. He walked me to the door. Rienacker followed at a short distance. 'And if you are successful, you will not find me wanting in generosity.'

And if I wasn't successful? For the moment, I preferred to forget that possibility.

12

It was nearly light by the time I got back to my apartment. The 'painting-out' squad was hard at work on the streets, obliterating the nocturnal daubings of the KPD – 'Red Front will Win' and 'Long Live Thälmann and Torgler' – before the city awoke to the new day.

I had been asleep for no more than a couple of hours when the sound of sirens and whistles wrenched me violently from my quiet slumbers. It was an air-raid practice.

I buried my head under the pillow and tried to ignore the area warden hammering on my door; but I knew that I would only have to account for my absence later on, and that failure to provide a verifiable explanation would result in a fine.

Thirty minutes later, when the whistles had blown and the sirens cranked to sound the all-clear, there seemed little point in going back to bed. So I bought an extra litre off the Bolle milkman and cooked myself an enormous omelette.

Inge arrived at my office at just after nine. Without much ceremony she sat down on the other side of my desk and watched me finish making some case notes.

'Did you see your friend?' I asked her after a moment.

'We went to the theatre.'

'Yes? What did you see?' I found that I wanted to know everything, including details that had no bearing on the man's possible knowledge of Paul Pfarr.

'*The Base Wallah*. It was rather weak, but Otto seemed to enjoy it. He insisted on paying for the tickets, so I didn't need the petty cash.'

'Then what did you do?'

'We went to Baarz's beer restaurant. I hated it. A real Nazi place.

Everyone stood and saluted the radio when it played the *Horst Wessel Song* and *Deutschland Über Alles*. I had to do it too, and I hate to salute. It makes me feel like I'm hailing a taxi. Otto drank rather a lot and became very talkative. I drank quite a lot myself actually – I feel a bit rough this morning.' She lit a cigarette. 'Anyway, Otto was vaguely acquainted with Pfarr. He says that Pfarr was about as popular as a ferret in a gumboot at the DAF, and it's not difficult to see why. Pfarr was investigating corruption and fraud in the Labour Union. As a result of his investigations, two treasurers of the Transport Workers Union were dismissed and sent to KZs, one after the other; the chairman of the Koch Strasse shop-committee of Ullstein's, the big printing works, was found guilty of stealing funds and executed; Rolf Togotzes, the cashier of the Metal Workers Union, was sent to Dachau; and a lot more. If ever a man had enemies, it was Paul Pfarr. Apparently there were lots of smiling faces around the department when it became known that Pfarr was dead.'

'Any idea what he was investigating at the time of his death?'

'No. Apparently he played things very close to his chest. He liked to work through informers, amassing evidence until he was ready to make formal charges.'

'Did he have any colleagues there?'

'Just a stenographer, a girl by the name of Marlene Sahm. Otto, my friend, if you can call him that, took quite a shine to her, and asked her out a couple of times. Nothing much came of it. That's the story of his life, I'm afraid. But he remembered her address though.' Inge opened her handbag and consulted a small notebook. 'Nollendorfstrasse, Number 23. She'll probably know what he had been getting up to.'

'He sounds like a bit of a ladies' man, your friend Otto.'

Inge laughed. 'That's what he said about Pfarr. He was pretty sure that Pfarr was cheating on his wife, and that he had a mistress. He saw him with a woman on several occasions at the same nightclub. He said that Pfarr seemed embarrassed at being discovered.

Otto said she was quite a beauty, if a bit flashy. He thought her name was Vera, or Eva, or something like that.'

'Did he tell the police that?'

'No. He says that they never asked. On the whole he'd rather not get involved with the Gestapo unless he has to.'

'You mean that he hasn't even been questioned?'

'Apparently not.'

I shook my head. 'I wonder what they're playing at.' I thought for a minute, and then added, 'Thanks for doing that, by the way. I hope it wasn't too much of a nuisance.'

She shook her head. 'How about you? You look tired.'

'I was working late. And I didn't sleep all that well. Then this morning there was a damned air-raid practice.' I tried to massage some life into the top of my head. I didn't tell her about Goering. There was no need for her to know more than she had to. It was safer for her that way.

That morning she was wearing a dress of dark-green cotton with a fluted collar and cavalier cuffs of stiffened white lace. For a brief moment I fed myself on the fantasy that had me lifting her dress up and familiarizing myself with the curve of her buttocks and the depth of her sex.

'This girl, Pfarr's mistress. Are we going to try and find her?'

I shook my head. 'The bulls would be bound to hear about it. And then it could get awkward. They're quite keen on finding her themselves, and I wouldn't want to start picking that nostril with one finger already in there.' I picked up the phone and asked to be connected to Six's home telephone number. It was Farraj, the butler, who answered.

'Is Herr Six, or Herr Haupthändler, at home? It's Bernhard Günther speaking.'

'I'm sorry, sir, but they're both away at a meeting this morning. Then I believe they'll be attending the opening of the Olympic Games. May I give either of them a message, sir?'

'Yes, you can,' I said. 'Tell them both that I'm getting close.'

'Is that all, sir?'

'Yes, they'll know what I mean. And make sure that you tell both of them, Farraj, won't you.'

'Yes, sir.'

I put the phone down. 'Right,' I said. 'It's time we got going.'

It was a ten-pfennig ride on the U-Bahn to the Zoo Station, repainted to look especially smart for the Olympic fortnight. Even the walls of the houses backing on to the station had been given a new coat of white. But high above the city, and where the Hindenburg airship droned noisily back and forwards towing an Olympic flag, the sky had gathered a surly gang of dark-grey clouds. As we left the station, Inge looked upwards and said: 'It would serve them right if it rained. Better still, if it rained for the entire fortnight.'

'That's the one thing they can't control,' I said. We approached the top of Kurfürstenstrasse. 'Now then, while Herr Haupthändler is away with his employer, I propose to have a squint at his rooms. Wait for me at Aschinger's restaurant.' Inge began to protest, but I continued speaking: 'Burglary is a serious crime, and I don't want you around if the going gets tough. Understand?'

She frowned, and then nodded. 'Brute,' she muttered, as I walked away.

Number 120 was a five-storey block of expensive-looking flats, of the sort that had a heavy black door that was polished so keenly they could have used it as a mirror in a negro jazz-band's dressing room. I summoned the diminutive caretaker with the enormous stirrup-shaped brass door-knocker. He looked about as alert as a doped tree sloth. I flashed the Gestapo warrant disc in front of his rheumy little eyes. At the same time I snapped 'Gestapo' at him and, pushing him roughly aside, I stepped quickly into the hall. The caretaker oozed fear through every one of his pasty pores.

'Which is Herr Haupthändler's apartment?'

Realizing that he was not about to be arrested and sent to a KZ, the caretaker relaxed slightly. 'The second floor, apartment five. But he's not at home right now.'

I snapped my fingers at him. 'Your pass-key, give it to me.' With eager, unhesitating hands, he produced a small bunch of keys and removed one from the ring. I snatched it from his trembling fingers.

'If Herr Haupthändler returns, ring once on the telephone, and then replace the receiver. Is that clear?'

'Yes, sir,' he said, with an audible gulp.

Haupthändler's were an impressively large suite of rooms on two levels, with arched doorways and a shiny wooden floor covered with thick Oriental rugs. Everything was neat and well-polished, so much so that the apartment seemed hardly lived in at all. In the bedroom were two large twin beds, a dressing-table, and a pouffe. The colour scheme was peach, jade-green and mushroom, with the first colour predominating. I didn't like it. On each of the two beds was an open suitcase, and on the floor were empty carrier-bags from several large department stores including C & A, Grunfeld's, Gerson's and Tietz. I searched through the suitcases. The first one I looked in was a woman's, and I was struck by the fact that everything in it was, or at least looked, brand-new. Some of the garments still had the price tags attached, and even the soles of the shoes were unworn. By contrast the other suitcase, which I presumed must belong to Haupthändler himself, contained nothing that was new, except for a few toiletries. There was no diamond necklace. But lying on the dressing-table was a wallet-sized folder containing two Deutsche Lufthansa air-tickets, for the Monday evening flight to Croydon, London. The tickets were returns, and booked in the name of Herr and Frau Teich-müller.

Before leaving Haupthändler's apartment I called the Adlon Hotel. When Hermine answered I thanked her for helping me with the Princess Mushmi story. I couldn't tell if Goering's people in the Forschungsamt had tapped the telephone yet; there were no audible clicks, nor any extra resonance in Hermine's voice. But I knew that if they really had put a tap on Haupthändler's telephone, then I ought to see a transcript of my conversation with

Hermine later on that day. It was as good a way as any of testing the true extent of the Prime Minister's cooperation.

I left Haupthändler's rooms and returned to the ground floor. The caretaker emerged from his office and took possession of his pass-key again.

'You will say nothing of my being here to anyone. Otherwise it will go badly for you. Is that understood?' He nodded silently. I saluted smartly, something Gestapo men never do, preferring as they do, to remain as inconspicuous as possible, but I was laying it on for the sake of effect.

'Heil Hitler,' I said.

'Heil Hitler,' repeated the caretaker, and, returning the salute, he managed to drop the keys.

'We've got until Monday night to pull this one back,' I said, sitting down at Inge's table. I explained about the air-tickets and the two suitcases. 'The funny thing was that the woman's case was full of new things.'

'Your Herr Haupthändler sounds like he knows how to look after a girl.'

'*Everything* was new. The garter-belt, the handbag, the shoes. There wasn't one item in that case that looked as though it had been used before. Now what does that tell you?'

Inge shrugged. She was still slightly piqued at having been left behind. 'Maybe he's got a new job, going door-to-door, selling women's clothes.'

I raised my eyebrows.

'All right then,' she said. 'Maybe this woman that he's taking to London doesn't have any nice clothes.'

'More like, doesn't have any clothes at all,' I said. 'Rather a strange kind of woman, wouldn't you say?'

'Bernie, just you come home with me. I'll show you a woman without any clothes.'

For a brief second I entertained myself with the idea. But I went on, 'No, I'm convinced that Haupthändler's mystery girlfriend is starting out on this trip with a completely new wardrobe, from top to toe. Like a woman with no past.'

'Or,' said Inge, 'a woman who is starting afresh.' The theory was taking shape in her mind even as she was speaking. With greater conviction, she added, 'A woman who has had to sever contact with her previous existence. A woman who couldn't go home and pick up her things, because there wasn't time. No, that can't be right. She has until Monday night after all. So perhaps she's afraid to go home, in case there's someone waiting for her there.' I nodded approvingly, and was about to develop this line of reasoning, but found that she was there ahead of me. 'Perhaps,' she said, 'this woman was Pfarr's mistress, the one the police are looking for. Vera, or Eva, I forget which.'

'Haupthändler in this with her? Yes,' I said thoughtfully, 'that could fit. Maybe Pfarr gives his mistress the brush-off when he finds out that his wife is pregnant. The prospect of fatherhood has been known to bring some men to their senses. But it also happens to spoil things for Haupthändler, who might himself have had ambitions as far as Frau Pfarr was concerned. Maybe Haupthändler and this woman Eva got together and decided to play the part of the wronged lover – in tandem, so to speak – and also make a little money into the bargain. It's not unlikely that Pfarr might have told Eva about his wife's jewellery.' I stood up, finishing my drink.

'Then maybe Haupthändler is hiding Eva somewhere.'

'That makes three maybes. More than I'm used to having over lunch. Any more and I'll get sick.' I glanced at my watch. 'Come on, we can think about it some more on the way.'

'On the way where?'

'Kreuzberg.'

She levelled a well-manicured finger at me. 'And this time, I'm not being left somewhere safe while you get all the fun. Understood?'

I grinned at her, and shrugged. 'Understood.'

*

The Kreuzberg, the Hill of the Cross, lies to the south of the city, in Viktoria Park, near Tempelhof Airport. It's where Berlin's artists gather to sell their pictures. Just a block away from the park, Chamissoplatz is a square surrounded by high, grey, fortress-like tenements. Pension Tillessen occupied the corner of Number 17, but with its closed shutters pasted over with Party posters and KPD graffiti, it didn't look as though it had been taking guests since Bismarck grew his first moustache. I went to the front door and found it locked. Bending down, I peered through the letter-box, but there was no sign of anyone.

Next door, at the office of Heinrich Billinger, 'German' Account-ant, the coalman was delivering some brown-coal briquets on what looked like a bakery tray. I asked him if he could recollect when the pension had closed. He wiped his smutty brow, and then spat as he tried to remember.

'It never was what you might call a regular pension,' he declared finally. He looked uncertainly at Inge, and choosing his words carefully, added: 'More what you might call a house of ill-repute. Not a regular out-and-out bawdy house, you understand. Just the sort of place where you used to see a snapper take her sledge. I remember as I saw some men coming out of there only a couple of weeks ago. The boss never bought coal regular like. Just the odd tray here and there. But as to when it closed, I couldn't tell you. If it is closed, mind. Don't judge it by the way it looks. Seems to me as how it's always been in that state.'

I led Inge round the back, to a small cobbled alleyway that was lined with garages and lock-ups. Stray cats sat mangily self-contained on top of brick walls; a mattress lay abandoned in a doorway, its iron guts spilling on to the ground; someone had tried to burn it, and I was reminded of the blackened bed-frames in the forensic photographs Illmann had shown me. We stopped beside what I took to be the garage belonging to the pension and looked through the filthy window, but it was impossible to see anything.

'I'll come back for you in a minute,' I said, and clambered up the drainpipe at the side of the garage and onto the corrugated iron roof.

'See that you do,' she called.

I walked carefully across the badly rusted roof on all fours, not daring to stand up straight and concentrate all my weight on one point. At the back of the roof I looked down into a small court-yard which led on to the pension. Most of the windows in the rooms were shrouded with dirty net curtains, and there was no sign of life at any of them. I searched for a way down, but there was no drainpipe, and the wall to the adjoining property, the German accountant's, was too low to be of any use. It was fortunate that the rear of the pension obscured the view to the garage of anyone who might have chanced to look up from poring over a dull set of accounts. There was no choice but to jump, although it was a height of over four metres. I made it, but it left the soles of my feet stinging for minutes afterwards, as if they had been beaten with a length of rubber hosing. The back door to the garage was not locked and, but for a pile of old car tyres, it was empty. I unbolted the double doors and admitted Inge. Then I bolted them again. For a moment we stood in silence, looking at each other in the half darkness, and I nearly let myself kiss her. But there are better places to kiss a pretty girl than a disused garage in Kreuzberg.

We crossed the yard, and when we came to the back door of the pension, I tried the handle. The door stayed shut.

'Now what?' said Inge. 'A lock-pick? A skeleton key?'

'Something like that,' I said, and kicked the door in.

'Very subtle,' she said, watching the door swing open on its hinges. 'I assume you've decided that there's nobody here.'

I grinned at her. 'When I looked through the letter-box I saw a pile of unopened mail on the mat.' I went in. She hesitated long enough for me to look back at her. 'It's all right. There's nobody here. Hasn't been for some time, I'd bet.'

'So what are we doing here?'

'We're having a look around, that's all.'

'You make it sound as if we were in Grunfeld's department store,' she said, following me down the gloomy stone corridor. The only sound was our own footsteps, mine strong and purposeful, and hers nervous and half on tiptoe.

At the end of the corridor I stopped and glanced into a large and extremely smelly kitchen. Piles of dirty dishes lay in untidy stacks. Cheese and meat lay flyblown on the kitchen table. A bloated insect buzzed past my ear. One step in, the stink was overpowering. Behind me I heard Inge cough so that it was almost a retch. I hurried to the window and pushed it open. For a moment we stood there, enjoying the clean air. Then, looking down at the floor, I saw some papers in front of the stove. One of the doors to the incinerator was open, and I bent forward to take a look. Inside, the stove was full of burnt paper, most of it nothing more than ash; but here and there were the edges or corners of something that had not quite been consumed by the flames.

'See if you can salvage some of this,' I said. 'It looks like someone was in a hurry to cover his tracks.'

'Anything in particular?'

'Anything legible, I suppose.' I walked over to the kitchen doorway.

'Where will you be?'

'I'm going to take a look upstairs.' I pointed to the dumbwaiter. 'If you need me, just shout up the shaft there.' She nodded silently, and rolled up her sleeves.

Upstairs, and on the same level as the front door, there was even more mess. Behind the front desk were empty drawers, their contents lying on the threadbare carpet; and the doors of every cupboard had been wrenched off their hinges. I was reminded of the mess in Goering's Derfflingerstrasse apartment. Most of the bedroom floorboards had been ripped up, and some of the chimneys showed signs of having been probed with a broom. Then I went into the dining room. Blood had spattered the white wallpaper like an enormous graze, and on the rug was a stain the size of a dinner-plate. I stood on something hard, and bent down to pick up what looked like a bullet. It was a lead weight, encrusted with blood. I tossed it in my hand and then put it in my jacket pocket.

More blood had stained the wooden sill of the dumb-waiter. I leaned into the shaft to shout down to Inge and found myself retching, so strong was the smell of putrefaction. I staggered away. There was something sticking in the shaft, and it wasn't a late breakfast. Covering my nose and mouth with my handkerchief, I poked my head back into the shaft. Looking down I saw that the lift itself was stuck between floors. Glancing upwards I saw that as it crossed the pulley, one of the ropes supporting the lift had been jammed with a piece of wood. Sitting on the sill, with the top half of my body in the shaft, I reached up and pulled the piece of wood away. The rope ran past my face and beneath me the lift plummeted down to the kitchen with a loud bang. I heard Inge's shocked scream; and then she screamed again, only this time it was louder and more sustained.

I sprinted out of the dining room, down the stairs to the basement and found her standing in the corridor, leaning weakly on the wall outside the kitchen. 'Are you all right?'

She swallowed loudly. 'It's horrible.'

'What is?' I went through the doorway. I heard Inge say: 'Don't go in there, Bernie.' But it was too late.

The body sat to one side in the lift, huddled foetally like a daredevil ready to attempt Niagara Falls in a beer barrel. As I stared at it the head seemed to turn, and it took a moment for me to realize that it was covered with maggots, a glistening mask of worms feeding on the blackened face. I swallowed hard several times. Covering my nose and mouth once again, I stepped forward for a closer look, close enough so that I could hear the light rustling sound, like a gentle breeze through moist leaves, of hundreds of small mouth parts. From my small knowledge of forensics, I knew that soon after death, flies not only lay their eggs on a cadaver's moist parts such as the eyes and mouth, but also on open wounds. By the number of maggots feeding on the upper part of the cranium and on the right temple, it looked more than probable that the victim had been beaten to death. From the clothes I could tell that the body was that of a man, and judging by the obvious quality of his shoes, quite a wealthy one. I put my hand into the right-hand jacket pocket, and turned it inside out. Some loose change and scraps of paper fell to the floor, but there was nothing that might have identified him. I felt around the area of the breast pocket, but it seemed to be empty, and I didn't feel like squeezing my hand between his knee and the maggoty head to make sure. As I stepped back to the window to draw a decent breath, a thought occurred to me.

'What are you doing, Bernie?' Her voice seemed stronger now.

'Just stay where you are,' I told her. 'I won't be very long. I just want to see if I can find out who our friend is.' I heard her take a deep breath, and the scrape of a match as she lit a cigarette. I found a pair of kitchen scissors and went back to the dumb-waiter, where I cut the arm of the jacket lengthways up the man's forearm. Against the skin's greenish, purplish hue and marbled veining, the tattoo was still clearly visible, clinging to his forearm like a large, black insect which, rather than feast on the head with the smaller flies and worms, had chosen to dine alone, on a bigger piece of carrion. I've never understood why men get themselves tattooed. You would have thought there were better things to do than deface your own body. Still, it makes identifying someone relatively straightforward, and it occurred to me that it wouldn't be very long before every German citizen was the subject of compulsory tattooing. But right now, the imperial German eagle identified Gerhard Von Greis just as certainly as if I had been handed his Party card and passport.

Inge looked round the doorway. 'Do you have any idea who it is?' I rolled up my sleeve and put my arm into the incinerator. 'Yes, I do,' I said, feeling around in the cold ash. My fingers touched something hard and long. I drew it out, and regarded it objectively. It was hardly burnt at all. Not the sort of wood that burns easily. At the thicker end it was split, revealing another lead weight, and an empty socket for the one I had found on the carpet in the dining room upstairs. 'His name was Gerhard Von Greis, and he was a high-class squeeze-artist. Looks like he was paid off, permanently. Someone combed his hair with this.'

'What is it?'

'A length of broken billiard cue,' I said, and thrust it back into the stove.

'Shouldn't we tell the police?'

'We don't have the time to help them feel their way around. Not right now, anyway. We'd just spend the rest of the weekend answering stupid questions.' I was also thinking that a couple of days' more fees from Goering wouldn't go amiss, but I kept that one to myself.

'What about him – the dead man?'

I looked back at Von Greis's maggoty body, and then shrugged. 'He's in no hurry,' I said. 'Besides, you wouldn't want to spoil the picnic, would you?'

We collected up the scraps of paper that Inge had managed to salvage from the inside of the stove, and caught a cab back to the office. I poured us both large cognacs. Inge drank it gratefully, holding the glass with both hands like a small child who is greedy for lemonade. I sat down on the side of her chair and put my arm around her trembling shoulders, drawing her to me, Von Greis's death accelerating our growing need to be close.

'I'm afraid I'm not used to dead bodies,' she said with an embarrassed smile. 'Least of all badly decomposed bodies that appear unexpectedly in service-lifts.'

'Yes, it must have been quite a shock to you. I'm sorry you had to see that. I have to admit he'd let himself go a bit.'

She gave a slight shudder. 'It's hard to credit that it was ever human at all. It looked so . . . so vegetable; like a sack of rotten potatoes.' I resisted the temptation to make another tasteless remark. Instead I went over to my desk, laid out the scraps of paper from Tillessen's kitchen stove and glanced over them. Mostly they were bills, but there was one, almost untouched by the flames, that interested me a good deal.

'What is it?' said Inge.

I picked up the scrap of paper between finger and thumb. 'A pay-slip.' She stood up and looked at it more closely. 'From a pay-packet made up by the Gesellschaft Reichsautobahnen for one of its motorway-construction workers.'

'Whose?'

'A fellow by the name of Hans Jürgen Bock. Until recently, he was in the cement with somebody by the name of Kurt Mutschmann, a nutcracker.'

'And you think that this Mutschmann might have been the one who opened the Pfarrs' safe, right?'

'Both he and Bock are members of the same ring, as was the owner of the excuse for a hotel we just visited.'

'But if Bock is in a ring with Mutschmann and Tillessen, what's he doing working in motorway construction?'

'That's a good question.' I shrugged and added, 'Who knows, maybe he's trying to go straight? Whatever he's doing, we ought to speak to him.'

'Perhaps he can tell us where to find Mutschmann.'

'It's possible.'

'And Tillessen.'

I shook my head. 'Tillessen's dead,' I explained. 'Von Greis was killed, beaten with a broken billiard cue. A few days ago, in the police morgue, I saw what happened to the other half of that billiard cue. It was pushed up Tillessen's nose, into his brain.'

Inge grimaced uncomfortably. 'But how do you know it was Tillessen?'

'I don't for sure,' I admitted. 'But I know that Mutschmann is hiding, and that it was Tillessen who he went to stay with when he got out of prison. I don't think Tillessen would have left a body lying around his own pension if he could possibly have avoided it.

The last I heard, the police still hadn't made a positive ID on the corpse, so I'm assuming that it must be Tillessen.'

'But why couldn't it be Mutschmann?'

'I don't see it that way. A couple of days ago my informer told me that there was a contract out on Mutschmann, by which time the body with the cue up its nose had already been fished out of the Landwehr. No, it could only be Tillessen.'

'And Von Greis? Was he a member of this ring too?'

'Not this ring, but another one, and far more powerful. He worked for Goering. All the same, I can't explain why he should have been there.' I swilled some brandy around my mouth like a mouthwash, and when I had swallowed it, I picked up the telephone and called the Reichsbahn. I spoke to a clerk in the payroll department.

'My name is Rienacker,' I said. 'Kriminalinspektor Rienacker of the Gestapo. We are anxious to trace the whereabouts of an autobahn-construction worker by the name of Hans Jürgen Bock, pay reference 30–4–232564. He may be able to help us in apprehending an enemy of the Reich.'

'Yes,' said the clerk meekly. 'What is it that you wish to know?'

'Obviously, the section of the autobahn on which he is working, and whether or not he'll be there today.'

'If you will please wait one minute, I shall go and check the records.' Several minutes elapsed.

'That's quite a nice little act you have there,' said Inge.

I covered the mouthpiece. 'It's a brave man who refuses to cooperate with a caller claiming to be in the Gestapo.'

The clerk came back to the telephone and told me that Bock was on a work detail beyond the edge of Greater Berlin, on the Berlin-to-Hanover stretch. 'Specifically, the section between Brandenburg and Lehnin. I suggest that you contact the site-office a couple of kilometres this side of Brandenburg. It's about seventy kilometres. You drive to Potsdam, then take Zeppelin Strasse. After about forty kilometres you pick up the A-Bahn at Lehnin.'

'Thank you,' I said. 'And is he likely to be working today?'

'I'm afraid I don't know,' said the clerk. 'Many of them do work Saturdays. But even if he's not working, you'll probably find him in the workers' barracks. They live on site, you see.'

'You've been most helpful,' I said, and added with the pomposity that is typical of all Gestapo officers, 'I shall report your efficiency to your superior.'

13

'It's just typical of the bloody Nazis,' said Inge, 'to build the People's roads before the People's car.'

We were driving towards Potsdam on the Avus Speedway, and Inge was referring to the much delayed Strength Through Joy car, the KdF-Wagen. It was a subject she evidently felt strongly about.

'If you ask me, it's putting the cart before the horse. I mean, who needs these gigantic highways? It's not as if there's anything wrong with the roads we have now. It's not as if there are that many cars in Germany.' She turned sideways in her seat the better to see me as she continued speaking. 'I have this friend, an engineer, who tells me that they're building an autobahn right across the Polish Corridor, and that one is projected across Czechoslovakia. Now why else would that be but to move an army about?'

I cleared my throat before answering; it gave me a couple more seconds to think about it. 'I can't see the autobahns are of much military value, and there are none west of the Rhine, towards France. Anyway, on a long straight stretch of road, a convoy of trucks makes an easy target for an air attack.'

This last remark drew a short, mocking laugh from my companion. 'That's precisely why they're building up the Luftwaffe – to protect the convoys.'

I shrugged. 'Maybe. But if you're looking for the real reason why Hitler has built these roads, then it's much more simple. It's an easy way of cutting the unemployment figures. A man receiving state relief risks losing it if he refuses the offer of a job on the autobahns. So he takes it. Who knows, that may be what happened to Bock.'

'You should take a look at Wedding and Neukölln sometime,' she said, referring to Berlin's remaining strongholds of KPD sympathy.

'Well, of course, there are those who know all about the rotten pay and conditions on the autobahns. I suppose a lot of them think that it's better not to sign on for relief at all rather than risk being sent to work on the roads.' We were coming into Potsdam on the Neue Königstrasse. Potsdam. A shrine where the older residents of the town light the candles to the glorious, bygone days of the Fatherland, and to their youth; the silent, discarded shell of Imperial Prussia. More French-looking than German, it's a museum of a place, where the old ways of speech and sentiment are reverently preserved, where conservatism is absolute and where the windows are as well polished as the glass on the pictures of the Kaiser.

A couple of kilometres down the road to Lehnin, the picturesque gave way abruptly to the chaotic. Where once had been some of the most beautiful countryside outside Berlin, there was now the earth-moving machinery and the torn brown valley that was the half built Lehnin–Brandenburg stretch of autobahn. Closer to Brandenburg, at a collection of wooden huts and idle excavating equipment, I pulled up and asked a worker to direct me to the foreman's hut. He pointed at a man standing only a few metres away.

'If you want him, that's the foreman there.' I thanked him, and parked the car. We got out.

The foreman was a stocky, red-faced man of medium height, and with a belly that was bigger than a woman who has reached the full term of her pregnancy: it hung over the edge of his trousers like a climber's rucksack. He turned to face us as we approached, and almost as if he had been preparing to square up to me, he hitched up his trousers, wiped his stubbly jaw with the back of his shovel-sized hand and transferred most of his weight on to his back foot.

'Hallo there,' I called, before we were quite next to him. 'Are you the foreman?' He said nothing. 'My name is Günther, Bernhard Günther. I'm a private investigator, and this is my assistant, Fräulein Inge Lorenz.' I handed him my identification. The foreman nodded at Inge and then returned his gaze back to my licence. There was a literalness about his conduct that seemed almost simian.

'Peter Welser,' he said. 'What can I do for you people?'

'I'd like to speak to Herr Bock. I'm hoping he can help us. We're looking for a missing person.'

Welser chuckled and hitched up his trousers again. 'Christ, that's a funny one.' He shook his head and then spat onto the earth. 'This week alone I've had three workers disappear. Perhaps I should hire you to try and find them, eh?' He laughed again.

'Was Bock one of them?'

'Good God, no,' said Welser. 'He's a damn good worker. Ex-convict trying to live an honest life. I hope you're not going to spoil that for him.'

'Herr Welser, I just want to ask him one or two questions, not rubber him and take him back to Tegel Prison in my trunk. Is he here now?'

'Yes, he's here. He's very probably in his hut. I'll take you over there.' We followed him to one of several long, single-storey wooden huts that had been built at the side of what had once been forest, and was now destined to be the autobahn. At the bottom of the hut steps the foreman turned and said, 'They're a bit rough-and-ready, these fellows. Maybe it would be better if the lady didn't come in. You have to take these men as you find them. Some of them might not be dressed.'

'I'll wait in the car, Bernie,' said Inge. I looked at her and shrugged apologetically, before following Welser up the steps. He raised the wooden latch and we went through the door.

Inside, the walls and floor were painted a washed-out shade of yellow. Against the walls were bunks for twelve workers, three of them without mattresses and three of them occupied by men wearing just their underwear. In the middle of the hut was a pot-bellied stove made of black cast-iron, its stove-pipe going straight through the ceiling, and next to it a big wooden table at which four men were seated, playing skat for a few pfennigs. Welser spoke to one of the card players.

'This fellow is from Berlin,' he explained. 'He'd like to ask you a few questions.'

A solid slab of man with a head the size of a tree stump studied the palm of his big hand carefully, looked up at the foreman, and then suspiciously at me. Another man got up off his bunk and started to sweep the floor nonchalantly with a broom.

I've had better introductions in my time, and I wasn't surprised to see that it didn't exactly put Bock at his ease. I was about to utter my own codicil to Welser's inadequate reference when Bock sprang out of his chair, and my jaw, blocking his exit, was duly hooked aside. Not much of a punch, but enough to set off a small steam kettle between my ears and knock me sideways. A second or two later I heard a short, dull clang, like someone striking a tin tray with a soup ladle. When I had recovered my senses, I looked around and saw Welser standing over Bock's half-conscious body. In his hand he held a coal shovel, with which he had evidently struck the big man's head. There was the scrape of chairs and table legs as Bock's card-playing friends jumped to their feet.

'Relax, all of you,' yelled Welser. 'This fellow isn't a fucking bull, he's a private investigator. He's not come to arrest Hans. He just wants to ask him a few questions, that's all. He's looking for a missing person.' He pointed at one of the men in the skat game. 'Here you, give me a hand with him.' Then he looked at me. 'You all right?' he said. I nodded vaguely. Welser and the other man bent down and lifted Bock from where he lay in the doorway. I could see it wasn't easy; the man looked heavy. They sat him in a chair and waited for him to shake his head clear. Meanwhile the foreman told the rest of the men in the hut to go outside for ten minutes. The men in the bunks didn't put up any resistance and I could see that Welser was a man who was used to being obeyed, and quickly.

When Bock came round, Welser told him what he had told the rest of the hut. I could have wished that he had done it at the beginning.

'I'll be outside if you need me,' said Welser, and pushing the last man from the hut, he left the two of us alone.

'If you're not a polyp then you must be one of Red's boys.' Bock spoke sideways out of his mouth, and I saw that his tongue was several sizes too big for his mouth. Its tip remained buried in his cheek somewhere, so that all I saw was the large pink-coloured chew that was his tongue's thickest part.

'Look, I'm not a complete idiot,' he said more vehemently. 'I'm not so stupid that I'd get killed to protect Kurt. I really have no idea where he is.' I took out my cigarette case and offered him one. I lit us both in silence.

'Listen, first off, I'm not one of Red's boys. I really am a private investigator, like the man said. But I've got a sore jaw and unless you answer all my questions your name will be the one the boys up at the Alex draw out of the hat to make the trip to the blade for canning the meat at Pension Tillessen.' Bock stiffened in his chair. 'And if you move from that chair, so help me I'll break your damned neck.' I drew up a chair and put one foot on its seat so that I could lean on my knee while looking at him.

'You can't prove I was near the place,' he said.

I grinned at him. 'Oh, can't I?' I took a long pull at my smoke, and blew it in his face. I said: 'On your last little visit to Tillessen's joint you kindly left your pay-slip behind. I found it in the incinerator, next to the murder weapon. That's how I managed to track you down here. Of course it's not there now, but I could easily put it back. The police haven't yet found the body, but that's only because I haven't had time to tell them. That pay-slip puts you in an awkward situation. Next to the murder weapon, it's more than enough to send you to the block.'

'What do you want?'

I sat down opposite him. 'Answers,' I said. 'Look, friend, if I ask you to name the capital of Mongolia you'd better give me an answer or I'll have your fucking head for it. Do you understand?' He shrugged. 'But we'll start with Kurt Mutschmann, and what the two of you did when you came out of Tegel.'

Bock sighed heavily and then nodded. 'I got out first. I decided to try and go straight. This isn't much of a job, but it's a job. I didn't want to go back in the cement. I used to go back to Berlin for the odd weekend, see? Stay at Tillessen's bang. He's a pimp, or was. Sometimes he fixed me up with a bit of plum.' He tucked the cigarette into the corner of his mouth and rubbed the top of his head. 'Anyway, a couple of months after I got out, Kurt finished his cement and went to stay with Tillessen. I went to see him, and he told me that the ring were going to fix him up with his first bit of thieving.

'Well, the same night I saw him, Red Dieter and a couple of his boys turn up. He more or less runs the ring, you understand. They've got this older fellow with them, and start working him over in the dining room. I stayed out of the way in my room. After a while Red comes in and tells Kurt that he wants him to do a safe, and that he wants me to drive. Well, neither of us was too happy about it. Me, because I'd had enough of all that sort of thing. And Kurt because he's a professional. He doesn't like violence, mess, you know. He likes to take his time, too. Not just go straight ahead and do a job without any real planning.'

'This safe: did Red Dieter find out about it from the man in the dining room, the man being beaten up?' Bock nodded. 'What happened then?'

'I decided that I wanted nothing to do with it. So I went out through the window, spent the night at the doss-house on Frobestrasse, and came back here. That fellow, the one they had beaten up, he was still alive when I left. They were keeping him alive until they found out if he had told them the truth.' He took the cigarette stub out of his mouth and dropped it on the wooden floor, grinding it under his heel. I gave him another.

'Well, the next thing I hear is that the job went wrong. Tillessen did the driving, apparently. Afterwards, Red's boys killed him. They would have killed Kurt too, only he got away.'

'Did they double-cross Red?'

'Nobody's that stupid.'

'You're singing, aren't you?'

'When I was in the cement, in Tegel, I saw lots of men die on that guillotine,' he said quietly. 'I'd rather take my chances with Red. When I go I want to go in one piece.'

'Tell me more about the job.'

' "Just crack a nut," ' said Red. 'Easy to a man like Kurt, he's a real professional. Could open Hitler's heart. The job was middle of the night. Puzzle the safe and take some papers. That's all.'

'No diamonds?'

'Diamonds? He never said nothing about no bells.'

'Are you sure of that?'

'Course I'm sure. He was just to claw the papers. Nothing else.'

'What were these papers, do you know?'

Bock shook his head. 'Just papers.'

'What about the killings?'

'Nobody mentioned killings. Kurt wouldn't have agreed to do the job if he thought he was going to have to can anyone. He wasn't that kind of fellow.'

'What about Tillessen? Was he the type to shoot people in their beds?'

'Not a chance. That wasn't his style at all. Tillessen was just a fucking garter-handler. Beating up snappers was all he was good for. Show him a lighter and he'd have been off like a rabbit.'

'Maybe they got greedy, and helped themselves to more than they were supposed to.'

'You tell me. You're the fucking detective.'

'And you haven't seen or heard from Kurt since?'

'He's too smart to contact me. If he's got any sense, he'll have done a U-Boat by now.'

'Does he have any friends?'

'A few. But I don't know who. His wife left him, so you can forget her. She spent every pfennig he had earned, and when she'd finished she took off with another man. He'd die before he'd ask that bitch for help.'

'Perhaps he's dead already,' I suggested.

'Not Kurt,' said Bock, his face set against the thought. 'He's a clever one. Resourceful. He'll find a way out of it.'

'Maybe,' I said, and then: 'One thing I can't figure is you going straight, especially when you end up working here. How much do you make a week?'

Bock shrugged. 'About forty marks.' He caught the quiet surprise in my face. It was even less than I had supposed. 'Not much, is it?'

'So what's the deal? Why aren't you breaking heads for Red Dieter?'

'Who says I ever did?'

'You went inside for beating up steel pickets, didn't you?'

'That was a mistake. I needed the money.'

'Who was paying it?'

'Red.'

'And what was in it for him?'

'Money, same as me. Just more of it. His sort never gets caught. I worked that one out in the cement. The worst of it is that now that I've decided to go straight it seems like the rest of the country has decided to go bent. I go to prison and when I come out I find that the stupid bastards have elected a bunch of gangsters. How do you like that?'

'Well, don't blame me, friend, I voted for the Social Democrats. Did you ever find out who was paying Red to break the steel strikes? Hear any names maybe?'

He shrugged. 'The bosses, I suppose. Doesn't take a detective to work that one out. But I never heard any names.'

'But it was definitely organized.'

'Oh yes, it was organized all right. What's more it worked. They went back, didn't they?'

'And you went to prison.'

'I got caught. Never have been very lucky. You turning up here is proof of that.'

I took out my wallet and thumbed a fifty at him. He opened his mouth to thank me.

'Skip it.' I got to my feet and made for the hut door. Turning round, I said, 'Was your Kurt the type of puzzler to leave a nut he'd cracked open?'

Bock folded the fifty and shook his head. 'Nobody was ever tidier round a job than Kurt Mutschmann.'

I nodded. 'That's what I thought.'

'You're going to have quite an eye in the morning,' said Inge. She took hold of my chin and turned my head to get a better look at the bruise on my cheekbone. 'You'd better let me put something on that.' She went into the bathroom. We had stopped off at my apartment on our way back from Brandenburg. I heard her run the tap for a while, and when she returned she pressed a cold flannel to my face. As she stood there I felt her breath caress my ear, and I inhaled deeply of the haze of perfume in which she moved.

'This might help to stop the swelling,' she said.

'Thanks. A jaw-whistler looks bad for business. On the other hand, maybe they'll just think that I'm the determined type – you know, the kind who never lets up on a case.'

'Hold still,' she said impatiently. Her belly brushed against me, and I realized with some surprise that I had an erection. She blinked quickly and I supposed that she had noticed it too; but she did not step back. Instead, almost involuntarily, she brushed against me once more, only with a greater pressure than before. I lifted my hand and cradled her ample breast on my open palm. After a minute or so of that I took her nipple in between my finger and thumb. It wasn't difficult to find. It was as hard as the lid on a teapot, and just as big. Then she turned away.

'Perhaps we should stop now,' she said.

'If you're intending to stop the swelling, you're too late,' I told her. Her eyes passed lightly over me as I said it. Colouring a little, she folded her arms across her breasts and flexed her long neck against her backbone.

Enjoying the very deliberateness of my own actions, I stepped close to her and looked slowly down from her face, across her breasts and her belly, over her thighs to the hem of the green cotton dress. Reaching down I caught hold of it. Our fingers brushed as she took the hem from me and held it at her waist where I had placed it. Then I knelt before her, my eyes lingering on her underthings for long seconds before I reached up and slipped her knickers round her ankles. She steadied herself with one hand on my shoulder and stepped out of them, her long smooth thighs trembling slightly as she moved. I looked up at the sight I had coveted, and then beyond, to a face that smiled and then vanished as the dress rose up over her head, revealing her breasts, her neck and then her head again, which shook its cascade of shiny black hair like a bird fluttering the feathers on its wings. She dropped the dress to the floor and stood before me, naked but for her garter-belt, her stockings and her shoes. I sat back on my haunches and with an excitement that ached to be liberated I watched her slowly turn herself in front of me, showing me the profile of her pubic hair and her erect nipples, the long chute of her back and the two perfectly matched halves of her bottom, and then once more the swell of her belly, the dark pennant that seemed to prick the air with its own excitement, and the smooth, quivering shanks.

I picked her up and took her into the bedroom where we spent the rest of the afternoon, caressing, exploring and blissfully enjoying a feast of each other's flesh.

The afternoon drifted lazily into evening, with light sleep and tender words; and when we rose from my bed having satisfied our lust, we found our appetites the more ravenous.

I took her to dinner at the Peltzer Grill, and then dancing at the Germania Roof, in nearby Hardenbergstrasse. The Roof was crowded with Berlin's smartest set, many of them in uniform. Inge looked around at the blue glass walls, the ceiling illuminated with small blue stars and supported with columns of burnished copper, and the ornamental pools with their water-lilies, and smiled excitedly.

'Isn't this simply wonderful?'

'I didn't think that this was your sort of place,' I said lamely. But she didn't hear me. She was taking me by the hand and pulling me on to the less crowded of the two circular dance-floors.

It was a good band, and I held her tight and breathed through her hair. I was congratulating myself on bringing her here instead of, one of the clubs with which I was better acquainted, such as Johnny's or the Golden Horseshoe. Then I remembered that Neumann had said that the Germania Roof was one of Red Dieter's chosen haunts. So when Inge went to the ladies' room I called the waiter over to our table and handed him a five.

'This gets me a couple of answers to a couple of simple questions, right?' He shrugged, and pocketed the cash. 'Is Dieter Helfferrich in the joint tonight?'

'Red Dieter?'

'What other colours are there?' He didn't get that, so I left it. He looked thoughtful for a moment, as if wondering whether or not the ringleader of German Strength would mind his being identified in this way. He made the right decision.

'Yes, he's here tonight.' Anticipating my next question, he nodded over his shoulder in the direction of the bar. 'He's sitting in the booth furthest from the band.' He started to collect some empties from the table and, lowering his voice, added, 'It doesn't do to ask too many questions about Red Dieter. And that's for free.'

'Just one more question,' I said. 'What's his usual neck-oil?' The waiter, who had the lemon-sucking look of a warm boy, looked at me pityingly, as if such a question hardly needed to be asked.

'Red drinks nothing but champagne.'

'The lower the life the fancier the taste, eh? Send a bottle over to his table, with my compliments.' I handed him my card and a note. 'And keep the change if there is any.' He gave Inge the once-over as she came back from the ladies' room. I didn't blame him, and he wasn't the only one; there was a man sitting at the bar who also seemed to find her worthy of attention.

We danced again and I watched the waiter deliver the bottle of champagne to Red Dieter's table. I couldn't see him in his seat, but

I saw my card being handed over, and the waiter nodding in my direction.

'Look,' I said, 'there's something that I have to do. I won't be long, but I'll have to leave you for a short while. If there's anything you want just ask the waiter.' She looked at me anxiously as I accompanied her back to the table.

'But where are you going?'

'I have to see someone, someone here. I'll only be a few minutes.'

She smiled at me, and said: 'Please be careful.'

I bent forward and kissed her on the cheek. 'Like I was walking on a tightrope.'

There was a touch of the Fatty Arbuckle about the solitary occupant of the end booth. His fat neck rested on a couple of doughnut-sized rolls pressed tight against the collar of his evening shirt. The face was as red as a boiled ham, and I wondered if this was the explanation behind the nickname. Red Dieter Helfferich's mouth was set at a tough angle like it ought to have been chewing on a big cigar. When he spoke it was a medium-sized brown bear of a voice, growling from the inside of a short cave, and always on the edge of outrage. When he grinned, the mouth was a cross between early-Mayan and High Gothic.

'A private investigator, huh? I never met one.'

'That just goes to show there aren't enough of us around. Mind if I join you?'

He glanced at the label on the bottle. 'This is good champagne. The least I can do is hear you out. Sit down –' He lifted his hand and looked at my card again for effect '– Herr Günther.' He poured us both a glass, and raised his own in a toast. Cowled under brows the size and shape of horizontal Eiffel Towers were eyes that were too wide for my comfort, each revealing a broken pencil of an iris.

'To absent friends,' he said.

I nodded and drank my champagne. 'Like Kurt Mutschmann perhaps.'

'Absent, but not forgotten.' He uttered a brash, gloating laugh and sipped at his drink. 'It would seem that we'd both like to know where he is. Just to put our minds at rest, of course. To stop us worrying about him, eh?'

'Should we be worried?' I asked.

'These are dangerous times for a man in Kurt's line of work. Well, I'm sure I don't have to tell you that. You know all about that, don't you, fleabite, you being an ex-bull.' He nodded appreciatively. 'I've got to hand it to your client, fleabite, it showed real intelligence involving you rather than your former colleagues. All he wants is his bells back, no questions asked. You can get closer. You can negotiate. Perhaps he'll even pay a small reward, eh?'

'You're very well informed.'

'I am if that's all your client wants; and to that extent I'll even help you, if I can.' His face darkened. 'But Mutschmann – he's mine. If your fellow has got any misplaced ideas of revenge, tell him to lay off. That's my beat. It's simply a matter of good business practice.'

'Is that all you want? Just to tidy up the store? You're forgetting the small matter of Von Greis's papers, aren't you? You remember – the ones your boys were so anxious to talk to him about. Like where he'd hidden them or who he'd given them to. What were you planning to do with the papers when you got them? Try a little first-class blackmail? People like my client maybe? Or did you want to put a few politicians in your pocket for a rainy day?'

'You're quite well informed yourself, fleabite. Like I said, your client is a clever man. It's lucky for me he took you into his confidence instead of the police. Lucky for me, lucky for you; because if you were a bull sitting there telling me what you just told me, you'd be on your way to being dead.'

I leaned out of the booth to check that Inge was all right. I could see her shiny black head easily. She was freezing off a uniformed reveller who was wasting his best lines.

'Thanks for the champagne, fleabite. You took a fair-sized chance talking to me. And you haven't had much of a payout on your bet. But at least you're walking away with your stake-money.' He grinned.

'Well this time, the thrill of playing was all I wanted.'

The gangster seemed to find that funny. 'There won't be another. You can depend on it.'

I moved to go, but found him holding my arm. I expected him to threaten me, but instead he said:

'Listen, I'd hate you to think that I'd cheated you. Don't ask me why, but I'm going to do you a favour. Maybe because I like your nerve. Don't turn round, but sitting at the bar is a big, heavy fellow, brown suit, sea-urchin haircut. Take a good look at him when you go back to your table. He's a professional killer. He followed you and the girl in here. You must have stepped on someone's corns. It looks as though you must be this week's rent money. I doubt he'll try anything in here, out of respect for me, you understand. But outside . . . fact is, I don't much like cheap gunmen coming in here. Creates a bad impression.'

'Thanks for the tip. I appreciate it.' I lit a cigarette. 'Is there a back way out of here? I wouldn't want my girl to get hurt.'

He nodded. 'Through the kitchens and down the emergency stairs. At the bottom there's a door that leads onto an alley. It's quiet there. Just a few parked cars. One of them, the light-grey sports, belongs to me.' He pushed a set of keys towards me. 'There's a lighter in the glove-box if you need it. Just leave the keys in the exhaust pipe afterwards, and make sure you don't mark the paintwork.'

I pocketed the keys and stood up. 'It's been nice talking to you, Red. Funny things, fleabites; you don't notice one when you're first bitten, but after a while there's nothing more irritating.'

Red Dieter frowned. 'Get out of here, Günther, before I change my mind about you.'

On the way back to Inge I glanced over at the bar. The man in the brown suit was easy enough to spot, and I recognized him as the man who had been looking at Inge earlier on. At our table Inge was finding it easy, if not particularly pleasant, to resist the negligible charm of a good-looking but rather short SS officer. I hurried Inge to her feet and started to draw her away. The officer held my arm. I looked at his hand and then in his face.

'Slow down, shorty,' I said, looming over his diminutive figure like a frigate coming alongside of a fishing boat. 'Or I'll decorate your lip and it won't be with a Knight's Cross and oak leaves.' I pulled a crumpled five-mark note from out of a pocket and dropped it onto the tabletop.

'I didn't think you were the jealous type,' she said, as I moved her towards the door.

'Get into the lift and go straight down,' I told her. 'When you get outside, go to the car and wait for me. There's a gun under the seat. Better keep it handy, just in case.' I glanced over at the bar where the man was paying for his drink. 'Look, I haven't got time to explain now, but it's got nothing to do with our dashing little friend back there.'

'And where will you be?' she said. I handed her my car keys.

'I'm going out the other way. There's a big man in a brown suit who's trying to kill me. If you see him coming towards the car, go home and phone Kriminalinspektor Bruno Stahlecker at the Alex. Got that?' She nodded.

For a moment I pretended to follow her, and then turned abruptly away, walking quickly through the kitchens and out of the fire door.

Three flights down I heard footsteps behind me in the almost pitch dark of the stairwell. As I scampered blindly down I wondered if I could take him; but then I wasn't armed and he was. What was more, he was a professional. I tripped and fell, scrambling up again even as I hit the landing, reaching out for the banister and wrenching myself down another flight, ignoring the pain in my elbows and forearms, with which I had broken my fall. At the top of the last flight I saw a light underneath a door and jumped. It was further than I thought but I landed well, on all fours. I hit the bar on the door and crashed out into the alley.

There were several cars, all of them parked in a neat row, but it wasn't difficult to spot Red Dieter's grey Bugatti Royale. I unlocked the door and opened the glove-box. Inside there were several small paper twists of white powder and a big revolver with a long barrel, the sort that puts a window in an eight-centimetre-thick mahogany door. I didn't have time to check whether it was loaded, but I didn't think that Red was the sort who kept a gun because he liked playing Cowboys and Indians.

I dropped to the ground and rolled under the running-board of the car parked next to the Bugatti, a big Mercedes convertible. At that moment my pursuer came through the fire door, hugging the well-shadowed wall for cover. I lay completely still, waiting for him to step into the moonlit centre of the alley. Minutes passed, with no sound or movement in the shadows, and after a while I guessed that he had edged along the wall in the cover of the shadow, until he was far enough away from the cars to cross the alley in safety before doubling back. A heel scraped on a cobble-stone behind me, and I held my breath. There was only my thumb which moved, slowly and steadily pulling back the revolver's hammer with a scarcely audible click, and then releasing the safety. Slowly I turned and looked down the length of my body. I saw a pair of shoes standing squarely behind where I was lying, framed neatly by the two rear wheels of the car. The man's feet took him away to my right, behind the Bugatti, and, realizing that he was on to its half-open door, I slid in the opposite direction, to my left, and out from underneath the Mercedes. Staying low, beneath the level of the car's windows, I went to the rear and peered around its enormous trunk. A brown-suited figure crouched beside the rear tyre of the Bugatti in almost exactly the same position as me, but facing in the opposite direction. He was no more than a couple of metres away. I stepped quietly forward, bringing the big revolver up to level it at arm's length at the back of his hat.

'Drop it,' I said. 'Or I'll put a tunnel through your goddamned head, so help me God.' The man froze, but the gun stayed put in his hand.

'No problem, friend,' he said, releasing the handle of his auto-matic, a Mauser, so that it dangled from his forefinger by the trigger guard. 'Mind if I put the catch on it? This little baby's got a hair-trigger.' The voice was slow and cool.

'First pull the brim of your hat down over your face,' I said.

'Then put the catch on like you had your hand in a bag of sand. Remember, at this range I can hardly miss. And it would be too bad to mess up Red's nice paintwork with your brains.' He tugged at his hat until it was well down over his eyes, and after he had seen to the Mauser's safety catch he let the gun drop to the ground where it clattered harmlessly on the cobbles.

'Did Red tell you I was following you?'

'Shut up and turn around,' I told him. 'And keep your hands in the air.' The brown suit turned and then dropped his head back onto his shoulders in an effort to see beyond the brim of his hat.

'You going to kill me?' he said.

'That depends.'

'On what?'

'On whether or not you tell me who's signing your expenses.'

'Maybe we can make a deal.'

'I don't see that you've got much to trade,' I said. 'Either you talk or I fit you with an extra pair of nostrils. It's that simple.'

He grinned. 'You wouldn't shoot me in cold blood,' he said.

'Oh, wouldn't I?' I poked the gun hard against his chin, and then dragged the barrel up across the flesh of his face to screw it under his cheekbone. 'Don't be so sure. You've got me in the mood to use this thing, so you'd better find your tongue now or you'll never find it again.'

'But if I sing, then what? Will you let me go?'

'And have you track me down again? You must think I'm stupid.'

'What can I do to convince you that I wouldn't?'

I stepped away from him, and thought for a moment. 'Swear on your mother's life.'

'I swear on my mother's life,' he said readily enough.

'Fine. So who's your client?'

'You'll let me go if I tell you?'

'Yes.'

'Swear on your mother's life.'

'I swear on my mother's life.'

'All right then,' he said. 'It was a fellow called Haupthändler.'

'How much is he paying you?'

'Three hundred now and –' He didn't finish the sentence. Stepping forward I knocked him cold with one blow of the revolver's butt. It was a cruel blow, delivered with sufficient power to render him insensible for a long time.

'My mother is dead,' I said. Then I picked up his weapon and pocketing both guns I ran back to the car. Inge's eyes widened when she saw the dirt and oil covering my suit. My best suit.

'The lift's not good enough for you? What did you do, jump down?'

'Something like that.' I felt around under the driver's seat for the pair of handcuffs I kept next to my gun. Then I drove the seventy or so metres back to the alley.

The brown suit lay unconscious where I had dropped him. I got out of the car and dragged him over to a wall a short way up the alley, where I manacled him to some iron bars protecting a window. He groaned a little as I moved him, so I knew I hadn't killed him. I went back to the Bugatti and returned Red's gun to the glove-box. At the same time I helped myself to the small paper twists of white powder. I didn't figure that Red Dieter was the type to keep cooking-salt in his glove-box, but I sniffed a pinch anyway. Just enough to recognize cocaine. There weren't many of the twists. Not more than a hundred marks' worth. And it looked like they were for Red's personal use.

I locked the car and slid the keys inside the exhaust, like he'd asked. Then I walked back to the brown suit and tucked a couple of the twists into his top pocket.

'This should interest the boys at the Alex,' I said. Short of killing him in cold blood, I could think of no more certain way of ensuring that he wouldn't finish the job he'd started.

Deals were for people that met you with nothing more deadly in their right hand than a shot of schnaps.

14

The next morning it was drizzling, a warm fine rain like the spray from a garden-sprinkler. I got up feeling sharp and rested, and stood looking out of the windows. I felt as full of life as a pack of sled-dogs.

We got up and breakfasted on a pot of Mexican mixture and a couple of cigarettes. I think I was even whistling as I shaved. She came into the bathroom and stood looking at me. We seemed to be doing a lot of that.

'Considering that someone tried to kill you last night,' she said, 'you're in a remarkably good frame of mind this morning.'

'I always say that there's nothing like a brush with the grim reaper to renew the taste for life.' I smiled at her, and added, 'That, and a good woman.'

'You still haven't told me why he did it.'

'Because he was paid to,' I said.

'By whom? The man in the club?' I wiped my face and looked for missed stubble. There wasn't any, so I put down my razor.

'Do you remember yesterday morning that I telephoned Six's house and asked the butler to give both his master and Haupthändler a message?'

Inge nodded. 'Yes. You said to tell them that you were getting close.'

'I was hoping it would spook Haupthändler into playing his hand. Well, it did. Only rather more quickly than I had expected.'

'So you think he paid that man to kill you?'

'I know he did.' Inge followed me into the bedroom where I put on a shirt, and watched me as I fumbled with the cuff-link on the arm that I had grazed, and that she had bandaged. 'You know,' I said, 'last night posed just as many questions as it answered.

There's no logic to anything, none at all. It's like trying to make up a jigsaw, with not one but two sets of pieces. There were two things stolen from the Pfarrs' safe; some jewels and some papers. But they don't seem to fit together at all. And then there are the pieces which have a picture of a murder on them, which can't be made to fit with those belonging to the theft.'

Inge blinked slowly like a clever cat, and looked at me with the sort of expression that makes a man feel *meschugge* for not having thought of it first. Irritating to watch, but when she spoke I realized just how stupid I really was.

'Perhaps there never was just one jigsaw,' she said. 'Perhaps you've been trying to put one together when there were two all along.' It took a moment or two to let that one sink all the way in, helped at the end with the flat of my hand smacking against my forehead.

'Shit, of course.' Her remark had the force of revelation. It wasn't one crime I was staring in the face, trying to understand. It was two.

We parked on Nollendorfplatz in the shadow of the S-Bahn. Overhead, a train thundered across the bridge with a noise that possessed the whole square. It was loud; but it wasn't enough to disturb the soot from the great factory chimneys of Tempelhof and Neukölln that caked the walls of the buildings which ringed the square, buildings which had seen many better days. Walking westwards into lower-middle-class Schöneberg, we found the five-storey block of apartments on Nollendorfstrasse where Marlene Sahm lived, and climbed up to the fourth floor.

The young man who opened the door to us was in uniform – some special company of SA that I failed to recognize. I asked him if Fräulein Sahm lived there and he replied that she did and that he was her brother.

'And who are you?' I handed him my card and asked if I might speak to his sister. He looked more than a little put out at the intrusion and I wondered if he had been lying when he said that she was his sister. He ran his hand through a large head of straw-coloured hair, and glanced back over his shoulder before standing aside.

'My sister is having a lie-down right now,' he explained. 'But I will ask her if she wishes to speak with you, Herr Günther.' He closed the door behind us, and tried to fix a more welcoming expression to his face. Broad and thick-lipped, the mouth was almost negroid. It smiled broadly now, but quite independently of the two cold blue eyes that flicked between Inge and myself as if they had been following a table-tennis ball.

'Please wait here a moment.'

When he left us alone in the hall, Inge pointed above the sideboard where there hung not one, but three pictures of the Führer. She smiled.

'Doesn't look like they're taking any chances as far as their loyalty is concerned.'

'Didn't you know?' I said. 'They're on special offer at Woolworth's. Buy two dictators, and you get one free.'

Sahm returned, accompanied by his sister Marlene, a big, handsome blonde with a drooping, melancholic nose and an underhung jaw that lent her features a certain modesty. But her neck was so muscular and well-defined as to appear almost inflexible; and her bronzed forearm was that of an archer or a keen tennis player. As she strode into the hallway I caught a glimpse of a well-muscled calf that was the shape of an electric lightbulb. She was built like a rococo fireplace.

They showed us into the modest little sitting room, and, with the exception of the brother, who stood leaning against the doorway and looking generally suspicious of myself and Inge, we all sat down on a cheap brown-leather suite. Behind the glass doors of a tall walnut cabinet were enough trophies for a couple of school prize-givings.

'That's quite an impressive collection you have there,' I said awkwardly, to no one in particular. Sometimes I think my small-talk falls a couple of centimetres short.

'Yes, it is,' said Marlene, with a disingenuous look that might have passed for modesty. Her brother had no such reserve, if that's what it was.

'My sister is an athlete. But for an unfortunate injury she would be running for Germany in the Olympiad.' Inge and I made sympathetic noises. Then Marlene held up my card and read it again.

'How can I help you, Herr Günther?' she said.

I sat back on the sofa and crossed my legs before launching into my patter. 'I've been retained by the Germania Life Assurance Company to make some investigations concerning the death of Paul Pfarr and his wife. Anyone who knew them might help us to find out just what did happen and enable my client to make a speedy settlement.'

'Yes,' said Marlene with a long sigh. 'Yes, of course.'

I waited for her to say something before eventually I prompted her. 'I believe you were Herr Pfarr's secretary at the Ministry of the Interior.'

'Yes, that's right I was.' She was giving no more away than a card-player's eyeshade.

'Do you still work there?'

'Yes,' she said with an indifferent sort of shrug.

I risked a glance at Inge, who merely raised a perfectly pencilled eyebrow at me by way of response. 'Does Herr Pfarr's department investigating corruption in the Reich and the DAF still exist?'

She examined the toes of her shoes for a second, and then looked squarely at me for the first time since I had seen her. 'Who told you about that?' she said. Her tone was even, but I could tell that she was taken aback.

I ignored her question, trying to wrong-foot her. 'Do you think that's why he was killed – because somebody didn't like him snooping and blowing the whistle on people?'

'I – I have no idea why he was killed. Look, here, Herr Günther, I think –'

'Have you ever heard of a man by the name of Gerhard Von Greis? He's a friend of the Prime Minister, as well as being a blackmailer. You know, whatever it was that he passed on to your boss cost him his life.'

'I don't believe that –' she said, and then checked herself. 'I can't answer any of your questions.'

But I kept on going. 'What about Paul's mistress, Eva or Vera, or whatever her name is? Any idea why she might be hiding? Who knows, maybe she's dead too.'

Her eyes quivered like a cup and saucer in an express dining-car. She gasped at me and stood up, her hands clenched tightly at her sides. 'Please,' she said, her eyes starting to well up with tears. The brother shouldered himself away from the doorway, and moved in front of me, much in the manner of a referee stopping a boxing-match.

'That's quite enough, Herr Günther,' he said. 'I see no reason why I should allow you to interrogate my sister in this fashion.'

'Why not?' I asked, standing up. 'I bet she sees it all the time in the Gestapo. And a lot worse besides that.'

'All the same,' he said, 'it seems quite clear to me that she does not wish to answer your questions.'

'Strange,' I said. 'I had come to much the same conclusion.' I took Inge by the arm and moved towards the door. But as we were leaving I turned and added, 'I'm not on anyone's side, and the only thing I'm trying to get is the truth. If you change your mind, please don't hesitate to contact me. I didn't get into this business to throw anyone to the wolves.'

'I never had you down as the chivalrous type,' Inge said when we were outside again.

'Me?' I said. 'Now wait a minute. I went to the Don Quixote School of Detection. I got a B-plus in Noble Sentiment.'

'Too bad you didn't get one for Interrogation,' she said. 'You know, she got really rattled when you suggested that Pfarr's mistress might be dead.'

'Well, what would you have me do – pistol-whip it out of her?'

'I just meant that it was too bad she wouldn't talk, that's all. Maybe she will change her mind.'

'I wouldn't bet on it,' I said. 'If she does work for the Gestapo then it stands to reason that she's not the sort who underlines verses in her Bible. And did you see those muscles? I bet she's their best man with a whip or a rubber truncheon.'

We picked up the car and drove east on Bülowstrasse. I pulled up outside Viktoria Park.

'Come on,' I said. 'Let's walk awhile. I could do with some fresh air.'

Inge sniffed the air suspiciously. It was heavy with the stink of the nearby Schultheis brewery. 'Remind me never to let you buy me any perfume,' she said.

We walked up the hill to the picture market where what passed for Berlin's young artists offered their irreproachably Arcadian work for sale. Inge was predictably contemptuous.

'Have you ever seen such absolute shit?' she snorted. 'From all these pictures of the muscle-bound peasants binding corn and ploughing fields you would think we were living in a story by the Brothers Grimm.'

I nodded slowly. I liked it when she became animated on a subject, even if her voice was too loud and her opinions of the sort that could have landed both of us in a KZ.

Who knows, with a bit more time and patience she might have obliged me to re-examine my own rather matter-of-fact opinion of the value of art. But as it was, I had something else on my mind. I took her by the arm and steered her to a collection of paintings depicting steel-jawed storm-troopers that was arranged in front of an artist who looked anything but the Aryan stereotype. I spoke quietly.

'Ever since leaving the Sahms' apartment, I've had the idea that we were being followed,' I said. She looked around carefully. There were a few people milling around, but none that seemed especially interested in the two of us.

'I doubt you'll spot him,' I said. 'Not if he's good.'

'Do you think it's the Gestapo?' she asked.

'They're not the only pack of dogs in this town,' I said, 'but I guess that's where the smart money is. They're aware of my interest in this case and I wouldn't put it past them to let me do some of their legwork.'

'Well, what are we going to do?' Her face looked anxious, but I grinned back at her.

'You know, I always think that there's nothing that's quite as much fun as trying to shake off a tail. Especially if it might turn out to be the Gestapo.'

15

There were only two items in the morning mail, and both had been delivered by hand. Away from Gruber's inquisitive, hungry-cat stare, I opened them, and found that the smaller of the two envelopes contained a solitary square of cardboard that was a ticket for the day's Olympic track-and-field events. I turned it over, and on the back were written the initials 'M.S.' and '2 o'clock'. The larger envelope bore the seal of the Air Ministry and contained a transcript of calls that Haupthändler and Jeschonnek had made and received on their respective telephones during Saturday, which, apart from the one I had made myself from Haupthändler's apartment, was none. I threw the envelope and its contents into the waste-paper basket and sat down, wondering if Jeschonnek had already bought the necklace, and just what I would do if I was obliged to follow Haupthändler to Tempelhof Airport that same evening. On the other hand, if Haupthändler had already disposed of the necklace I couldn't imagine that he would have been waiting for the Monday evening flight to London just for the hell of it. It seemed more likely that the deal involved foreign currency, and that Jeschonnek had needed the time to raise the money. I made myself a coffee and waited for Inge to arrive.

I glanced out of the window and, seeing that the weather was dull, I smiled as I imagined her glee at the prospect of another shower of rain falling upon the Führer's Olympiad. Except that now I was going to get wet too.

What had she called it? 'The most outrageous confidence-trick in the history of modern times.' I was searching in the cupboard for my old rubberized raincoat when she came through the door.

'God, I need a cigarette,' she said, tossing her handbag onto a chair and helping herself from the box on my desk. With some amusement she looked at my old coat and added, 'Are you planning to wear that thing?'

'Yes. Fräulein Muscles came through after all. There was a ticket for today's games in the mail. She wants me to meet her in the stadium at two.'

Inge looked out of the window. 'You're right,' she laughed, 'you'll need the coat. It's going to come down by the bucket.' She sat down and put her feet up on my desk. 'Well, I'll just stay here on my own, and mind the shop.'

'I'll be back by four o'clock at the latest,' I said. 'Then we have to go to the airport.'

She frowned. 'Oh yes, I was forgetting. Haupthändler is planning to fly to London tonight. Forgive me if I sound naive, but exactly what are you going to do when you get there? Just walk up to him and whoever it is he's taking with him and ask them how much they got for the necklace? Maybe they'll just open their suitcases and let you take a look at all their cash, right there in the middle of Tempelhof.'

'Nothing in real life is ever all that tidy. There never are neat little clues that enable you to apprehend the crook with minutes to spare.'

'You sound almost sad about it,' she said.

'I had one ace in the hole which I thought would make things a bit easier.'

'And the hole fell in, is that it?'

'Something like that.'

The sound of footsteps in the outer office made me stop. There was a knock at the door, and a motorcyclist, a corporal in the National Socialist Flying Corps, came in bearing a large buff-coloured envelope of the same sort as the one I had consigned earlier to the waste-paper basket. The corporal clicked his heels and asked me if I was Herr Bernhard Günther. I said that I was, took the envelope from the corporal's gauntleted hands and signed his receipt slip, after which he gave the Hitler Salute and walked smartly out again.

I opened the Air Ministry envelope. It contained several type-written pages that made up the transcript of calls Jeschonnek and Haupthändler had made the previous day. Of the two, Jeschonnek, the diamond dealer, had been the busier, speaking to various people regarding the illegal purchase of a large quantity of American dollars and British sterling.

'Bulls-eye,' I said, reading the transcript of the last of Jeschonnek's calls. This had been to Haupthändler, and of course it also showed up in the transcript of the other man's calls. It was the piece of evidence I had been hoping for: the evidence that turned theory into fact, establishing a definite link between Six's private secretary and the diamond dealer. Better than that, they discussed the time and place for a meeting.

'Well?' said Inge, unable to restrain her curiosity a moment longer.

I grinned at her. 'My ace in the hole. Someone just dug it out. There's a meet arranged between Haupthändler and Jeschonnek at an address in Grünewald tonight at five. Jeschonnek's going to be carrying a whole bagful of foreign currency.'

'That's a hell of an informant you have there,' she said, frowning. 'Who is it? Hanussen the Clairvoyant?'

'My man is more of an impresario,' I said. 'He books the turns, and this time, anyway, I get to watch the show.'

'And he just happens to have a few friendly storm-troopers on the staff to show you to the right seat, is that it?'

'You won't like it.'

'If I start to scowl it will be heartburn, all right?'

I lit a cigarette. Mentally I tossed a coin and lost. I would tell it to her straight. 'You remember the dead man in the service-lift?'

'Like I just found out I had leprosy,' she said, shuddering visibly.

'Hermann Goering hired me to try and find him.' I paused, waiting for her comment, and then shrugged under her bemused stare. 'That's it,' I said. 'He agreed to put a tap on a couple of telephones – Jeschonnek's and Haupthändler's.' I picked up the transcript and waved it in front of her face. 'And this is the result.

Amongst other things it means that I can now afford to tell his people where to find Von Greis.'

Inge said nothing. I took a long angry drag at my cigarette and then stubbed it out like I was hammering a lectern. 'Let me tell you something: you don't turn him down, not if you want to finish your cigarette with both lips.'

'No, I suppose not.'

'Believe me, he's not a client that I would have chosen. His idea of a retainer is a thug with a machine-pistol.'

'But why didn't you tell me about it, Bernie?'

'When Goering takes someone like me into his confidence, the table stakes are high. I thought it was safer for you that you didn't know. But now, well, I can't very well avoid it, can I?' Once again I brandished the transcript at her. Inge shook her head.

'Of course you couldn't refuse him. I didn't mean to appear awkward, it's just that I was, well, a bit surprised. And thank you for wanting to protect me, Bernie. I'm just glad that you can tell someone about that poor man.'

'I'll do it right now,' I said.

Rienacker sounded tired and irritable when I called him.

'I hope you've got something, pushbelly,' he said, 'because Fat Hermann's patience is worn thinner than the jam in a Jewish baker's sponge-cake. So if this is just a social call then I'm liable to come and visit you with some dog-shit on my shoes.'

'What's the matter with you, Rienacker?' I said. 'You having to share a slab in the morgue or something?'

'Cut the cabbage, Günther, and get on with it.'

'All right, keep your ears stiff. I just found your boy, and he's squeezed his last orange.'

'Dead?'

'Like Atlantis. You'll find him piloting a service-lift in a deserted hotel on Chamissoplatz. Just follow your nose.'

'And the papers?'

'There's a lot of burnt ash in the incinerator, but that's about all.'

'Any ideas on who killed him?'

'Sorry,' I said, 'but that's your job. All I had to do was find our aristocratic friend, and that's as far as it goes. Tell your boss he'll be receiving my account in the post.'

'Thanks a lot, Günther,' said Rienacker, sounding less than pleased. 'You've got –' I cut across him with a curt goodbye, and hung up.

I left Inge the keys to the car, telling her to meet me in the street outside Haupthändler's beach house at 4.30 that afternoon. I was intending to take the special S-Bahn to the Reich Sports Field via the Zoo Station; but first, and so that I could be sure of not being followed, I chose a particularly circuitous route to get to the station. I walked quickly up Königstrasse and caught a number two tram to Spittel Market where I strolled twice around the Spindler Brunnen Fountain before getting onto the U-Bahn. I rode one stop to Friedrichstrasse, where I left the U-Bahn and returned once more to street level. During business hours Friedrichstrasse has the densest traffic in Berlin, when the air tastes like pencil shavings. Dodging umbrellas and Americans standing huddled over their Baedekers, and narrowly missing being run over by a Rudesdorfer Peppermint van, I crossed Tauberstrasse and Jägerstrasse, passing the Kaiser Hotel and the head office of the Six Steel Works. Then, continuing up towards Unter den Linden, I squeezed between some traffic on Französische Strasse and, on the corner of Behrenstrasse, ducked into the Kaiser Gallery. This is an arcade of expensive shops of the sort that are much patronized by tourists and it leads onto Unter den Linden at a spot next to the Hotel Westminster, where many of them stay. If you are on foot it has always been a good place to shake a tail for good. Emerging on to Unter den Linden, I crossed over the road and rode a cab to the Zoo Station, where I caught the special train to the Reich Sports Field.

The two-storey-high stadium looked smaller than I had expected, and I wondered how all the people milling around its perimeter would ever fit in. It was only after I had gone in that I realized that it was actually bigger on the inside than on the outside, and this by virtue of an arena that was several metres below ground level.

I took my seat, which was close to the edge of the cinder track and next to a matronly woman who smiled and nodded politely as I sat down. The seat to my right, which I imagined was to be occupied by Marlene Sahm, was for the moment empty, although it was already past two o'clock. Just as I was looking at my watch the sky released the heaviest shower of the day, and I was only too glad to share the matron's umbrella. It was to be her good deed of the day. She pointed to the west side of the stadium and handed me a small pair of binoculars.

'That is where the Führer will be sitting,' she said. I thanked her, and although I wasn't in the least bit interested, I scanned a dais that was populated with several men in frock-coats, and the ubiquitous complement of SS officers, all of them getting as wet as I was. Inge would be pleased, I thought. Of the Führer himself, there was no sign.

'Yesterday he didn't come until almost five o'clock,' explained the matron. 'Although with weather as atrocious as this, he could be forgiven for not coming at all.' She nodded down at my empty lap. 'You don't have a programme. Would you care to know the order of events?' I said that I would, but found to my embarrassment that she intended not to lend me her programme but to read it aloud.

'The first events on the track this afternoon are the heats of the 400-metre hurdles. Then we have the semi-finals and final of the 100-metres. If you'll allow me to say so, I don't think the German has a chance against the American negro, Owens. I saw him running yesterday and he was like a gazelle.' I was just about to start out on some unpatriotic remark about the so-called Master Race when Marlene Sahm sat down next to me, so probably saving me from my own potentially treasonable mouth.

'Thank you for coming, Herr Günther. And I'm sorry about yesterday. It was rude of me. You were only trying to help, were you not?'

'Certainly.'

'Last night I couldn't sleep for thinking about what you said about –' and here she hesitated for a moment. 'About Eva.'

'Paul Pfarr's mistress?' She nodded. 'Is she a friend of yours?'

'Not close friends, you understand, but friends, yes. And so early this morning I decided to put my trust in you. I asked you to meet me here because I'm sure I'm being watched. That's why I'm late too. I had to make sure I gave them the slip.'

'The Gestapo?'

'Well, I certainly don't mean the International Olympic Committee, Herr Günther.' I smiled at that, and so did she.

'No, of course not,' I said, quietly appreciating the way in which modesty giving way to impatience made her the more attractive. Beneath the terracotta-coloured raincoat she was unbuttoning at the neck, she wore a dress of dark blue cotton, with a neckline that allowed me a view of the first few centimetres of a deep and well-sunburnt cleavage. She started to fumble inside her capacious brown-leather handbag.

'So then,' she said nervously. 'About Paul. After his death I had to answer a great many questions, you know.'

'What about?' It was a stupid question, but she didn't say so.

'Everything. I think that at one stage they even got round to suggesting that I might be his mistress.' From out of the bag she produced a dark-green desk diary and handed it to me. 'But this I kept back. It's Paul's desk diary, or, rather, the one he kept himself, his private one, and not the official one that I kept for him: the one that I gave to the Gestapo.' I turned the diary over in my hands, not presuming to open it. Six, and now Marlene, it was odd the way people held things back from the police. Or maybe it wasn't. It all depended on how well you knew the police.

'Why?' I said.

'To protect Eva.'

'Then why didn't you simply destroy it? Safer for her and for you too I would have thought.'

She frowned as she struggled to explain something she perhaps only half understood herself. 'I suppose I thought that in the proper hands, there might be something in it that would identify the murderer.'

'And what if it should turn out that your friend Eva had something to do with it?'

Her eyes flashed and she spoke angrily. 'I don't believe it for a second,' she said. 'She wasn't capable of harming anyone.'

Pursing my lips, I nodded circumspectly. 'Tell me about her.'

'All in good time, Herr Günther,' she said, her mouth becoming compressed. I didn't think Marlene Sahm was the type ever to be carried away by her passion or her tastes, and I wondered whether the Gestapo preferred to recruit this kind of woman, or simply affected them that way.

'First of all, I'd like to make something clear to you.'

'Be my guest.'

'After Paul's death I myself made a few discreet inquiries as to Eva's whereabouts, but without success. But I shall come to that too. Before I tell you anything I want your word that if you manage to find her you will try to persuade her to give herself up. If she is arrested by the Gestapo it will go very badly for her. This isn't a favour I'm asking, you understand. This is my price for providing you with the information to help your own investigation.'

'You have my word. I'll give her every chance I can. But I have to tell you: right now it looks as though she is in it up to her hatband. I believe that she's planning to go abroad tonight, so you'd better start talking. There's not much time.'

For a moment Marlene chewed her lip thoughtfully, her eyes gazing emptily at the hurdlers as they came up to the starting line. She remained oblivious of the buzz of excitement in the crowd that gave way to silence as the starter raised his pistol. As he fired she began to tell me what she knew.

'Well, for a start there's her name: it's not Eva. That was Paul's name for her. He was always doing that, giving people new names. He liked Aryan names, like Siegfried, and Brünhilde. Eva's real name was Hannah, Hannah Roedl, but Paul said that Hannah was a Jewish name, and that he would always call her Eva.'

The crowd gave a great roar as the American won the first heat of the hurdles.

'Paul was unhappy with his wife, but he never told me why. He and I were good friends, and he confided in me a great deal, but I never heard him speak about his wife. One night he took me to a gaming club, and it was there that I ran across Eva. She was working there as a croupier. I hadn't seen her in months. We first met working for the Revenue. She was very good with figures. I suppose that's why she became a croupier in the first place. Twice the pay, and the chance to meet some interesting people.'

I raised my eyebrows at that one: I, for one, have never found the people who gamble in casinos to be anything less than dull; but I said nothing, not wishing to cut her thread.

'Anyway, I introduced her to Paul, and you could see they were attracted. Paul was a handsome man, and Eva was just as good-looking, a real beauty. A month later I met her again and she told me that she and Paul were having an affair. At first I was shocked; and then I thought it was really none of my business. For a while – maybe as long as six months – they were seeing quite a lot of each other. And then Paul was killed. The diary should provide you with dates and all that sort of thing.'

I opened the diary and turned to the date of Paul's murder. I read the entries written on the page.

'According to this he had an appointment with her on the night of his death.' Marlene said nothing. I started to turn back the pages. 'And here's another name I recognize,' I said. 'Gerhard Von Greis. What do you know about him?' I lit a cigarette and added: 'It's time you told me all about your little department in the Gestapo, don't you think?'

'Paul's department. He was so proud of it, you know.' She sighed profoundly. 'A man of great integrity.'

'Sure,' I said. 'All the time he was with this other woman, what he really wanted was to be back home with the wife.'

'In a funny way that's absolutely true, Herr Günther. That's exactly what he wanted. I don't think he ever stopped loving Grete. But for some reason he started hating her as well.'

I shrugged. 'Well, it takes all sorts. Maybe he just liked to wag his tail.' She stayed silent for a few minutes after that one, and they ran the next heat of the hurdles. Much to the delight of the crowd, the German runner, Nottbruch, won the race. The matron got very excited at that, standing up in her seat and waving her programme.

Marlene rummaged in her bag again, and took out an envelope.

'This is a copy of a letter originally empowering Paul to set up his department,' she said, handing it to me. 'I thought you might like to see it. It helps to put things in perspective, to explain why Paul did what he did.'

I read the letter. It went as follows:

The Reichsführer SS and	Berlin NW7
Chief of the German Police in	6 November 1935
the Reich Ministry of the	Unter den Linden, 74
Interior	Local Tel. 120 034
o–KdS g2(o/R V) No. 22 11/35	Trunk Call 120 037

Express letter to Hauptsturmführer Doktor Paul Pfarr

I write to you on a very serious matter. I mean corruption amongst the servants of the Reich. One principle must apply: public servants must be honest, decent, loyal and comradely to members of our own blood. Those individuals who offend against this principle – who take so much as one mark – will be punished without mercy. I shall not stand idly by and watch the rot develop.

As you know, I have already taken measures to root out corruption within the ranks of the SS, and a number of dishonest men have been eliminated accordingly. It is the will of the Führer that you should be empowered to investigate and root out corruption in the German Labour Front, where fraud is endemic. To this end you are promoted to the rank of Hauptsturmführer, reporting directly to me.

Wherever corruption forms, we shall burn it out. And at the end of the day, we shall say that we performed this task in love of our people.

Heil Hitler!
(signed)
Heinrich Himmler

'Paul was very diligent,' Marlene said. 'Arrests were made and the guilty punished.'

' "Eliminated",' I said, quoting the Reichsführer.

Marlene's voice hardened. 'They were enemies of the Reich,' she said.

'Yes, of course.' I waited for her to continue, and seeing her rather unsure of me I added, 'They had to be punished. I'm not disagreeing with you. Please go on.'

Marlene nodded. 'Finally, he turned his attention to the Steel Workers Union, and quite early on he became aware of certain rumours regarding his own father-in-law, Hermann Six. In the beginning he made light of it. And then, almost overnight, he was determined to destroy him. After a while, it was nothing short of an obsession.'

'When was this?'

'I can't remember the date. But I do remember that it was about the time that he started working late, and not taking telephone calls from his wife. And it wasn't long after that he started to see Eva.'

'And exactly how was Daddy Six misbehaving?'

'Corrupt DAF officials had deposited the Steel Workers Union and Welfare Fund in Six's bank –'

'You mean, he owns a bank as well?'

'A major shareholding, in the Deutsches Kommerz. In return, Six saw to it that these same officials were given cheap personal loans.'

'What did Six get out of it?'

'By paying low interest on the deposit to the detriment of the workers, the bank was able to improve the books.'

'Nice and tidy then,' I said.

'That's just the half of it,' she said with an outraged sort of chuckle. 'Paul also suspected that his father-in-law was skimming the union's funds. And that he was churning the union's investments.'

'Churning,' I said. 'What's that?'

'Repeatedly selling stocks and shares and buying others so that each time you can claim the legal percentages, The commission if you like. That would have been split between the bank and the union officials. But trying to prove it was a different story,' she said. 'Paul tried to get a tap on Six's telephone, but whoever it is that arranges these things refused. Paul said that somebody else was already tapping his phone and that they weren't about to share. So Paul looked for another way to get to him. He discovered that the Prime Minister had a confidential agent who had certain information that was compromising to Six, and for that matter to many others. His name was Gerhard Von Greis. In Six's case, Goering was using this information to make him toe the economic line. Anyway, Paul arranged to meet Von Greis and offered him a lot of money to let him take a look at what he had on Six. But Von Greis refused. Paul said he was afraid.'

She looked around as the crowd, anticipating the semi-final of the 100-metres, grew more excited. With the hurdles cleared off the track, there were now several sprinters warming up, including the man the crowd had come to see: Jesse Owens. For a moment, her attention was devoted entirely to the negro athlete.

'Isn't he superb?' she said. 'Owens I mean. In a class of his own.'

'But Paul did get hold of the papers, didn't he?'

She nodded. 'Paul was very determined,' she said, distractedly. 'At such times, he could be quite ruthless, you know.'

'I don't doubt it.'

'There is a department in the Gestapo at Prinz Albrecht Strasse, which deals with associations, clubs and the DAF. Paul persuaded them to issue a "red tab" on Von Greis, so that he could be arrested immediately. Not only that, but they saw to it that Von Greis was picked up by Alarm Command, and taken to Gestapo headquarters.'

'What is Alarm Command exactly?' I said.

'Killers.' She shook her head. 'You wouldn't want to fall into their hands. Their brief was to scare Von Greis: to scare him badly enough to convince him that Himmler was more powerful than Goering, that he should fear the Gestapo before he should fear the Prime Minister. After all, hadn't Himmler taken control of the Gestapo away from Goering in the first place? And then there was the case of Goering's former chief of Gestapo, Diels, being sold down the river by his former master. They said all of these things to Von Greis. They told him that the same would happen to him, and that his only chance was to cooperate, otherwise he would find himself facing the displeasure of the Reichsführer SS. That would mean a KZ for sure. Of course, Von Greis was convinced. What man in their hands would not have been? He gave Paul everything he had. Paul took possession of a number of documents which he spent several evenings examining at home. And then he was killed.'

'And the documents were stolen.'

'Yes.'

'Do you know something of what was in these documents?'

'Not in any detail. I never saw them myself. I only know what he told me. He said that they proved beyond all shadow of a doubt, that Six was in bed with organized crime.'

At the gun Jesse Owens was away to a good start, and by the first thirty metres he was powering fluently into a clear lead. In the seat next to me the matron was on her feet again. She had been wrong, I thought, to describe Owens as a gazelle. Watching the tall, graceful negro accelerate down the track, making a mockery of crackpot theories of Aryan superiority, I thought that Owens was nothing so much as a Man, for whom other men were simply a painful embarrassment. To run like that was the meaning of the earth, and if ever there was a master-race it was certainly not going to exclude someone like Jesse Owens. His victory drew a tremendous cheer from the German crowd, and I found it comforting that the only race they were shouting about was the one they had just seen.

Perhaps, I thought, Germany did not want to go to war after all. I looked towards that part of the stadium that was reserved for Hitler and other senior Party officials, to see if they were present to witness the depth of popular sentiment being demonstrated on behalf of the black American. But of the leaders of the Third Reich there was still no sign.

I thanked Marlene for coming, and then left the stadium. On the taxi-ride south towards the lakes, I spared a thought for poor Gerhard Von Greis. Picked up and terrified by the Gestapo, only to be released and almost immediately picked up, tortured and killed by Red Dieter's men. Now that's what I call unlucky.

We crossed Wannsee Bridge, and drove along the coast. A black sign at the head of the beach said, 'No Jews Here', which prompted the taxi-driver to an observation. 'That's a fucking laugh, eh? "No Jews Here." There's nobody here. Not with weather like this there isn't.' He uttered a derisive laugh for his own benefit.

Opposite the Swedish Pavilion restaurant a few die-hards still entertained hopes of the weather improving. The taxi-driver continued to pour scorn on them and the German weather as he turned into Koblanck Strasse, and then down Lindenstrasse. I told him to pull up on the corner of Hugo-Vogel Strasse.

It was a quiet, well-ordered and leafy suburb consisting of medium to large-sized houses, with neat front lawns and well-clipped hedges. I spotted my car parked on the pavement, but could see no sign of Inge. I looked around anxiously for her while I waited for my change. Feeling something was wrong, I managed to over-tip the driver, who responded by asking me if I wanted him to wait. I shook my head, and then stepped back as he roared off down the road. I walked down towards my car, which was parked about thirty metres down the road from Haupthändler's address. I checked the door. It wasn't locked, so I sat inside and waited a while, hoping that she might come back. I put the desk diary that Marlene Sahm had given me inside the glove-box, and then felt around under the seat for the gun I kept there. Putting it into my coat pocket, I got out of the car.

The address I had was a dirty-brown, two-storey affair with a run-down, dilapidated look about it. The paint was peeling from the closed shutters, and there was a 'For Sale' sign in the garden. The place looked as though it hadn't been occupied in a long time. Just the kind of place you'd choose to hide out in. A patchy lawn surrounded the house, and a short wall separated it from the pavement, on which a bright blue Adler was parked, facing downhill. I stepped over the wall, and went round the side, stepping carefully over a rusting lawnmower and ducking under a tree. Near the back corner of the house I took out the Walther and pulled back the slide to load the chamber and cock the weapon.

Bent almost double, I crept along beneath the level of the window, to the back door, which was slightly ajar. From somewhere inside the bungalow I could hear the sound of muffled voices. I pushed the door open with the muzzle of my gun and my eyes fell upon a trail of blood on the kitchen floor. I walked quietly inside, my stomach falling uncomfortably away beneath me like a coin dropped down a well, worried that Inge might have decided to take a look around on her own and been hurt, or worse. I took a deep breath and pressed the cold steel of the automatic against my cheek. The chill of it ran through the whole of my face, down the nape of my neck and into my soul. I bent down in front of the kitchen door to look through the keyhole. On the other side of the door was an empty, uncarpeted hallway and several closed doors. I turned the handle.

The voices were coming from a room at the front of the house and were clear enough for me to identify them as belonging to Haupthändler and Jeschonnek. After a couple of minutes there was a woman's voice too, and for a moment I thought it was Inge's, until I heard this woman laugh. Now that I was more impatient to know what had become of Inge than I was to recover Six's stolen diamonds and collect the reward, I decided that it was time I confronted the three of them. I'd heard enough to indicate that they weren't expecting any trouble, but as I came through the door,

I fired a shot over their heads in case they were in the mood to try something.

'Stay exactly where you are,' I said, feeling that I'd given them plenty of warning, and thinking that only a fool would pull a gun now. Gert Jeschonnek was just such a fool. It's difficult at the best of times to hit a moving target, especially one that's shooting back. My first concern was to stop him, and I wasn't particular how I did it. As it turned out, I stopped him dead. I could have wished not to have hit him in the head, only I wasn't given the opportunity. Having succeeded in killing one man, I now had the other to worry about, because by this time Haupthändler was on me, and wrestling for my gun. As we fell to the floor, he yelled to the girl who was standing lamely by the fireplace to get the gun. He meant the one which had fallen from Jeschonnek's hand when I blew his brains out, but for a moment the girl wasn't sure which gun it was that she was supposed to go for, mine or the one on the floor. She hesitated long enough for her lover to repeat himself, and in the same instant I broke free of his grasp and whipped the Walther across his face. It was a powerful backhand that had the follow-through of a match-winning tennis stroke, and it sent him sprawling, unconscious, against the wall. I turned to see the girl picking up Jeschonnek's gun. It was no time for chivalry, but then I didn't want to shoot her either. Instead I stepped smartly forward, and socked her on the jaw.

With Jeschonnek's gun safely in my coat pocket, I bent down to take a look at him. You didn't have to be an undertaker to see that he was dead. There are neater ways of cleaning a man's ears than a 9 mm bullet. I fumbled a cigarette into my dry mouth and sat down at the table to wait for Haupthändler and the girl to come round. I pulled the smoke through clenched teeth, kippering my lungs, and hardly exhaling at all, except in small nervous puffs. I felt like someone was playing the guitar with my insides.

The room was barely furnished, with only a threadbare sofa, a table and a couple of chairs. On the table, lying on a square of felt, was Six's necklace. I threw the cigarette away, and tugged the diamonds towards me. The stones, clacking together like a handful of marbles, felt cold and heavy in my hand. It was hard to imagine a woman wearing them: they looked about as comfortable as a canteen of cutlery. Next to the table was a briefcase. I picked it up and looked inside. It was full of money – dollars and sterling as I had expected – and two fake passports in the names of a Herr and Frau Rolf Teichmüller, the names that I had seen on the air-tickets in Haupthändler's apartment. They were good fakes, but not hard to obtain provided you knew someone at the passport office and were prepared to pay some big expenses. I hadn't thought of it before, but now it seemed that with all the Jews who had been coming to Jeschonnek to finance their escapes from Germany, a fake-passport service would have been a logical and highly profitable sideline.

The girl moaned and sat up. Cradling her jaw and sobbing quietly, she went to help Haupthändler as he himself twisted over on to his side. She held him by the shoulders as he wiped his bloody nose and mouth. I flicked her new passport open. I don't know that you could have described her, as Marlene Sahm had done, as a beauty, but certainly she was good-looking, in a well-bred, intelligent sort of way – not at all the cheap party-girl I'd had in mind when I'd been told that she was a croupier.

'I'm sorry I had to sock you, Frau Teichmüller,' I said. 'Or Hannah, or Eva, or whatever it is you or somebody else is calling you at the moment.'

She glared at me with more than enough loathing to dry her eyes, and mine besides. 'You're not so smart,' she said. 'I can't see why these two idiots thought it was necessary to have you put out of the way.'

'Right now I should have thought it was obvious.'

Haupthändler spat on the floor, and said, 'So what happens now?'

I shrugged. 'That depends. Maybe we can figure out a story: crime of passion, or something like that. I've got friends down at the Alex. Perhaps I can get you a deal, but first you've got to help me. There was a woman working with me – tall, brown hair, well-built, and wearing a black coat. Now there's some blood on the kitchen floor that's got me worried about her, especially as she seems to be missing. I don't suppose you would know anything about that, would you?'

Eva snorted with laughter. 'Go to hell,' said Haupthändler.

'On the other hand,' I said, deciding to scare them a little. 'Pre-meditated murder, well, that's a capital crime. Almost certain when there's a lot of money involved. I saw a man beheaded once – at Lake Ploetzen Prison. Goelpl, the state executioner, even wears white gloves and a tail-coat to do the job. That's rather a nice touch, don't you think?'

'Drop the gun, if you don't mind, Herr Günther.' The voice in the doorway was patient, but patronizing, as if addressing a naughty child. But I did as I was told. I knew better than to argue with a machine pistol, and a brief glance at his boxing-glove of a face told me that he wouldn't hesitate to kill me if I so much as told a bad joke. As he came into the room, two other men, both carrying lighters, followed.

'Come on,' said the man with the machine pistol. 'On your feet, you two.' Eva helped Haupthändler to stand. 'And face the wall. You too, Günther.'

The wallpaper was cheap flock. A bit too dark and sombre for my taste. I stared hard at it for several minutes while I waited to be searched.

'If you know who I am, then you know I'm a private investigator. These two are wanted for murder.'

I didn't see the India Rubber so much as hear it sweep through the air towards my head. In the split second before I hit the floor and lost consciousness I told myself that I was getting tired of being knocked out.

16

Glockenspiel and big bass drum. What was that tune again? *Little Anna of Tharau is the One I Love*? No, not so much a tune as a number 51 tram to the Schönhauser Allee Depot. The bell clanged and the car shook as we raced through Schillerstrasse, Pankow, Breite Strasse. The giant Olympic bell in the great clock-tower tolling to the opening and closing of the Games. Herr Starter Miller's pistol, and the crowd yelling as Joe Louis sprinted up towards me and then put me on the deck for the second time in the round. A four-engined Junkers monoplane roaring through the night skies to Croydon taking my scrambled brains away with it. I heard myself say:

'Just drop me off at Lake Ploetzen.'

My head throbbed like a hot Dobermann. I tried raising it from the floor of the car, and found that my hands were handcuffed behind me; but the sudden, violent pain in my head made me oblivious to anything else but not moving my head again . . .

. . . a hundred thousand jackboots goose-stepping their way up Unter den Linden, with a man pointing a microphone down at them to pick up the awe-inspiring sound of an army crunching like an enormous great horse. An air-raid alarm. A barrage being laid down on the enemy trenches to cover the advance. Just as we were going over the top a big one exploded right above our heads, and blew us all off our feet. Cowering in a shell-hole full of incinerated frogs, with my head inside a grand piano, my ears ringing as the hammers hit the strings, I waited for the sound of battle to end . . .

Groggy, I felt myself being pulled out of the car, and then half carried, half dragged into a building. The handcuffs were removed, and I was sat down on a chair and held there so as to stop me falling off it. A man smelling of carbolic and wearing a uniform went through my pockets. As he pulled their linings inside out, I felt the collar of my jacket sticky against my neck, and when I touched it I found that it was blood from where I had been sapped. After that someone took a quick look at my head and said that I was fit enough to answer a few questions, although he might just as well have said I was ready to putt the shot. They got me a coffee and a cigarette.

'Do you know where you are?' I had to stop myself from shaking my head before mumbling that I didn't.

'You're at the Königs Weg Kripo Stelle, in the Grunewald.' I sipped some of my coffee and nodded slowly.

'I am Kriminalinspektor Hingsen,' said the man. 'And this is Wachmeister Wentz.' He jerked his head at the uniformed man standing beside him, the one who smelt of carbolic. 'Perhaps you'd care to tell us what happened.'

'If your lot hadn't hit me so hard I might find it easier to remember,' I heard myself croak.

The Inspektor glanced at the sergeant, who shrugged blankly. 'We didn't hit you,' he said.

'What's that?'

'I said, we didn't hit you.'

Gingerly, I touched the back of my head, and then inspected the dried blood on my fingers' ends. 'I suppose I did this when I was brushing my hair, is that it?'

'You tell us,' said the Inspektor. I heard myself sigh.

'What is going on here? I don't understand. You've seen my ID, haven't you?'

'Yes,' said the Inspektor. 'Look, why don't you start at the beginning? Assume we know absolutely nothing.'

I resisted the rather obvious temptation, and started to explain as best I was able. 'I'm working on a case,' I said. 'Haupthändler and the girl are wanted for murder —'

'Now wait a minute,' he said. 'Who's Haupthändler?'

I felt myself frown and tried harder to concentrate. 'No, I remember now. They're calling themselves the Teichmüllers now.

Haupthändler and Eva had two new passports, which Jeschonnek organized.'

The Inspektor rocked on his heels at that. 'Now we're getting somewhere. Gert Jeschonnek. The body we found, right?' He turned to his sergeant who produced my Walther PPK at the end of a piece of string from out of a paper bag.

'Is this your gun, Herr Günther?' said the sergeant.

'Yes, yes,' I said tiredly. 'It's all right, I killed him. It was self-defence. He was going for his gun. He was there to make a deal with Haupthändler. Or Teichmüller, as he's now calling himself.' Once again I saw the Inspektor and the sergeant exchange that look. I was starting to get worried.

'Tell us about this Herr Teichmüller,' said the sergeant.

'Haupthändler,' I said correcting him angrily. 'You have got him, haven't you?' The Inspektor pursed his lips and shook his head. 'The girl, Eva, what about her?' He folded his arms and looked at me squarely.

'Now look, Günther. Don't give us the cold cabbage. A neighbour reported hearing a shot. We found you unconscious, a dead body, and two pistols, each of them fired, and a lot of foreign currency. No Teichmüllers, no Haupthändler, no Eva.'

'No diamonds?' He shook his head.

The Inspektor, a fat, greasy, weary-looking man with tobacco-stained teeth, sat down opposite me and offered me another cigarette. He took one himself and lit us both in silence. When he spoke again his voice sounded almost friendly.

'You used to be a bull, didn't you?' I nodded, painfully. 'I thought I recognized the name. You were quite a good one too, as I recall.'

'Thanks,' I said.

'So I don't have to tell you of all people how this looks from my side of the charge-sheet.'

'Bad, eh?'

'Worse than bad.' The Inspektor rolled his cigarette between his lips for a moment, and winced as the smoke stung his eyeballs. 'Want me to call you a lawyer?'

'Thanks, no. But as long as you're in the mood to do an ex-bull a favour, there is one thing you could do. I've got an assistant, Inge Lorenz. Perhaps you would telephone her and let her know I'm being held.' He gave me a pencil and paper and I wrote down three phone numbers. The Inspektor seemed a decent sort of fellow, and I wanted to tell him that Inge had gone missing after driving my car to Wannsee. But that would have meant them searching my car and finding Marlene Sahm's diary, which would undoubtedly have incriminated her. Maybe Inge had been taken ill, and had caught a cab somewhere, knowing that I'd be along to pick up the car. Maybe.

'What about friends on the force? Somebody up at the Alex perhaps.'

'Bruno Stahlecker,' I said. 'He can vouch that I'm kind to children and stray dogs, but that's about it.'

'Too bad.' I thought for a moment. About the only thing that I could do was call the two Gestapo thugs who had ransacked my office, and throw them what I'd learned. It was a fair bet they'd be very unhappy with me, and I guessed that calling them would as likely win me an all-expenses trip to a KZ, as letting the local Inspektor charge me with Gert Jeschonnek's murder.

I'm not a gambling man, but they were the only cards I had.

Kriminalkommissar Jost drew thoughtfully on his pipe.

'It's an interesting theory,' he said. Dietz stopped playing with his moustache for long enough to snort contemptuously. Jost looked at his Inspektor for a moment, and then at me. 'But as you can see, my colleague finds it somewhat improbable.'

'That's putting it lightly, mulemouth,' muttered Dietz. Since scaring my secretary and smashing my last good bottle he seemed to have got uglier.

Jost was a tall, ascetic-looking man, with a face that wore a stag's permanently startled expression, and a scrawny neck that stuck out of his shirt collar like a tortoise in a rented shell. He allowed himself a little razor-blade of a smile. He was about to put his subordinate very firmly in his place.

'But then theory is not his strong point,' he said. 'He's a man of action, aren't you, Dietz?' Dietz glowered back, and the Kommissar's smile widened a fraction. Then he removed his glasses and began to clean them in such a way as might serve to remind anyone else in the interrogation-room that he regarded his own intellectualism as something superior to a vitality that was merely physical. Replacing his glasses he removed his pipe and gave way to a yawn that bordered on the effete.

'That's not to say that men of action do not have a place in Sipo. But after all is said and done, it is the men of thought who must make the decisions. Why do you suppose that the Germania Life Assurance Company did not see fit to inform us of the existence of this necklace?' The way he moved imperceptibly on to his question almost took me unawares.

'Perhaps nobody asked them,' I said hopefully. There was a long silence.

'But the place was gutted,' said Dietz in an anxious sort of way. 'Normally the insurance company would have informed us.'

'Why should they?' I said. 'There hadn't been a claim. But just to be neat they retained me, in case there should be.'

'Are you telling us that they knew that there was a valuable necklace in that safe,' said Jost, 'and yet were prepared not to pay out on it; that they were prepared to withhold valuable evidence?'

'But did you think to ask them?' I repeated again. 'Come now, gentlemen, these are businessmen we're talking about, not the Winter Relief. Why should they be in such a hurry to get rid of their money that they press someone to make a claim and take several hundred thousand Reichsmarks off their hands? And who should they pay out to?'

'The next of kin, surely,' said Jost.

'Without knowing who had title, and to what? Hardly,' I said.

'After all, there were other items of value in that safe which had nothing to do with the Six family, is that not so?' Jost looked blank. 'No, Kommissar, I think your men were too busy worrying about the papers belonging to Herr Von Greis to bother with finding out what else might have been in Herr Pfarr's safe.'

Dietz didn't like that one bit. 'Don't get smart with us, mule-mouth,' he said. 'You're in no position to charge us with incompetence. We've got enough to kick you all the way to the nearest KZ.'

Jost pointed the stem of his pipe at me. 'In that at least he is right, Günther,' he said. 'Whatever our shortcomings were, you are the man with his neck on the block.' He sucked on his pipe, but it was empty. He started to fill it again.

'We'll check your story,' he said, and ordered Dietz to telephone the Lufthansa desk at Tempelhof to see if there was a reservation for the evening flight to London in the name of Teichmüller. When Dietz said there was, Jost lit his pipe; between puffs he said: 'Well then, Günther, you're free to leave.'

Dietz was beside himself, although that was only to be expected; but even the Grunewald station Inspektor seemed rather puzzled at the Kommissar's decision. For my part, I was as taken aback as either of them at this unexpected turn of events. Unsteadily I got to my feet, waiting for Jost to give Dietz the nod that would have him knock me down again. But he just sat there, puffing his pipe and ignoring me. I crossed the room to the door and turned the handle. As I went out I saw that Dietz had to look away, for fear that he might lose control and disgrace himself in front of his superior. Of the few pleasures that were left to me that evening, the prospect of Dietz's rage was sweet indeed.

As I was leaving the station, the desk-sergeant told me that there had been no reply from any of the telephone numbers that I'd given him.

Outside in the street, my relief at being released quickly gave way to anxiety for Inge. I was tired, and I thought I probably needed a few stitches in my head, but when I hailed a cab I found myself telling the driver to take me to where Inge had parked my car in Wannsee.

There was nothing in the car that gave any clue as to her whereabouts, and the police car parked in front of Haupthändler's beach house cancelled any hope I might have entertained of searching the place for some trace of her, always supposing that she had gone inside. All I could do was drive around Wannsee awhile on the chance that I might see her.

My apartment seemed especially empty, even with the radio and all the lights turned on. I telephoned Inge's apartment in Charlottenburg, but there was no reply. I called the office, I even called Müller, on the *Morgenpost*; but he knew as little about Inge Lorenz, who her friends were, if she had any family and where they lived, as it seemed I did myself.

I poured myself a massive brandy and drank it in one gulp, hoping to anaesthetize myself against a new kind of discomfort I was feeling – the kind that was deep in my gut: worry. I boiled up some water for a bath. By the time it was ready I'd had another large one, and was getting ready for my third. The tub was hot enough to parboil an iguana but, preoccupied with Inge and what might have happened, I hardly noticed.

Preoccupation submitted to puzzlement as I tried to fathom why it was that Jost had let me go on the strength of an interrogation lasting hardly as much as one hour. Nobody could have persuaded me that he believed everything that I had told him, despite his pretence to being something of a criminologist. I knew his reputation, and it wasn't that of a latter-day Sherlock Holmes. From what I had heard of him Jost had the imagination of a gelded carthorse. It went against everything he believed in to release me on such a desultory piece of cross-checking as a phone call to the Lufthansa desk at Tempelhof.

I dried myself and went to bed. For a while I lay awake, rummaging through the ill-fitting drawers in the dilapidated cabinet of my head, hoping that I might find something that would make things appear clearer to me. I didn't find it, and I didn't think I was going to. But if Inge had been lying next to me, I might have told her that my guess was that I was free because Jost had superiors who wanted Von Greis's papers at any cost, even if that meant using a suspected double-murderer to do it.

I would also have told her that I was in love with her.

17

I awoke feeling hollower than a dug-out canoe, and disappointed that I didn't have a bad hangover to occupy my day.

'How do you like that?' I muttered to myself as I stood by my bed, and squeezed my skull in search of a headache. 'I suck the stuff up like a hole in the ground and I can't even get a decent tomcat.'

In the kitchen I made myself a pot of coffee that you could have eaten with a knife and fork, and then I had a wash. I made a bad job of shaving; slapping on some cologne, I nearly passed out.

There was still no reply from Inge's apartment. Cursing myself and my so-called speciality in finding missing persons, I called Bruno at the Alex and asked him to find out if the Gestapo might have arrested her. It seemed the most logical explanation. When a lamb is missing from the flock, there's no need to go hunting tiger if you live on the same mountain as a wolf pack. Bruno promised to ask around, but I knew that it might take several days to find out something. Nevertheless, I hung about my apartment for the rest of the morning in the hope that Bruno, or Inge herself, might call. I did a lot of staring at the walls and the ceiling, and I even got to thinking about the Pfarr case again. By lunchtime I was in the mood to start asking more questions. It didn't take a brick wall to fall on me to realize that there was one man who could provide a lot of the answers.

This time the huge wrought-iron gates to Six's property were locked. A length of chain had been wrapped and padlocked around the centre bars; and the small 'Keep Out' sign had been replaced with one that read: 'Keep Out. No Trespassers'. It was as if Six had suddenly grown more nervous about his own security.

I parked close to the wall and, having put the gun from my

bedside-drawer in my pocket, I got out of the car and climbed onto the roof. The top of the wall was easily reached, and I pulled myself up to sit astride the parapet. An elm tree provided an easy climb down to ground level.

There was little or no growl that I could recall, and I hardly heard the sound of the dogs' paws as they galloped across the fallen leaves. At the last second I heard a heavy, panting breath which made the hair on the back of my neck stand up on end. The dog was already leaping at my throat as I fired. The shot sounded small beneath the trees, almost too small to kill something as fierce as the Dobermann. Even as it fell dead at my feet the wind was already bearing the noise away, and in the opposite direction from the house. I let out the breath that unconsciously I had held while firing, and with my heart beating like a fork in a bowlful of egg-white, I turned instinctively, remembering that there had been not one, but two dogs. For a second or two, the leaves rustling in the trees overhead camouflaged the other's low growl. The dog came forward uncertainly, appearing in the clearing between the trees and keeping its distance from me. I stepped back as slowly it approached its dead brother, and when it dipped its head to sniff at the other's open wound, I raised my gun once more. In a sudden gust of wind, I fired. The dog yelped as the bullet kicked it off its feet. For a moment or two it continued breathing, and then it lay still.

Pocketing the gun, I moved into the trees and walked down the long slope in the direction of the house. Somewhere the peacock was calling, and I had half a mind to shoot that too if it were unlucky enough to be stumbled upon. Killing was very much on my mind. It is quite common in a homicide for the murderer to get warmed up for the main event by disposing of a few innocent victims, such as the family pets, along the way.

Detection is all about chain-making, manufacturing links: with Paul Pfarr, Von Greis, Bock, Mutschmann, Red Dieter Helfferich and Hermann Six, I had a length of something strong enough to put my weight on. Paul Pfarr, Eva, Haupthändler and Jeschonnek was shorter, and altogether different.

It wasn't that I intended killing Six. It was just that if I was unsuccessful in obtaining a few straight answers then I hadn't ruled it out as a possibility. So it was with some embarrassment then that, with these thoughts passing through my mind, I came across the millionaire himself, standing under a great fir tree, smoking a cigar and humming quietly.

'Oh, it's you,' he said, quite unperturbed to see me turn up on his property with a gun in my hand. 'I thought it was the groundsman. You'll want some money, I suppose.'

For a brief moment I didn't know what to say to him. Then I said: 'I shot the dogs.' I put the gun back into my pocket.

'Did you? Yes, I thought I heard a couple of shots.' If he felt any fear or irritation at this piece of information, he did not show it.

'You'd better come up to the house,' he said, and began to walk slowly towards the house, with me following a short way behind.

When we got within sight of the house I saw Ilse Rudel's blue BMW parked outside, and I wondered if I would see her. But it was the presence on the lawn of a large marquee that prompted me to break the silence between us.

'Planning a party?'

'Er, yes, a party. It's my wife's birthday. Just a few friends, you know.'

'So soon after the funeral?' My tone was bitter, and I saw that Six had noticed it too. As he walked along he searched first the sky and then the ground for an explanation.

'Well, I'm not –' he began. And then: 'One can't – one cannot mourn one's loss indefinitely. Life must go on.' Recovering some of his composure he added: 'I thought that it would be unfair to my wife to cancel her plans. And of course, we both have a position in society.'

'We mustn't forget that, must we?' I said. Leading us up to the front door, he said nothing, and I wondered if he was going to call for help. He pushed it open, and we stepped into the hall.

'No butler today?' I observed.

'It's his day off,' said Six, hardly daring to catch my eye. 'But there is a maid if you would like some refreshment. You must be quite warm after your little excitement.'

'Which one?' I said. 'Thanks to you I've had several "little excitements".'

He smiled thinly. 'The dogs, I mean.'

'Oh yes, the dogs. Yes, I am quite warm as it happens. They were big dogs. But I'm quite a shot, even though I say so myself.' We went in to the library.

'I enjoy shooting myself. But only for sport. I don't suppose I've ever shot anything bigger than a pheasant.'

'Yesterday, I shot a man,' I said. 'That's my second one in as many weeks. Since I started to work for you, Herr Six, it's become a bit of a habit with me, you know.' He stood awkwardly in front of me, his hands clasped behind his neck. He cleared his throat and threw the cigar butt into the cold fireplace. When eventually he spoke, he sounded embarrassed, as though he were about to dismiss an old and faithful servant who had been caught stealing.

'You know, I'm glad you came,' he said. 'As it happens I was going to speak to Schemm, my lawyer, this afternoon, and arrange for you to be paid. But since you are here I can write you a cheque.' And so saying he went over to his desk with such alacrity that I thought he might have a gun in the drawer.

'I'd prefer cash, if you don't mind.' He glanced up at my face, and then down at my hand holding the butt of the automatic in my jacket pocket.

'Yes, of course you would.' The drawer stayed shut. He sat down in his chair and rolled back a corner of the rug to reveal a small safe sunk in the floor.

'Now that's a handy little nut. You can't be too careful these days,' I said, relishing my own lack of tact. 'You can't even trust the banks, can you?' I peered innocently across the desk. 'Fire-proof, is it?' Six's eyes narrowed.

'You'll forgive me, but I seem to have lost my sense of humour.' He opened the safe, and withdrew several packets of banknotes. 'I believe we said five per cent. Would 40,000 close our account?'

'You could try it,' I said, as he placed eight of the packets on the desk. Then he closed the safe, rolled back the carpet, and pushed the money towards me.

'They're all hundreds, I'm afraid.'

I picked up one of the bundles and tore the paper wrapping off. 'Just as long as they've got Herr Liebig's picture on them,' I said.

Smiling thinly, Six stood up. 'I don't think we need ever meet again, Herr Günther.'

'Aren't you forgetting something?'

He began to look impatient. 'I don't think so,' he said testily.

'Oh, but I'm sure you are.' I put a cigarette in my mouth and struck a match. Bending my head towards the flame I took a couple of quick puffs and then dropped the match into the ashtray. 'The necklace.' Six remained silent. 'But then, you already have it back, don't you?' I said. 'Or at least you know where it is, and who has got it.'

His nose wrinkled with distaste, as if it detected a bad smell. 'You're not going to be tiresome about this are you, Herr Günther? I do hope not.'

'And what about those papers? The evidence of your involvement with organized crime that Von Greis gave to your son-in-law. Or do you imagine that Red Dieter and his associates are going to persuade the Teichmüllers to tell them where they are? Is that it?'

'I've never heard of a Red Dieter, or –'

'Sure you have, Six. He's a crook, just like you. During the steel strikes he was the gangster you paid to intimidate your workers.'

Six laughed and lit his cigar. 'A gangster,' he said. 'Really, Herr Günther, your imagination is running away with you. Now, if you don't mind, you've been very handsomely paid, so if you will please leave I would be most grateful. I'm a very busy man, and I have a lot of things to do.'

'I guess things are difficult without a secretary to help. What if I were to tell you that the man calling himself Teichmüller, the one that Red's thugs are probably beating the shit out of right now, is really your private secretary, Hjalmar Haupthändler?'

'That is ridiculous,' he said. 'Hjalmar is visiting some friends in Frankfurt.'

I shrugged. 'It's a simple matter to get Red's boys to ask Teich-müller what his real name is. Perhaps he's already told them; but then, Teichmüller is the name on his new passport, so they could be forgiven for not believing him. He purchased it from the same man he was planning to sell the diamonds to. One for him and one for the girl.'

Six sneered at me. 'And does this girl have a real name too?' he said.

'Oh yes. Her name is Hannah Roedl, although your son-in-law preferred to call her Eva. They were lovers, at least they were until she murdered him.'

'That's a lie. Paul never had a mistress. He was devoted to my Grete.'

'Come off it, Six. What did you do to them that made him turn his back on her? That made him hate you bad enough to want to put you behind bars?'

'I repeat, they were devoted to each other.'

'I admit it's possible that they might have become reconciled to each other not long before they were killed, with the discovery that your daughter was pregnant.' Six laughed. 'And so Paul's mistress decided to get her own back.'

'Now you really are being ridiculous,' he said. 'You call yourself a detective and you don't know that my daughter was physically incapable of having children.'

I felt my jaw. 'Are you sure about that?'

'Good God, man, do you think it's something that I might have forgotten? Of course I'm sure.'

I walked round Six's desk and looked at the photographs that were arranged there. I picked one of them up, and stared grimly at the woman in the picture. I recognized her immediately. It was the woman from the beach house at Wannsee; the woman I had socked; the woman who I had thought was Eva, and was now call-ing herself Frau Teichmüller; the woman who in all probability had killed her husband and his mistress: it was Six's only daughter, Grete. As a detective, you have to expect to make mistakes; but it is nothing short of humiliating to come face to face with evidence of your own stupidity; and it is all the more galling when you discover that the evidence has been staring you in the face all along.

'Herr Six, this is going to sound crazy, I know, but I now believe that at least until yesterday afternoon your daughter was alive, and preparing to fly to London with your private secretary.'

Six's face darkened, and for a moment I thought he was going to attack me. 'What the hell are you babbling about now, you bloody fool?' he roared. 'What do you mean "alive"? My daughter is dead and buried.'

'I suppose that she must have come home unexpectedly and found Paul in bed with his bit of brush, both of them drunk as cats. Grete shot them both and then, realizing what she had done, she telephoned the only person she felt she could turn to, Haupthändler. He was in love with her. He would have done anything for her, and that included helping her to get away with murder.'

Six sat down heavily. He was pale and trembling. 'I don't believe it,' he said. But it was clear that he was finding my explanation only too plausible.

'I expect it was his idea to burn the bodies and make it look like it was your daughter who had died in bed with her husband, and not his mistress. He took Grete's wedding-ring and put it on the other woman's finger. Then he had the bright idea of taking the diamonds out of the safe and making it look like a burglary. That's why he left the door open. The diamonds were to stake their new life somewhere. New lives and new identities. But what Haupthändler didn't know was that somebody had already been in the safe that evening and removed certain papers that were compromising to you. This fellow was a real expert, a puzzler not long out of prison. A neat worker too. Not the sort to use explosives or do anything untidy like leave a safe door open. As drunk as they were, I'll bet that Paul and Eva never even heard him. One of Red's boys, of course. Red used to carry out all your dodgy little schemes, didn't he? While Goering's man Von Greis had these documents, things were merely inconvenient. The Prime Minister is a pragmatist. He could use the evidence of your previous criminality to ensure that you were useful to him, and make you toe the Party's economic line. But when Paul and the Black Angels got hold of them, that was altogether more uncomfortable. You knew that Paul wanted to destroy you. Backed into a corner you had to do something. So, as usual, you got Red Dieter to take care of it.

'But later on, with Paul and the girl dead, and the diamonds gone from the safe, it looked to you as though Red's man had been greedy, and that he'd taken more than he was supposed to. Not unreasonably you concluded that it was he who had killed your daughter, and so you told Red to put things right. Red managed to kill one of the two burglars, the man who had driven the car; but he missed the other, the one who had opened the safe, who therefore still had the papers and, you assumed, the diamonds. That's where I came in. Because you couldn't be sure that it wasn't Red himself who had double-crossed you, and so you probably didn't tell him about the diamonds, just as you didn't tell the police.'

Six took the dead cigar from out of the corner of his mouth and laid it, unsmoked, on the ashtray. He was starting to look very old.

'I have to hand it to you,' I said. 'Your reasoning was perfect: find the man with the diamonds and you would find the man with the documents. And when you found out that Helfferich hadn't hazed you, you put him on my tail. I led him to the man with the diamonds and, you thought, the documents too. At this very moment your German Strength associates are probably trying to persuade Herr and Frau Teichmüller to tell them where Mutschmann is. He's the man who really has the documents. And naturally they won't know what the hell he's talking about. Red won't like that. He's not a very patient man, and I'm sure I don't have to remind you of all people of what that means.'

The steel magnate stared into space, as if he had not heard one word I had said. I grabbed the lapels of his jacket, hauled him to his feet, and slapped him hard.

'Did you hear what I said? These murderers, these torturers, have your daughter.' His mouth went as slack as an empty douche-bag. I slapped it again.

'We've got to stop them.'

'So where's he got them?' I let him go and pushed him away from me.

'On the river,' he said. 'The Grosse Zug, near Schmöckwitz.'

I picked up the telephone. 'What's the number?'

Six swore. 'It's not on the phone,' he gasped. 'Oh Christ, what are we going to do?'

'We'll have to go there,' I said. 'We could drive there, but it would be quicker by boat.'

Six sprang round the desk. 'I've got a slipper at a mooring close by. We can drive there in five minutes.'

Stopping only to collect the boat keys and a can of petrol, we took the BMW and drove to the shores of the lake. The water was busier than on the previous day. A stiff breeze had encouraged the presence of a large number of small yachts, and their white sails covered the surface of the water like the wings of hundreds of moths.

I helped Six remove the green tarpaulin from the boat, and poured petrol into the tank while he connected the battery and started the engine. The slipper roared into life at the third time of asking, and the five-metre polished-wood hull strained at the mooring ropes, eager to be up-river. I threw Six the first line, and having untied the second I stepped quickly into the boat beside him. Then he wrenched the wheel to one side, punched the throt-tle lever and we jerked forwards.

It was a powerful boat and as fast as anything that even the river-police might have had. We raced up the Havel towards Spandau, Six holding the white steering-wheel grimly, oblivious to the effect that the slipper's enormous wake was having on the other waterway craft. It slapped against the hulls of boats moored under trees or beside small jetties, bringing their irate owners out on deck to shake their fists and utter shouts that were lost in the noise of the slipper's big engine. We went east on to the Spree.

'I hope to God we're not too late,' shouted Six. He had quite recovered his former vigour, and stared resolutely ahead of him, the man of action, with only a slight frown on his face to give a clue to his anxiety.

'I'm usually an excellent judge of a man's character,' he said, as if by way of explanation, 'but if it's any consolation to you, Herr Günther, I'm afraid I gravely underestimated you. I had not expected you to be as doggedly inquisitive. Frankly, I thought you'd do precisely what you were told. But then you're not the kind of man who takes kindly to being told what to do, are you?'

'When you get a cat to catch the mice in your kitchen, you can't expect it to ignore the rats in the cellar.'

'I suppose not,' he said.

We continued east, up-river, past the Tiergarten and Museum Island. By the time we turned south towards Treptower Park and Köpenick, I had asked him what grudge his son-in-law had had against him. To my surprise he showed no reluctance to answer my question; nor did he affect the indignant, rose-tinted viewpoint that had characterized all his previous remarks concerning members of his family, living and dead.

'As well-acquainted with my personal affairs as you are, Herr Günther, you probably don't need to be reminded that Ilse is my second wife. I married my first wife, Lisa, in 1910, and the following year she became pregnant. Unfortunately things went badly and our child was still-born. Not only that, but there was no possibility of her having another child. In the same hospital was an unmarried girl who had given birth to a healthy child at about the same time. She had no way of looking after it, so my wife and I persuaded her to let us adopt her daughter. That was Grete. We never told her she was adopted while my wife was alive. But after she died, Grete discovered the truth, and set about trying to trace her real mother.

'By this time of course Grete was married to Paul, and was devoted to him. For his part, Paul was never worthy of her. I suspect he was rather more keen on my family name and money than he was on my daughter. But to everyone else they must have seemed like a perfectly happy couple.

'Well, all that changed overnight when Grete finally tracked down her real mother. The woman was a gypsy from Vienna, working in a Bierkeller on Potsdamer Platz. If it was a shock to Grete it was the end of the world to that little shit Paul. Something called racial impurity, whatever that amounts to, gypsies running the Jews a close second for unpopularity. Paul blamed me for not having informed Grete earlier. But when I first saw her I didn't see a gypsy child, but a beautiful healthy baby, and a young mother who was as keen as Lisa and I that we should adopt her and give her the best in life. Not that it would have mattered if she'd been a rabbi's daughter. We'd still have taken her. Well, you remember what it was like then, Herr Günther. People didn't make distinctions like they do these days. We were all just Germans. Of course, Paul didn't see it that way. All he could think of was the threat Grete now posed to his career in the SS and the Party.' He laughed bitterly.

We came to Grünau, home of the Berlin Regatta Club. On a large lake on the other side of some trees, a 2,000-metre Olympic rowing course had been marked out. Above the noise of the slipper's engine could be heard the sound of a brass band, and a public-address system describing the afternoon's events.

'There was no reasoning with him. Naturally, I lost my temper with him, and called him and his beloved Führer all sorts of names. After that we were enemies. There was nothing I could do for Grete. I watched his hate breaking her heart. I urged her to leave him, but she wouldn't. She refused to believe that he wouldn't learn to love her again. And so she stayed with him.'

'But meanwhile he set out to destroy you, his own father-in-law.'

'That's right,' said Six. 'While all the time he sat there in the comfortable home that my money had provided for them. If Grete

222

did kill him as you say, then he certainly had it coming. If she hadn't done it I might have been tempted to have arranged it myself.'

'How was he going to finish you?' I asked. 'What evidence was there that was so compromising to you?'

The slipper reached the junction of Langer See and Seddinsee. Six throttled back and steered the boat south in the direction of the hilly peninsula that was Schmöckwitz.

'Clearly your curiosity knows no bounds, Herr Günther. But I'm sorry to disappoint you. I welcome your assistance, but I see no reason why I should answer all your questions.'

I shrugged. 'I don't suppose it matters much now,' I said.

The Grosse Zug was an inn on one of the two islands between the marshes of Köpenick and Schmöckwitz. Less than a couple of hundred metres in length, and no more than fifty wide, the island was tightly packed with tall pine trees. Close to the water's edge there were more signs saying 'Private' and 'Keep Out' than on a fan-dancer's dressing-room door.

'What is this place?'

'This is the summer headquarters of the German Strength ring. They use it for their more secret meetings. You can see why, of course. It's so out of the way.' He started to drive the boat round the island, looking for somewhere to moor. On the opposite side we found a small jetty, to which were tied several boats. Up a short grassy slope was a cluster of neatly painted boathouses, and beyond it the Grosse Zug Inn itself. I collected up a length of rope and jumped off the slipper on to the jetty. Six cut the engine.

'We'd best be careful how we approach the place,' he said, joining me on the jetty, and tying up the front of the boat. 'Some of these fellows are inclined to shoot first and ask questions later.'

'I know just how they feel,' I said.

We walked off the jetty and up the slope towards the boathouses. Excepting the other boats, there was nothing to indicate that there was anyone else on the islet. But closer to the boathouses, two armed men emerged from behind an upturned boat.

Their faces wore expressions that were cool enough to cope with me telling them that I was carrying bubonic plague. It's the sort of confidence that only a sawn-off can give you.

'That's far enough,' said the taller of the two. 'This is private property. Who are you and what are doing here?' He didn't lift the gun from his forearm where it was cradled like a sleeping baby, but then he did not have to lift it very far to get off a shot. Six made the explanations.

'It's desperately important that I see Red.' He thumped his fist into the palm of his hand as he spoke. It made him seem rather melodramatic, I thought. 'My name is Hermann Six. I can assure you gentlemen he'll want to see me. But please hurry.'

They stood there shuffling uncertainly. 'The boss always tells us if he's expecting anyone. And he didn't say anything about you two.'

'Despite that, you can depend on it that there'll be hell to pay if he finds out you turned us away.'

Shotgun looked at his partner, who nodded and walked away towards the inn. He said: 'We'll wait here while we check it out.'

Wringing his hands nervously, Six called out after him: 'Please hurry. It's a matter of life or death.'

Shotgun grinned at that. I guessed he was used to matters of life and death where his boss was concerned. Six produced a cigarette and fed it nervously into his mouth. He snatched it out again without lighting it.

'Please,' he said to Shotgun. 'Are you holding a couple on the island, a man and a woman? The – the –'

'The Teichmüllers,' I said.

Shotgun's grin disappeared under a whole pantomine of dumb. 'I don't know nothing,' he said dully.

We kept looking anxiously at the inn. It was a two-storey affair, white-painted with neat, black shutters, a windowbox full of geraniums and a high mansard roof. As we watched, smoke started to come out of the chimney, and when the door finally opened

I half expected an old woman to come out carrying a tray of gingerbread. Shotgun's pitman beckoned us forward.

We moved Indian-file through the door, with Shotgun bringing up the rear. The two stumpy barrels gave me an itch in the back of my neck: if you have ever seen someone shot with a sawn-off at close range, you would know why. There was a small hallway with a couple of hatstands, only nobody had bothered to check his hat. Beyond that was a small room, where somebody was playing the piano like he had a couple of fingers missing. At the far end there was a round bar and some stools. Behind it were lots of sports trophies and I wondered who had won them and why. The Most Murders in One Year perhaps, or The Cleanest Knockout With an India Rubber – I had a nominee for that award myself if I could find him. But probably they had just bought them to make the place look more like what it was supposed to be – the headquarters of an ex-convicts' welfare association.

Shotgun's partner grunted. 'This way,' he said, and led us towards a door beside the bar.

Through the door the room was like an office. A brass lamp hung from one of the beams on the ceiling. There was a long walnut chaise-longue in the corner by the window, and next to it, a big bronze of a naked girl, the sort that looks as though the model must have had a bad accident with a circular saw. There was more art on the panelled walls, but of the sort that normally you only find in the pages of midwives' textbooks.

Red Dieter, his black shirt-sleeves rolled up, and his collar off, stood up from the green-leather sofa and flicked his cigarette into the fire. Glancing first at Six and then at me, he looked uncertain as to whether he ought to look welcoming or worried. He didn't get time to make a choice. Six stepped forwards, and caught him by the throat.

'For God's sake what have you done with her?' From a corner of the room another man came to my assistance, and each of us taking one of the old man's arms, we pulled him off.

'Hold up, hold up,' yelled Red. He straightened his jacket and tried to control his natural indignation. Then he glanced around his person, as if to check that his dignity was still intact.

Six continued to shout. 'My daughter, what have you done with my daughter?'

The gangster frowned and looked quizzically at me. 'What's he fucking talking about?'

'The two people your boys snatched from the beach house yesterday,' I said urgently. 'What have you done with them? Look, there's no time for an explanation now, but the girl is his daughter.'

He looked incredulous. 'You mean, she's not dead after all?' he said.

'Come on, man,' I said.

Red swore, his face darkened like dying gaslight, his lips quivering like he had just chewed on broken glass. A thin, blue vein stood off his square forehead like a piece of ivy on a brick wall. He pointed at Six.

'Keep him here,' he growled. Red shouldered his way through the men outside like an angry wrestler. 'If this is one of your tricks, Günther, I'll personally fillet your fucking nose.'

'I'm not that stupid. But as it happens, there is one thing that's puzzling me.'

At the front door Red stopped and glared at me. His face was the colour of blood, almost purple with rage. 'And what's that?'

'I had a girl working with me. Name of Inge Lorenz. She disappeared from the area of the beach house in Wannsee not long before your boys tapped me on the head.'

'So why ask me?'

'You've already kidnapped two people, so a third along the way might not be too much for your conscience to bear.'

Red almost spat in my face. 'What's a fucking conscience, then?' he said, and carried on through the door.

Outside the inn I hurried after him in the direction of one of the boathouses. A man came out, buttoning up his flies. Misinterpreting his boss's purposeful stride, he grinned.

'You come to give her one as well, boss?'

Red drew level with the man, looked blankly at him for a second, and then punched him hard in the stomach. 'Shut your stupid mouth,' he roared, and kicked his way through the boat-house door. I stepped over the man's gasping body and followed him inside.

I saw a long rack on which were laid several eight-oar boats, and tied to it was a man stripped to the waist. His head hung down, and there were numerous burns on his neck and shoulders. I guessed that it was Haupthändler, although as I came closer I could see that his face was so badly contused as to be unrecognizable. Two men stood idly by, paying no attention to their captive. They were both smoking cigarettes, and one of them wore a set of brass knuckles.

'Where's the fucking girl?' screamed Red. One of Haupthändler's torturers jabbed a thumb across his shoulder.

'Next door, with my brother.'

'Hey, boss,' said the other man. 'This coat still won't talk. Do you want us to work on him some more?'

'Leave the poor bastard alone,' he growled. 'He knows nothing.'

It was almost dark in the adjoining boathouse, and it took several seconds for our eyes to become accustomed to the gloom.

'Franz. Where the fuck are you?' We heard a soft groan, and the slap of flesh against flesh. Then we saw them: an enormous figure of a man, his trousers round his ankles, bent over the silent and naked body of Hermann Six's daughter, tied face down over an upturned boat.

'Get away from her, you big ugly bastard,' yelled Red.

The man, who was the size of a luggage locker, made no move to obey the order, not even when it was repeated at greater volume and at closer range. Eyes shut, his shoe-box of a head lying back on the parapet that was his shoulders, his enormous penis squeezing in and out of Grete Pfarr's anus almost convulsively, his knees bent like a man whose horse had escaped from underneath him, Franz stood his ground.

Red punched him hard on the side of the head. He might as well

227

have been hitting a locomotive. The very next second he pulled out a gun and almost casually blew his man's brains out.

Franz dropped cross-legged to the ground, a collapsing chimney of a man, his head spurting a smoke-plume of burgundy, his still erect penis leaning to one side like the mainmast of a ship that has crashed onto the rocks.

Red pushed the body to one side with the toe of his shoe as I started to untie Grete. Several times he glanced awkwardly at the stripes that had been cut deep onto her buttocks and thighs with a short whip. Her skin was cold, and she smelt strongly of semen. There was no telling how many times she had been raped.

'Fuck, look at the state of her,' groaned Red, shaking his head. 'How can I let Six see her like this?'

'Let's hope she's alive,' I said, taking off my coat, and spreading it on the ground.

We laid her down, and I pressed my ear to her naked breast. There was a heartbeat, but I guessed that she was in deep shock.

'Is she going to be all right?' Red sounded naive, like a schoolboy asking about his pet rabbit. I looked up at him and saw that he was still holding the gun in his hand.

Summoned by the shot, several German Strength men were standing awkwardly at the back of the boathouse. I heard one of them say, 'He killed Franz'; and then another said, 'There was no call to do it,' and I knew we were going to have trouble. Red knew it too. He turned and faced them.

'The girl is Six's daughter. You all know Six. He's a rich and powerful man. I told Franz to leave her alone but he wouldn't listen. She couldn't have taken any more. He'd have killed her. She's only just alive now.'

'You didn't have to shoot Franz,' said a voice.

'Yeah,' said another. 'You could have slugged him.'

'What?' Red's tone was incredulous. 'His head was thicker than the oak on a nunnery door.'

'Not now it isn't.'

Red bent down beside me. With one eye on his men he murmured, 'You got a lighter?'

'Yes,' I said. 'Look, we don't stand a chance in here, nor does she. We've got to get to a boat.'

'What about Six?'

I buttoned the coat over Grete's naked body, and gathered her up in my arms. 'He can take his chances.'

Helfferich shook his head. 'No, I'll go back for him. Wait for us on the jetty as long as you can. If they start shooting, then get the hell away. And in case I don't, I know nothing about your girl, fleabite.' We walked slowly towards the door, Red leading the way. His men stepped back sullenly to allow us through, and once outside we separated, and I walked back down the grassy slope to the jetty and to the boat.

I laid Six's daughter on the slipper's back seat. There was a rug in a locker and I took it out and put it over her still unconscious body. I wondered whether if she came round I might have another chance to ask her about Inge Lorenz. Would Haupthändler be any more cooperative? I was just thinking about going back to get him when from the direction of the inn I heard several pistol shots. I slipped the boat's line, started the engine and took the gun out of my pocket. With my other hand I held onto the jetty to stop the boat drifting. Seconds later I heard another volley of shots and what sounded like a riveter working along the stern of the boat. I rammed the throttle forwards and spun the wheel away from the jetty. Wincing with pain I glanced down at my hand, imagining that I had been hit, but instead I found an enormous splinter of wood from the jetty sticking out of the palm of my hand. Breaking off the largest part of it I turned and fired off the rest of my clip in the direction of the figures now appearing on the retreating jetty. To my surprise they threw themselves on their bellies. But behind me something heavier than a pistol had opened up. It was only a warning burst, but the big machine-gun cut through the trees and the wood of the jetty like metallic rain drops, sending up splinters, chopping off branches and slicing through foliage. Looking to my front again, I had just enough time to pull the throttle into reverse and steer away from the police-launch. Then I cut the engine and instinctively raised my hands high above my head, dropping my gun onto the floor of the boat as I did so.

It was then that I noticed the neat red caste-mark in the centre of Grete's forehead, from which a hair's breadth trickle of blood was now bisecting her lifeless features.

18

Listening to the systematic destruction of another human spirit has a predictably lowering effect on one's own fibre. I imagine that that was how it was intended to be. The Gestapo is nothing if not thoughtful. They let you eavesdrop on another's agony to soften you up on the inside; and only then do they get to work on the outside. There is nothing worse than a state of suspense about what is going to happen, whether it's waiting for the results of some tests at a hospital, or the headsman's axe. You just want to get it over with. In my own small way it was a technique I had used myself at the Alex when I'd let men, suspects, sweat themselves into a state where they were ready to tell you everything. Waiting for something lets your imagination step in to create your own private hell.

But I wondered what it was that they wanted from me. Did they want to know about Six? Did they hope that I knew where the Von Greis papers were? And what if they tortured me and I didn't know what they wanted me to tell them?

By the third or fourth day alone in my filthy cell, I was beginning to wonder if my own suffering was to be an end in itself. At other times I puzzled as to what had become of Six and Red Helfferich, who were arrested with me, and of Inge Lorenz.

Most of the time I just stared at the walls, which were a kind of palimpsest for those previous unfortunates who had been its occupants. Oddly enough there was little or no abuse for the Nazis. More common were recriminations between the Communists and the Social Democrats as to which of these two 'fallen women' was responsible for allowing Hitler to get elected in the first place: the Sozis blamed the Pukers, and the Pukers blamed the Sozis.

Sleep did not come easily. There was an evil-smelling pallet, which I avoided on my first night of incarceration, but as the days passed and the slop-bucket became more malodorous, I ceased to be so fastidious. It was only on the fifth day, when two SS guards came and hauled me out of my cell, that I realized just how badly I smelled: but it was nothing compared to their stink, which is of death.

They frog-marched me through a long urinous passage to a lift, and this took us up five floors to a quiet and well-carpeted corridor which, with its oak-panelled walls and gloomy portraits of the Führer, Himmler, Canaris, Hindenburg and Bismarck, had the air of an exclusive gentleman's club. We went through a double wooden door the height of a tram and into a large bright office where several stenographers were working. They paid my filthy person no attention at all. A young SS Hauptsturmführer came round an ornate sort of desk to look disinterestedly at me.

'Who's this?' With a click of his heels, one of the guards stood to attention and told the officer who I was.

'Wait there,' said the Hauptsturmführer and walked over to a polished mahogany door on the other side of the room, where he knocked and waited. Hearing a reply he poked his head round the door and said something. Then he turned and jerked his head at my guards who shoved me forwards.

It was a big, plush office with a high ceiling and some expensive leather furniture, and I saw that I wasn't going to get the routine Gestapo chat over the kind of script that would have to involve the twin prompts of blackjack and brass knuckles. Not yet anyway. They wouldn't risk spilling anything on the carpet. At the far end of the office was a French window, a set of bookshelves and a desk behind which, sitting in comfortable armchairs, were two SS officers. These were tall, sleek, well-groomed men with supercilious smiles, hair the colour of Tilsiter cheese and well-behaved Adam's apples. The taller of the pair spoke first, to order the guards and their adjutant out of the room.

'Herr Günther. Please sit down.' He pointed to a chair in front of the desk. I looked behind as the door shut, and then shuffled forwards, my hands in my pockets. Since they had taken away my shoelaces and braces at my arrest, it was the only way I had of keeping my trousers up.

I hadn't met senior SS officers before and so I was not certain as to the rank of the two who faced me; but I guessed that one was probably a colonel, and the other, the one who continued speaking, was possibly a general. Neither one of them seemed to be any older than about thirty-five.

'Smoke?' said the general. He held out a box and then tossed me some matches. I lit my cigarette and smoked it gratefully. 'Please help yourself if you want another.'

'Thanks.'

'Perhaps you would also like a drink?'

'I wouldn't say no to some champagne.' They both smiled simultaneously. The second officer, the colonel, produced a bottle of schnaps and poured a glassful.

'I'm afraid we don't run to anything so grand round here,' he said.

'Whatever you've got, then.' The colonel stood up and brought me the drink. I didn't waste any time with it. I jerked it back, cleaned my teeth and swallowed with every muscle in my neck and throat. I felt the schnaps flush right the way down to my corns.

'You'd better give him another,' said the general. 'He looks as though his nerves are a bit shaky.' I held out my glass for the refill.

'My nerves are just fine,' I said, nursing my glass. 'I just like to drink.'

'Part of the image, eh?'

'And what image would that be?'

'Why, the private detective of course. The shoddy little man in the barely furnished office, who drinks like a suicide who's lost his nerve, and who comes to the assistance of the beautiful but mysterious woman in black.'

'Someone in the SS perhaps,' I suggested.

He smiled. 'You might not believe it,' he said, 'but I have a passion for detective stories. It must be interesting.' His face was of an unusual construction. Its central feature was its protruding, hawk-like nose, which had the effect of making the chin seem weak; above the thin nose were glassy blue eyes set rather too close together, and slightly slanting, which lent him an apparently world-weary, cynical air.

'I'm sure that fairy-stories are a lot more interesting.'

'But not in your case, surely. In particular, the case you have been working on for the Germania Life Assurance Company.'

'For which,' the colonel chipped in, 'we may now substitute the name of Hermann Six.' The same type as his superior, he was better-looking if apparently less intelligent. The general glanced over a file that was open on the desk in front of him, if only to indicate that they knew everything there was to know about me and my business.

'Precisely so,' he murmured. After a short while he looked up at me and said: 'Why ever did you leave Kripo?'

'Coal,' I said.

He stared blankly at me. 'Coal?'

'Yeah, you know, mouse, gravel . . . money. Speaking of which, I had 40,000 marks in my pockets when I checked into this hotel. I'd like to know what's happened to it. And to a girl who was working with me. Name of Inge Lorenz. She's disappeared.'

The general looked at his junior officer, who shook his head. 'I'm afraid we know nothing about any girl, Herr Günther,' said the colonel. 'People are always disappearing in Berlin. You of all people should know that. As to your money, however, that is quite safe with us for the moment.'

'Thanks, and I don't mean to sound ungrateful, but I'd sooner leave it in a sock underneath my mattress.'

The general put his long, thin, violinist's hands together, as if he was about to lead us in prayer, and pressed their fingertips against his lips meditatively. 'Tell me, did you ever consider joining the Gestapo?' he said.

I figured it was my turn to try a little smile.

'You know, this wasn't a bad suit before I was obliged to sleep in it for a week. I may smell a bit, but not that badly.'

He gave an amused sort of sniff. 'The ability to talk as toughly as your fictional counterpart is one thing, Herr Günther,' he said. 'Being it is quite another. Your remarks demonstrate either an astonishing lack of appreciation as to the gravity of your situation, or real courage.' He raised his thin, gold-leaf eyebrows and started to toy with the German Horseman's Badge on his left breast-pocket. 'By nature I am a cynical man. I think that all policemen are, don't you? So normally I would be inclined to favour the first assessment of your bravado. However, in this particular case it suits me to believe in the strength of your character. Please do not disappoint me by saying something really stupid.' He paused for a moment. 'I'm sending you to a KZ.'

My flesh turned as cold as a butcher's shop-window. I finished what was left of my schnaps, and then heard myself say: 'Listen, if it's about that lousy milk bill . . .'

They both started grinning a lot, enjoying my obvious discomfort.

'Dachau,' said the colonel. I stubbed out my cigarette and lit another. They saw my hand shake as I held the match up.

'Don't worry,' said the general. 'You'll be working for me.' He came round the desk and sat on its edge in front of me.

'And who are you?'

'I am Obergruppenführer Heydrich.' He waved his arm at the colonel and folded his arms. 'And this is Standartenführer Sohst of Alarm Command.'

'Pleased to meet you, I'm sure.' I wasn't. Alarm Command were the special Gestapo killers that Marlene Sahm had talked about.

'I've had my eye on you for some time,' he said. 'And after that unfortunate little incident at the beach house in Wannsee I have had you under constant observation, in the hope that you might lead us to certain papers. I'm sure you know the ones I mean. Instead you gave us the next best thing – the man who planned their theft. Over the past few days, while you've been our guest, we've been checking your story. It was the autobahn worker, Bock, who told us where to look for this Kurt Mutschmann fellow – the safecracker who now has the papers.'

'Bock?' I shook my head. 'I don't believe it. He wasn't the sort to turn informer about a friend.'

'It's quite true, I can assure you. Oh, I don't mean he told us exactly where to find him, but he put us on the right track, before he died.'

'You tortured him?'

'Yes. He told us that Mutschmann had once told him that if he were ever really wanted so that he was desperate, then he should probably think of hiding in a prison, or a KZ. Well, of course, with a gang of criminals looking for him, not to mention ourselves, then desperate is exactly what he must have been.'

'It's an old trick,' explained Sohst. 'You avoid arrest for one thing by having yourself arrested for another.'

'We believe that Mutschmann was arrested and sent to Dachau three nights after the death of Paul Pfarr,' said Heydrich. With a thin, smug smile he added: 'Indeed, he was almost begging to be arrested. It seems that he was caught red-handed, painting KPD slogans on the wall of a Kripo Stelle in Neukölln.'

'A KZ isn't so bad if you're a Kozi,' chuckled Sohst. 'In comparison with the Jews and the queers. He'll probably be out in a couple of years.'

I shook my head. 'I don't understand,' I told them. 'Why don't you simply have the commandant at Dachau question Mutschmann? What the hell do you need me for?'

Heydrich folded his arms and swung his jackbooted leg so that his toe was almost kicking my kneecap. 'Involving the commandant at Dachau would also mean having to inform Himmler, which I don't want to do. You see, the Reichsführer is an idealist. He would undoubtedly see it as his duty to use these papers to punish those he perceived to be guilty of crimes against the Reich.'

I recalled Himmler's letter to Paul Pfarr which Marlene Sahm had shown me at the Olympic Stadium and nodded.

'I, on the other hand, am a pragmatist, and would prefer to use the papers in a rather more tactical way, as and where I require.'

'In other words, you're not above a bit of blackmail yourself. Am I right?'

Heydrich smiled thinly. 'You see through me so easily, Herr Günther. But you must understand that this is to be an undercover operation. Strictly a matter for Security. On no account should you mention this conversation to anyone.'

'But there must be somebody among the SS at Dachau that you can trust?'

'Of course there is,' said Heydrich. 'But what do you expect him to do, march up to Mutschmann and ask him where he has hidden the papers? Come now, Herr Günther, be sensible.'

'So you want me to find Mutschmann, and get to know him.'

'Precisely so. Build his trust. Find out where he's hidden the papers. And having done so, you will identify yourself to my man.'

'But how will I recognize Mutschmann?'

'The only photograph is the one on his prison record,' said Sohst, handing me a picture. I looked at it carefully. 'It's three years old, and his head will have been shaved of course, so it doesn't help you much. Not only that, but he's likely to be a great deal thinner. A KZ does tend to change a man. There is, however, one thing that should help you to identify him: he has a noticeable ganglion on his right wrist, which he could hardly obliterate.'

I handed back the photograph. 'It's not much to go on,' I said. 'Suppose I refuse?'

'You won't,' said Heydrich brightly. 'You see, either way you're going to Dachau. The difference is that working for me, you'll be sure to get out again. Not to mention getting your money back.'

'I don't seem to have much choice.'

Heydrich grinned. 'That's precisely the point,' he said. 'You don't. If you had a choice, you'd refuse. Anyone would. Which is why I can't send one of my own men. That and the need for secrecy. No, Herr Günther, as an ex-policeman, I'm afraid you fit the bill perfectly. You have everything to gain, or to lose. It's really up to you.'

'I've taken better cases,' I said.

'You must forget who you are now,' said Sohst quickly. 'We have arranged for you to have a new identity. You are now Willy Krause, and you are a black-marketeer. Here are your new papers.' He handed me a new identity card. They'd used my old police photograph.

'There is one more thing,' said Heydrich. 'I regret that verisimilitude requires a certain amount of further attention to your appearance, consistent with your having been arrested and interrogated. It's rare for a man to arrive at Columbia Haus without the odd bruise. My men downstairs will take care of you in that respect. For your own protection, of course.'

'Very thoughtful of you,' I said.

'You'll be held at Columbia for a week, and then transferred to Dachau.' Heydrich stood up. 'May I wish you good luck.' I took hold of my trouser band and got to my feet.

'Remember, this is a Gestapo operation. You must not discuss it with anyone.' Heydrich turned and pressed a button to summon the guards.

'Just tell me this,' I said. 'What's happened to Six and Helfferich, and the rest of them?'

'I see no harm in telling you,' he said. 'Well then, Herr Six is under house-arrest. He is not charged with anything, as yet. He is still too shocked at the resurrection and subsequent death of his daughter to answer any questions. Such a tragic case. Unfortunately, Herr Haupthändler died in hospital the day before yesterday, having never recovered consciousness. As to the criminal known as Red Dieter Helfferich, he was beheaded at Lake Ploetzen at six o'clock this morning, and his entire gang sent to the KZ at Sachsenhausen.' He smiled sadly at me. 'I doubt that any harm will come to Herr Six. He's much too important a man to suffer any lasting damage because of what has happened. So you can see, of all the other leading players in this unfortunate affair, you are the only one who is left alive. It merely remains to be seen if you can

238

conclude this case successfully, not only as a matter of professional pride, but also your personal survival.'

The two guards marched me back to the elevator, and then to my cell, but only to beat me up. I put up a struggle but, weak from lack of decent food and proper sleep, I was unable to put up more than a token resistance. I might have managed one of them alone, but together they were more than a match for me. After that I was taken to the SS guardroom, which was about the size of a meeting hall. Near the double-thick door sat a group of SS, playing cards and drinking beer, their pistols and blackjacks heaped on another table like so many toys confiscated by a strict schoolmaster. Facing the far wall, and standing at attention in a line, were about twenty prisoners whom I was ordered to join. A young SS Sturmmann swaggered up and down its length, shouting at some prisoners and booting many in the back or on the arse. When an old man collapsed onto the stone floor, the Sturmmann booted him into unconsciousness. And all the time new prisoners were joining the line. After an hour there must have been at least a hundred of us.

They marched us through a long corridor to a cobbled courtyard where we were loaded into Green Minnas. No SS men came with us inside the vans, but nobody said much. Each sat quietly, alone with his own thoughts of home and loved ones whom he might never see again.

When we got to Columbia Haus we climbed out of the vans. The sound of an aeroplane could be heard taking off from nearby Tempelhof Flying Field, and as it passed over the Trojan-grey walls of the old military prison, to a man we all glanced wistfully up into the sky, each of us wishing that he were among the plane's passengers.

'Move, you ugly bastards,' yelled a guard, and with many kicks, shoves and punches, we were herded up to the first floor and paraded in five columns in front of a heavy wooden door. A menagerie of warders paid us close and sadistic attention.

'See that fucking door?' yelled the Rottenführer, his face twisted to one side with malice, like a feeding shark. 'In there we finish you as men for the rest of your days. We put your balls in a vice, see? Stops you getting homesick. After all, how can you want to go home to your wives and girlfriends if you've nothing left to go home with?' He roared with laughter, and so did the menagerie, some of whom dragged the first man kicking and screaming into the room, and closed the door behind them.

I felt the other prisoners shake with fear; but I guessed that this was the corporal's idea of a joke, and when eventually it came to my own turn, I made a deliberate show of calm as they took me to the door. Once inside they took my name and address, studied my file for several minutes, and then, having been abused for my supposed black-marketeering, I was beaten up again.

Once in the main body of the prison I was taken, painfully, to my cell, and on the way there I was surprised to hear a large choir of men singing *If You Still Have a Mother*. It was only later on that I discovered the reason for the choir's existence: its performances were made at the behest of the SS to drown out the screams from the punishment cellar where prisoners were beaten on the bare buttocks with wet sjamboks.

As an ex-bull I've seen the inside of quite a few prisons in my time: Tegel, Sonnenburg, Lake Plœtzen, Brandenburg, Zellengefängnis, Brauweiler; every one of them is a hard place, with tough discipline; but none of them came close to the brutality and dehumanizing squalor that was Columbia Haus, and it wasn't long before I was wondering if Dachau could be any worse.

There were approximately a thousand prisoners in Columbia. For some, like me, it was a short-stay transit prison, on the way to a KZ; for others, it was a long-stay transit camp on the way to a KZ. Quite a few were only ever to get out in a pine box.

As a newcomer on a short stay I had a cell to myself. But since it was cold at night and there were no blankets, I would have welcomed a little human warmth around me. Breakfast was coarse rye wholemeal bread and ersatz coffee. Dinner was bread and potato gruel. The latrine was a ditch with a plank laid across it, and you were obliged to shit in the company of nine other prisoners at any one time. Once, a guard sawed through the plank and some of the prisoners ended up in the cesspit. At Columbia Haus they appreciated a sense of humour.

I had been there for six days when one night, at around midnight, I was ordered to join a vanload of prisoners for transport to Putlitzstrasse Railway Station, and from there to Dachau.

Dachau is situated some fifteen kilometres north-west of Munich. Someone on the train told me that it was the Reich's first KZ. This seemed to me to be entirely appropriate, given Munich's reputation as the birthplace of National Socialism. Built around the remains of an old explosives factory, it stands anomalously near some farmland in pleasant Bavarian countryside. Actually, the countryside is all there is that's pleasant about Bavaria. The people certainly aren't. I felt sure that Dachau wasn't about to disappoint me in this respect, or in any other. At Columbia Haus they said that Dachau was the model for all later camps: that there was even a special school there to train SS men to be more brutal. They didn't lie.

We were helped out of the wagons with the usual boots and rifle-butts, and marched east to the camp entrance. This was enclosed by a large guardhouse underneath which was a gate with the slogan 'Work Makes You Free' in the middle of the iron grille-work. The legend was the subject of some contemptuous mirth among the other prisoners, but nobody dared say anything for fear of getting a kicking.

I could think of lots of things that made you free, but work wasn't one of them: after five minutes in Dachau, death seemed a better bet.

They marched us to an open square which was a kind of parade ground, flanked to the south by a long building with a high-pitched roof. To the north, and running between seemingly endless rows of prison huts, was a wide, straight road lined with tall poplar trees. My heart sank as I began to appreciate the full magnitude of the task that lay before me. Dachau was huge. It might take months even to find Mutschmann, let alone befriend him convincingly enough to learn where he had hidden the papers. I was beginning to doubt whether the whole exercise simply wasn't the grossest piece of sadism on Heydrich's part.

The KZ commander came out of the long hut to welcome us. Like everybody in Bavaria, he had a lot to learn about hospitality. Mostly he had punishments on offer. He said that there were more than enough good trees around to hang every one of us. He finished by promising us hell, and I didn't doubt that he would be as good as his word. But at least there was fresh air. That's one of the two things you can say for Bavaria: the other has something to do with the size of their women's breasts.

They had the quaintest little tailor's shop at Dachau. And a barber's shop. I found a nice off-the-peg in stripes, a pair of clogs, and then had a haircut. I'd have asked for some oil on it but that would have meant pouring it on the floor. Things started to look up when I got three blankets, which was an improvement on Columbia, and was assigned to an Aryan hut. This was quarters for 150 men. Jewish huts contained three times that number.

It was true what they said: there's always somebody else who is worse off than you. That is, unless you were unfortunate enough to be Jewish. The Jewish population in Dachau was never large, but in all respects Jews were the worst off. Except maybe the questionable means of attaining freedom. In an Aryan hut the death rate was one per night; in a Jewish hut it was nearer seven or eight.

Dachau was no place to be a Jew.

Generally the prisoners reflected the complete spectrum of opposition to the Nazis, not to mention those against whom the Nazis were themselves implacably hostile. There were Sozis and Kozis, trade unionists, judges, lawyers, doctors, schoolteachers, army officers. Republican soldiers from the Spanish Civil War, Jehovah's Witnesses, Freemasons, Catholic priests, gypsies, Jews, spiritualists, homosexuals, vagrants, thieves and murderers. With the exception of some Russians, and a few former members of the Austrian cabinet, everyone in Dachau was German. I met a convict who was a Jew. He was also a homosexual. And if that weren't enough, he was also a Communist. That made three triangles. His luck hadn't so much run out as jumped on a fucking motorcycle.

Twice a day we had to assemble at the Appellplatz for Parade, and after roll-call came the Hindenburg Alms – floggings. They fastened the man or woman to a block and gave you an average of twenty-five on the bare arse. I saw several shit themselves during a beating. The first time I was ashamed for them; but after that someone told me it was the best way you had of spoiling the concentration of the man wielding the whip.

Parade was my best chance for looking at all the other prisoners. I kept a mental log of those men I had eliminated, and within a month I had succeeded in ruling out over 300 men.

I never forget a face. That's one of the things that makes you a good bull, and one of the things that had prompted me to join the force in the first place. Only this time my life depended on it. But always there were newcomers to upset my methodology. I felt like Hercules trying to clean the shit out of the Aegean stables.

How do you describe the indescribable? How can you talk about something that made you mute with horror? There were many more articulate than me who were simply unable to find the words. It is a silence born of shame, for even the guiltless are guilty. Shorn of all human rights, man reverts back to the animal. The starving steal from the starving, and personal survival is the only consideration, which overrides, even censors, the experience. Work sufficient to destroy the human spirit was the aim of Dachau, with death the unlooked-for by-product. Survival was through the vicarious suffering of others: you were safe for a while when it was another man who was being beaten or lynched; for a few days you might eat the ration of the man in the next cot after he had expired in his sleep.

*

To stay alive it is first necessary to die a little.

Soon after my arrival at Dachau I was put in charge of a Jewish work-company building a workshop on the north-western corner of the compound. This involved filling handcarts with rocks weighing anything up to thirty kilos and pushing them up the hill out of the quarry and to the building site, a distance of several hundred metres. Not all the SS in Dachau were bastards: some of them were comparatively moderate and managed to make money by running small businesses on the side, using the cheap labour and pool of skills that the KZ provided, so it was in their interest not to work the prisoners to death. But the SS supervising the building site were *real* bastards. Mostly Bavarian peasants, formerly unemployed, theirs was a less refined type of sadism than that which had been practised by their urban counterparts at Columbia. But it was just as effective. Mine was an easy job: as company leader I was not required myself to shift the blocks of stone; but for the Jews working in my kommando it was back-breaking work all the way. The SS were always setting deliberately tight schedules for the completion of a foundation, or a wall, and failure to meet the schedule meant no food or water. Those who collapsed through exhaustion were shot where they fell.

At first I took a hand myself, and the guards found this hugely amusing; and it was not as if the work grew any lighter as a result of my participation. One of them said to me:

'What, are you a Jew-lover or something? I don't get it. You don't have to help them, so why do you bother?'

For a moment I had no answer. Then I said: 'You don't get it. That's why I have to bother.'

He looked rather puzzled, and then frowned. For a moment I thought he was going to take offence, but instead he just laughed and said: 'Well, it's your fucking funeral.'

After a while I realized that he was right. The heavy work was killing me, just like it was killing the Jews in my kommando. And so I stopped. Feeling ashamed, I helped a convict who had collapsed, hiding him under a couple of empty handcarts until he had sufficiently recovered to continue working. And I kept on doing it, although I knew I was risking a flogging. There were informers everywhere in Dachau. The other convicts warned me about them, which seemed ironic since I was half way to being one myself.

I wasn't caught in the act of hiding a Jew who had collapsed, but they started questioning me about it, so I had to assume I'd been fingered, just like I'd been warned. I was sentenced to twenty-five strokes.

I didn't dread the pain so much as I dreaded being sent to the camp hospital after my punishment. Since the majority of its patients were suffering from dysentery and typhoid, it was a place to avoid at all costs. Even the SS never went there. It would be easy, I thought, to catch something and get sick. Then I might never find Mutschmann.

Parade seldom lasted longer than one hour, but on the morning of my punishment it was more like three.

They strapped me to the whipping frame and pulled down my trousers. I tried to shit myself, but the pain was so bad that I couldn't concentrate enough to do it. Not only that, but there was nothing to shit. When I'd collected my alms they untied me, and for a moment I stood free of the frame before I fainted.

For a long time I stared at the man's hand which dangled over the edge of the cot above me. It never moved, not even a twitch of fingers, and I wondered if he were dead. Feeling unaccountably impelled to get up and look at him I raised myself up off my stomach and yelled with pain. My cry summoned a man to the side of my cot.

'Jesus,' I gasped, feeling the sweat start out on my forehead. 'It hurts worse now than it did out there.'

'That's the medicine, I'm afraid.' The man was about forty, rabbit-toothed, and with hair that he'd probably borrowed from an old mattress. He was terribly emaciated, with the kind of body that looked as though it belonged properly in a jar of formaldehyde, and there was a yellow star sewn to his prison jacket.

'Medicine?' There was a loud note of incredulity in my voice as I spoke.

'Yes,' drawled the Jew. 'Sodium chloride.' And then more briskly: 'Common salt to you, my friend. I've covered your stripes with it.'

'Good God,' I said. 'I'm not a fucking omelette.'

'That may be so,' he said, 'but I am a fucking doctor. It stings like a condom full of nettles, I know, but it's about the only thing I can prescribe that will stop the weals going septic.' His voice was round and fruity, like a funny actor's.

'You're lucky. You I can fix. I wish I could say the same for the rest of these poor bastards. Unfortunately there's only so much that one can do with a dispensary that's been stolen from a cook-house.'

I looked up at the bunk above me, and the wrist which dangled over the edge. Never had there been an occasion when I had looked upon human deformity with such pleasure. It was a right wrist with a ganglion. The doctor lifted it out of my sight, and stood on my cot to check on its owner. Then he climbed down again, and looked at my bare arse.

'You'll do,' he said.

I jerked my head upwards. 'What's wrong with him?'

'Why, has he been giving you trouble?'

'No, I just wondered.'

'Tell me, have you had jaundice?'

'Yes.'

'Good,' he said. 'Don't worry, you won't catch it. Just don't kiss him or try to fuck him. All the same, I'll see that he's moved onto another bunk, in case he pisses on you. Transmission is through excretory products.'

'Transmission?' I said. 'Of what?'

'Hepatitis. I'll get them to put you on the top bunk and him on the bottom. You can give him some water if he gets thirsty.'

'Sure,' I said. 'What's his name?'

The doctor sighed wearily. 'I really haven't the faintest idea.'

Later on, when, with a considerable degree of discomfort, I had been moved by the medical orderlies on to the bunk above, and its previous occupant had been moved below, I looked down over the edge of my pallet at the man who represented my only way out of Dachau. It was not an encouraging sight. From my memory of the photograph in Heydrich's office, it would have been impossible to identify Mutschmann but for the ganglion, so yellow was his pallor and so wasted his body. He lay shivering under his blanket, delirious with fever, occasionally groaning with pain as cramp racked his insides. I watched him for a while and to my relief he recovered consciousness, but only long enough to try, unsuccessfully, to vomit. Then he was away again. It was clear to me that Mutschmann was dying.

Apart from the doctor, whose name was Mendelssohn, and three or four medical orderlies, who were themselves suffering from a variety of ailments, there were about sixty men and women in the camp hospital. As hospitals went it was little more than a charnel-house. I learned that there were only two kinds of patient: the sick, who always died, and the injured, who sometimes also got sick.

That evening, before it grew dark, Mendelssohn came to inspect my stripes.

'In the morning I'll wash your back and put some more salt on,' he said. Then he glanced disinterestedly down below at Mutschmann.

'What about him?' I said. It was a stupid question, and only served to arouse the Jew's curiosity. His eyes narrowed as he looked at me.

'Since you ask, I've told him to keep off alcohol, spicy food and to get plenty of rest,' he said drily.

'I think I get the picture.'

'I'm not a callous man, my friend, but there is nothing I can do to help him. With a high-protein diet, vitamins, glucose and methionine, he might have had a chance.'

'How long has he got?'

'He still manages to recover consciousness from time to time?' I nodded. Mendelssohn sighed. 'Difficult to say. But once coma has set in, a matter of a day or so. I don't even have any morphine to give him. In this clinic death is the usual cure that is available to patients.'

'I'll bear it in mind.'

'Don't get sick, my friend. There's typhus here. The minute you find yourself developing a fever, take two spoonfuls of your own urine. It does seem to work.'

'If I can find a clean spoon, I'll do just that. Thanks for the tip.'

'Well, here's another, since you're in such a good mood. The only reason that the Camp Committee meets here is because they know the guards won't come unless they absolutely have to. Contrary to outward appearances, the SS are not stupid. Only a madman would stay here for any longer than he has to.

'As soon as you can get about without too much pain, my advice to you is to get yourself out of here.'

'What makes you stay? Hippocratic oath?'

Mendelssohn shrugged. 'Never heard of it,' he said.

I slept for a while. I had meant to stay awake and watch Mutschmann in case he came round again. I suppose I was hoping for one of those touching little scenes that you see in the movies, when the dying man is moved to unburden his soul to the man crouching over his deathbed.

When I awoke it was dark, and above the sound of the other inmates of the hospital coughing, and snoring, I heard the unmistakeable sound, coming from the cot underneath, of Mutschmann retching. I leaned over and saw him in the moonlight, leaning on one elbow, clutching his stomach.

'You all right?' I said.

'Sure,' he wheezed. 'Like a fucking Galapagos tortoise, I'm going to live for ever.' He groaned again, and painfully, through clenched teeth, said: 'It's these damned stomach cramps.'

'Would you like some water?'

'Water, yes. My tongue is as dry as –' He was overcome by

another fit of retching. I climbed down gingerly, and fetched the ladle from a bucket near the bed. Mutschmann, his teeth chattering like a telegraph button, drank the water noisily. When he'd finished he sighed and lay back.

'Thanks, friend,' he said.

'Don't mention it,' I said. 'You'd do the same for me.'

I heard him cough his way through what sounded like a chuckle. 'No I fucking wouldn't,' he rasped. 'I'd be afraid of catching something, whatever it is that I've got. I don't suppose you know, do you?'

I thought for a moment. Then I told him. 'You've got hepatitis.'

He was silent for a couple of minutes, and I felt ashamed. I ought to have spared him that agony. 'Thanks for being honest with me,' he said. 'What's up with you?'

'Hindenburg Alms.'

'What for?'

'Helped a Jew in my work kommando.'

'That was stupid,' he said. 'They're all dead anyway. Risk it for someone who's got half a chance, but not for a Jew. Their luck is long gone.'

'Well, yours didn't exactly win the lottery.'

He laughed. 'True enough,' he said. 'I never figured on going sick. I thought I was going to get through this fuck-hole. I had a good job in the cobbler's shop.'

'It's a tough break,' I admitted.

'I'm dying, aren't I?' he said.

'That's not what the doc says.'

'No need to give me the cold cabbage. I can see it in the lead. But thanks anyway. Jesus, I'd give anything for a nail.'

'Me too,' I said.

'Even a roll up would do.' He paused. Then he said: 'There's something I've got to tell you.'

I tried to conceal the urgency that was crowding my voice-box. 'Yes? What's that then?'

'Don't fuck any of the women in this camp. I'm pretty sure that's how I got sick.'

'No, I won't. Thanks for telling me.'

The next day I sold my food ration for some cigarettes, and waited for Mutschmann to come out of his delirium. It lasted most of the day. When eventually he regained consciousness he spoke to me as if our previous conversation had been only a few minutes earlier.

'How's it going? How are the stripes?'

'Painful,' I said, getting off my bunk.

'I'll bet. That bastard sergeant with the whip really lays it on like fuck.' He inclined his emaciated face towards me, and said: 'You know, it seems to me that I've seen you somewhere.'

'Well now, let's see,' I said. 'The Rot Weiss Tennis Club? The Herrenklub? The Excelsior, maybe?'

'You're putting me on.' I lit one of the cigarettes and put it between his lips.

'I'll bet it was at the Opera – I'm a big fan, you know. Or perhaps it was at Goering's wedding?' His thin yellow lips stretched into something like a smile. Then he breathed in the tobacco smoke as if it was pure oxygen.

'You are a fucking magician,' he said, savouring the cigarette. I took it from his lips for a second before putting it back again. 'No, it wasn't any of those places. It'll come to me.'

'Sure it will,' I said, earnestly hoping that it wouldn't. For a moment I thought of saying Tegel Prison, but rejected it. Sick or not, he might remember differently, and then I'd be finished with him.

'What are you? Sozi? Kozi?'

'Black-marketeer,' I said. 'How about you?'

The smile stretched so that it was almost a rictus. 'I'm hiding.'

'Here? From whom?'

'Everyone,' he said.

'Well, you sure picked one hell of a hiding place. What are you, crazy?'

'Nobody can find me here,' he said. 'Let me ask you something: where would you hide a raindrop?' I looked puzzled until he answered, 'Under a waterfall. In case you didn't know it, that's Chinese philosophy. I mean, you'd never find it, would you?'

'No, I suppose not. But you must have been desperate,' I said.

'Getting sick . . . was just unlucky . . . But for that I'd have been out . . . in a year or so . . . by which time . . . they'd have given up looking.'

'Who would?' I said. 'What are they after you for?'

His eyelids flickered, and the cigarette fell from his unconscious lips and onto the blanket. I drew it up to his chin and tapped out the cigarette in the hope that he might come round again for long enough to smoke the other half.

During the night, Mutschmann's breathing grew shallower, and in the morning Mendelssohn pronounced that he was on the edge of coma. There was nothing that I could do but lie on my stomach and look down and wait. I thought of Inge a lot, but mostly I thought about myself. At Dachau, the funeral arrangements were simple: they burned you in the crematorium and that was it. End of story. But as I watched the poisons work their dreadful effect on Kurt Mutschmann, destroying his liver and his spleen so that his whole body was filled with infection, mostly my thoughts were of my Fatherland and its own equally appalling sickness. It was only now, in Dachau, that I was able to judge just how much Germany's atrophy had become necrosis; and as with poor Mutschmann, there wasn't going to be any morphine for when the pain grew worse.

There were a few children in Dachau, born to women imprisoned there. Some of them had never known any other life than the camp. They played freely in the compound, tolerated by all the guards, and even liked by some, and they could go almost anywhere, with the exception of the hospital barrack. The penalty for disobedience was a severe beating.

Mendelssohn was hiding a child with a broken leg under one of the cots. The boy had fallen while playing in the prison quarry, and had been there for almost three days with his leg in a splint when the SS came for him. He was so scared he swallowed his tongue and choked to death.

When the dead boy's mother came to see him and had to be told the bad news, Mendelssohn was the very model of professional sympathy. But later on, when she had gone, I heard him weeping quietly to himself.

'Hey, up there.' I gave a start as I heard the voice below me. It wasn't that I'd been asleep; I just hadn't been watching Mutschmann as I should have been. Now I had no idea of the invaluable period of time for which he had been conscious. I climbed down carefully and knelt by his cot. It was still too painful to sit on my backside. He grinned terribly and gripped my arm.

'I remembered,' he said.

'Oh yes?' I said hopefully. 'And what did you remember?'

'Where I seen your face.' I tried to appear unconcerned, although my heart was thumping in my chest. If he thought that I was a bull then I could forget it. An ex-convict never befriends a bull. It could have been the two of us washed away on some desert island, and he would still have spat in my face.

'Oh?' I said nonchalantly. 'Where was that, then?' I put his half-smoked cigarette between his lips and lit it.

'You used to be the house-detective,' he croaked. 'At the Adlon. I once cased the place to do a job.' He chuckled hoarsely. 'Am I right?'

'You've got a good memory,' I said, lighting one myself. 'That was quite some time ago.'

His grip tightened. 'Don't worry,' he said. 'I won't tell anyone. Anyway, it's not like you were a bull, is it?'

'You said you were casing the place. What particular line of criminality were you in?'

'I was a nutcracker.'

'I can't say as I recall the hotel safe ever being robbed,' I said. 'At least, not as long as I was working there.'

'That's because I didn't take anything,' he said proudly. 'Oh, I opened it all right. But there was nothing worth taking. Seriously.'

'I've only got your word for that,' I said. 'There were always rich people at the hotel, and they always had valuables. It was very rare that there wasn't something in that safe.'

'It's true,' he said. 'Just my bad luck. There really was nothing that I could take that I could ever have got rid of. That's the point, you see. There's no point in taking something you can't shift.'

'All right, I believe you,' I said.

'I'm not boasting,' he said. 'I was the best. There wasn't anything I couldn't crack. Here, I bet you'd expect me to be rich, wouldn't you?'

I shrugged. 'Perhaps. I'd also expect you to be in prison, which you are.'

'It's because I am rich that I'm hiding here,' he said. 'I told you that, didn't I?'

'You mentioned something about that, yes.' I took my time before I added: 'And what have you got that makes you so rich and wanted? Money? Jewels?'

He croaked another short laugh. 'Better than that,' he said. 'Power.'

'In what shape or form?'

'Papers,' he said. 'Take my word for it, there's an awful lot of people who'd pay big money to get their hands on what I've got.'

'What's in these papers?'

His breathing was shallower than a *Der Junggeselle* cover-girl.

'I don't know exactly,' he said. 'Names, addresses, information. But you're a clever sort of fellow, you could work it.'

'You haven't got them here, have you?'

'Don't be stupid,' he wheezed. 'They're safe, on the outside.' I took the dead cigarette from his mouth and threw it onto the floor. Then I gave him the rest of mine.

'It'd be a shame . . . for it never to be used,' he said breathlessly. 'You've been good . . . to me. So I'm going to do you a favour . . . Make 'em sweat, won't you? This'll be worth . . . a lorry load . . . of gravel . . . to you . . . on the outside.' I bent forwards to hear him speak. 'Pick 'em up . . . by the nose.' His eyelids flickered. I took him by the shoulders and tried to shake him back to consciousness.

Back to life.

I knelt there by him for some time. In the small corner of me that still felt things, there was a terrible and terrifying sense of abandonment. Mutschmann had been younger than I was, and strong, too. It wasn't too difficult to imagine myself succumbing to illness. I had lost a lot of weight, I had bad ringworms and my teeth felt loose in their gums. Heydrich's man, SS Oberschutze Bürger, was in charge of the carpenter's shop, and I wondered what would happen to me if I went ahead and gave him the code-word that would get me out of Dachau. What would Heydrich do to me when he discovered that I didn't know where Von Greis's papers were? Send me back? Have me executed? And if I didn't blow the whistle, would it even occur to him to assume that I had been unsuccessful and that he should get me out? From my short meeting with Heydrich, and what little I had heard of him, it seemed unlikely. To have got so near and failed at the last was almost more than I could bear.

After a while I reached forwards and drew the blanket over Mutschmann's yellow face. A short stub of a pencil fell onto the floor, and I looked at it for several seconds before a thought crossed my mind and a glint of hope once more shone in my heart. I drew the blanket back from Mutschmann's body. The hands were tightly bunched into fists. One after the other I prised them open. In Mutschmann's left hand was a piece of brown paper of the sort that the prisoners in the cobbler's shop used to wrap shoe repairs for the SS guards in. I was too afraid of there being nothing to open the paper immediately. As it was, the writing was almost illegible, and it took me almost an hour to decipher the note's contents. It said,

'Lost property office, Berlin Traffic Dept. Saarlandstr. You lost briefcase sometime July on Leipzigerstr. Made of plain brown hide, with brass lock, ink-stain on handle. Gold initials K.M. Contains postcard from America, Western novel, *Old Surehand*, Karl May and business papers. Thanks. K.M.'

It was perhaps the strangest ticket home that anyone ever had.

19

It seemed that there were uniforms everywhere. Even the newspaper-sellers were wearing SA caps and greatcoats. There was no parade, and certainly there was nothing Jewish on Unter den Linden that could be boycotted. Perhaps it was only now, after Dachau, that I fully realized the true strength of the grip that National Socialism had on Germany.

I was heading towards my office. Situated incongruously between the Greek Embassy and Schultze's Art Shop, and guarded by two storm-troopers, I passed the Ministry of the Interior from which Himmler had issued his memo to Paul Pfarr regarding corruption. A car drew up outside the front door, and from it emerged two officers and a uniformed girl whom I recognized as Marlene Sahm. I stopped and started to say hallo and then thought better of it. She passed me by without a glance. If she recognized me she did a good job disguising it. I turned and watched her as she followed the two men inside the building. I don't suppose I was standing there for more than a couple of minutes, but it was long enough for me to be challenged by a fat man with a low brimmed hat.

'Papers,' he said abruptly, not even bothering to show a Sipo pass or warrant disc.

'Says who?'

The man pushed his porky, poorly shaven face at me and hissed: 'Says me.'

'Listen,' I said, 'you're sadly mistaken if you think you are possessed of what is cutely known as a commanding personality. So cut the shit and let's see some ID.' A Sipo pass flashed in front of my nose.

'You boys are getting lazy,' I said, producing my papers. He snatched them away for examination.

'What are you doing hanging around here?'

'Hanging? Who's hanging?' I said. 'I stopped to admire the architecture.'

'Why were you looking at those officers who got out of the car?'

'I wasn't looking at the officers,' I said. 'I was looking at the girl. I love women in uniforms.'

'On your way,' he said, tossing my papers back at me.

The average German seems to be able to tolerate the most offensive behaviour from anyone wearing a uniform or carrying some sort of official insignia. In everything except that I consider myself to be a fairly typical German, because I have to admit that I am naturally disposed to be obstructive to authority. I suppose you would say that it's an odd attitude for an ex-policeman.

On Königstrasse the collectors for the Winter Relief were out in force, shaking their little red collecting-boxes under everyone's noses, although November was only a few days old. In the early days the Relief had been intended to help overcome the effects of unemployment and the depression, but now, and almost universally, it was regarded as nothing more than financial and psychological blackmail by the Party: the Relief raised funds but, just as importantly, it created an emotional climate in which people were trained to do without for the sake of the Fatherland. Each week the collection was the charge of a different organization, and this week it was the Railwaymen.

The only railwayman I ever liked was my former secretary Dagmar's father. I had no sooner bitten my lip and handed over 20 pfennigs to one of them, than farther up the road I was solicited by another. The small glass badge you got for contributing didn't so much protect you from further harassment as mark you out as a good prospect. Still, it wasn't that which made me curse the man, fat as only a railwayman can be, and push him out of my way, but the sight of Dagmar herself disappearing round the sacrificial column that stands outside the Town Hall.

Hearing my hurried footsteps she turned and saw me before

I reached her. We stood awkwardly in front of the urn-like monument with its huge white-lettered motto which read 'Sacrifice for the Winter Relief'.

'Bernie,' she said.

'Hallo,' I said. 'I was just thinking about you.' Feeling rather awkward, I touched her on the arm. 'I was sorry to hear about Johannes.' She gave me a brave smile, and drew her brown wool coat closer about her neck.

'You've lost a lot of weight, Bernie. Have you been ill?'

'It's a long story. Have you got time for a coffee?'

We went to the Alexanderquelle on Alexanderplatz where we ordered real mocha and real scones with real jam and real butter.

'They say that Goering's got a new process that makes butter from coal.'

'It doesn't look like he's eating any of it then.' I laughed politely. 'And you can't buy an onion anywhere in Berlin. Father reckons they're using them to make poison gas for the Japs to use against the Chinese.'

After a while I asked her if she was able to discuss Johannes. 'I'm afraid there's not really much to tell,' she said.

'How did it happen?'

'All I know is that he was killed in an air-raid on Madrid. One of his comrades came to tell me. From the Reich I received a one-line message which read: "Your husband died for Germany's honour." In a pig's eye, I thought.' She sipped her coffee. 'Then I had to go and see someone at the Air Ministry, and sign a promise that I wouldn't talk about what had happened, and that I wouldn't wear mourning. Can you imagine that, Bernie? I couldn't even wear black for my own husband. It was the only way I could get a pension.' She smiled bitterly, and added: ' "You are Nothing, Your Nation is Everything." Well, they certainly mean it.' She took out her handkerchief and blew her nose.

'Never underestimate the National Socialists when it comes to the pantheistic,' I said. 'Individuals are an irrelevance. These days your own mother takes your disappearance for granted. Nobody cares.'

Nobody except me, I thought. For several weeks after my release from Dachau, the disappearance of Inge Lorenz was my only case. But sometimes even Bernie Günther draws a blank.

Looking for someone in Germany in the late autumn of 1936 was like trying to find something in a great desk drawer that had crashed to the floor, the contents spilled and then replaced according to a new order so that things no longer came easily to hand, or even seemed to belong in there. Gradually my sense of urgency was worn away by the indifference of others. Inge's former colleagues on the newspaper shrugged and said that really, they hadn't known her all that well. Neighbours shook their heads and suggested that one needed to be philosophical about such things. Otto, her admirer at the DAF, thought she'd probably turn up before very long. I couldn't blame any of them. To lose another hair from a head that's already lost so many seems merely inconvenient.

Sharing quiet, lonely evenings with a friendly bottle, I often tried to imagine what might have become of her: a car accident; some kind of amnesia perhaps; an emotional or mental breakdown; a crime she had committed which necessitated an immediate and permanent disappearance. But always I was led back to abduction and murder and the idea that whatever had happened had been related to the case I had been working on.

Even after two months had passed, when you might normally have expected the Gestapo to have admitted to something, Bruno Stahlecker, lately transferred out of the city to a little Kripo station of no account in Spreewald, failed to come up with any record of Inge having been executed or sent to a KZ. And no matter how many times I returned to Haupthändler's house in Wannsee, in the hope that I might find something that would provide me with a clue to what had happened, there never was anything.

Until Inge's lease expired I often went back to her apartment looking for some secret things she had not seen fit to share with me. Meanwhile, the memory of her grew more distant. Having no photograph, I forgot her face, and came to realize how little I had really known about her, beyond rudimentary pieces of information. There had always seemed to be so much time to find out all there was to know.

As the weeks turned into months, I knew my chances of finding Inge grew smaller as an almost arithmetically inverse proportion. And as the trail grew colder, so did hope. I felt – I knew – that I would never see her again.

Dagmar ordered some more coffee, and we talked about what each of us had been doing. But I said nothing of Inge, or of my time in Dachau. There are some things that can't be discussed over morning coffee.

'How's business?' she asked.

'I bought myself a new car, an Opel.'

'You must be doing all right then.'

'What about you?' I asked. 'How do you live?'

'I'm back home with my parents. I do a lot of typing at home,' she said. 'Students' theses, that sort of thing.' She managed a smile. 'Father worries about me doing it. You see, I like to type at night, and the sound of my typewriter has brought the Gestapo round three times in as many weeks. They're on the lookout for people writing opposition newspapers. Luckily the sort of stuff that I'm churning out is so worshipful of National Socialism that they're easy to get rid of. But Father worries about the neighbours. He says they'll start to believe that the Gestapo is after us for something.'

After a while I suggested that we go to see a film.

'Yes,' she said, 'but I don't think I could stand one of those patriotic films.'

Outside the café we bought a newspaper.

On the front page there was a photograph of the two Hermanns, Six and Goering, shaking hands: Goering was grinning broadly, and Six wasn't smiling at all: it looked like the Prime Minister was going to have his way regarding the supply of raw materials for the German steel industry after all. I turned up the entertainments section.

'How about *The Scarlet Empress* at the Tauentzienpalast?' I said. Dagmar said that she'd seen it twice.

'What about this one?' she said. '*The Greatest Passion*, with Ilse Rudel. That's her new picture, isn't it? You like her, don't you? Most men seem to.' I thought of the young actor, Walther Kolb, who Ilse Rudel had sent to do murder for her, and had himself been killed by me. The line-drawing on the newspaper advertisement showed her wearing a nun's veil. Even when I had discounted my personal knowledge of her, I thought the characterization questionable.

But nothing surprises me now. I've grown used to living in a world that is out of joint, as if it has been struck by an enormous earthquake so that the roads are no longer flat, nor the buildings straight.

'Yes,' I said, 'she's all right.'

We walked to the cinema. The red *Der Stürmer* showcases were back on the street corners and, if anything, Streicher's paper seemed more rabid than ever.

PHILIP KERR

THE PALE CRIMINAL

'Blends high-powered storytelling with a rich piece of historical re-creation' *Independent*

The second in Philip Kerr's iconic 'Berlin Noir' trilogy, *The Pale Criminal* sees detective Bernie Gunther return to hunt one of the most evil killers in human history.

Bernie Gunther is back on the mean streets of Berlin with his new partner, Bruno Stahlecker, another ex-police officer. But on a seemingly straightforward stakeout Bruno is killed, and Bernie suddenly finds himself tapped for a much bigger job.

A serial sex murderer is killing Aryan teenage girls in Berlin - and what's worse, he's making utter fools of the police. Gunther is forced to accept a temporary post in Obergruppenfuehrer Reinhard Heydrich's state Security Service, with a team of men underneath him tasked purely with hunting the killer.

But can he trust his team any more than he can trust his superiors?

'Kerr makes his star turns - Heydrich, Himmler, et al - eerily believable' *The Times*
'Powerful period flavour; a gruff, subversive hero; Kerr delivers the good' *Literary Review*
'Echoes of Raymond Chandler...vivid and well-researched' *Evening Standard*

PHILIP KERR

A GERMAN REQUIEM

'Philip Kerr is the contemporary master of the morally complex thriller...'
New York Observer

The third in Philip Kerr's universally loved Berlin Noir trilogy, *A German Requiem* sees detective Bernie Gunther enter the new and terrifying world of post-war Vienna.

In the bitter winter of 1947 the Russian Zone is closing ever more tightly around Berlin. So when an enigmatic Russian colonel asks Bernie Gunther to go to Vienna, where his ex-Kripo colleague Emil Becker faces a murder charge, Bernie doesn't hesitate for long. Despite an unsavoury past, Gunther is convinced that the shooting of an American Nazi-hunter is one crime Becker didn't commit.

But Vienna is not the peaceful haven Bernie expects it to be. Communism is the new enemy, and with the Nuremberg trials over, some strange alliances are being forged against the Red Menace - alignments that make many wartime atrocities look lily-white by comparison.

'Richly satisfying mystery...evokes the noir sensibilities of Raymond Chandler and Ross Macdonald while breaking important new ground of its own' *LA Times*